SUMMER OF THE
VAMPIRE

As the sizzling summer sun sets,
a darker pleasure awaits…

SUMMER HOLIDAY
with a
VAMPIRE

Michele Hauf

Kendra Leigh Castle

Lisa Childs

Caridad Piñeiro

Laura Kaye

MILLS & BOON

First published in Great Britain 2013
by Mills & Boon, an imprint of Harlequin (UK) Limited, Eton House,
18-24 Paradise Road, Richmond, Surrey TW9 1SR

SUMMER HOLIDAY WITH A VAMPIRE
© Harlequin Books S.A. 2013

The publisher acknowledges the copyright holders of the individual works as follows:

Stay © Michele Hauf 2012
Vivi and the Vampire © Kendra Sawicki 2012
Island Vacation © Lisa Childs 2012
Honour Calls © Caridad Piñeiro Scordato 2009
In the Service of the King © Laura Kaye 2012

ISBN: 978 0 263 90671 4

013-0713

Harlequin (UK) policy is to use papers that are natural, renewable and recyclable products and made from wood grown in sustainable forests. The logging and manufacturing processes conform to the legal environmental regulations of the country of origin.

Printed and bound by
CPI Group (UK) Ltd, Croydon, CR0 4YY

Contents

Stay   9

Vivi and the Vampire   139

Island Vacation   267

Honour Calls   377

In the Service of the King   441

STAY

Michele Hauf

Michele Hauf has been writing romance, action-adventure and fantasy stories for more than twenty years. If she followed the adage 'write what you know,' all her stories would have snow in them. Fortunately, she steps beyond her comfort zone and writes about countries she has never visited and creatures she has never seen. Michele can be found on Facebook and Twitter and at michelehauf.com. You can also write to Michele at: PO Box 23, Anoka, MN 55303, USA.

Chapter 1

Lucian Bellisario staggered down the streets of Paris. At his back, the setting sun shimmered silver in his hematite hair. He was—and he hated to admit this—exhausted. Light-headed and drained, there was but one means to rally.

He needed hot, mortal blood pulsing with life.

Veering toward his antique shop nestled in the shadow of the Eiffel Tower, he scanned the streets. He sought a lone walker, someone who would meet his eyes and smile, project onto him their assumption that he was not threatening.

And then he would threaten them.

He didn't clutch at the wound over his heart because he wouldn't draw attention to himself in that manner.

Had to maintain decorum. The inch-wide puncture had healed, but the pain lingered.

His best friend, Certainly Jones, had needed his help. The dark witch had required fresh vampire blood for a spell. Lucian happened to have plenty of blood coursing through his veins, and being a vampire, he'd fit the bill.

The steel pipe, shoved between his ribs to facilitate a steady stream of blood onto the witch's hands while he'd spoken a doppelganger spell, had served but a nuisance to Lucian. Not thick enough to burst his heart, he'd only had it in a few minutes. Long enough to drain much blood from his system and deplete his energy, resulting in a now ravenous hunger.

More than once, he'd been CJ's guinea pig for new magic spells over the decades.

"The things I do for friends," he muttered.

A slender woman wearing a studious skirt and blouse stood before a door that featured an Art Nouveau–style nymph draped over the shop name, L'Extraordinaire. He'd painted the door decades ago. Seeing his approach, she smiled warmly at him.

Lucian could smell her misfortunate trust from ten paces. Human blood, infused with sweet innocence and polite acceptance. Easy enough to entice her into an embrace that would satisfy his needs.

But he was not a brute, or a creature. Never did he

swoop in and attack a female, even when hounded by hunger.

"Mademoiselle?" He pulled a key out of his leather coat pocket, and smiled a smile that had conquered hundreds, perhaps thousands. He was not one to boast.

"Is the shop closed?" she asked. A breeze shifted her straight brown hair over a slender shoulder. An American, to judge her accent. He liked foreigners. Visitors were transitory; they usually did not return, and that made feeding his hunger so much neater.

Lucian's fangs tingled to sink in, there, at the smooth white column of her neck. The erotic sensation stirred his loins as strongly as it did his thirst. Blood and sex often complemented one another.

"Closed? Temporarily, while I was out, er...giving blood."

"Oh, they have the Red Cross here in France? That's generous of you. Needles freak me out, so I've never been able to donate."

"The intrusion of something sharp into flesh is but a small sacrifice if you know it will help another," he said with an ill-concealed smirk that slipped to amusement as he turned his head toward the door. He shoved the key in the lock, and invited his next meal inside. "Welcome to my dusty little corner of the ancient and overlooked."

Crossing the threshold, she moved through the ill-sorted chaos, her eyes scanning the shadowed recesses behind centuries-old furniture, glassware that had been held by kings, and folded damasks and linens that may have seen lusty nights of royal passion.

Lucian preferred the shop disordered, as opposed to the neat and fancy showplaces on the Champs-élysées that overcharged to cover the upkeep and false provenances they assigned to their objets d'art. A monthly dusting from a cleaning girl he kept on retainer—and enthralled after his bite—suited him fine and well.

Normally, he did not look to feed his hunger via customers, but circumstances as they were, he wasn't about to hold off this craving much longer. Her simple prettiness beckoned his interest though, and he decided he could manage a few minutes of restraint.

"What are you looking for?"

"I'm not sure." Her black-framed glasses glinted in the dull sunlight as she ran a hand over a dented copper serving tray. "A friend of mine loaned her apartment to me for a couple weeks. It's my first vacation overseas. I thought I'd repay her with a pretty little something to decorate her bedroom."

"Trinkets are under the glass case," Lucian directed, allowing her to wander the creaky floorboards and browse.

He paced behind her, hands behind his back, indulging in the provocative tease of her blood. Yet above the metallic sweetness rose the scent of peaches, seasoned with nutmeg and cinnamon. Like some kind of pie? Odd, but strangely appealing. He hadn't consumed mortal food in ages.

"Actually, she needs furnishings," she mused. "Her apartment is remarkably bare."

Pushing her glasses up her nose, the woman leaned over an Edwardian pot cupboard to get a better view of the mirror tilted against the wall, and tucked away as if it had no appeal to the owner. It did not. Hugging one side, a sinuous faerie glided, her arm curving along the top of the frame.

Horrible reminder, that.

"I see you've an eye for your pretty reflection," he tried, fighting against his fangs' insistent stirring to descend.

Frowning at the comment, she cast a glower at him. Soft blue eyes reflected the last rays of sun struggling through the windows.

"Forgive my manners. Lucian Bellisario." He offered his hand.

The woman stared at his hand for so long he had to give it a good long look himself. Following CJ's spell, he'd washed off all his blood. Had he missed a spot?

Finally, she put her hand in his, and it was like sunshine sliding into his cold, tired grasp. He wasn't cold-blooded, but blood loss contributed to his chilliness. He clasped her warmth with both hands and wished it would not end. It was an odd thought for him, a man who did not make connections, save those fleeting one-bite stands which had become his mien. The urge to savor her skin colliding with his was strong, but too soon, he'd have to destroy this genial masquerade with an essential bite.

"And you are?" he prompted.

Tugging from his firm grip, and stepping back, she dragged her eyes from what he suspected had been his mouth, to the immaculate design of his dark suit. Fortunately, he'd removed the crisp white shirt before the spell, so she couldn't have sighted a bloodstain.

"Magen Sloan." Again she met his eyes, this time more daring. Her mouth parted and he almost leaned forward to kiss her. He had managed to connect with her trusting innocence.

Lucian swallowed his aching need. *Just a few moments to enjoy her sweetness before you destroy it all.*

"The Belle Époque era interests me," she said. "I think the mirror will be perfect."

"Bohemia, eh?" Lucian could not prevent the note of distaste on his tone.

He walked around her, his gaze tracking the subtle pulse at her throat, the flex of her neck muscles with each turn of her head. A trace of a grin revealed a soft blush in cheeks too smooth for porcelain. She avoided sunlight. Or she was a workaholic.

"You look far too practical for such a decadent piece, Magen Sloan."

Touching the rim of her glasses, she lifted her chin in defense. "I have a surprising wild side." Then she gaped, covering her mouth with her fingers. "I can't believe I said that."

"I'm pleased you did," he said with a flirtatious smile, finding the banter eased his raging hunger. "Behind those studious glasses and beneath that equally studious gray skirt and blazer, I'll wager *Mademoiselle Pratique* indulges in a wild thing or two."

"Well, I—" He'd caught her off guard, and ill-prepared to deal with a stranger who offered intimate conversation. The challenge heightened the peach/blood scent of her deliciously. "How much for the mirror?"

Lucian leaned back, his hip nudging the counter, and crossed his arms. An assessing gaze stripped away her practical blazer and he imagined dragging his fingers down the fake pearl buttons dotting her white blouse. The shop was cool this late-September day, yet the skin on her neck and cheeks flushed as if she stood beneath a high sun.

A few moments more of indecently teasing conversation and he'd have her blood simmered to a delicious brew.

But the mirror offended him.

"It's cracked along the bottom," he offered. "I can

let you have it for four hundred euros." An obscenely low price.

"A little crack doesn't bother me. Cracks add character. Much like a foreign accent increases a man's appeal. Oh." Pale pink lips parting, she again seemed to catch herself before thinking.

"Are you all right, *mademoiselle?* You look flustered. Is the price too high?"

"No, actually, you're just right. I mean—oh. I'm sorry. I don't know what I'm saying."

"You, mademoiselle, were flirting with me."

"It was the jet lag talking. I only arrived in the city yesterday afternoon."

"Sure."

Blowing out a breath that lifted the soft brown bangs above her brows, she said, "I confess, this is going to be one hell of a vacation if all the men are as disarming as you."

He lifted a brow.

"It's your sexy accent," she added with a flutter of her fingers as she drew up her purse and set it on the counter. "So uh, do you deliver? The apartment where I'm staying is close, just across the river from here."

"Of course. I'll send the delivery boy out later this evening if that will work for you."

"Oh, yes." She dug out her wallet and credit card, and

a business card that did not say Magen Sloan, but instead Lisa Cooper. "That's the place."

"Very good, *mademoiselle*."

He took her credit card and hissed as the fleeting touch of their fingers sent electrifying tingles up his arm and to his teeth. Why he hadn't already bitten her baffled Lucian. They were alone. She was not on the defense. And she stood so close.

It was that damned mirror. Getting rid of the thing was an opportunity he could not resist.

He went through the motions of writing up a bill and slashing the credit card. "Is your friend practical, as well?"

"Does practical bother you, Monsieur Bellisario?"

Her use of his name emboldened his want and Lucian clutched the credit card, the plastic edges gouging into his palm.

Soon. Continue with the small talk, and then—

Magen signed the receipt. Closing his eyes, Lucian inhaled deeply. She smelled like a treat he'd not been able to indulge in for over a century. "Actually, practical baffles me," he said, forcing calm and handing her back the credit card. "But you did mention your surprisingly wicked side. That appeals to me." He handed her the receipt. The cuff of his sleeve brushed her wrist and she gasped. "Now for my transaction."

"What transaction?"

He leaned in, blocking her against the counter with his body, and placing his hands to either side of her tiny waist. She inhaled, which lifted her breasts, and renewed her sweet scent. "Monsieur?"

"You are a gorgeous woman, Magen Sloan, and you smell like peaches."

"That's my perfume. You, uh…" She looked aside nervously, then managed to draw her gaze onto his, a bold move that set his heart racing faster than it had when the silver tube had been crammed into it. "…like peaches?"

"I believe I will find the taste exquisite when drunk slowly and directly from the source."

"I don't understand. Oh." She sighed as he ran his fingertips along her neck, tracing the vein, melding her heat into his pores. "Are you…? Lucian," she said, not as a question, but an acceptance.

And he bent his head to her neck and pierced her skin and vein with his fangs. Delicate fingers clutched his arms and squeezed, but she did not cry out. Instead, a tiny gasp tickled his ear. Her sweetness poured into his mouth and Lucian groaned. He wrapped an arm about her back and tugged her closer, unwilling to relinquish his prize, this necessary renewal.

"Ohmygod," she whispered. "You're…biting…"

The swoon enveloped her with an orgasmic tremor that vibrated through her being and against Lucian's hardened muscles. Every part of him was hard, from his biceps and abs, to his thighs and even his cock. Her surrender quickened him. Her blood was rich and thick, like fresh peaches fallen from the tree.

She would be difficult to never see again.

As she sank in his arms, he supported her weight, an elbow catching the counter, and, having taken enough blood to quench his hunger, he licked the wound to seal it. With a kiss above her ear, he smoothed out her straight brown hair and adjusted her glasses.

"I needed that," he whispered. "Thank you. You'll be woozy, but you should manage the walk home, yes?"

She nodded.

"You won't remember my bite," he continued, persuading the altered memory into her thoughts, as vampires were able. "Just a pleasant evening at the antique shop with a stranger whose name you won't recall. Go now, my delicious one."

Magen turned and headed toward the door. Stroking her neck, she called out, "You'll deliver the mirror?"

He had intended to have a delivery boy bring it over, but...

Lucian licked his lips. Mmm... Another bite of Magen Sloan would be just the thing. It went completely against his character, but—he'd enthrall her again. She would never be the wiser.

"Of course. I'll stop by in a few hours. And I like my

wine red," he called. "I cannot abide white wine. De-classé."

"Red," Magen said as she gripped the brass doorknob and stepped outside.

Magen found a corkscrew in the kitchen drawer and set it next to the bottle of red wine. She was no connoisseur so she hoped she'd purchased something, at the least, palatable. Her giddiness over the anticipated arrival of Lucian Bellisario actually made her titter.

"He's so sexy. And I'm in Paris. On vacation." Clasping her hands to her lips, she wondered aloud, "Might I have an illicit affair with a gorgeous Frenchman who whispers sweet nothings to me in a language I can't understand, and won't need to understand because it'll all be about the sex?"

She shook her head, chuckling. "You are getting carried away with your crazy self, *Mademoiselle Pratique*."

His eyes had glittered when he'd named her that. Combined with his accent? Mercy! He'd absolutely smoldered.

"I made the right choice," she whispered. "To adventure."

A spur-of-the-moment decision to take a vacation had come after watching her seventy-year-old neighbor lady wave goodbye to the mailman. Again. The woman was having an affair with the silver postal fox, Magen knew, because every other day he went to her front door with her mail and didn't come out for approximately forty-five minutes. When he did reappear, Magen could only think, *now he's going to my mailbox, and handling my mail. Ugh.*

But seriously? Her seventy-year-old neighbor was getting some action, and Magen spent her days staring out the office window dreaming she had the same. She'd needed a change in her life. Adventure!

Yet Magen knew well when she'd told her friends she was going to Paris for almost two weeks, when she'd said the word *adventure,* what she'd been thinking was *affair.* A silly fantasy.

Or was it?

Not if she could help it.

This foray was also a research trip. The historical novel she was writing had demanded she come to the source for more information. But if she could work in an affair on the side, then this trip would prove more than a mere tax write-off.

She ran her fingers down her throat, and strayed to the sore spot on the side of her neck. "Didn't think they had mosquitoes in Paris," she muttered. "I leave Minnesota and find them here. Ha!"

Strolling into the bedroom, she wondered briefly if she should cover up the red marks with some foundation, but decided if she could stop touching them they'd look fine. Didn't itch, and she couldn't remember getting them. She'd spent the afternoon walking the city, breathing in the air and fighting jet lag. Now she felt as if she could go all night. Must be the giddiness she still felt since meeting Lucian.

A rap at the door set her heart racing.

"Ohmygosh. He's here. Keep calm, Magen, and don't let your mouth run faster than your thoughts. No stupid comments this time. Just be cool."

If she managed as much, this vacation could prove far more intriguing than a boring research trip.

Chapter 2

Lucian couldn't recall how or why he'd acquired this mirror. He was particular to avoid antiquities from the late 1800s, the oft-glamorized Belle Époque. Too many bad memories.

The woman had homed in on it as if it were the only piece in his shop. He should be thankful to be rid of it.

The slim, rather colorless Magen Sloan was not like his usual sort of female. Not gregarious, nor flirtatious, nor even sensual. She was…astute. And plain.

And he couldn't decide why he'd wanted to make the delivery himself—which he never did. To see her again? Sure. But why? For another bite? He didn't need blood now that she'd quenched his thirst. As well, he didn't do *the second time*. It went against his very marrow. And even though he'd not combined sex with blood extraction earlier, they couldn't all become his blood-donation lovers.

You were compelled by her blushes and apparent unease when speaking to you. And those sudden bold looks, as if she defied her own mien with such a rash connection.

Or it had been her taste, he decided. He simply wanted another taste of American peach pie.

Greeted by an effusive, yet blushing Magen, Lucian accepted her invitation to enter and strode across the small living area to the window, the mirror hefted under one arm.

"You've an awful view. The Eiffel Tower is on the other side of the building. Not that having such a monstrosity in one's backyard provides for a better sight."

"You're kidding me," she said. "The Eiffel Tower is a world-famous landmark. Who wouldn't want to look at that?"

He turned, taking in her slim gray skirt. She had removed the blazer and the way the white blouse hugged her body, emphasizing high, ample breasts, pleased him. But still, too stiff and proper, she.

"I've that damned tower directly outside my window," he said. "And let me tell you, there are days I wish it was not. It's always in the way. There's much more to see in Paris than the Iron Lady."

"Then why don't you move?"

He smirked. The one thing keeping him fixed in place was his neighbor. "Because where I am is where I belong. Been there…" Far longer than she could fathom—or accept. "Forever, it seems."

"Set it over by the wall," she directed, clasping her hands gleefully at the prospect of such a prize. "You've wrapped it nicely."

"Standard for all deliveries. You want me to unwrap it?"

"Yes, please. I'm going to put it in the bedroom."

"Then let me bring it in there." Her openmouthed gape pricked his lascivious notions to undo her, transform her into something less than practical. "It's very heavy," he said. "I'm not sure you can lift it."

"Of course." She led him down the hallway to the bedroom, which boasted a bed and armoire and a free-standing wardrobe rack hung with colorful feminine clothing.

He tore away the brown paper and untied the string, letting the wrappings fall to the tiled floor, which had seen wear over the centuries. He deftly avoided standing directly before the silver-backed glass. Didn't need the mortal wondering why he cast no reflection.

"Lisa is going to love it," Magen said as she studied the faerie carved into the wood frame and traced a wing. "She's got a touch of green paint on her. The green faerie, eh?"

Lucian smirked at the cliché reference to absinthe, and

again, the abominable Belle Époque era. He glanced to the bed where an assortment of dresses had been neatly laid out. "You unpacking?"

"Planning my wardrobe for the week. I can't decide on the black or the red for the Moulin Rouge."

Seriously? This woman was all about the one period in time he most abhorred.

"The Moulin Rouge," he said, finding the words felt like blood-tainted absinthe on his tongue. "Decided to hit all the tourists traps then, eh?"

"Of course! I have the Louvre on my list. And Nôtre Dame and the Pantheon, and I must do the catacombs."

"Bunches of dirty old skulls, and a long laborious walk, that."

"Still. I've never been in Paris and I want to make the most of the time I have. Though, I am doing a sort of working vacation. Historical research to be done. I think I'll go with the red."

The ruffles flirting about the skirt hem would attract more than a few male eyes. Lucian winced to consider *Mademoiselle Pratique* being fawned over by the rabble who frequented the hedonistic nightclub. "You don't plan to go alone?"

"I am. I don't know anyone in the city."

"The Moulin Rouge is no place for a lone woman. Especially not a tourist lacking street smarts." She would be the proverbial rabbit surrounded by wolves. He didn't care much for wolves. "Why the Moulin Rouge, if I may ask? We've established you are practical. Unless your surprisingly wild side demands you go?"

"It's actually research."

He lifted a brow, unsure how a nightclub could provide information for any sort of research.

"I'm a freelance writer, and I'm working on a story that involves the nightclub, set during the Belle Époque. I'm particularly interested in the dancers who performed at the Moulin Rouge and their costumes."

"I see. You are aware it's been completely torn down and rebuilt since its heydays at the turn of the last century?"

"Yes, but still, I want to get a feel for the place. It's a writer thing. You wanted wine?"

She scampered into the kitchen, and Lucian followed. Upon noting her struggle with the corkscrew, he took over and expertly removed the cork to the encouraging ring of her giggle. Cheap wine to judge the garish label, but at least it wasn't white. He poured into the waiting goblets, and handed her a glass. Her swoon was obvious, and he couldn't help a lascivious smirk. He'd become jaded by beautiful women, some drenched in diamonds and demanding his attention, a few sexy models who frequented the clubs, the occasional lonely widow browsing the jewelry store counter, even a serious young artist sitting in the shade of a local park.

When had he last been the subject of a girlish giggle? It felt…refreshing.

Yet a familiar tingle jittered at the base of his fangs. She was no different than the others, save genuine innocence, and those unsexy spectacles. And peaches.

"To the impracticality of the moment," he offered, and tinged his glass against hers.

"Yes. To not being practical!"

"So." He wandered into the living room and lingered before the window. *"Vous êtes touriste?"*

"I don't understand the language. But, please, say something in French again."

He lifted a brow at her, and said, *"Le français vous plaît?"*

Beaming, she stepped closer to him, her blue eyes sweeping his face and down the front of his shirt. She'd had a few sips of wine, but her inhibitions were already noticeably loosening. Lucian could recognize desire a mile away. Sweet little tourist girl. She'd be chum in the hands of those who frequented the Moulin Rouge.

"Votre naïveté me plaît," he said. *Your innocence appeals to me.*

Magen breathed a sigh and touched him, right there, over his strangely speeding heart.

"I love the sound of the spoken French language," she said. "It's so seductive."

Seriously? It was the French? *"J'ai remarqué. Tes mamelons sont durs."*

"Mmm, I don't know what you just said, but if you've in mind to seduce me, Monsieur Bellisario, you are saying all the right things."

"Is that so?" He smirked at his crass comment about her hard nipples, and yet, she would never be the wiser. "I've never given much thought to the power of the language. And yet, here you are, standing in my arms. I have discovered, quite by accident, *Mademoiselle Pratique's* weakness."

"Say that in French."

He did so, and she then asked, quite out of the blue, "Are you interested in me, Lucian?"

"Yes," came out tentatively. She'd caught him unprepared for such a bold question.

"Why?"

Hell, one of those women who needed to talk and discuss everything? But he could not disregard her closeness, and those pert nipples. Blood and sex, anyone?

"Because you're cute," he said, speaking what came to mind, "and not like my usual woman. And, also, because of your accidental boldness. It's a weird juxtaposition with your studious appearance. And you smell like peaches."

She licked her lips. Lucian's erection grew harder. He twisted his head to loosen his tightening muscles.

"Magen, I must warn you, I'm a rogue. I conquer. I love them and leave them. I don't do…"

"Practical?"

"Exactly."

"Oh." A sigh, and then she looked up through her lush lashes. Her voice lowering to a sexy whisper, she wondered, "What about surprisingly wild?"

"Now that, I can work with that."

"Good, because I can't stop myself from what I need to do now."

She tilted up on tiptoes and kissed him. The slide of her hard leather shoe cruised up along his ankle. Her fingers glided up his chest. The woman in the practical clothing and serious glasses had found her brazen core and unleashed it.

"Oh." She leaned back, but did not step from his embrace. "I can't believe I just did that."

"I can't believe you're so startled you did." He pressed another kiss to her exquisite, small mouth, compelled by her innocent brazen. "*Je serai condamné.* If a few foreign words can coax you into my arms, I have to wonder what would happen if I spoke nothing but French to you, *mon amant.*"

"It's always been a fantasy of mine to have a Frenchman whisper sweet nothings to me."

"Sorry to disappoint you. I'm Italian."

"Oh? Oh."

She melted away from him, so he clutched her about the waist. Couldn't let this one get away on a technicality. Not when she had stirred him to a curious twist of want and desire. And she had no clue those fading red marks at her neck had been courtesy of him.

She giggled. "I'm silly, aren't I? Wow, this wine is potent."

"The cheap stuff always is." He took her goblet and set it aside along with his on a nearby table he recognized as mid-19th century. Acanthus leaves. Always the insipid acanthus leaves.

Nuzzling against her neck, Lucian drew in the gorgeous scent of her. Wine, peaches, and warm, salty skin. Keeping his lips over his teeth, he bit gently at her neck. So tempting to sink them in deeply. He allowed a skim of tooth to skin. It stirred his desire and hardened his erection to steel.

"Mmm, are you a vampire?" she asked playfully.

He'd heard the comment before after such a move. Thanks to the media, vampires—and the fantastical belief in them—were commonplace. He always used it to his advantage. "I am." He bit harder but did not break the skin. "I understand the vampire's bite is supposed to be erotic."

"Yes, but I'd never want to become a creature of the night. I imagine it would be a lonely life. Well, you know, if they were real."

She'd nailed that one on the head. Lonely, and... unfulfilling. Interesting though, she'd not concluded it was horrible, disgusting or even sacrilege.

"You're like a man who has stepped out of my dreams," she whispered. "I...I want you, Lucian."

He slid a hand along her leg, lifting it high to hug his thigh. They always wanted him. Because of the bite.

Yet, it had been hours since he'd bitten her. Any orgasmic effects from the blood extraction had long left her system. So she wanted him...for him?

Magen's fingers worked at his shirt buttons, and quickly her warm palm seared against his skin. Lucian sucked in air and held her arms, almost defensively, as he vacillated with his inner devil. Bite her, and fuck her and be done with her.

Or...make love to this practical, yet strangely sensual, woman who had melted against his heart with but a few French words?

He lifted Magen into his arms, and, kissing her hot neck, carried her into the bedroom and laid her on the bed. He tore off his shirt. She slipped down her skirt to reveal—

"Those are not practical undergarments, *Mademoiselle Pratique*."

Dashing a finger along the pink lace scalloping her bra, she again gave him that devastating look up through her lashes. "I did mention my surprisingly wild side."

The rosy flush that colored her cheeks and chest invited him to skate his tongue over the pink lace, and beyond, to taste the heat of her.

Screw the bite. He wanted to indulge in the carnal pleasures tonight.

Such novelty.

Lucian's hard biceps pulsed as he crawled above her on the bed, a predatory glint in his dark eyes. Briefly, Magen admonished herself for jumping off a cliff with no safety net below. Having sex with a man she just met? Scandalous.

And then she abandoned her inner angel, and pulled the handsome foreigner down for a long, deep kiss that defied her to push him away and ask him to leave.

Never.

His mouth slicked down her throat and his seeking tongue traced a tingling path to her bra, which he quickly removed and tossed to the floor, while muttering something about pink being a new favorite color. Hot breaths hushed across her nipples; one, then the other, slowly, as if stoking kindle to a flame. He looked to her, defying her to chicken out, to push him away and pull on her clothes.

No way. Not tonight. She had come to Paris exactly for this.

"Yes," she said on a gasping hush.

His tongue danced about her nipple. Magen thrust her

head back in the soft feather pillow, closing her eyes to fully experience the sensation. He teased her expertly, licking and nipping gently, then pausing until she almost cried out for him to continue, but before she could, he began again.

Gliding her hands down his back, she marveled at his structure. Solid, with muscles like leather straps that pulsed and undulated under her exploring fingers. He smelled faintly of spicy aftershave, and a little like dust, perhaps from his antique shop.

"*Mon amant*, you want this?"

"Yes. What does *mon amant* mean?"

"My lover," he said. He tongue tickled down her belly and circled there, marking her lazily. "The panties will have to go." The trace of his tongue along the lacy border of her panties coaxed up Magen's hips.

Her insides screamed for him to go quickly, to not stop and to grant her the fantasy affair she desired, yet the practical synapses in her brain that were still firing despite the erotic deluge managed to plead for a slow, restrained seduction.

And Magen had to agree with her practical side.

Raking her fingers through his soft, dark hair, she moaned when his teeth snagged the lace and tugged. So glad she'd gone with the bikini wax at the salon, she smiled to herself as she watched her panties go flying and land by the mirror across the room.

But Lucian would not allow her mind to stray from what he was doing. He found her sensitive spot at the apex of her thighs, and tongued it expertly. Slow, then hard, then lightly, then in swift repetitive strokes.

She clutched for…something, anything, wanting it to be Lucian's hot, hard body beneath her fingers, yet only landed a clump of the sheets, which she squeezed as the orgasm fired through her core and swept her off into a place more wonderful than Paris, or her wild imagination could ever take her.

Magen Sloan had just fulfilled her wildest fantasy.

Chapter 3

The following day, Lucian strode about Magen's borrowed apartment before the window with the terrible view. The setting sun gleamed gold on the windows across the street. They had just finished making love for perhaps the third time since breakfast, and Magen was in the shower humming.

And he was still here.

"What the hell?"

Clad in but his jeans, he looked about the apartment. Velvet pillows that had once been neatly placed upon the couch were strewn on the floor because they'd made love there moments ago. Pieces of Magen's clothing forged a path to the bedroom, because despite her good intentions of getting dressed, he had stripped her as quickly as she had donned them. Teacups sat half-empty on the kitchen table alongside hard cheese and bread. A wine bottle lay on the floor by the window.

"I never..." He winced. "Stay."

What was so different about this woman that he had been here twenty-four hours, and had made love to her in every position possible and had even learned a new one from her? And he had not bitten her again, since first meeting her in the shop.

"Incredible."

It was almost as if he enjoyed her company. As if he didn't need to take from her whatever he could get and then cast her aside.

"That makes little sense." Women were...disposable. Relationships were...not a word in his lexicon.

"Mon amant," she called softly from around the corner. A long, bare leg teased, followed by a peek of her kiss-reddened lips.

As if a magnet, Lucian was at her side, kissing her mouth, still wet from the shower, and gliding his hands down her back as the towel slipped away. There, at the curve of her hip, he liked to rest his hand as it fit about her and claimed her. As if starved for blood as he had been yesterday afternoon, he couldn't get enough of her now, yet drinking her blood was the furthest thing from his thoughts.

"I was thinking while I was showering," she said. "You have to know I don't make a habit of sleeping with strangers. It's not who I am. I would never—well, I mean, I did, and it was amazing. But only with you."

"Then you must also know this is not a habit of mine."

"This?"

"This." He kissed her neck. No, no desire to sink in his fangs. Inhaling her soapy clean scent did enough to rocket up his libido—not that it had come down. "Staying. One-night stands are my thing."

"I see." Her body curved away from his. "You didn't have to bring the mirror. You did say you were going to have someone else deliver it."

"I know that. But I genuinely wanted to see you again. You seem to have enchanted me, *Mademoiselle Pratique*." He slipped his fingers about her breast, finding he knew the shape of it, the exact way to cup his fingers to encompass her, for he'd studied her so closely over the past day. "Tell me you won't put a bra on these gorgeous breasts tonight?"

"Monsieur, I may have a wild side, but no bra?"

He bent to suckle at her, and she cooed in that soft, sighing manner that felt like music across his skin.

"All right," she said. "You've convinced me. Shouldn't we get going soon?"

"The Moulin Rouge stays open all night. We'll get there in time."

Chapter 4

In fact, they didn't head to the Moulin Rouge until two days later. Magen couldn't argue against sex with Lucian, even after he'd brought her to orgasm, over and over, and she felt achy and tired. Exhausted, really. Yet blissfully drowsy with wonder and satisfaction.

Lying next to him, breathing in his skin and holding him, she could do all day. And they had. She'd even almost forgotten his mention of not doing the *stay*. Almost. But, heck, if she was worthy of the man breaking a rule like that, then she wasn't about to complain.

He'd gone down to fetch her lunch and then later, went out for wine and cheese. The past three days had been a decadent indulgence in all her wildest fantasies.

He'd said he wasn't the kind of guy to stay, let alone see a woman a second time after their initial encounter.

So that must mean she'd won him over. Yet how, baffled Magen. She was no seductress. And Lucian Bellisario put sexy off the scale and out into the stratosphere. But she wasn't about to question the match. Best to enjoy this fantasy while she could.

Lucian had needed to stop by the shop and check emails before they continued to the nightclub, so Magen browsed the jewelry counter while waiting. The pieces he offered were gemstones set in silver, platinum and gold. All very pricey.

"Find something that appeals to you, *mon amant?*"

That he called her an endearment in French never ceased to send a titillating shiver down Magen's spine and across her breasts. Her tightening nipples drew his eyes, and she reveled in the quiet power she had over him.

"I'm not sure. What is that? I think there's a piece slipped down the side between the glass."

He leaned over the counter to inspect and reached under the glass to fish for the tiny bit of brass chain that just peeked out. "You're right. Hell, this thing? I thought I'd sold that decades—I mean, years ago."

She snagged it before he could protest. Magen laid the necklace on the display-counter glass. A green glass-winged faerie was set in ornamental brass she associated with the Belle Époque era. "It almost looks like—"

"Fouquet," he offered. "It's a sorry old piece."

"Sorry? It's gorgeous. I want to wear it. Please?" she begged when his frown surprised her. She'd only gotten smiles and coos and agreements from him the past few days. "I don't want you to give it to me. Just let me borrow it for tonight?"

"It doesn't go with your red dress."

"Even better. It'll stand out." She took the cleaning cloth tucked aside the register and rubbed it over the brass. "The green faerie. She's been showing up a lot in my life since I arrived in Paris. Oh, pretty please, my handsome lover?"

She walked her fingers up his shirt, and flicked her nails under his chin, a move that generally found his cock hardening against her stomach when they were lying in bed.

"Just for tonight," he said.

Magen squealed, and the words *I love you* touched the tip of her tongue, but she fought them back. To say such words would be a jerk reaction to the gift of wearing the valuable necklace, nothing more. Nothing was going to spoil this fantasy, especially not love.

Magen walked hand in hand with Lucian through the dazzling neon chaos of the Moulin Rouge. The faerie necklace hung low at her neckline, or rather, her décolletage. She loved that word for cleavage. Anything spoken in French zoned right into the desire center of her brain. Like Lucian. *L'homme* was the word for man. And what a man. His smoldering, dark eyes and the way he parted his lips and pressed his tongue to the back of his top teeth as he pumped his steel-hard erection inside her was a sloe-eyed hungry look that turned her insides melty and warm.

"Would you like to get something to eat?" he asked as they passed the restaurant nestled inside the club.

"No, but I would like a sip of absinthe."

His hungry look switched abruptly to shock.

"Research," she explained. "Please?"

He nodded. "Just a sip, then. *Mon Dieu, je vais brûler.*" He stepped up to the bar.

While Magen waited, she watched the show onstage. It was a rock opera version of Dracula that mixed in touches of ballet, Cirque du Soleil and Broadway. The lead, who played Dracula to a swooning Lucy in red ballet tutu, was gorgeous, but not as handsome as her date.

When Lucian returned with her drink, he snuggled up behind her, handing around the glass of pale green liquid from behind. He whispered in her ear, "Don't go all loopy on me now."

Smiling, she vacillated between concentrating on the taste, and the intensity of Lucian's closeness. His body lured her to seek his innate warmth, drawing her back until her shoulder rested against his chest. He smelled—

well, she couldn't get beyond the smell of the absinthe. Sharp and like licorice. And the first sip?

"Oh, this is awful."

With a chuckle, he claimed her glass and held it high to catch the glinting neon lights in the cloudy liquid. "It never was good. Its notoriety is what gave it fame. All hype, if you ask me. You like the show?"

"I don't understand what they are singing, and, yet, I feel the sexy mood. But maybe that's because I'm standing in your arms."

He swept an arm about her shoulder and looked toward the stage. "Ah, Dracula. Another hyped-up media darling. So, do you think you've seen enough?" He set the absinthe on a passing waiter's tray.

"Almost. Let's walk down this hallway where it looks like they feature some historical displays."

Lucian paused before a framed Art Nouveau poster that featured a dancer with ruffled skirts. Magen commented it looked like Toulouse Lautrec's work.

"No. Toulouse would have never painted that," he said with some authority.

She studied him keenly. Beyond their bedroom antics she knew little about the man's interests. "You speak of the past as if you've walked through it."

"I, well…" With a jaunty tilt of his head, he cast her a devilish grin. "As I told you that first night we met, I am a vampire."

"I see. And you've walked through the centuries?"

"Just the twentieth and late nineteenth centuries."

He put his hand against the wall, over her shoulder, leaning in so she was but inches from his mouth. Despite the blaring music from the main ballroom, the red-fabric walls darkened the empty hallway, granting them a certain intimacy.

"If you were a vampire," she said, "I would let you bite me."

"I bet you'd taste like peaches." He nuzzled aside her cheek, his nose tracing her ear.

"Show me your fangs, *mon amant*," she said teasingly.

Lucien tapped her jaw with a finger, grinned widely, then parted his lips to reveal his incisors, which looked rather sharp, but were no longer than his other teeth.

"Tease," she said and turned to walk right into the framed poster on the wall.

Magen caught herself against the glass. It featured an image of a cancan dancer wearing maroon skirts. The name painted in bold pink across the bottom declared her Magenta, Dazzling Queen of the Night.

Placing her palms against the glass, she suddenly felt her body burst with light, as if she'd been blasted by a star, though she felt no pain, only a strange feeling of... claiming.

"Must have been a famous dancer," Lucian commented. His voice sounded distant, muted. He tugged her firmly to move along.

Yet Magen remained, fixed to the poster. The world receded. Her heartbeats muffled. *Knowing* embodied her. She gasped, narrowing her gaze on the poster. What was happening?

"Magen?"

Lucian's sure presence prickled up her spine. Suddenly his closeness irritated, and the faded mosquito bites at her neck burned like flame. The sensation of something hard and sharp pricking her neck washed over her, and crimson flooded her vision.

"Vampire," Magen gasped.

And her world went black.

Before fainting into his arms, Magen had whispered *vampire*. That word disturbed Lucian more than it should. Was she recalling their playful banter? Confused by the obnoxious entertainment out in the main ballroom? She had seemed different before fainting, and her voice had sounded deeper, not the high, yet sure tone of *Mademoiselle Pratique*.

Lying upon a fainting sofa in a dressing room they'd been offered by the manager, Magen awoke with a start. Lucian offered a smile and squeezed her arm. "You fainted."

Magen sat up and blinked, taking in the dark violet-damask walls and the strip lighting paralleling a wall-size dressing mirror, which Lucian had conveniently covered with a black shawl he'd found on a chair.

"I'm still at the Moulin Rouge. I…" She ran a palm over her neck, landing on the faerie necklace Lucian wished she had never spotted wedged against the glass. "I feel different."

"Did you hit your head out in the hallway?"

"No, I…don't think so?" She frowned and touched her temple.

Of course she hadn't hit her head. She'd been staring at that damned poster of Magenta as if it had meant something to her. She could never know how much it meant to him. How it haunted him. He should have never accompanied her to this place.

"You're a…vampire?" When she looked at him, it was with older eyes, more knowing. Almost familiar, that gaze. "Lucian?"

"Let's get you home," he suggested. "We can talk about this later."

She nodded. "Yes, I want to go home. She's so tired of this place."

Lucian paused in helping her to stand from the red-velvet couch. "She?"

"Huh?"

"You said *she* is tired?"

"I did? Me. I'm tired. I'm sorry I flaked out on our date by fainting."

"Don't worry about it. I'll hail a cab."

The faster he got out of this memory trap, the better.

The cabbie let them off in the eighth quarter, and Lucian escorted Magen up to her apartment. He looked out the window, avoiding eye contact with her. "Did you get a good look over the place for your research?"

"I think so. But now I'm curious about Magenta, Dazzling Queen of the Night. When I looked at the Magenta poster it was almost as if… I felt her presence. In me."

"In you? Like what? Some kind of reincarnated soul?" His laughter was deep and accusing.

Magen dropped the shawl she'd wrapped about her shoulders. He shouldn't be so cruel. She hadn't deserved his cut. He should wrap her in his arms and strip away her clothes, because damn, if he wasn't already comfortable with the sweet American tourist and already craved her skin against his. She had done something to him the past few days. Softened him. Made him want something more than a quick bite and a fast fuck. She had opened his heart to the possibilities that could come with the stay.

She called you vampire.

He did need to get to the root of that out-of-the-blue accusation. Should he reveal his truth? Could he? She wouldn't be in Paris much longer. It hardly seemed worth the headache and the sure argument and then abandonment.

No, keep her while you can. You've never had such closeness with a woman.

From his position by the door, Lucian noticed Magen's walk took on a decidedly slinky rhythm as she approached the window where outside velvet-gray clouds streaked across the half-moon. Reaching up, she tugged out a pin from her updo and her glossy hair swept her neck and across her shoulders. It was a practiced move, not one he expected from his American tourist. Though certainly he had unburied her sensuality and set it free.

"Lucian," she cooed in an odd tone.

That voice pierced his skin and ran through his veins like ice. He'd heard it before, but not for over a century. And he was imagining it now. *Had to be.*

His mention of reincarnation, and that poster—combined with the ridiculous Dracula show—had put him out of sorts as much as she was.

"You feeling all right, *mon amant?*"

Magen turned and grabbed him by the shoulders and pulled him in for an urgent kiss. Not breaking the kiss, Lucian swept her up and landed on the couch with her in his arms. She tasted like the sweet anise bite of absinthe. Beneath his roaming palms, her skin was hot and flushed, her breath coming heavily.

Nuzzling his nose along her jaw, he dared to graze a fang over her skin, to dally with his control. He walked a fine line—to reveal his nature or not? He wanted to possess her in every way possible, and he could still bring the taste of her peach-sweet blood to the tip of his tongue with recall. But dare he?

"Oh, I remember this," she cooed.

That voice—so familiar—startled him so much, he pushed away from her wanting embrace and stood.

Curling up a leg, she sat upright and leaned forward, employing a kittenish flutter of lash along with a brazenly slinky shift of her shoulder that set her dress sleeve sliding down to expose the cusp of a breast.

"My lover, the vampire," she said. Licking her lips, she pierced him with a coy smirk. "Bite me, Lucian. Give me your wicked kiss."

"Magen?" Reason was not at hand. He bent to study her face and saw her practical blue irises and pale pink mouth, but in his very being Lucian felt the seductress beneath the innocence tap at a part of him he'd long thought excised. "What are you playing at?"

"It's no play, *mon amant*." She fondled the faerie necklace. That damned necklace! "She brought me back, and now I want more."

"More?" He raked his fingers through his hair. "This is insanity. Magen, you sound like—"

She skated her tongue across her lower lip, bowing her

head and looking up at him with the devastating knowing that cut him to the core.

And in that moment, Lucian's heart stopped beating. And then it dropped to his gut.

Magenta had returned to haunt him.

Chapter 5

Her voice was Magen's, but lower, more confident. Sure of herself. Lucian felt as though he were standing before…his former lover.

"This is not happening." He put up a palm, as if he were Certainly Jones, the dark witch, and a gesture of his hand could revert the moment to him and sweet, practical Magen Sloan from America. "You are not her. You cannot be."

He backed toward the door.

Could reincarnation be possible? But more disturbing—she knew he was vampire? He had persuaded that memory from Magen. She hadn't said a thing to him during their days-long sex session. The persuasion must have gone afoul. She remembered, only it had been a delayed memory, perhaps like amnesia. Which didn't

explain why she thought she was Magenta. Or how she
could sound like her and...remember.

Would she remember it all?

Lucian staggered to the door and gripped the handle.
"I have to get away from here."

"Not until you bite me again, lover!" Magen rushed to
meet him at the door and pressed her back against it so
her body was sandwiched between him and his escape.

His chest heaved against hers. She smelled different.
Like lilacs.

No, that had been her scent. She used to bathe in it so
she would smell like flowers and salt when they made
love in his apartment following a show.

"Lucian." Her pupils were wide, her lips parted. She
toyed her finger along his jaw and tapped his tight mouth.
"I know what you're hiding behind that scowl. A hunger for this."

She tilted her head aside, exposing the long, pale column of neck he'd earlier had under his mouth. But then
he had kissed Magen softly with little intention of sinking in his fangs.

Lucian breathed out. He could not tear his gaze from
the pulsing vein. Sustenance. He didn't need it. But he
would never pass it up. He indulged in blood as a woman
indulged in jewelry or chocolate.

She nodded, silently granting him permission.

He kissed her neck, hard, growling at the connection,

the extreme control the act gave him. She tangled her fingers into his hair. Drawing in the scent of her arousal, he licked her vein hungrily.

He should push her aside and march out of here. Everything about Magen Sloan was wrong for him. And yet it felt so damned right. She had become bold and seductive, and that enamored him. And made him hard and hot for her blood.

But whose blood did he really crave right now?

He stroked his tongue along her neck. "Tell me your name."

"You know my name, lover."

He wasn't aware of sliding his hands up her torso to cup her breasts, a natural reaction to holding Magen's sensual body so close. Her nipples beaded against his chest. Her arousal salted her blood and he wanted to know her. Own her.

Taste her.

No matter who she was.

Lucian bit into flesh and vein. Heat spurted against the roof of his mouth. Her fingernails dug into his shoulders and she clung to him as he sucked in her blood. Her sweet, hot, dizzyingly delicious blood. It tasted, not like Magen's sweet peach blend, but instead...

"Oh, Lucian, *mon amour,* you are a marvelous vampire."

...like absinthe.

He pulled away with the taste of wormwood on his tongue. Beyond the disturbing taste, something bothered him more. She'd spoken perfect French.

Magen's lips curled into a saucy tease, and she stroked her bleeding neck. *"Prends du plus, mon amant, c'était bien longtemps."* Take more, lover, it was so long ago.

Absinthe and blood curled down Lucian's throat. "No, it can't be."

A vixen unleashed, blood flowing down her neck and staining her red dress, Magen grabbed his shirt front. "You are frightened of me, Lucian?"

"No. Yes."

He shoved her aside and tugged open the door, racing away from the horrors of his past.

This night, the vampire fled the victim.

Magen came to with a start. Water splashed and she slipped, flailing to slap her palms on the edge of the tub.

"A bath?"

She was sitting naked in the tub, soaking, with lemon-scented bubble bath frothing about her breasts. "When did I—?"

She never took baths. It was too...*impractical.* And lately her showers had been shared with Lucian. Where was he?

She listened, but did not hear him pattering about the apartment through the open bathroom door.

Time had slipped away. And yet, she had been aware of the passing time. She'd known when she'd kissed Lucian earlier, and then he'd fled as if the devil were on his heels.

Something, or someone, had overtaken her upon return from the Moulin Rouge. Or had it occurred at the nightclub? That something had slipped into her skin and spoken through her, moved her body as another person would, and said things—

"In French."

She touched her throat and sat up. The air in the bathroom was chilly due to the window having been left open a crack so she sank down into the warm water.

"I had a sip of absinthe." It had tasted awful, so bitter, and she didn't like anise. "I've never been so drunk that I can't recall the things I've done."

But she did recall racing to the door to stop Lucian from leaving—because she'd wanted him to bite her.

Magen stroked her neck, feeling new, tender wounds. For reasons beyond her grasp, she knew they had not been inflicted by a nuisance insect. "A vampire?"

Had the man actually bitten her? And she had asked him to.

"Magenta asked," she said with no doubt. "The dancer from the Moulin Rouge. The one…" Lucian had said something about reincarnation. Could it possibly be? "Ohmygod, this is so weird. And amazing. And…"

Troubling.

She got out of the tub and wrapped a towel around her body. Checking the mirror, she studied the two red spots on her neck. "They've begun to heal quickly."

She remembered the startled look on Lucian's face, though she hadn't been herself, but rather had been sitting inside her body witnessing, as the other woman had used it and had spoken to Lucian as if she'd known him.

How could that be?

And he had reacted as if he had known her, running his hands over her body, kissing her with such familiarity. Of course, he did know her body well, so that hadn't been unusual.

Magen wandered into the dark bedroom and flicked on the lamp by the bed. She dried off and climbed into bed, pulling the sheets up around her breasts. Despite feeling as though Lucian should be nestled beside her, his hand fitted against her hip and his mouth tasting her skin, she took solace in being alone right now. She pondered what had occurred.

"Am I really a reincarnation of a cancan dancer?" Wouldn't that make for some awesome research material? "But how was she able to...?" She glanced around the darkness. "Are you in this room?"

She put a hand over her chest. "Or are you in here?"

She didn't know how reincarnation worked. Could the former person occupy the current person? Sounded far wackier than she could concoct, a writer who supplemented her historical writing with the occasional fantasy novel.

Could she call her back? Dare she? What if Magenta was able to take over her body for lengthy periods, and she, Magen, could not control her?

And, yet, she wanted her to return, so she could learn all she could about the fascinating woman she may have once been.

He lived across the river from where Magen was staying. Lucian rushed through the streets. Visions haunted his thoughts, and he had difficulty determining what was real and what was not. Everything was toned in red. Screams clamored against the sounds of car horns and shouts from tourists gathered outside the Eiffel Tower, which was lit up in a dazzling display of wasted electricity.

He landed in the lobby of his building and shuffled toward the stairs, closing the door with a slam and sliding down onto the steps. Catching his head in his hands, he shook it to fend off the images. A couple dancing in a small studio beneath torn drapes. Candles flickering madly, the wax running across a chipped tile floor. Real chills wracked his body as the visions segued to skulls and rats, and a wooden stake dripping with blood. The taste of wormwood coiled on his tongue.

"It can't be," he said. "How is this possible?"

Even after her transformation, Magenta had always feared her death. She'd thought she would be buried in a pauper's grave where the rats would gnaw at her bones.

"It was an accident," he whispered. "I drank too much. *She* had drunk too much."

She'd been addicted to absinthe. Had consumed it constantly. He'd never had a taste for the wicked brew, save for when it was lacing her blood. He'd become drunk on it, too, without lifting the glass to his lips.

That night haunted him relentlessly over the decades. A night he regretted. And, yet, she had tried to kill him first.

And now it had returned to haunt him again. But how? Through Magen's blood? It didn't make sense. And, yet, in the moment when he'd bitten her, and she had spoken French, and crept toward him like a vixen on the hunt, he'd known it was Magenta.

Swallowing the awful taste of absinthe-laced blood, Lucian let his head fall against the wall. The vindictive woman he had once loved, only to be spurned after her fickle love had turned sour, had returned to take revenge upon him.

Chapter 6

Magen woke, dressed and made scrambled eggs and coffee, and was out of the door like a breeze. She wanted answers. She wanted to return to the Moulin Rouge. She wanted Lucian to enfold her in his arms, kiss away her worries and tell her everything was not as strange and horrifying as she suspected.

She wanted… Well, she wanted a lot before ten o'clock in the morning.

Knowing Lucian's hours were a bit later—for he always slept until noon—and knowing the Moulin Rouge didn't open until evening, she curbed her enthusiasm and decided a stroll to the Louvre would distract her from the excitement and strange revelations of last night.

Besides, she intended to see as many sights as possible while here. And despite her vacation having been highjacked by a nineteenth-century cancan dancer and, possibly, a sexy vampire, she was determined to get some touristing done.

Could he really be a vampire? It had been their silly banter, she tried to convince herself. Combined with the weirdness of Magenta, and she wasn't sure what was real anymore.

Once at the Louvre, she headed straight for the *Mona Lisa,* yet was disappointed to discover the painting quite small. Not that she'd expected it to be large, but after all its hype, it was a quiet little piece hung on a big white wall behind bulletproof glass.

Sighing, she took in the rest of the paintings in the room, finding Veronese's *Wedding at Cana* on the wall opposite the *Mona Lisa* was so large, it perhaps should be put to blame for making DaVinci's masterpiece appear so infinitesimal. Then again, *La Joconde* could probably hold her own against the ribald wedding party.

Around noon, and after getting a coffee and pastry at the Louvre's Starbucks, Magen pondered heading over to Lucian's antique shop. It was the only place she knew to find him, and the shop was near the Eiffel Tower. Perhaps he lived in the neighborhood? Strange that he hadn't invited her to his place yet. On the other hand, once they melted into each other's arms, their intensity and desire to become one another had kept them in place, which had always been Lisa's apartment.

She needed answers about why she had thought he was a vampire, and with the evidence of a bite on her neck, she suspected what the answer would be.

So why go to him? He's dangerous, could bite you again, maybe even turn you into one.

"Nonsense."

Her practical side wrangled with her apprehension. If he was a vampire, she had no reason to fear him. He wouldn't change her unless she wanted that, if he even could. And he'd only given her a small bite. She was already healed and—

"What are you thinking?"

Outside the Louvre, in the Cour Napoléon, near the glass and metal pyramid, Magen found a seat on the bench before one of seven triangular granite pools.

"I'm going to talk to the vampire," she said out loud, surprised at the shaky tone of her voice.

Because she needed answers to the more pressing question: Had she actually been Magenta last night? When he'd stood in her apartment and had bitten her, had it been because Magenta had urged him to do so? It was a crazy thought, and she wasn't sure how to present it to him, but she had to know.

"I'm not sure what happened," Lucian said into the cell phone as he strode down the shady street toward his building, a bouquet of pink roses in one hand. Sunglasses in place, he worried little for the UV rays harming his skin. He'd chosen this location because four-story buildings across the street always shadowed his walk, no matter where the sun sat in the sky.

He'd called his best friend, CJ, whom he'd woken.

"She had a different voice, and she sounded like..." He winced. "You know."

"And she said something about reincarnation?"

"Actually, I was the one to bring that up. It was the first idea that popped into my brain. But do you think it's possible?"

"I'm not sure I subscribe to soul renewal, at least not soul rebirth. Seems a lot of work if you ask me."

"Right. But ghosts are real," Lucian argued. "Vampires are real. Hell, witches summon demons and all that crazy stuff. So why not reincarnation?"

"You going to see her again?"

"I'm not sure. She knows I bit her. It's not so much I can't deal with her knowing what I am, but that she'll know I persuaded her and manipulated her mind."

"So she means something to you," CJ suggested.

"Absolutely. I haven't been away from her for more than an hour since I met her days ago."

CJ whistled. "Lucian, this is interesting. You are a rascal, a rogue extraordinaire. You don't do the stay."

"Tell me about it!"

"I think you need to see her again," CJ suggested.

He did want to see Magen again. And he did not. Because if faced with Magenta, he wasn't prepared for that reunion. But how to stay away from the woman he— well, he wouldn't go *there*. Could he? Love? No, it was too early. He knew Magen's body, but there was much to learn about her life yet.

The last woman he'd truly known, body, soul and mind, had been Magenta. His fickle lover, who had died in his arms.

A little over a hundred years ago, he'd poured out his grief to CJ over many drunken nights of guilt and torture. He'd thought he'd gone beyond the need for forgiveness, but had he? Did he think he could earn forgiveness from an innocent American woman who had no clue what skeletons danced in his closet?

"Magen Sloan is sweet and plain and has a mind of her own. She's not impressed by me, yet a few French words have her begging for more."

"Not your type, that's for sure. That's why she attracts you so much. Maybe you want to be tamed."

"I don't know."

"Sounds like she's got a good start. You spending all your time with her is damning evidence."

"Guilty as charged. But what if she's not…herself. I can't deal with this, man. Magenta was…"

He stopped at the entrance to his building and tilted

back his head, closing his eyes. Never had a woman muddled him so. Or was it two women?

"You can't run from your past forever," CJ said. "You've been lucky to avoid something like this for so long. Talk to you later, man. I have a warm witch nestled up against me, and am not fool enough to ignore her for one moment longer."

The phone clicked off, and Lucian shoved the cell in his pocket. When a woman with practical brown hair and a pressed gray skirt called to him from across the street, he waved and forced on a smile.

"And so it begins."

Chapter 7

Lucian waved at her. Magen crossed the street. The antique shop was around the corner, so she guessed this must be his residence. With little more than a brush of his lips across hers in greeting, he then nodded for her to follow him through the brass- and marble-clad lobby.

Seeing him for the first time in daylight, Magen lost her apprehension. He'd been outside walking in the sunshine. *Not a vampire.* And yet…

She couldn't disregard the bite marks on her neck. Had it been some kind of weird sexual fetish? The guy liked to gnaw on necks? Taste blood? She wasn't as repulsed as she should be. When it had happened, it had felt so good. Hell, she could have sworn she'd had something very close to an orgasm at the time.

On the other hand, every time the man touched her

she achieved some kind of sexual explosion. Stars sparkled and the earth's gravity wobbled. It was that good.

She was about to ask if biting was his thing, when the elevator doors glided open. Together in the small enclosure, she breathed in his cologne, which was woodsy, like cedar, and then she got distracted wondering if coffins were still made from cedar.

"I'm pleased you've found my place," he said.

"We have things to talk about."

"We do. But I confess it'll be hard to converse when you smell so good. Peaches again. I should ask—why peaches?"

"My mother used to bake peach pies."

"Used to?"

"She ran away with a lover years ago. Haven't heard from her since."

He quirked a brow.

So she was from hoyden stock. And, yes, she'd traveled to Paris seeking a passionate affair with a man who would whisper sexy French bon mots in her ear. Magen Sloan's wild side, revealed. It was high time.

"Those are beautiful," she said of the roses.

"Yes, I thought so. Uh, I'm sorry. For rushing out last night. Things got weird—" The elevator dinged, and the door slid open. He winked and let her exit the elevator first.

An elderly woman was setting a trash bag outside

her door, the only other apartment on the floor. Lucian rushed to help her. "Evelyn, you should let me take that out for you."

"Oh, Lucian, you spoil me. What is this?"

"I was thinking of you. They are the color of the blush in your cheeks." He handed her the flowers and kissed her on the cheek.

Magen sighed. Such a romantic gesture. The woman must be in her eighties. She couldn't feel jealous the flowers hadn't been meant for her.

"And who is this?"

"Oh, I'm sorry. Madame de Tour, this is Magen Sloan, a...client of the shop and new friend. Magen, this is the one and only Madame Evelyn de Tour."

Trying not to be miffed by the cold label of *friend,* Magen shook the woman's crepe-skinned hand. An elegant sweep of silver hair curled upon her head and her gray eyes brightened with a smile. Thin, she stood remarkably straight and Magen wondered if she might have been a dancer for her carriage.

"She's not like the others," Evelyn commented, then stepped inside her apartment, and blew Lucian a kiss. "Have a lovely afternoon, you two."

Lucian closed her door, and directed Magen into his apartment.

She made a beeline for the window overlooking the Eiffel Tower. It soared through the sky across a park directly before his building. "Wow. You do have an amazing view."

"As I've said—"

"A monstrosity. You are a nut. I can't see how this view could ever get boring."

"Trust me, it gets dull. Wine?"

"Uh, no. It's early."

He shrugged, and leaned against the wall, arms crossing over his broad chest. Too far away. Why hadn't he swept her into his arms and ravished her with kisses and whispers in French?

Same reason you're keeping your distance. Weird, as he'd said in the elevator.

His hair was loose and curly, easily raked over his ears. Magen wanted to try the move, yet something in his dark gaze cautioned her. And his mouth, slightly open, did not show her the teeth she was so curious about, yet that manner he had of pressing his tongue to the backs of his top teeth was so sexy.

"So I'm not like the others, eh?"

"The others?" he wondered.

"Madame de Tour just said?"

"Ah. The others. Yes, well, I am a bachelor. I do have lovers. I'm sure she made an assumption."

"And how am I so different from these other lovers that your dear old neighbor recognizes it?"

"Don't speak rudely of Evelyn. We've been friends for decades."

"Really? How is that possible? You don't look a day over thirty. She must have been your babysitter."

"I'm much older. But, then, you already suspect as much, don't you?"

"Why don't you come out with it and tell me?" Her hand started to shake, so Magen put it behind her back.

Be bold, she whispered inwardly. Or had that been a whisper from within?

Either way, time to get some answers. "Are you a vampire?"

He tilted his head and nodded. A simple acknowledgment to a tremendous question.

"It's true, then."

"You've caught me out. How is the bite?" he asked. "It's not sore?"

She rubbed her neck. "No, it's fine now, but—*you bit me.* And I think you also bit me when I was in your shop, yet I can't remember—"

He approached her, but Magen took a step back, and her shoulders met the wall. He remained four feet from her, his hands up to placate. "Don't be afraid."

"I'm not afraid. Maybe a little. I feel more betrayal than fear to know you've been so intimate with me on the sly."

"You make it sound cheap."

"Well, what was it?"

"Magen, when I bite someone I can make them forget. I did it in the antique shop because I had to. I was famished. I'd just...given blood."

"So you said. You seriously donate blood?"

"It's not as you assume. It was for a friend. He needed it for a spell."

"A spell?" Chest tightening, her mouth grew dry. "I don't think I want to hear this."

"You don't need details. Suffice, yes, I am a vampire. I drink blood to survive. You were there when I needed blood desperately, and I hadn't thought to see you again, so I persuaded the memory of my bite from you."

"But you did return with the mirror. And you've been with me, in my bed, every day since. You didn't think it would have been wise to mention this sometime?"

"Magen—how does one come out with a fact like that? Hello, how do you do? You're pretty and you smell nice. I adore making love to you, and by the by, I also drink blood to survive."

Despite the revelation creatures of the night actually existed, Magen couldn't ignore the betrayal creeping along her veins, tightening and poking. He could have given her some version of that confession when they'd teasingly danced around the topic.

"So you're a vampire." She inhaled and let out her breath, her shoulders falling. "Give me some time with that one. But there's the other thing that happened last night in my apartment I need to understand."

"You coaxed me to bite you, if I recall correctly. *Mademoiselle Pratique* showing me a new fetish?"

"Did I? Or was it someone else? I think it wasn't me, but instead Magenta."

"Oh, Magen. The reincarnation thing? It was a stupid suggestion. Reincarnation isn't for real."

He made show of laughing but it was false. Magen wondered what he was trying to cover up so skillfully as he had his bite.

"I felt her inside me, Lucian. And I know things. Like I can see myself on a bed with a lover who speaks to me in French and we are in love and nothing else matters. Not even the world."

"Not even the world," he muttered. Then, adjusting his tone and dropping his frown, he forced a smile. "Sounds like you watch too many movies."

"Sounds like you're trying to cover something up. It's so deep, the feeling. I felt the fabrics on my body and smelled the absinthe."

He sucked in a breath. "That's because you drank absinthe at the nightclub."

"Maybe. I don't know how to describe it. I was her. Or I'm her soul living again. Something. I don't have words to figure it out. I need your help because for some reason, Magenta seemed to know you last night."

He scoffed and turned to pace toward the window, hands akimbo, his back to her.

"How long have you lived?" she asked.

Shaking his head, he sighed and said, "Born in 1870. Changed to vampire in 1898. Lived in Paris all my life. Never wanted to leave. I'm basically happy with my life, as depraved as it has a tendency to be."

"Do you consider what we've had these past few days depraved?" She tugged in her lower lip with her teeth, hoping against hope—

"Never. Magen, what we have is…different. It's not me."

"So you've said." Was he getting ready to brush her off? How could he? Well, she wasn't going to let him off without learning the truth. "Did you ever go to the Moulin Rouge…back then?"

"Are you implying I might have actually known Magenta?" He put up his hand and protested with a "No!" And, then, "What kind of coincidence would it be that I should know the woman who died, and then over a century later, her reincarnation returns to my shop and I bite her? The odds are incredible."

They were, but not impossible.

"How did she die?" Magen asked.

"I—" Lucian slapped his arms across his chest.

He knew how she had died, and he had known her.

Magen felt it as a heat rising in her neck and a sudden simple knowing.

I loved him. Nothing could keep us apart. Not even the world.

She shook her head at the intrusive voice. "Were you lovers?"

He turned to face her, his lips pressed tightly and his eyes narrowed, fighting something, unwilling to relent.

And then, he nodded.

And Magen sucked in a breath as the brightness overcame her and she felt Magenta slink into her being.

Lucian could not shake the eerie feeling he stood before, not Magen, but instead a woman he had known so long ago.

She fluttered her thick, dark lashes and stroked a finger along her décolletage. It wasn't a Magen move. She was not adept at flirting. As she drew her fingers down her shirt, slowly over her breasts, and eased them over her hips, he shook his head, wishing it away.

Whatever *it* was.

"Why are you doing this to her?" he hissed at the woman. "Is it really you? You've come for me, haven't you?"

Magen stepped forward, sliding her hands aside his neck before he could comprehend what she intended, and kissed him. Magen's sweet mouth commanded him with the intensity of contact, yet the overwhelming memory—and the taste of absinthe—clued him this was not *Mademoiselle Pratique.*

Lucian pushed her away and swiped a hand over his mouth. The cloudy green-white liquid swirled at the back of his throat and he coughed, as if he'd actually taken a sip of the horrible concoction.

"How are you doing this? Is it true? That she is your reincarnation?"

"I don't want to talk about silly stuff." Magen advanced, and he stepped backward. "Don't you want me, lover? Or does remorse keep you from embracing me?"

"Remorse?" Hell, he'd felt that for years. Decades. Only recently could he think about what he'd done with some semblance of understanding, of *almost* not blaming himself. "Get out of her. Whatever you're doing to her, you can't. She has her own life."

"She invited me in," Magen cooed. She slicked her tongue along her lower lip. "Though it was a rather long wait."

"Yeah? Well, I'm inviting you to leave!" He gripped her and shoved her toward the door. Opening it, he pushed her out into the hallway and slammed the door behind her.

Lucian leaned against the wall, tossing back his head. He'd handled that wrong. But he was at odds right now. He needed to think about this. He could not face her.

Not even the world.

Not when she was…her.

Magen wandered down the hallway from Lucian's apartment, disoriented after their fight. He'd been fighting with Magenta. She'd been aware of their conversation, yet hadn't been able to influence the words that had come out of her mouth. Magenta's words. She had come upon her so suddenly.

What remorse had she spoken about?

She glanced to the closed door. She'd leave him alone. The whole becoming another person thing took a lot out of her, and she needed to sit down.

"Magen, is it?" Madame de Tour stood in her open doorway, an elegant vision in gray chiffon and white lace.

"Hello. Yes, Magen." *I think.*

Magenta was gone. For now.

"You look tired. I heard Lucian yelling. For such a charming man, he does have a volatile temper. Won't you come in for some tea?"

The idea of taking refuge from an angry vampire… She didn't want to walk home until she'd had a few moments to collect herself. And Evelyn's kind smile spoke to her bruised heart.

"Just a few minutes, then I'll have to find my way home."

"I've ginger spice. Always brew a cup in the afternoon," Evelyn said as she gestured Magen to sit on the floral couch. "His bark is worse than his bite, *chérie,* trust me on that one."

Apparently the woman wasn't aware her next-door neighbor was a vampire.

Yet that wasn't the most troubling thing right now. More than the vampire, *Magenta* was the thing that troubled her most. Her strange mental state, or rather, could it be deemed a mental takeover?

Magen bent a leg and settled onto the couch next to a thick pillow embroidered with soft blue velvet roses. "You've known Lucian for a long time?"

"A dear friend," Evelyn said, handing her a cup of tea on a saucer. "And, yes, quite some time. Did he…mention how long?"

"I know what he is."

Evelyn's shoulders relaxed.

"How did you learn he was…" Magen didn't want to say the word, not until she knew for sure Evelyn was aware of his true nature. "What he is?"

"He told me quickly. We were closer in age then. I know you'll ask—he's never bitten me. Ours is a true friendship. About a decade after we'd met, the apartment next door went up for sale and I let him know. He snatched it up for the view, of all things. Nowadays he curses the tower. Most days we'll share tea. He always brings me flowers. How did the two of you meet?"

Magen smiled over the brim of the teacup. "I went into his shop looking for a gift. I was immediately taken with him. I confess, a man who speaks French does it for me. You know what I mean? Maybe not. You're French. Anyway, I wonder now if that's just his...way."

"You mean the vampiric persuasion? No, Lucian would never utilize the thrall to gain a woman's attention. He doesn't need it. He has an intoxicating aura about him. An innate charm."

"And yet his charm feels...predatory."

"He's a rascal, but yet, predator is a good term. It is his nature."

"I suppose. I know I've no right to ask, but I'm curious because you two share a long history. Have the two of you...?"

"No, we are strictly friends, and both prefer it that way. I'm not much for scoundrels, and he prefers his women younger than myself."

"Must be weird to know the man, and to age, and to know he's growing older, yet he remains the same on the outside."

"At times it can be disconcerting. But who would grow tired of Lucian Bellisario's handsome facade?" The woman winked, and Magen relaxed.

"I feel sorry for him," Evelyn continued. "Immortality extends his life indefinitely. Yet can you imagine what a permanent relationship would present to him? It could be a nightmare. He either takes a mortal woman as partner, and thus, must experience her aging while he does not. Or he takes a non-mortal woman who would live as long as him. Don't you think he might tire of her after so long? So instead he's a lone seeker of comfort and connection he knows he can never truly possess."

"One-night stands? No commitment?"

"Exactly. That's why you are different. He's never introduced me to a woman before. They never last so long."

"We have a weird connection."

"Tell me about it?"

"I came to Paris to do some historical research," Magen said. "I'm writing a story set in the late 1800s. I wasn't planning on it, but now I'm wondering if I should include reincarnation in the plot."

Evelyn scoffed over a sip of tea. "Reincarnation is ballyhoo."

"You don't believe in it?"

"Not at all."

"But you believe in vampires."

"And witches, and, oh, Lucian introduced me to a werewolf once. Very sexy, that man. You'd never think it for all the hair on his chest—er, well. Ahem. And I know about faeries and demons and other unsavory sorts. Ghosts exist, as well."

"So why not reincarnation?"

"The soul is not so egotistic, is it? Perhaps clever enough to haunt another soul, but to take over an entity the moment it is conceived and come into this world to experience another life?"

"What if I told you I'm beginning to believe I am a reincarnated cancan dancer?"

The woman shrugged and set down her teacup, before moving to sit beside Magen. "Dreams tend to convince. Will you let me read your palm?"

"Oh." Magen immediately thought of circus sideshow acts. She believed in palm reading as much as Evelyn believed in reincarnation. But it wouldn't hurt to humor the woman. "Is it something you've trained for?"

Evelyn's warm, soft fingers stroked Magen's right hand. "Intuition is a knowing. Nothing but. You've fine, graceful hands. Don't do much physical work, do you?"

"I use hand cream to keep them soft. I'm a writer, so my hands are my tools for creation."

"I can see that. Long and sinewy fingers. You've the writer's fork, here. This is your lifeline, here. Just one, you see. Not two, or even split. Oh."

"Oh?"

"This line right here, it crosses the heart line. Oh, dear. That's not good." She set down Magen's hand and stood, rubbing the back of her neck where a tendril of gray hair spilled over her wrist.

"What did you see?" She studied her palm, seeing nothing more than lines and flesh.

"I believe you are being haunted, *chérie*."

"Haunted? No, she...occupied me. I was Magenta—"

"Magenta? Oh, double dear."

"Just a bit ago when Lucian and I—she comes forth when he—"

"Tastes your blood?" The woman shuddered. "It makes sense. Have you an object that belonged to her? An item of clothing or piece of jewelry?"

"I don't think—" Magen tapped the base of her throat, recalling that after finding the faerie necklace was when weird things had started to occur. "I wore a necklace that night. Lucian let me borrow it. He hadn't realized he owned it until I saw it wedged in the jewelry case in his shop. He didn't mention how he came to own it. Do you think the necklace could have been hers?"

"Very possible. But no matter. If I am correct, and you are being haunted, you need an exorcism, nothing but."

Magen pressed a palm to her chest, unsure how to take in this information. An exorcism? Haunted? The woman couldn't know such things.

But no matter if she were haunted, or indeed reincarnated, it wasn't good that Magenta was coming up and taking over her body.

"You must tell Lucian," Evelyn suggested. "He'll know the right people to contact."

"I need to think about all this." Magen stood, but the sudden movement made her sway and she caught her head in her palm and Evelyn helped her to sit back down.

"You've been through much," the woman said. "You'll stay here and rest a bit. You're tired, and I've a mind to watch over you. No arguments."

Magen nodded, and by the time her head hit the couch arm, her eyelids fluttered and she was out.

Chapter 8

Magen aimed her camera at the Trocadero across the river. She knew the building was called something else now, but due to her research she tended to know the city by eighteenth- and nineteenth-century terms. Though she did recall some of the odd names they'd renamed various landmarks following the Revolution. Nôtre Dame as the Temple du Reason? That just wasn't right.

The day had screamed for her to take a walk and put out of mind all the craziness from yesterday, so she'd headed out walking. And going to Lucian had been out of the question. Much as she pined to melt into his arms and feel his body tremor next to hers in bliss, he should be the one to approach her.

Who was she trying to fool? She planned to go to his place in a bit. Screw chivalry, she wanted more of his kisses. And his body. But she was trepid about getting into it with him now. Would he bite her? Could she accept that? And still the thing about Magenta needed to be resolved.

Tracking to the right through the camera lens she focused on the Louvre's glass pyramid and snapped a few shots. Another twist brought up a man's face—right there.

Magen was startled and dropped the camera. Lucian reached over the bridge railing and caught it in a move so fast it could have only been vampiric reflexes.

"Are you following me?"

"Yes. I uh...spoke to Evelyn this morning. She said you stayed awhile yesterday afternoon."

"She offered me tea and good conversation. And you didn't come after me."

"I couldn't. Things were—"

"I know. Weird."

He handed her the camera and she tucked it in her jacket pocket. "Evelyn told me what she read on your palm."

"Don't tell me you believe that fortune-telling stuff."

He leaned against the railing, heels of his palms to the cement, and met her eye to eye. "You believe in vampires, why can't I believe in fortune-tellers?"

"Not fair. When one is bitten, is it really a choice to

believe? As for what Evelyn said, I'm still not sure about the idea of a spirit haunting me."

"It does sound far-fetched, but Evelyn said spirits don't reincarnate. And I tend to place her soundly in the corner of wisdom."

Magen had to agree with his assessment of Evelyn. She reminded her of her grandmother, a woman who had always had gentle advice and great chocolate-chip cookies on hand, all while looking dazzling in a smart dress and pearls.

"So you're going to let it continue?" he asked.

"I'm not sure. There is so much I want to learn about her."

"Magen, she takes over your body. How is that in any way acceptable to you?"

"It's not. I don't want her to do that, but…"

"But you won't stop it."

"How can I?"

"You need to exorcise her."

"That's assuming she's a spirit and I'm not—"

He grabbed her by the shoulders. "You're not, Magen. Please, believe me on this one."

"I think you're worried she'll tell me something you don't want me to know."

"Magen! What is there to tell? You've figured out we used to be lovers."

"Yes, but what happened between you and Magenta,

Lucian? It had to have been awful for the woman to now seek you through these means. Nothing could keep you apart, not even—"

He stopped her with a hand flat before her face. "Don't. She used to say that. It's not your right to say that."

Not even the world.

They must have been madly in love. Magen wanted to know more, to be allowed into that part of the man she had begun to care about—yes, a vampire. Lucian had a heart, and a soul, and he was being hurt by Magenta's presence.

"I want to know you," she said. "Beyond our bodies against one another and our mouths taking and giving so sweetly. And for reasons beyond my knowledge we've been drawn to one another, so I think it's permissible to ask it of you. Will you tell me about you and her?"

He scanned across the river, seeming to want to look anywhere but at her. Her heart dropped at his reluctance. Something awful had torn him away from Magenta.

He took her hand, kissed the back of it, and started to walk. "Come with me to the shop. I'll tell you there."

Once at the shop, Lucian left Magen sitting on a dusty damask chaise, circa the seventeenth century, and excused himself to go rummage around in the office. He was in there for an inordinate amount of time, and Magen almost got up to go look for him, when he reappeared with a sketchbook. He handed it to her, and sat down beside her.

"Open it," he said, brushing a kiss across her temple. "There's but the one painting."

Smoothing her palm over the bruised red-velvet cover, she then turned it aside and gasped at the beautiful painting. The woman's eyes captured her attention, the brilliant emerald irises outlined by kohl and highlighted by mesmerizing arched black brows. Thick black hair splayed across a damask spread, for she lay on her back, looking up at the painter. An elaborate headdress dangled a bejeweled pendant onto her porcelain forehead, the jewels matching the violet corset that cinched up her breasts.

"She's gorgeous," Magen said quietly. "Magenta?"

"Yes. The only painting I made of her."

Magen exhaled shallowly, feeling as though she were intruding on a deeply personal part of Lucian's life. As if she peeked through a keyhole while he and Magenta had made love. And yet, she was glad he trusted her to reveal this—a peek into the man's heart.

The stroke of his finger along her cheek startled her, but she dipped her head toward the touch. "You've the same porcelain skin," he commented wistfully.

"But I'm not her."

"You're not. And for that I am glad."

Glad because it made it easier for him to dismiss her?

She shouldn't think like that. It wasn't as if she had a claim to him.

Much as she wanted to.

"She is so beautiful. I don't understand why she chose me…."

"It could be the necklace. It was a favorite piece of hers. I can't believe it's been in the display case all this time…."

For now, the necklace was sitting on Lisa's dresser, abandoned after Lucian had undressed her during one of their lovemaking sessions. Neither had regarded it since.

"Did you love her?"

"In a desperate, pining way that young rogues tend to when they've realized a beautiful woman actually deigns to grant him her attentions," he said, gazing out the dusty window. "An actress always, Magenta used to dramatically declare we'd be together forever. No one could tear us apart. Not even the world."

Magen swallowed. How dare she have said those same words to him?

"It wasn't real love," he said. "On either of our parts."

Relieved to know that, Magen felt she still hadn't heard the whole story.

"Perhaps it was love. I was transformed to a vampire about a month before Magenta and I got together. Zara Destry was the name of my creator. Never saw the bitch again. She didn't leave me with the important detail that I could have prevented my own vampirism if only I didn't take mortal blood before the full moon."

Magen threaded one of her hands through his, while she traced the painted arc of Magenta's lips with the other.

"It was a new and dangerous thing for me. I had no one to teach me how the vampire functioned, how much blood I needed, when I needed it, when to stop. Or, how not to turn a mortal into a vampire."

Magen sucked in a breath at his pause. And she knew. It was an awful knowing. "You don't have to say any more."

"I transformed her to vampire," he said quietly. "One night while drunk on absinthe—Magenta loved the green faerie—is when it happened. I didn't drink it—couldn't abide the taste, yet it infused her blood and made me drunk, as well.

"Surprisingly, she reveled in her vampirism. Yet, it made me jealous as hell. Magenta had a certain agreement with the owner of the Moulin Rouge, clients to entertain. I knew she was never faithful to me, and had accepted that. But once she came into her fangs, her bloodlust grew insatiable. I begged her to be discreet. She blamed me for everything and insisted her life would be better without me. I had to agree, yet felt I had to keep an eye on her, or someone would turn up dead.

"That someone should have been me." He sighed heavily. "She actually carved a stake. The bitch. I believe she instigated the argument as a means to rile me, to give her good reason to stake me. We were in an absinthe haze again, but I saw the stake coming for me. I wrestled her for it. It swung free from her clutches, and the next thing I knew…"

Magen swallowed and sought Lucian's gaze.

"Did you know a new vampire does not ash completely?" he said quietly. "Older vamps do. But the recently transformed ones? No. They simply die, their hearts burst. Magenta's dead green eyes accused me as she lay there with the stake in her heart."

"Oh, Lucian."

He pressed the back of her hand to his heart. "You don't know how many times I've offered my soul to whatever dark demon would take it if only to change that night. To give back the young soul I stole from this world, despite her duplicitous, fickle ways. I just wanted her to be alive, and to have never transformed her and destroyed her life."

Magen didn't know what to say, so instead remained silent, allowing him this pain, this moment of grief. Closing the sketchbook, she pressed her palm to the rough velvet.

"So now you know," he finally said. "Magenta is dead. Is still dead. She has not been reincarnated in you. And now she's using you in some twisted means of revenge against me. That's got to be it."

Magen exhaled a breath. "I never thought of it that way."

She touched her chest, unsure now. Could Magenta be using her as revenge against Lucian? Surely, Magenta had lured her to Lucian in order to dredge up his past. It made terrible sense. It had been an accident, the dancer's death, to judge from the manner in which Lucian had described it. But a tormented soul such as Magenta must see it differently.

He tugged her closer and she found herself snuggling into the hug and tilting her head onto his strong, broad shoulder. Never had she felt so right sitting in someone's arms, surrounded by his cedar scent. Yet they were so different. They weren't even the same kind of being.

He and Magenta had been the same, as brief as it had been.

Jealousy stabbed Magen much like she imagined a stake to the heart would feel. She had to be rid of Magenta. She'd had her time with the man.

Now it was Magen's turn.

"What do I have to do to get this person, this soul or spirit, or whatever she is, out of me?"

"I don't know. I'm going to talk to a friend about it."

"Another fortune-teller?"

"Actually, he's a vampire who works for Himself."

"Himself?"

"The devil. Robbie Titan is the devil's fixer. And because of his alliance with the dark prince, he knows everything the devil does. If anyone can help us, he might be able to."

"I don't think I want to meet this guy."

"You're not going to. I would never introduce you into my world, Magen." He kissed the crown of her head. "I've made that mistake once. It's not for the faint of heart."

"I think Magenta has already inducted me into it."

"I'm sorry for that."

"Somehow, I don't think it was your fault. Unless… When you bit me in the antique shop…. I wonder if that was Magenta's way in? And then when I put on the necklace and went to the Moulin Rouge it opened the doorway wide for her to enter?"

"I didn't consider that. It's—I don't know. What baffles me is you don't seem offended by the fact I'm a vampire."

"I don't think I am. You won't change me?"

"Never. I swear it."

"Then I'm strangely cool with it."

"*Mademoiselle Pratique*'s wild side strikes again."

He kissed her and tilted up her chin to deepen the kiss. It was not a distracted connection, but rather, she felt all of him focus on her as he lingered, tasting her. All she wanted to do was fall into bed with him and have him whisper sweet French words to her.

"I want you to stay at my place," he said. "So I can keep you close. Protect you."

"Yes, I don't want to be alone now that the idea of a spirit inside me is starting to sink in. But won't being near you bring her up more often?"

"Possibly. But I'll get us some answers today. Promise."

Chapter 9

"You going to tell me what the devil's assistant guy said?" Magen asked as Lucian poured her a second glass of red wine from his private vintage bottled in the Rhône valley.

"Robbie is the devil's fixer," Lucian corrected. "And he said we need a soul bringer to collect Magenta's soul after we exorcise her from you. And to do that, we need a witch who practices dark magic. I left a message with Thoroughly Jones. He'll be the one we want to work with. He's an expert in releasement."

"Releasement?"

"Of souls and haunts, and other nasty things. But not so adept with removing demons, as he wasn't able to remove the infestation from his brother, CJ, but that's another story entirely."

"So what does releasement involve?"

"I'm not sure. I've never exorcised a spirit from someone before. Though, Robbie did say something about bloodsexmagic."

"Blood, sex..." She gaped. "Is it dangerous?"

He tilted his head. "Again, I have no clue. Save for my best friend, Certainly Jones—TJ's brother—I've avoided witches and magic even though the Protection spell was dropped decades ago."

"The Protection spell?"

"Almost a millennia ago, witches put a great Protection spell upon their blood so it would be poisonous to vampires. My kind used to enslave them and drain them of their magic. Yet now the spell has been lifted, you'll find we're cautious around witches. Trust me, Magen, if TJ can help us, we'll be in good hands."

"I trust you."

She rolled the rim of the goblet along her lower lip. She'd stepped into an utterly insane plot, yet all she wanted to do was feel this man's touch on her skin, to know more than the blissful pain of his bite.

"Are you attracted to me for more than my blood?" she asked quietly.

"I didn't once bite you when we were engaged in our days-long sexfest. I am attracted to you, Magen, first and foremost. Your blood?"

She tilted her head.

"It is exquisite."

He bridged their distance in what seemed like some super-vampire move. Magen found herself in his arms, pressed against his long, lean body, trapped within his delving gaze. So much there, she knew she could stare into his eyes a lifetime and never know him completely. He'd walked the world for over a century, an exile from another age. He'd been responsible for another woman's death—she wouldn't think about that right now.

But you should. What if he accidentally kills you?

"I am attracted to your peach scent and lush mouth." He kissed her once, twice. "Your practical hair and, yes, even these ghastly glasses which have the saving grace of drawing attention to your sky-bright eyes. And your determination, a woman alone in the big city, set on discovering a dangerous truth, who easily accepts the vampire sitting beside her, even after he's taken her blood without permission."

"Your bite is something I imagine no woman could resist."

Her heart beat rapidly and her breasts rose and fell as his eyes wandered down over them, his fingers slowly moving along the neckline of her blouse.

"So it's not just the fact I spoke French to you?"

"The French language does provide for some amazing foreplay."

"Je veux te lecher de tête à pied." I want to lick you *from head to toe.*

"Yes," she said on a sigh as his fingers unbuttoned her blouse and parted the silk.

Growing bold with desire, Magen pushed him,and he landed on the couch. Stretching his arms across the back, he studied her with his deep, focused gaze, a boyish grin parting his lips. His look stroked her skin, from her neck and down over her breasts, to sliding about her belly and lower, where her core hummed and tingled in anticipation of more than a look, but instead, a touch.

"Votre beauté m'accable." Your beauty overwhelms *me.*

"I think that means you're pleased," she said.

"You're so beautiful, Magen."

More beautiful than Magenta? she wanted to ask. *No. Unless you want an unwelcome visitor, don't think about her now. This is not a ménage a trois.*

She clasped Lucian's big, wide hand. Kissing his fingertips, she worked her way to his palm with her tongue. "You've the hands of an artist. Why did you stop painting?"

"I didn't, not right away. But over the years, my interest in creating art faded. Some days I think I've secluded myself in the past with my business. And yet, old things intrigue me because I know about them. And it is a quiet life, which I prefer."

"And here I had you pegged for a guy who hit the nightclubs on the weekends. You do have a type, and I suspect those women are usually found dancing in dark clubs."

"I would never deny it. But those women are also easy to leave behind. Not like you." He stroked her hair, his eyes tracing her face. "You're someone a man would like to keep hold of for a long time."

She nestled her head on his shoulder. "I've only a few more days in Paris, then it's back to Minnesota."

"What holds you there? Have you family? Friends?"

"Just my father, who travels all over the world for business. I've lots of friends. And I've my writing."

"I've heard the northern states are an excellent breeding ground for my kind. It's cold and dark there. But I couldn't fathom all that snow."

"Paris gets snow."

"Not so much you have to wear snowshoes or get out a special machine to blow the snow from your drive. No, I'm a Parisian, through and through."

"Would you ever travel to the States to visit me?"

"I would travel the world to see you, Magen." He traced a finger along her panties, and her stomach muscles tensed in anticipation. "You've captured my heart."

"I've never captured a man's heart before."

"Do handle it with care."

"Absolutely." She traced his mouth with a finger.

"Let me see your fangs." He opened his mouth and she watched as his fangs lowered. Snow-white and pin-sharp, they looked deadly, yet she knew the pleasure those fangs could give her was deliciously worth the pain. "Does that hurt when they come down?"

"No, it feels damn good. I get the same expectant feeling as if you would stroke your fingers over my cock."

Said manly appendage was noticeably hard against her thigh right now. "And how often do you have to drink blood?"

"Once or twice a week. Not a lot."

"Could you drink from only one person? For, you know, as long as you were together with that person?"

"I could. But I wouldn't want to weaken you, Magen. But a bite now and then—"

"Feels so good." She pushed aside her hair. "Bite me, Lucian."

"An irresistible offer. Let me take your body first, then we'll top it off with a bite later."

He turned her to sit upon his lap, and his hand glided down to caress her thigh, while the other slid up to clasp her breast and massage the nipple through the pink lace. His groan against her neck shivered across her skin. It was as if his breaths and moans and satisfied hums had become a part of her very makeup; she could read him through those telling sounds, and he was in predatory mode. His prey? Her pleasure.

Magen threaded her fingers through his hair, which lifted her breasts high, and his fingers slipped down the pink lace. Her body hummed, and she wanted the hand on her thigh to move higher, yet he lingered, taking his time, kissing his way along her shoulder. His fangs skimmed her flesh, increasing the erotic electricity of his touch, but he didn't break skin, and she didn't want him to. Yet.

"Es-tu mouillé pour moi?"

Finally, his fingers glided over her panties, and Magen squirmed as the gentle pressure pulsed against her sensitive nub. Tearing her panties down, he slid his hand between her thighs and she couldn't spread her legs for the panties, but that only increased the sensations of his probing touch. He slid inside her, then stroked high upon her sex, slicking across her. She gripped his legs beneath her, and was frustrated he was still dressed, and then it didn't matter—he knew how to control her, and this was not some vampire trick of the mind.

She clutched his hand at her breast and squeezed her nipple, igniting the defiant pain that felt so damn good.

"Merde, oui," he whispered and kissed her jaw beneath her ear. "Come for me, *mon amant.*"

The French words. His deep, raspy voice. His masterful control of her sex with but a flick of his finger. The heat of his breath hushing over her neck. It all combined to bring forth a tremendous orgasm that tilted her hips up to receive his expert strokes. Magen exhaled, gliding in the perfect moment, unashamed at her unabashed foray into intimacy with this enigmatic stranger.

He was dangerous. Forbidden. He was *Mademoiselle Pratique*'s fantasy affair.

She turned and pulled his shirt over his head, and hastily unbuttoned his jeans. He tilted her closer with a hand to her back, bringing her breast to his mouth where he suckled and nipped, and drew her in deeply, while she fumbled to unzip him. Only after a while, did he lift his hips to aid her efforts, and she tugged down his jeans, his penis springing up against her palm. She rubbed her mons over the hot, hard shaft, covering it with her wetness, and leaned in to kiss his mouth as he groaned in delicious satisfaction.

"I've my own form of persuasion," she said against his mouth, and gave his cock a firm, long stroke.

"So you do—aaahhhh. *Ma petite pêche est une impudente.*"

"If that means please, then I'm inclined to give you what you want."

"S'il vous plaît," he said on a breathless gasp. "Put me inside you, *mon amant.*"

Settling onto his firm, thick shaft, Magen abandoned the practical, hometown girl and unfurled the brazen seductress she had embraced since arriving in Paris.

Lucian clasped her hips, lifting her effortlessly up and down upon him. He was so thick she felt him tug at her.

And when she sensed he was close to the verge, he pulled her closer, and moved in to kiss her neck over the vein. Hot breaths matched her racing huffs. And as his teeth entered her, he moaned loudly and his hips bucked hard against hers. And Magen surrendered to the duel penetration.

She had come to Paris for a vacation and had found a vampire lover.

The afterglow did not follow their sexy liaison.

Lucian suddenly stumbled away from Magen's embrace and landed on the floor, legs sprawled and hands clasping his head. Magen wasn't sure what was wrong, but he seemed to be in pain.

"What is it?"

"The *danse macabre.* Oh, Christ. This only happens when I've— It's her! You should go. This won't be pretty. Ah!"

Magen gathered her clothes while her lover moaned and beat his head against the base of the couch. And then she paused. She couldn't feel sorry for him. She wanted to see this. *She deserved to see this.*

"No, that's not what I want…"

And her vision blackened for a moment, and when she opened her eyes, Magenta laughed to see her killer caught in the throes of her nightmares.

Chapter 10

As a detour from the grocery store, Magen stopped into the hardware store. Not sure why she was here, she wandered the aisles looking over the familiar yet French labels. Her thoughts were on Lucian. Made her warm and snuggly, and also stirred up her desire for him. More kisses, more sex, and, yes, more bites.

Without Magenta.

Then her thoughts turned sour. The ghost or spirit—whatever she was—had been there last night, reveling in his pain. Drinking her blood had brought Magenta's nightmares to Lucian's memory in a physically vivid way; she knew that from having watched, even though it had been through Magenta's perspective. Magen wasn't even sure who had left his apartment—her or Magenta—

but she had been glad to get away and not have to witness his torturous cries.

Wincing, she pressed her fingers to her temples. Rarely did she get a headache. This didn't feel like one so much as a hot pressure crawling under her skin. Hell, would she experience the same nightmares?

You will do as I direct.

Magen shook her head. Magenta couldn't come out here. Not now.

Heading toward the front of the store, she paused before a stack of wood dowels she suspected were used to create furniture and stroked her fingers along one. The hardness of the wood appealed and reminded her of the slick, hard shaft between Lucian's legs. Mmm… He had wielded that weapon expertly, and she couldn't wait to get back to it.

He's mine! Not yours!

"No, he's not," Magen whispered. "Get out of me."

She smiled at a passing woman carrying an armload of light bulbs. Before turning to leave, Magen grabbed one of the dowels and slapped it against her palm.

And Magenta smiled.

After talking with Thoroughly Jones, Lucian was nervous about telling Magen the plan. TJ said he could definitely exorcise the spirit from Magen's body, but he also confirmed it would require bloodsexmagic. As well, a sort of restaging of the time period was required in order to make the surroundings inviting for the spirit to come up, because TJ sensed the spirit would balk once she figured out what they were trying to do.

So Lucian now left the Moulin Rouge with a garment bag over his shoulder. He'd had to use persuasion on the manager. Their clothing had to be authentic, and he'd no desire to stalk the antique stores for something similar. He'd return it tomorrow, if Magen agreed to this crazy idea tonight. "Magen. Magenta," he muttered. "Even their names are similar."

Why hadn't he noticed that before? And how odd, the events that had finally brought them all together?

"Something to do with that damned necklace. She'll have to wear it for sure."

He tossed the garment bag in the back of his Mercedes, where another garment bag lay; he'd taken his outfit to get pressed. He'd gotten it out of the back of his closet. Some things a man liked to hang on to. And much as he'd fled his memories of the time period, he still liked to occasionally look at his paintings and remember his bohemian days when the world had been his to crush against his chest, and he had always been happy no matter that he'd rarely claimed more than a few livres in his pocket.

Now he could afford to buy anything he required to make him happy. But the one thing he wanted wasn't to be purchased and hung up on the wall or even worn. If she went home to Minnesota, he would be devastated. He wanted a chance with Magen Sloan.

How to seduce the thoroughly practical yet secretly brazen *Mademoiselle Pratique* to stay with him? Could he accompany her home? He could see himself visiting the States, but Paris was his home.

Perhaps this relationship was doomed, spirit or no spirit.

No, he wanted her to stay. He wanted. As simple as that. He wanted everything he felt when with Magen, the companionship, the excitement, the closeness and even the burgeoning love.

But who was he to deserve such things?

Sighing, he drove toward Magen's building. Waiting for him was one woman he could entirely see fitting into his life. But the other woman who had fit herself into Magen's soul was not welcome. And yet, she was owed revenge. By rights, he should allow Magenta her revenge. Perhaps it would lift the heavy chains from his soul. Could she grant him the forgiveness he sought?

But Magen would suffer in the process. He couldn't have that.

How to please them both?

Never before had he been so at odds over a woman. And that excited him about her. She turned his head into a messy place, and he liked that just fine.

When she greeted him at the door, she immediately inquired after what was inside the garment bags.

"You can't look until we get to TJ's home. That is where the witch wants to perform the spell."

"What do we have to do?" she asked, staring at the bags. Her eyes sparkled. "Does he think he can exorcise the spirit?"

"He's positive he can." He pulled her to him, and kissed her long and firmly so she wouldn't ever again forget to kiss him when he walked through the door. "That's more like it."

"Sorry." Her body hugged his as if only she had been formed to fit against him. Love. He wanted it. "Those garment bags distracted me. You can't bring in a surprise like that and expect a girl to think straight."

"It's clothing from the time period in which…"

"Oh. When you and, uh…she?"

Neither wanted to speak her name, because neither wanted to invoke the pesky spirit.

"I went to the Moulin Rouge and got the costume that was framed on the wall. She actually wore it. If that doesn't conjure her up, I don't know what will."

"This is so awesome for my research! I can't wait to try it on."

He pressed a finger to her mouth and shook his head. "You can wait. You don't want to wear the thing a moment longer than necessary."

She nodded, her eager expression growing somber. "You're right. I know this is serious and dangerous. I want to get rid of her so it's just you and me."

"I can't argue that."

"Really? Because I have to wonder…."

"You think I'd prefer it if she stayed in you?"

Magen shrugged.

"Absolutely not. She was my past. A wicked, fickle past who tried to stake me. You? Well. I hope you are my future. Just you."

"I'd like that." Her kiss touched the cool shadows of his heart, a place he'd never thought capable of feeling light again. Perhaps he was worthy of love after all. "So that's all we do? Get dressed up and wait?"

"Not exactly. TJ said we have to create an atmosphere to draw up the spirit."

"Usually she's come up when you—Oh."

"Yes, when I bite your pretty neck and when we get amorous."

"Right. Like last night. So we have to make love, in costume. Where is the witch going to be?"

"Waiting." He winced. There was no good way to explain this. "He has to be nearby to exorcise the spirit once she comes forth."

"So, we're going to have sex while a witch watches?"

"I don't think he'll watch. TJ is discreet."

She clutched her throat and he could feel her courage

seep out through her pores. He pressed her against his heart. There is where she belonged. "It's what must be done. And when she is gone, we'll have only each other. It's what I want more than anything."

She nodded. "Then sex with an audience it is. But could we do it alone one more time before then? I'd like the practice."

"Ah? I do love your surprisingly wild side, *Mademoiselle Pratique*."

"How do you say *kiss me* in French?"

"Embrasse-moi."

"Ask and you shall receive."

Unbuttoning his shirt, Magen pressed kisses to Lucian's chest, strapped tightly with muscles that flexed under her touch, the skin growing hotter with each lash of her tongue to skin, nipples and the fine dark hair queued down the center of his chest.

"My turn." He pulled down the zipper at the side of her pencil skirt, and hissed as his fingers brushed her skin. "No panties, you vixen. Did you do this for me?"

"You don't think I normally walk around without underthings, do you?"

"It shouldn't be something you do for me, but because it makes you feel good. Everything in life should make you feel good."

"Mmm…" She swept her hand over the front of his trousers. "This feels great."

Quickly, she unzipped him. He wore dark boxer briefs that hugged his legs and cupped his erection, revealing its long, hard length. She bent to tug down his briefs, and with but a glide of his hand over her head, she decided to stay down on her knees and stroke him.

His sigh ended with a groan as she touched her tongue to the bold, hot head of him. She interpreted his satisfaction by the gasps and moans and his encouraging hand on her head, his fingers clenching and unclenching at her hair. She loved to make him speechless like this, and she loved to taste him, up and down, dancing and swirling her tongue and then sucking him into her mouth.

Gazing up at her lover's closed eyes and clenched jaw, she smiled to herself. This sexy Frenchman—vampire— was all hers.

When she sensed his shudders would lead to an orgasm, she tightened her grip about the base of his erection to prolong the moment. Standing, she glided her tongue up his hard belly and to each nipple, before kissing him deeply and hooking a leg up on his hip.

He slammed her against the wall by the window, and hooked up her other leg so she encircled his hips.

"Inside me," she commanded. "All the hot, hardness of you."

"You bring me so close to the edge," he said, his teeth nipping at her earlobe after he spoke. "You want it?"

"Yes, all of you."

He entered her with a growl, and seared her with his hot shaft. Magen clawed into his shoulders at the sweet pleasure of it. His kisses, fast and hard along her jaw, traveled down her neck, and with the intrusion of his fangs her world took off into the stratosphere. She felt him come inside her as her orgasm swept her into a throaty cry of joy.

And the brightness surrounded in a loopy sparkle of pleasure and falling. Falling inward, away from her lover. She tried to grasp for him, but it was too late.

"Oh, my lover, you always did know how to pleasure me."

"Get the hell out of her, Magenta!" Lucian shoved away from her, and tugged up his pants. "You can't do this to her! You want a piece of me?"

"I have had a piece and a taste, and soon enough, all of you."

She strode toward the window and glided her hand along the table. Naked from the waist down, her blouse unbuttoned, the streetlight shone on her skin. Lucian struggled between adoring her and wanting to strangle her.

When he saw what she picked up from the table,

Lucian gasped. "What the hell?" He glared at Magen, who tapped the pointed dowel against her chin. "That's a bloody stake!"

Magenta stroked her lips with her tongue, eyeing him cattily.

"You carved that?" Wood shavings sat in a neat pile near the stake, which had been honed to a fine point. "Magen?"

"She is getting too possessive of you. Stupid chit." She rushed for him, but he dodged her swinging hand, feeling the stake whisk by his shoulder. "I will have my revenge, Lucian!"

Yes, she must be allowed revenge. But sacrifice his life so the damned spirit could find some peace? There was no guarantee his death would exorcise Magenta from Magen's body. And damn it, he wasn't about to give up the one good thing he had just to please a pissed-off spirit.

"Get rid of it. Right now. You! Get out of her!"

She clutched the stake to her chest, defiantly lifting her chin.

When he thought she would protest, Lucian almost put his hands to her throat, but he resisted. "Magen, please, I know you're in there. Don't let her win. You're strong. Fight her. For me."

The woman snarled and again lunged for him. This time he stood against the wall, waiting, willing her to miss. And as the woman's body collided against his, he heard the stake jam into the wall beside his ear with a crunch.

He exhaled. His heart stuttered. Close one.

"I did it," Magen gasped. "I stopped her."

"For now," he whispered, and pulled his lover into a hug. It was her, all her. For now. "But she's getting stronger."

He grabbed the garment bags. "Get dressed. We need to go now. I'll not rest peacefully until the bitch is sent to either Above or Beneath, wherever it is she belongs."

Chapter 11

"Did you contact the soul bringer?" Lucian asked TJ.

Magen had been introduced to TJ, a tall, lean man with long black hair and a twinkle to his eye. He wore all black and embodied her image of a practitioner of dark magic, what with his sinuous movements and slightly evil facade.

At the kitchen counter, she'd gotten a wave from a woman, introduced as Star, who was chopping greens for a salad. When finished, she'd escorted Magen into the bathroom to help her change.

Star helped tug up the dress, which was a torso- and hip-hugging corset, with sheer layers of spangled pink chiffon for the skirt. A high kick would expose her lacking underwear. She suspected this dress had been used in such a manner when Magenta had taken the stage to perform the cancan.

It was gorgeous, but Magen felt a shiver as she stared at her reflection in the mirror.

Are you in there?

Of course the dancer was, but she could not tell when Magenta was going to come out. She had influenced her in the hardware store. She'd made her go after Lucian with a stake! Yet she suspected she would stay in hiding tonight if she had any clue what they intended.

Star's bright green eyes studied her from over her shoulder. The petite woman, whom Magen understood could shift into cat form, was so smiley. "Don't worry. You're in good hands with my husband. TJ will be respectful."

"I trust anyone Lucian trusts. Though I don't understand why your husband practices dark magic."

"It's not evil, like you might guess. Dark is required to balance the universe against the light. But if I told you how we met you'd be shocked."

"Oh, now you have to tell me."

Star smirked. "He captured me, in a cage, and took me home with him, and forced me to have sex with him to summon a demon."

Magen's mouth dropped open.

"I could have refused him at any time, but seriously?

Having sex with that man is no burden. I adore my Thoroughly Jones."

"But he put you in a cage?"

"I was in cat shape."

"Oh," Magen said, as if that made all the difference.

This realm of otherworldly beings was too odd, and yet fascinating. In a few days she'd met a vampire, a witch and a familiar. What a vacation! And what a coup for her fictional research.

She studied the dress, smoothing her hands down the tight bodice. "Do you think he'll like it?"

"It's gorgeous. But it's not whether or not Lucian will like it, but rather, will it freak the hell out of him. Didn't he...murder this woman?"

"It was an accident. Self-defense, actually, because she had tried to kill him first."

Magen's smile wilted. Defending her vampire lover's indiscretions? It felt so not right, and yet, she had empathy for Lucian. He had been a newly turned vampire. He'd had no mentor, no one to teach him the ways of his kind. He would have never committed such a heinous act had he not been under the influence of absinthe. She believed that to her very soul.

"TJ and I will stay on the other side of the loft, in the living room," Star explained. The entire loft was open, no walls, not even one separating the bedroom from the kitchen. "I'll put some music on. Loud. I set up an old Chinese screen at the end of the bed to give you some privacy."

"We're going to be…on the bed?"

Star took her hand and gave it a good squeeze. "It'll be okay. You want to exorcise this spirit, yes?"

Magen nodded effusively.

"Then sometimes a girl's gotta engage in work sex, as I like to call it."

Lucian had explained to Magen on the way here that familiars served as conduits to bring demons to this realm—via sex. The familiar was brought to orgasm, then, her body relaxed and open, the witch stepped in and conjured a demon through her body. It didn't hurt, and it was an accepted practice in the world of the familiar.

"Work sex," Magen muttered. "That sounds…"

"Don't think about it too much, it'll only give you the shivers. Just think of it as a night with a handsome vampire. I know you mortals tend to romanticize the vampire. Lucian's is not an easy life, nor would a relationship with him prove uncomplicated. But if you really feel deeply for him…?"

"Oh, yes."

"Then do what you can to keep him." She gave Magen's hand a tug. "You ready?"

"No, but let's do this anyway."

* * *

A vision walked toward him. And Lucian's heart dropped to his stomach.

For a moment it was not Magen but Magenta striding confidently, sashaying her chiffon-laden hips and tracing the neckline of her low-cut costume where the faerie necklace dangled. He remembered that gown. He'd not gotten to remove it from her because her manager never let her take the costumes off the premises. It had been fine with him. Made it easier to strip her and plunge between the sheets. They'd spent an inordinate amount of time in bed. Loving, talking, sleeping, eating. Consuming absinthe.

The sudden taste of absinthe on his tongue darkened his memories and he snapped back to the present.

Magen stood before him, admiring his attire. The ivory silk waistcoat was hand-embroidered with colorful flowers, and the damask coat had been one of his favorites. His shirt collar was cut high and starched, jutting under his jaw, and the trousers fit perfectly because they were bespoke. With his liquid diet, he'd maintain the same form for eternity.

She ran her palm over the waistcoat. "You look like a time traveler stepped out of the late-nineteenth century," she said.

"We make quite the pair, eh?" He was feeling nervous, and that was new to him. He didn't mind having sex while others were in the vicinity. It was the teasing his dead lover back part that made his fingers tingle and his words come carefully. "You good with this?"

She nodded. "It's what has to be done."

"Then let's summon Magenta."

Upon the big four-poster bed, they kissed. They touched. Lucian's mouth painted scintillating trails over her skin. Highlighted by the glow from dozens of lit candles, Magen's body hummed with imminent orgasm. He'd yet to strip her from the dress, and that was fine with her. She didn't need to get naked with two others in the apartment, even if the classical tunes wavering out from the speakers didn't cover their murmurs and moans so much as draw attention to the two elephants in the room.

A wave of incense curled above their heads, imbuing the room with rosemary—for release, TJ had stated of the scent. Magen sighed and struggled beneath Lucian's embrace for a moment to breathe.

"Is it them?" he asked, his eyes searching hers. "Are you nervous?"

"No. Yes. Are you? I feel—this isn't normal for us. It's just…off. I don't feel like she's anywhere close inside me."

"She must know what we're trying to do."

"Maybe if you bit me?"

"No." His intense stare softened her nerves. In his arms she felt safe. "TJ said that had to wait until the spirit showed herself. The blood has to come at the right time for the releasement to work."

His shirt unbuttoned to reveal his hard abs, she stroked his chest with a swath of the chiffon. "*Embrasse-moi.* Maybe if I think about her, about dancing and the wild abandon of the Moulin Rouge?"

"No." Lucian slid off the bed and tugged his pants closed and buttoned them. His jaw pulsing, he said decisively, "Stay right here. I know what will bring her up."

Chapter 12

The slotted silver spoon clinked against the glass rim. Jade absinthe glinted, a liquid jewel in the tumbler. Lucian placed a sugar cube on top of the flat spoon—from TJ's collection—and then held it under the dripping faucet to slowly introduce cold water into the drink.

In a few minutes the louche came up, alchemizing the liquid to a milky lime. It smelled…like a horrific memory. But as he stirred the liquid, purposefully tinking the spoon against the glass, he noted Magen sat up on the bed and peered around the Chinese screen.

"Got you," he whispered. "Come to me, oh, Dazzling Queen of the Night."

Magen slid off the bed and, amidst a swirl of incense, slowly approached, her eyes heavy-lidded, her tongue dashing out to lick her lips. The gown was open to reveal her breasts, which she stroked lazily, seductively.

"Lucian, you wicked boy," Magenta purred. "Give me."

He sipped the awful drink. It was acrid and dry. He hated it. And he hated doing this to Magen. But *she* had arrived. His worst nightmare.

He tipped the glass to her lips. She took it with her hand and attempted to tilt it back farther, but he controlled how much she could get. A sip for now. A slow tease.

Purring, she kissed him with her absinthe-laced lips. "Not only are you wicked, but you're a naughty fanged one. Trying to catch me out? What does that nasty witch wait for, lover? Do you want them to watch us make love? You were never an exhibitionist when I was alive."

Her purr turned to a growl, and she dragged a fingernail down his cheek abrading his flesh. "When I was alive," she repeated harshly. "You bastard."

She grabbed something from the counter and swung toward him. Icy pain entered Lucian's gut. Gaping, he gripped the steel handle of the butcher knife jutting out from his stomach.

Magenta laughed and grabbed the glass of absinthe, drinking it down and spinning about. A graceful pirouette splayed out the spangled skirts in a move Magen could not know were it not for her spirit passenger.

"Bite her," TJ commanded.

Lucian cast the dark witch a glance. Did he not see the knife sticking out of his gut? The blood dripping over his fingers and to the floor?

Fuck it. No blade was going to kill him. And the spirit had been granted some revenge. It had better be enough.

He gripped Magen's hair and tugged her body against his, abruptly stopping her dance. Roughly shoving aside her jaw, he sank his fangs into her neck. Her fingernails clawed at his arms. Magenta fighting him, not Magen.

Or maybe it was both? He was being rough, but she'd angered him, and his gut hurt like a mother. As much as he had ever loved her, he now wanted her gone.

Blood streamed over his tongue, tainted with absinthe, crashing into his memories like a flaming battering ram aimed to bring down the ramparts. He wanted to stop. He could not stop.

You must. Don't kill another. Find salvation while there is yet a chance.

Lucian grasped Magenta by the face and peered into, not Magen's eyes, but the eyes of the woman he had once loved foolishly. "Please, Magenta, can you forgive me?"

It hurt his heart to ask such a thing. He had no right. He had murdered her! But his soul needed rest as much as did hers. There was no bringing her back, no restoring her heartbeat, so he must seek peace for them both.

"It was the absinthe," he whispered, fighting the shaking tones that belied confidence. At her neck, blood bubbled and spilled down her pale skin. "It muddled us both. You loved the green faerie."

"You're too rough with me!"

"Look at me, Magenta. Remember us? Your wicked ways? You never really loved me. You wanted to stake me."

"You staked me!"

"It was the damned absinthe!"

"You blame a drink for your indiscretion?"

No. No, never. He was not so callous or self-righteous. "I did it. I killed you. It was not the drink. Our struggle—we both hated each other in that moment. Please. Give me some peace."

Magenta sighed, drawing her fingers over the scratch on his cheek. "Absinthe was my lover, more than you were. My wicked green lover brought us down. You were but a plaything, but I did love you."

"Only until you had to service one of your clients."

"Bastard."

"I'm sorry. I loved you, too, in my own way. We were caught up in the blood and the newness of our power as vampires. Admit it, Magenta, you loved the hunt, the hot, fresh blood."

"True. I adored drinking blood. More so than you ever did. I do, Lucian. I do forgive you."

He closed his eyes and pressed his forehead to hers.

"Thank you. I know I don't deserve it, but I think you need it. Can you...move on?"

"I don't know how. Lucian, I've been stuck here so long, wandering the ether, trying to communicate with you, but you never noticed me until the one who wore my necklace came along."

"It was good you were able to grasp on to Magen, if only so you can now find peace."

"But you love her now."

He couldn't deny those burgeoning emotions for Magen, but with the knife embedded in his gut, it would be wiser not to say as much to this vengeful spirit.

"The soul bringer," he said. "When he comes, you go with him, yes?"

She nodded. "Kiss me first."

He bent to kiss her, but she touched his lips. "Not her. Kiss *me,* Lucian. Only me."

"Only you," he murmured, and kissed her.

And it was not Magen, but instead Magenta in his arms, sighing, melting against his body, forgiving and giving him some small peace from the travesty he had been haunted by for over a century. In her kiss he said thank-you and goodbye, and...nothing will ever destroy the memory of our love, as tainted as it had been. Not even the world.

He felt her clasp the knife, still embedded in his gut,

and push against it. Trying to end him—to take him with her? She'd always been determined.

He would not go. Not when Magen could give him a new and bright future.

"You ready, TJ?" he yelled, wincing at the pain the blade inflicted.

The witch was already chanting, his arms held aloft at his sides, and head bowed. The releasement was spoken in Latin. At TJ's direction, he resumed drinking from her, to keep the blood flowing out. Metallic and tainted with wormwood, he had to force himself to consume the awful blend. The last memories of absinthe trickled across his tongue, and in its wake shone a promising future in the rich peach taste of Magen's blood.

The witch stepped forward, swiping a finger through the blood on Magen's neck. She'd gone limp now, but her eyes were open.

TJ drew an *X* on Magen's forehead with his bloody finger. "I cast you out, Magenta Price du Lounge by all that is sacred to the witch's rede and the laws of this mortal realm. Cross over to Above or Beneath. May the universe guide you. Hold her."

Taking his mouth from her neck, Lucian supported Magen, who stumbled as if drunk. The witch pressed his palm to her forehead and recited more Latin spellwork. With one final command she vacated the body.

Magen stiffened and gasped as her body jerked once as if giving up the ghost.

Lucian felt a hot brightness move through his body and burst out the back of his rib cage. Magen went limp in his arms. He and TJ followed the bobbling light that lingered over their heads. A corpse light. Magenta's soul.

And suddenly a man with a top hat and cane appeared in the kitchen, arms held out and head lifted.

"The soul bringer," TJ whispered. "Blackthorn Regis."

The corpse light wavered toward Blackthorn. The soul bringer had come to collect what he had not taken over a century earlier. Had he missed it, forgotten about it or merely not cared? Damn him, for letting Magenta's spirit wander.

Magnetically drawn to the soul bringer, Magenta's soul hovered above his head. When he opened his mouth, the soul slid down his throat. He nodded to Lucian and TJ and dematerialized.

The air changed, growing light and cooler. Lucian sucked in a breath and wiped the blood from his lips. It tasted like peaches, and that made him smile.

TJ bent to help him lift Magen. "Put her on the bed."

"Is the spirit gone?"

TJ nodded. "We did it."

"I need to take her home."

"Right, but first you gotta take care of that." He pointed to Lucian's gut.

"Right. Give it a yank."

"In the bathroom," Star said, suddenly appearing in the kitchen. "I don't want blood all over the kitchen floor. Go on. I'll tend your woman. You boys made a big mess."

Magen was aware Lucian drove her to Lisa's apartment. He carried her up in the elevator and into the bedroom to lay her on the bed. She still wore the dancer's costume, and when she tugged at the bodice, he loosened the ties in the back for her.

Exhaustion overwhelmed her, and it was all she could do to whisper, "Thank you."

Her vampire lover kissed her mouth and whispered he would leave her to get some rest, and she should call him as soon as she woke. At his gut, a crimson blossom stained the beautiful waistcoat. She'd been aware when Magenta had stabbed him, and had allowed it because she'd been in Magenta's soul and realized she had needed the revenge.

Cruel of her, and yet, the man was a vampire. He could take it. And she'd instinctually known that unless it had pierced his heart, he'd survive the injury.

"Je t'aime," he whispered.

She didn't need an interpreter to know he'd said *I love you.*

"Stay," she said, giving his hand a tug.

Stay. Something the man had never done until he'd met her. It was asking a lot, she knew.

He snuggled up beside her on the bed, one strong arm wrapping across her stomach, his fingers cupping beneath her breast. Only then did she feel safe and relaxed enough to drift off to sleep.

Chapter 13

Magen Sloan was not the reincarnation of Magenta, Dazzling Queen of the Night. And hallelujah for that.

While here in Paris, she'd discovered what she'd hoped to learn for her research, yet had decided against writing the story in that particular time period. Some ghosts were best left to haunt the ether. But certainly she could use the paranormal revelations to plot out a new novel. A vampire romance? Stranger things could happen.

And she had fulfilled her fantasy to have an affair with a sexy Frenchman. Okay, so he was Italian. She wasn't going to take off points for that small discrepancy.

Yet, she felt even more at odds than ever.

There were many arguments against continuing her affair with Lucian Bellisario. Besides the fact she didn't live in the same country as him, he was a freaking vampire. And vampire romances were fictional. They'd never be able to have a real relationship. Because they were two different people. Hell, they were two entirely different breeds.

"Not so different."

Lucian had once been human. He lived as a human and held a job and paid his rent and ate—okay, so his diet was vastly different than hers. But he didn't kill.

Only that one time. And she was glad he'd won instead of Magenta.

Magen stroked her neck where he'd bitten her countless times, yet the skin was smooth, unscarred. *A relationship is possible, you just have to want it to be possible.* If a haunting were possible, then surely romancing a vampire could hold promise?

"I am *Mademoiselle Pratique,*" she whispered. "Can't do the odd stuff."

Yet she had. And she had enjoyed the parts that hadn't involved being haunted.

As well, Lucian had gotten the forgiveness he needed to move forward. And now the spirit was gone, what had she to fear?

"I can't stay."

She had a life in the States. Family. Sort of. Her father breezed into the city once or twice a year for a day to kiss her, take her out for a meal, then off to adventure once again. He'd been to Paris more times than she could count. And he loved his life because he was doing what made him happy.

So why wasn't she? She was a freelance writer—who could do her job anywhere, in any city.

Something tugged at Magen's heart. And this time it was not a vindictive spirit. Why not be true to herself?

With a decisive nod, she shimmied up her tight pencil skirt, and tugged down her lace panties.

The afternoon sun beamed through the antique shop's dusty windows. Lucian inhaled the scents of the past, yet quickly corrected his senses that if he ever smelled absinthe again, it would be too soon.

The door closed, and Magen wheeled her suitcase down the wood floor toward him. His smile of greeting dropped, as did his hopeful expectations. Hell, his heart clenched and he felt something akin to real fear. "You're leaving?"

"My flight departs in three hours." She parked the suitcase and stood before it. "I purchased a round-trip ticket."

"I see." He didn't approach her, only stepped back to lean against the counter, crossing his arms over his chest. The same position he'd taken the first day she'd come in here. Only this time it wasn't curious but defensive. "How you feeling? No signs of Magenta?"

"She's gone for good. How about you? I can't imagine the mental toll it must have taken on you to carry such memories for so long. We've been through a lot."

"That we have." He tapped his lower lip and looked up at her from a bowed head. "I know we only had a short time but... I meant what I said to you last night. I do love you, Magen."

She inhaled and announced, "I love you, too."

"So you can just leave me like this?"

"Lucian, I have a life in Minnesota. Mostly. Sure, as a writer I could work anywhere, but I do have friends."

"I understand." No, he didn't. Didn't want to, at any rate. Friends could be reached with letters—hell, email and Skype. What was wrong with him that she couldn't give him a chance? Besides the obvious, that is.

He wanted to ask her to stay.

"I would never ask you to sacrifice so much," he said instead. "And I've already stated I'm a Parisian through and through."

"You belong here. It is your home. You..." She stroked her neck, and his fangs tingled sensuously at the sight of the pulsing vein.

Would he ever know such desire, such unabashed passion again? The discovery of Magen had been fraught with a wicked haunting but after all that? She'd won him over with her innocent appeal and peach-sweet skin. But apparently the vampire he was held no appeal for her. The truth never did win him permanency in the relationship department. Yet why couldn't he accept the rejection this time around?

"You know when I was a kid," she said, "our teacher used to have us write a report on what we did on our summer vacations."

"Is that so? I imagine this year's report would shock the hell out of your teacher."

"Might get an *A,* though."

They chuckled softly.

"So, this is it?" He wouldn't look at her. Mustn't force her to stay when she'd likely had more than her share of Paris and vampires and ghosts for a lifetime.

"I haven't exactly said what I *really* want," she started. With a heavy exhale, she drew up a breath and an irrepressible smile. "Just so you know, I'm not wearing any panties right now."

Lucian's heart did a double-beat. "*Mon amant,* that sounds perfectly impractical."

"I know." She blushed, stroking her neck. "I mean, can you imagine if I were in an accident—"

He pressed a finger to her lips. "Don't speak. I'll take your lacking underthings as a yes to staying. At least a little longer. And if you agree, then you'd better kiss me now."

Magen lifted up on her tiptoes and kissed him. And then she tilted down to lick his neck and followed with a playful bite. "I'm all yours, *mon amant.*"

* * * * *

VIVI AND THE VAMPIRE

Kendra Leigh Castle

Praised for both her world-building and her vibrant characters, **Kendra Leigh Castle**'s greatest pleasure is spinning romantic tales for those who like their heroes a little on the nocturnal side. A Navy wife, she currently lives in Maryland with her husband, three children and a menagerie of pets. She can be found online on Facebook, Twitter and at www.kendraleighcastle.com.

Chapter 1

"No."

Justin glared over the top of the itinerary that his sister appeared to be trying to shove up his nose. Dru, as stubborn as always, simply tipped her chin down and tried to stare him into submission. He didn't miss the determined glint in her eyes, either. It was never a good sign.

"Dru." Justin sighed, shoving one hand through his short crop of ebony hair. "I don't have time for a vacation. I don't *need* a vacation. Your heart is in the right place, and I appreciate that—mostly—but this is out of the question."

She rolled her eyes, removed the printed itinerary from beneath his nose, and perched on the edge of the massive mahogany desk she often accused him of hiding behind. Which was ridiculous, of course. It was piled high with work because he had an insane amount of responsibility as the king of the underground city of Terra Noctem, a magically protected enclave that had existed in various places for thousands of years to house members of the night races who wished to live free among their own kind. He also sat at the head of the Necromancium, the governing council of all the world's night creatures. Between mediating interspecies disputes, keeping his people hidden from humankind while also making an obscene amount of money off of them, and lately, fending off demon attacks, he was a busy man.

As he had been since the early days of the Roman Empire.

It was a long time to have your sister nagging at you, but the vampire who'd turned them both had said very complimentary things about the particular flavor of his family's blood. And he was glad to have a sibling to go through eternity with. Usually. When she wasn't trying to send him off on some pointless vacation.

"Damn it, Justin, have you taken a look in a mirror lately? You look tired. Vampires aren't supposed to look tired. And you're really walking the line between pale and pasty these days."

He glared balefully up at her. "You want me to turn myself into a stain on someone's tanning bed? That's cruel, Dru. I thought you loved me."

His attempt at humor fell predictably flat.

Dru growled and slapped the itinerary down onto the desk in front of him. It had a cover sheet emblazoned with the words *The Most Excellent Summer Vacation of Septimus Junius Iustinianus* and a picture of a buff life-guard with Justin's head photoshopped onto the body. "Justin," Dru said, leaning down directly into his face. "I do love you. That's why I went and worked this all out ahead of time. You know very well I can handle things for a week. I'm a phone call away if you need a monarchy fix. You'll be *fine*." Her eyes softened as they searched his face, and he knew she saw more than anyone did. Especially the things he didn't want anyone to see.

"You need this," she said. "Working yourself into a second death isn't going to help anyone."

Justin blew out a breath and leaned back in his chair while Dru crossed her arms over her chest and looked at him the way a parent looked at a particularly beloved and frustrating child. Part of him, a large part, knew she was right. It had been ages since he'd done anything just for himself. And he *was* tired, though it was the sort of soul-deep weariness that no amount of sleep would fix.

"I know what you're doing, Dru. And it's very sweet. But a week isn't long enough for me to find the sort of woman who'd put up with me and all of this, even if I was inclined to go looking. Which I'm not."

"Which is insane," she replied, not unkindly. "You're lonely, little brother. You've been lonely way too long.

I know *you* won't look…. But if you get out of the city for a while, the right woman might just find you on her own." Then she grinned, the smile lighting up what was already a breathtakingly beautiful face. "If nothing else, getting laid should do you a world of good. And I'm not the only one who thinks so."

Justin huffed out a laugh, too accustomed to Dru's bluntness to be offended. He didn't miss the chance to tweak her, though. She wasn't the only one who paid attention to her sibling's personal life…or lack thereof.

"Oh? So if I agree to this, does this mean you won't argue when I send you and that ill-tempered fallen angel off on a trip so you can finally jump one another instead of the usual heated glaring?"

She wrinkled her nose at him and pushed a long lock of pale blond hair out of her face. Everyone knew about the tension between Dru and Meresin, one of a small band of Fallen who'd rejoined the Necromancium after deserting Hell. One of them, Raum, had actually become one of Justin's most trusted advisors…. And it didn't hurt that Raum's mate, Ember, was a favorite of anyone who met her. Meresin, on the other hand, was angry, uncommunicative and generally unpleasant. A typical fallen angel.

Justin supposed it could work, if neither of them killed the other first.

"Low blow. No. Meresin is…" Dru waved her hand,

as though looking to pluck the right descriptor out of the air, and then finally just shook her head, frowning. "No."

That he'd finally flustered her made Justin smile. And, when she fixed him with the most pathetically woebegone expression she could muster, he knew he was going to have to take pity on her. He looked at the ridiculous picture on the cover of her "gift," looked at Dru's pleading expression, and heaved another sigh. Immediately, his sister leaped to her feet and squealed.

"You'll go!" She clapped her hands together like an excited child, which was at considerable odds with the crimson corset and tight black pants she was wearing. She got the strangest kick out of dressing like a Goth vampire wannabe.

"Yes, well, since you'll never let me hear the end of it if I don't. And it was sweet of you. In an annoying, bossy sort of way."

Dru laughed, grabbed his face between her hands, and planted a noisy kiss in the middle of his forehead.

"You just wait! You'll be begging me to be your vacation planner every year. I've got *so much* great stuff planned." As she chattered at him happily, Justin's thoughts drifted to what Dru had said earlier. About him being lonely. He wasn't lonely. He was just…focused. Driven. Busy.

Anyway, if he had never found a woman who suited him in all these centuries, vampire or otherwise, then it was never going to happen. And certainly not on some silly weeklong vacation to a place he was pretty sure was generally vampire-free.

He wasn't lonely, damn it.

But he would go, for Dru. And then maybe she'd realize that not everyone needed a mate to be happy. That some mythical perfect woman wasn't lurking out there just waiting to pounce on an overworked two-thousand-year-old vampire.

That he was just fine on his own.

Chapter 2

Her vamp-free vacation was off to a roaring start.

Vivi settled her hands on her hips and glared at the two bloodsuckers arguing over her. All she'd wanted was a quiet walk on a moonlit beach, a little peace and quiet after months of chasing, staking and risking life and limb on a nightly basis. Instead, she got…this.

"I saw her first," the taller one said, stepping forward so that he was toe to toe with his adversary. "Go find another snack. This one's mine."

Vivi bristled, her eyes narrowing. "Hey," she said. "Watch who you're calling a snack, buddy. You don't even know what you're—"

"I've been following her for half an hour," the other vamp sneered, his eyes glinting red in the darkness. "And if you think I'm going to let you have her, you can just bite me, asshole."

Teeth were bared. Growling ensued. Typical vamp posturing.

Over *her*. Why did she feel like she'd suddenly been warped into a paranormal version of *Wild Kingdom?*

Vivi looked between her would-be suitors, each trying to out-badass the other, and wondered whether they'd even notice if she walked away. They might be hungry, but they also smelled like a distillery. It wasn't the first time she'd been grateful that vampires could still metabolize, and often enjoyed, alcohol.

"Boys," she said. Neither looked at her. Vivi sighed, reached behind her, and pulled a small, slim device from where it had been tucked beneath her shirt against her lower back.

"Boys," she said, a little more firmly. The tall vamp shoved the shorter one.

"You really think you can take me, punk? Try it," he snarled.

With a flick of Vivi's thumb, gleaming silver blades shot out of each end of the device with a neat little *snick*. That, at last, got the bickering vamps' attention in a big way. Both heads snapped toward her, the looks of surprise priceless. Vivi smiled sweetly.

"So here's the thing," she said. "I'm on vacation. I'm not in the mood for death and dismemberment this evening, and besides, I happen to really like this shirt. Blood, as I'm sure you know, is a bitch to get out. So why don't you two clear out of town and we'll call it good. Deal?"

"Shit," the shorter vamp muttered. "Later." He vanished so quickly into the shadows cast by the dim lights of the bars in the distance that it was almost as though he'd never been there. The other vamp, sadly, didn't look like he was going to accommodate her. Vivi pursed her lips and looked at the immortal creature determined to ruin her evening.

"You think a little stake like that is going to scare me?" he asked, his lips parting in a sharp grin. The points of his elongated incisors glittered in the half-light. "I've seen worse. And you're pretty small for a Hunter. Not too intimidating, sweetheart."

"Insults," Vivi said. "Nice. And as I'm sure you are intimately aware, size isn't everything."

He snorted. "Honey, I'm going to have a good time showing you otherwise."

It wasn't stupidity after all. This one was much older than the one who'd run off, Vivi realized. She'd been a Hunter long enough that she could tell the differences fairly quickly. It didn't worry her too much…yet. She'd danced with worse characters and come out on top. Still, it would have made her more comfortable if there'd been backup somewhere, anywhere, nearby. Vamps were formidable adversaries, even the weaker ones. There were good reasons why Hunters always ran in pairs.

Unless, you know, they weren't *actively hunting*.

Vivi stayed very still, making sure not to look him directly in the eye when she spoke to him. Falling prey to a thrall was the kiss of death, usually. And he was definitely trying to catch her gaze.

"You want me, you'll have to come and get me," she said.

His grin widened. "With pleasure. I like a woman with spirit."

He lunged at her so quickly that Vivi barely dodged him, spinning away and nicking him with the tip of one of the blades. She sliced him along one side to make a point. He hissed as a thin line of crimson soaked through his white shirt. The cocky grin morphed into a grimace. The vamp had been pretty before…they all were…but the monster underneath was now much closer to the surface.

"You'll pay for that."

"Heard it before," she snapped. "Try another one."

Silken sand shifted between her toes, and to her right, the ocean lapped the beach in a rhythmic dance. Vivi listened with half an ear, wistfully thinking of her hotel room that overlooked all this, and her plans to fall asleep listening to the endless rush of the waves.

The thought only distracted her for an instant—but that was all it took for the vamp to take advantage.

He knocked her off balance, smacked the retractable stake out of hand, and slammed her to the ground before she could do so much as squeak. It was as humiliating as it was terrifying. Vamps never got the better of her, Vivi thought, thrashing frantically as her attacker chuckled above her. She got in a solid knee and knocked the wind out of him, then tried to roll away. But he had her back in seconds, dragging her through the sand to lay beneath him once again and looking decidedly less amused by her.

Rule one in Vampire Engagement: never let the vamp get the upper hand. Because if they do, you'll never get it back. Vivi recalled that as she locked eyes with him, his seeming to expand and fill with unholy light, ready to swallow her whole. She couldn't breathe, couldn't move...didn't want to... Oh, God, he was thralling her....

Vivi felt her body go limp.

"You bitch," the vampire breathed. "Not so tough now, are you? I'm going to—"

"Get off her."

The intrusion of a third party was enough to make the vampire jerk his head to the side in surprise. That, in turn, snapped the thrall, and was enough of an opening for Vivi to knee the vampire again. This time, she went lower than his stomach. The effect was loud and instantaneous. He made a harsh gagging sound, his eyes widening, then shut them as he flopped to the ground beside Vivi and tried to fold himself in half, all while making soft little noises of pain.

Some things never got less debilitating. Lucky for her.

Vivi sprang to her feet before he could even think about recovering, but she had no intention of running. This vamp needed to be taught not to mess with a Hunter.

Of course, his bloody end was going to be pretty awkward with an audience.

"Thanks," she said, turning her head to look at whoever had come to her—well, all right, she supposed it *was* a rescue—just in time. "I definitely needed the ha..."

It was rare that Vivi forgot what she was saying in the middle of a sentence. Then again, she didn't make a habit of being rescued. Not in general, and certainly not by vampires. Especially not vampires like this one.

He was, in a word, *gorgeous*. Not that you couldn't say that about any vampire. It kind of went with the territory. Still, this one took it to an entirely new level. For the few seconds it took her to repair whatever had fried in her brain, Vivi stared openly at the tall, dark vampire who was glaring daggers down at her attacker. He had the sort of lean, muscular figure that managed to be completely drool-worthy even in a simple T-shirt and battered jeans. His feet were bare, too. And yet the whole beach-bum look he had going on was completely at odds with what she saw when she looked at his face, now turned in profile. This was a warrior, and a very ancient one. He practically oozed power. His sharp features were somehow regal, with a strong blade of a nose, a hard, seductive mouth and slashing brows the same shade of midnight as his hair. His skin was eerily perfect, like marble in the dim light.

Vivi shivered a little at his nearness, then flushed, appalled at herself. She was a Hunter, damn it! And getting hot for the enemy was one of the biggest no-nos in the book. She'd thought she was immune to the vampires' considerable charms…. Until right now.

"Adam, isn't it?" her rescuer said in a voice that was dark and silken. Vivi shivered again and only barely refrained from slapping herself.

Adam, who seemed to have recovered completely, scrambled to his feet. He looked, Vivi saw with satisfaction, completely terrified.

"I. It's you. I didn't… Please, your highness, I only wanted—"

"Shut up."

Vivi stared, looking more closely at him. *Your highness?* But there was no way. Everyone knew the vampire king never left his hidey-hole, wherever that was. Hell, the Hunters weren't even positive there still *was* a vampire king.

"You will apologize to the lady," the regal vampire said, his cool, even tone never changing. She would have thought he didn't care, except for the genuinely frightening way he was staring at Adam. It worked, too, because Adam turned quickly to her, his eyes wide, and tripped all over his words as he begged forgiveness. It was satisfying, in a way, though not nearly as much as if she'd gotten him to this point herself. Still, she had her life. Beggars couldn't be choosers.

"I'm so sorry. So, so sorry," Adam said. He swallowed hard, glanced at the other vampire, and then continued. "I am so, so, so, *so incredibly sorry*—"

"Um, yeah, I got it," Vivi interrupted, arching one brow. "I still ought to stake you."

"That won't be necessary," the other vampire said smoothly. "Adam, go home. And when I say home, I mean *my* home. Ask for Rayne. Tell him what you've done, and he'll see to your punishment."

Adam blanched. "But—"

"If you choose not to, I'll have you hunted down and killed. Painfully. It's this sort of thing that created Hunters in the first place." That sexy voice was as cold and emotionless as stone. To his credit, Adam seemed to recognize he was standing in front of two people who would stake him on the spot without any remorse. He nodded, slowly at first, then more decisively as he began to back away.

"Home. Rayne. Got it. I'll go right away…your highness."

Eyes still wide with terror, Adam turned and sprinted

off into the darkness, vanishing into shadow. The remaining vampire watched him go, his expression troubled.

"He's going to run," he said. "And then I'll have to spare people to get rid of him, since he obviously poses a threat. Bloody waste of time and resources." The he sighed, a gusty, forlorn sound that Vivi had never heard from a vamp before. They tended to be a pretty carefree crowd, what with the power and immortality and incredible beauty. That was the sigh of a man who carried the weight of the world on his shoulders.

Vivi felt a sinking sensation as she watched him, even as desire curled into a hard knot deep in her belly. There could be no doubt about who he was. Public Enemy Number One.

Fabulous.

"Why did I agree to come on this stupid vacation?" he asked no one in particular.

"I'm asking myself the same thing right now," she said, shaking her head. He looked at her, seeming a little surprised, as though he'd forgotten she was standing there. It didn't surprise Vivi. She doubted many mortals were really on his radar. Probably had his blood supply delivered to him in a crystal carafe. Still, her manners won out. He'd saved her ass. She was a killer, a scourge of his kind, but she was not rude.

"Thanks for that," she said, then stuck her hand out. "I'm Vivi. Vivi Martin."

His eyes, so dark they were like onyx, swept her from head to toe as though seeing her for the first time. It was the oddest sensation, as though he were drinking her in. Vivi flushed, the heat racing all over her skin. *No,* she told herself. *Bad. Down, girl. No.*

For all the good it did.

Finally, he reached out and took her hand in his. The contact, so simple, sizzled along her skin and brought every nerve ending in her body to quivering life. She had to bite back a whimper, fight not to just melt in front of him.

"Vivi," he said, a soft exhalation. "You're very welcome. Adam is far more dangerous than he looks." He paused. "Even for a seasoned Hunter."

She huffed out a laugh, pulling her hand back to herself as quickly as she could without being completely rude. "I noticed."

His smile was like the sun breaking through a stormy sky. If she'd entertained any notions of staking this guy tonight, they flew out the window immediately.

"I'm Justin," he said.

"Justin," Vivi repeated. With his name, everything clicked into place. "So you really *are* the vampire king." Then she smirked, only half joking. "I guess a truce is in order for tonight. Consider this your running start."

Chapter 3

He wanted to take her seriously. Hell, Justin knew he ought to. A woman didn't carry a spring-loaded stake unless she meant business.

It was just difficult to get around the fact that the Hunter standing in front of him, giving him a "go ahead, make my day" look, gave off a vibe that was far more sexy pixie than bloodthirsty commando. He imagined it had given her the upper hand in plenty of fights with his kind.

It would here, too, if he let it. Still, Justin found himself...intrigued. Enough that he was reluctant to just say goodbye and walk away.

"So," he said, reaching for a way to keep her standing there. "You come to the beach to hunt often?"

She laughed, which he took as a good sign. Justin

watched her shift her weight from one foot to the other, even her smallest movements imbued with grace. Vivi was a little thing, delicately built, though the frayed cutoff shorts and simple tank she wore revealed a lithe figure that was anything but boyish. Her heart-shaped face was dominated by a pair of big, thickly lashed eyes of a bright, forget-me-not blue, and framed by shining ebony hair that had been cut into a sleek angled bob that skimmed along her jawline.

And she had a wicked smile.

"I'm trying to be on vacation, actually. It isn't working." She paused, considering him. Her gaze was so direct as to be almost uncomfortable for him. He hadn't been given a real once-over by a beautiful woman in a long time. Of course, Dru would happily tell him that was because he never went anywhere. Which would be true.

"What about you?" she asked. "Business or pleasure? I had no idea this was some kind of vampire hot spot. And believe me, I tried to check and make sure it wasn't."

Justin shook his head. "Believe it or not, I'm trying to be on vacation, too. I just got in last night."

Her dark brows winged up. "Seriously? Vampire kings take vacations in slow little beach towns like Mirage?"

It was his turn to laugh. "They do now. My sister's idea. She thinks I work too much."

Vivi just stared for a moment. "Your sister. Okay. So you have a sister who is…"

"Also a vampire. Yes. It was just one of those things."

"Uh-huh." Vivi walked to pick up her stake where Adam had knocked it, retracted the blades and paused to look at him before tucking it into a back pocket. "I meant it about not stabbing you with this, by the way. Don't worry."

He grinned, amused by her cockiness. "Vivi. I'm over two thousand years old. You're, what, in your midtwenties? I'm not worried."

She blinked. "Twenty-six. And I'm better than you think."

"So am I."

Her flush, which he noted the moment her mind went into the gutter, was charming. Justin relaxed a little, hooking his thumbs into the front pockets of his jeans. How long had it been since he'd even flirted with someone? He'd forgotten how enjoyable it could be.

A light breeze ruffled his hair, carrying with it the scents of ocean and night. Justin inhaled deeply, catching another scent, light, like vanilla and apricot wound together: Vivi. Something stirred in him that had been dormant for far too long, awakening with a surprising amount of heat and hunger. She seemed to sense it, a wariness flickering in those bright blue eyes, her body tensing ever so slightly.

She would fight him if she had to. The thought was strangely arousing.

"I'm not going to try to bite you," Justin said. "I already ate."

She wrinkled her nose. "Great. Well, um, look, Justin…it's been real, but I think I'll get back to my vacation now. Keep out of my way and I'll forget you're here. Deal?"

The words came before he could think better of them…though once he spoke them, Justin found he had no interest in taking them back.

"Have dinner with me."

Her stunned expression was priceless. "Excuse me?"

Justin took a step toward her, then another. He made no attempt to thrall her even though her eyes were locked with his. She would accept his offer in good faith or not at all. To her credit, she didn't back away, though her tension increased the closer he got.

"Dinner. Or a drink. An evening with me." He paused, then gave her a slow smile. "You do owe me."

"I…but… I already said I wouldn't kill you. Doesn't that make us even?"

"Killing me would take more than just you, and more effort than you should be expending on your vacation anyway." He took another step, closing the distance between them until he was only a foot away from her. Still she didn't bolt, though she was beginning to look like she wanted to.

"You want me to…go out with you," she said slowly, as though trying to process the information herself.

"You're here alone. I'm here alone. And to be perfectly honest, I'm already bored out of my mind. But I promised my sister I'd spend a week away, at least attempting to enjoy myself."

Justin watched Vivi mull this, and found he wanted her to say yes. More, much more, than he'd counted on.

"You realize that my job involves, you know, killing vampires on a regular basis, right?" she asked. "This doesn't bother you?"

"Technically, you're not on the job. And if I'm not mistaken, the Hunter's Guild targets only vampires who are threatening humans in some way, not the average night crawler minding his or her own business. We're all few and far between…" He nearly finished with *up here,* but stopped himself. His interest in Vivi notwithstanding, it was dangerous to get too comfortable.

"True," she said. "But we're not all the same. I'm not as…zealous…as some. And if you think you wouldn't be considered a big prize for the higher-ups, you're nuts. You're the freaking vampire *king.*"

"Mmm," he murmured. "It doesn't work exactly how you think it does." Humans, even Hunters, had no true knowledge of Terra Noctem beyond rumors and whispers. If too much information got out about the location, the city would simply move and reappear elsewhere, an ancient magic he had always appreciated without ever understanding it. Apart from that, there were other, deadlier safeguards against human invasion.

He was the king of a city, not of his race. The vampires were a diverse lot, impossible to corral, impossible to rule. He had influence, yes. But the bloodthirsty troublemakers who had necessitated Hunters in the first place were no more influenced by him than they would be by any vampire. It was hard to begrudge Vivi her position, though he knew what she said was true. Some Hunters hated all vampires, unequivocally. It had the potential to become a problem someday, perhaps sooner rather than later.

But not yet. And not here.

Vivi was frowning at him. "You are a very weird man, Justin. Even for a vamp."

"Is that a yes, then?"

She sighed, rubbed her palms against her hips, and looked around as though searching for guidance in the warm Florida night. Finally, she looked back at him.

"One date? I mean, well, outing, whatever you want to call it. One, and you won't get all stalkerish on me after the fact or anything."

He nodded, though he had every intention of seeing her more than once this week. He'd just have to come up with a strategy when he had time to think about it. For the first time in ages, he'd met a woman who fascinated him, provoked him. Every time she spoke, he wondered whether that pink rosebud of a mouth would taste as sweet as it looked, whether her tongue was as clever with a kiss as it was with words.

He was betting on yes.

"When will we be doing this?" she asked. "I'm here for another six days."

"As am I," Justin replied. "A fortunate coincidence."

"Hmm," was all Vivi said. He was definitely making her nervous, but not afraid, Justin decided. It was, in his opinion, a good sign. Though he doubted a Hunter was what Dru had had in mind when she'd been poking at him to find a woman. Still, he was under no illusions. This was a temporary diversion. Though it had the potential to be an incredibly satisfying one.

"Tomorrow night," he decided. "I'll pick you up at sunset. Sound good?"

She gave him a funny little smile. "Good is an interesting term to use here. It sounds…workable, if you're dead set on this. I'm at the Palm. Room 624. Break in and try to pull a Count Dracula, and I swear to God I *will* stake you, no matter how cool you think you are."

Justin grinned. He couldn't help himself, though he supposed it was a sign of just how long he'd been celibate if he found a woman who kept threatening him with death quite so entertaining.

"That's convenient. I'm at the Palm, too. Royal Suite."

Vivi rolled her eyes. "Naturally. Okay, big shot. I'll be waiting in the lobby a little after sunset." She shook her head. "This should be interesting, at least."

"I have no doubt." On impulse, and because he knew it would fluster her, he took her hand in a single fluid movement, bowed and pressed his lips to it. Her skin was soft, enticing. Hunger, of several different sorts, had his chest tightening, his incisors lengthening.

"I look forward to it."

Then Justin straightened, turned and walked away before Vivi could change her mind.

He knew he would think of nothing but her until the sun set again. And for the first time in centuries, he savored the anticipation.

Chapter 4

Vivi almost managed to talk herself out of this…meeting/date/whatever thing…a hundred times over the course of the afternoon. But when the sun began to sink beneath the waves, she was touching up her lipstick one last time in her bathroom mirror and eyeing her sundress, hoping she'd managed to find the delicate balance between looking good without appearing to have tried too hard.

Vivi tucked her hair behind her ear and made a face at her reflection. She'd erred on the side of looking like she'd made an effort. But seriously? She hadn't been asked out in ages. It was a great excuse to be girly for once.

If only her date was anywhere close to her age. And mortal. That would have been awesome.

She pressed her lips together, cast a final, critical look at herself in the mirror and then turned to walk out into the bedroom. Vivi grabbed her slouchy striped bag from the bed, tossed her lipstick into its dark and frightening depths, and swung it onto her shoulder as she headed out the door.

The elevator ride down to the first floor gave her plenty of time to wonder what the hell she was doing. Yeah, Justin was gorgeous. Vamps with faces like his had been known to trip up even seasoned Hunters, and despite all of her experience, Vivi knew she was hardly the most hardened warrior in her guild. But she'd been nice and immune to vampire charms up until last night.

It made her feel only slightly better to think that most Hunters never had to try and resist flirting with the vampire king. Who was, fittingly, the hottest of the preternaturally hot.

She heaved a sigh when the doors opened.

"One night," she told herself quietly. "Not a big deal. Just one night."

Vivi stepped out into the airy lobby, warm with the colors of the beach with air stirred by large paddle fans. Her espadrilles made a muffled echo on the marble floors as she moved among milling guests of the hotel, some with bags, others waiting for friends or lovers. The number of Panama hats and Hawaiian shirts made her smile. She wondered whether Justin would turn up in one or the other...or both.

Her cell phone burst into song somewhere in the depths of her purse.

"Damn it," Vivi muttered. She rummaged for it as she made her way to a cozy cushioned bench tucked into a small seating area near the huge windows facing the beach. A glance around as she pulled it from her purse revealed nothing but a bunch of mortals. Her date wasn't here yet. Fortunately.

The ringtone, which was the *Ghostbusters* theme song, meant work.

"I'm on vacation," she said by way of greeting. "If there's not a full-scale demon invasion going on, like, right this second, I'm going to have to get back to you."

A soft, female laugh had the hair on the back of Vivi's neck rising. The sound might have come off as warm, except that she knew the laugh's owner, who was anything but.

"Don't worry, Vivi. Even if there was, I'm sure we'd get by while you lounged on the beach. It's important to have priorities, right?"

Vivi gritted her teeth a moment before she could answer. Of course it was Marina. Of *course* it was. After all, what was a first day of vacation without a call from your least favorite Hunter?

She wished she knew.

"It was a joke, Marina. Learn to take one. What do you need?"

"Not so much a need. Just a warning. Keep an eye out. We've got some buzz that an important vamp is in your area."

It was a struggle to keep her throat from closing up completely. "Oh?" she forced out, hoping she sounded casual. "You might want to define 'important,' Marina. All I've seen so far are beach bums and overweight dads. I didn't pick this place for the action."

Distaste curled through Marina's sharp voice. "Source says the vamp king may be out and about. I think that's bullshit, myself. These *things* don't do authority all that well. But the really old ones get a lot of respect. Bagging one would be a big deal…. And it would send the right message."

Vivi frowned. This was what had begun to bother her about some of the higher-up Hunters. She'd gotten into hunting because of the adventure, the challenge…and also because she was doing something good, keeping rogue bloodsuckers from hurting people. But she'd noticed, over time, that there were quite a few Hunters who regarded all vamps, not just the rogue ones, as targets. She'd been told it was instinct—the kind of instinct she would never have. Which was fine with her.

"Has this theoretical high-profile vamp harmed anyone? Caused any problems?" Vivi asked, already knowing the answer. Marina hated anyone with fangs, unequivocally.

"His *existence* is causing a problem. Getting away with leeching off of humans for hundreds, maybe thousands of years tells them they can all do it. Hit a target like that, the rest think twice about showing their faces."

Vivi closed her eyes. "Marina—"

"Just keep an eye out," Marina interjected, her voice going ice-cold. "Be careful, Vivi. You might be talented, and you might have Desmond talking you up to anyone who'll listen, but I see all the weak spots. Sympathy for the devil is just one of them. You slip up, I'll be right there making sure everyone knows it…right after I've finished cleaning up your mess."

The call ended before Vivi could say another word. By design, of course. Marina Ferrars always got the last word. And for whatever reason, she had hated Vivi's guts from day one. She just wasn't always so overt about it, probably because Desmond O'Meara, the man who headed up the Northeastern Hunter's Guild, really did favor Vivi. He'd been her biggest advocate since the day he'd recruited her.

And that fact continued to make Marina's head explode on a regular basis.

"Bitch," Vivi growled at her phone, her fingers gripping the edges of it harder than she needed to. She was tired of being Marina's hate object. And equally tired of the niggling little voice in the back of her mind that wondered, always and often, whether Marina and Hunters like her weren't just a little right about her. Whether the sense of justice she prided herself on, along with her aversion to senseless violence, would only get her—or worse, others—killed.

She dumped the phone back into her bag, then noted the silent arrival of a pair of polished brown shoes directly in her line of vision. Vivi took a deep breath, tried to steel herself against any effects Justin might have on her.

It's only tonight, she told herself.

Then she raised her eyes to meet those of the vampire king.

Chapter 5

The instant Vivi's eyes lifted to lock with his, Justin felt as though he'd been punched in the chest.

Some part of him had insisted, even hoped, that he'd imagined Vivi's effect on him last night. That he'd let the darkness and the years without a woman muddle his thoughts for one brief and intriguing interlude.

But here, in the softly lit lobby of his hotel, Vivi seemed even more vibrant to him. She reached up to brush her gleaming swing of blue-black hair away from her face and tuck it behind her ear. She looked wary, he noted. That made two of them. And yet here they were.

"I wondered if you'd be here yet," Justin said, forcing himself to keep his tone casual, relaxed.

Vivi arched one slim eyebrow ever so slightly. "I was here right at sunset," she said. "I like to be punctual."

He smirked. "Or you're just eager to get this over with."

Humor flickered across her face. "Actually, I'm more curious than anything. You're pretty old, right? What does a vamp like you *do* on a date? Aren't you completely bored by pretty much everything by now?"

"Not *everything*," Justin replied, amused to see color quickly staining Vivi's cheeks, though her gaze didn't waver. He could have meant any number of things, but her thoughts had headed right to his bed…. Exactly where he'd spent the day imagining her as he'd slept.

"Yeah, I suppose you do look like a shuffleboard-and-bingo kind of guy," Vivi said, and Justin surprised both of them by laughing, a sound so simple and genuine it was barely recognizable to him as his own. It really had been a long time since he'd gotten out, so long that he had stopped noticing the pressure he was always under. He felt…lighter. Happier, even.

Of course, it helped to have something—or rather, some*one*—so very distracting to focus on.

Vivi looked up at him, studying him as intently as if he were some exotic species. She was settled gracefully on a wicker love seat, shapely legs crossed at the ankle. From somewhere in the depths of the purse that sat beside her came a buzzing, accompanied by the unmistakable tones of the *Ghostbusters* theme song. Stifling a grin at her taste in ringtones, Justin waited to see what Vivi would do about it.

Her lips tightened just for a moment when her eyes shot to the bag.

Work, he supposed, and felt an odd twinge. He understood the purpose of the Hunters, understood the reasoning behind their existence even though he dearly wished mortals would just let the night races police their own members. But his understanding didn't extend to the increasing number of Hunters who killed his kind for sport.

Not all were like that. Not even most...yet. But Justin knew he'd be a fool not to keep the baser elements of her profession in mind tonight. Whatever else Vivi was, she was still a Hunter. What that title meant to her remained to be seen.

"Do you think that might be important?" Justin asked coolly when the ringing and vibrating started again.

If Vivi thought so, she didn't show it. "If the world was ending, I'd notice. Barring the apocalypse, the Hunters can manage without me for a week." She tipped her head to the side slightly, regarding Justin with a new, hard glint in her eye he didn't much like. "Or maybe you're wondering whether I've been telling my boss about you?" Her warm, melodious voice was deceptively calm, and a whole lot cooler.

"Not at all," Justin replied, sensing that he was suddenly on treacherous territory with Vivi.

"Good," Vivi said, more than a little stiffly. "Because if there's one thing no one ever has to question me on, it's my honor. You don't hurt anyone, I won't turn you in. Period."

"A simple code of ethics," Justin said. "I like it."

"You should. It's saved the ass of many a vampire."

When he laughed, genuinely amused by her, Justin saw Vivi's tension begin to dissipate. Her shoulders relaxed ever so slightly, and the curve of her lips softened. A puzzle, that even a hint of questioning her honor would put her back up this way. Much like a warrior, Justin thought, and smiled. Vivi would make an awfully small warrior...but he already had a feeling she was as fierce as ten men.

"Well, then. Shall we?" he asked, holding out his hand.

Vivi's smile was slow and sexy, with a quizzical lift of her brows. "Still determined to go out with the armed and dangerous vampire hunter?"

"Hoping I'd change my mind?"

Her pretty blue eyes went to steel. "Not a chance." She slipped her hand into his without another word and allowed him to help her rise, as regal as any queen. Her skin was soft and warm in his cool palm.

The shiver of pleasure that even that simple bit of contact caused drove home exactly how long it had been since he'd touched a woman. It had been even longer since he'd touched a mortal one. Too long. Her heat, her scent were both going to drive him mad.

"Well. Let's get this party started," Vivi said wryly, pulling her hand away as easily as she'd given it and starting toward the entrance. Justin fell into step beside her, drinking her in with a single sidelong look. Even in her wedge heels, Vivi was only barely taller than his shoulder. Justin let his eyes linger, allowing himself a moment to take in the floaty little sundress she wore. The thin material skimmed over her small, perfect curves, and thin straps revealed strong shoulders and creamy skin not yet kissed by the sun.

"Didn't you spend any time flopped on a towel today?" he asked. "I thought that was supposed to be a part of this whole beach-vacation thing."

Vivi turned her head to look at him. "Oh, yeah? You planning on trying it?"

"I didn't pick this place," he reminded her. "And you don't have the whole 'bursting into flames' thing as a deterrent to sunbathing. Why come here if you're going to avoid the actual beach?"

Vivi took a moment to answer. When she finally did, her voice held a note of embarrassment. "I slept half the day. My hours aren't much different than yours, you know. And anyway, I prefer the beach minus the crowds."

Justin's smile was slow, easy. In this, he understood Vivi perfectly.

"You prefer the night," he said. Not a question. A statement. And Vivi didn't bother to disagree, simply nodding.

"Always have." Her lips quirked with humor. "And there you have what is probably our one thing in common. I'd say 'check, please,' but we haven't even gotten out the door yet. Now what are we supposed to do? Sit around and stare at one another?"

Justin held open one of the big glass doors for her, watching her step through the doorway with that casual grace of hers.

"Doesn't sound so bad to me," he replied.

"Mmm-hmm," Vivi replied, arching one dark brow at him, a playful twinkle in her eye. "Don't worry. If you get boring, I'll come up with something."

The promise in those words had nothing to do with sex, Justin knew, but he found his mind rushing to roll around in the gutter anyway.

"You do know how to fight, right?" she asked over her shoulder, so casually that she might have been asking about the weather. Justin stared for a moment, then shook his head as he followed after her, wondering once again what he thought he was doing with this woman, in this place, tonight.

Chapter 6

A half hour and two drinks later, Vivi was aimlessly stirring her Malibu Bay Breeze and wondering how, exactly, she had managed to make a guy two thousand years older than her nervous. At least, that seemed to be the case with Justin, Vivi thought, watching him stare out at the dark ocean. He'd been very smooth in small doses. But here, alone with her under the stars, Justin didn't seem to know quite what to do with her.

It was kind of charming. And also kind of…awkward.

She tapped out a rhythm with her toes beneath the table, propped her chin on her fist, and looked around at the other customers enjoying the balmy spring night. They sat outside, on the wraparound deck of a restaurant and bar called the Wayfarer. Candles on the tables gave off a warm glow, as did the little white lights wrapped around the wood railings of the deck. A soft breeze made their candle flicker, the glow playing over Justin's strong features. Her chest tightened, just a little, at the dark beauty of him.

Then she pressed her lips together, irritated. After all this time, you'd think she would be a little more immune to vampire charms.

"So what's the deal with you, anyway?" she asked, reaching into the basket of fries in the center of the table.

Justin shifted his gaze back to her, pinning her with eyes almost as dark as the night. Depending on the angle, she'd noticed, there was a reddish tint in their depths. Otherwise, they were fathomless.

"What deal are we talking about?" Justin asked. She liked the sound of his voice, not too deep, a little husky. She liked his mouth, too. Very…lickable.

Damned Bay Breezes. I'm switching to water.

"*Your* deal," Vivi replied. "I've done plenty of talking. You've gotten an earful about my parents, my obnoxious older brother and how my apartment is too small for a dog, which sucks. But what about you? This sister of yours…where you're from…anything, really," she continued, gesturing with one hand. Justin watched her wave her French fry around, looking slightly mesmerized. When he volunteered nothing, she hissed out a breath through her nose. "How long has it been since you've been on an actual date, anyway?"

Justin's shoulders hunched ever so slightly. That was pretty much all the answer Vivi needed, but she was curious anyway.

"No, *seriously.*"

"A while," Justin finally said.

"Not an answer," Vivi replied, pausing to ask for a glass of water when the waitress wandered back over to see about refills. Justin's beer sat untouched in front of him, and she wondered if he actually liked the stuff, or if it was just a prop of sorts. Once the girl was gone, Vivi quickly refocused.

"So it's been a few months? A few years? What?"

Justin gave her a baleful look. "Is this really going that badly?"

Something about the way he said it humanized him in a way Vivi hadn't expected at all. Here he was, this all-powerful vampire king, totally mouthwatering...and he was a fish out of water. Empathy was the last thing she'd expected to feel tonight, but there it was. How often had she had disastrous dates just because she was a little different? It helped in being a Hunter. In dealing with the opposite sex, not so much. Most guys didn't want a woman who slayed things for a living. And if they did, there was usually something wrong with them.

"You're not doing *badly*," Vivi said, hoping to soften the observation. "You just seem like you don't, um...do this often." She offered him an apologetic little smile. "You seem a little uptight."

Justin reached up and rubbed a hand through his hair, a gesture he didn't even seem aware of. It left his dark crop of hair tousled.

"Well. I don't. Do this often."

At Vivi's raised eyebrows, he sighed and continued. "Okay. It's been a hundred years. Give or take."

Her mouth dropped open. She couldn't help it. "Give or take? Give or take *what*, exactly?"

"Another few hundred years," he muttered, looking back out toward the ocean.

Vivi stared. It took her a moment to collect herself enough to respond, but that didn't seem to bother Justin. He looked like he was considering jumping over the railing and tossing himself bodily into the waves to avoid further questioning.

"Well, that explains a lot," she finally said. "I don't really get it. At all. But okay."

Justin's lips pressed together in a hard line. "I did mention what I do for a living, right? It's a little time-consuming. I don't have time to date."

In response, Vivi widened her eyes, slapped both hands on the table before her, and made a loud, incredulous sound. The dramatic display earned her an amused snort from Justin, whose mouth seemed to be turning up despite his best efforts to look affronted.

"No *time?* You're undead royalty and probably surrounded by hot vampire women," Vivi said. "You have
eternity to play in! Why would you want to be a workaholic? A *celibate* workaholic, no less?"

Justin frowned, eyeing the fry she was still brandishing at him. "Hey."

"Hey, nothing. That's seriously messed up, Justin." Vivi shook her head, swirled the lukewarm fry in
ketchup, and popped it in her mouth to chew it contem-
platively. "And here I thought all vamps were worthless
hedonists."

"Not any more than all Hunters are murderous zeal-
ots," he replied, and though the tone was soft, the words
were anything but. Vivi shifted uncomfortably. Hunters
performed a service, and an honorable, just one! Was
that really how the vampires saw her kind?

"I... The vamps I get sent after..." she stammered,
surprised to find herself on the defensive like this. But,
then, she'd wanted conversation. She was certainly getting it.

"You only see the outliers," Justin interjected. "Most
vampires are little different than their mortal counter-
parts."

"Except for the eternity thing," Vivi pointed out. "And
the incredible strength. And the blood drinking. And the
abnormal hotness."

His smile was slow, sexy. And this time, the pool of

liquid heat deep in her belly didn't evaporate no matter how hard she willed it to.

"You think I look abnormal?" he asked, his dark eyes glittering with what she thought was humor. Vivi nodded, grateful for the turn of topic. The last thing she wanted to do was argue with him about the relative merits of staking the bad seeds littered among his kind.

"Yeah," she replied. "Really, really abnormal." Oh, was he ever.

Justin leaned forward slightly, never taking his eyes from her. Vivi swallowed hard, but didn't shrink back like her instincts told her to. If he started to thrall her, well, he'd find himself with a dagger in his trachea and an empty seat where she was now. The thought was comforting.

Because Justin was by far the oldest and most powerful vamp she'd ever encountered. And the fact that she felt so at ease with him unnerved her more than even the most violent bloodsuckers who'd crossed her path.

"I'm sure your line of work has its perks, too," Justin said.

Vivi grinned, though her heart was fluttering like a caged butterfly. "Nah. We're just like everyone else. Except for the sharp, pointy toys. And the high mortality rate."

"And the abnormal fearlessness. The last person I met who had such a blatant disregard for his own safety was over six feet tall and carried a sword and a shield." He looked her over very deliberately, making heat spiral up from her toes.

"You're...not similarly equipped."

Vivi rolled her eyes. "I would hope not. All of those things sound bulky. Height I don't need. Speed, on the other hand..."

She trailed off, looking out past the edge of the deck to the dark beach beyond. For a moment, she saw nothing. Then there was the barest flicker of movement, a shadow edged with the faintest hint of flame moving quickly along the water's edge.

"Vivi?"

"Hold that thought," she said, never taking her eyes from the shadow on the beach. Her blood was already up, her senses opening to the night.

"I'll be right back."

Chapter 7

Whatever Justin had expected on this date, it wasn't watching Vivi vault over the deck railing to go racing off into the darkness.

"Shit," he muttered, noting the chuckles and stares as he stood up. "She's...ah...a free spirit," he said to their waitress, who stared at him like he'd grown another head. He pulled two twenties from his wallet, tossed them onto the table and grabbed Vivi's purse. It was surprisingly heavy. Of course, the woman probably had a veritable armory in there.

Silently cursing himself for thinking any of this was a good idea, Justin leaped over the railing himself, landing in the silken sand and taking off in the direction he'd seen Vivi go. A single sniff of the air had his stomach sinking.

Brimstone. Great.

Did Hunters make a habit of tangling with *inferi* now, too?

Vivi had cut the unwitting demon off not far down the beach, and it was mere moments before Justin reached them. Her dagger sliced through inky blackness as she and the *inferi* circled one another, a woman versus a squat, red-skinned demon with horns protruding from its forehead. It was hideously ugly, stinking of brimstone, its dagger-sharp teeth bared in a grotesque parody of a smile.

It was also, as Justin well knew, easily as dangerous as a vampire. Often more so.

But here was Vivi, slashing away at it…. And damned if she didn't look like she was having the time of her life.

"That doesn't look like a vampire," Justin commented, dropping Vivi's purse in the sand at his feet. The *inferi,* realizing its meal had potentially just doubled, gave a grunt that was a combination of anger and pleasure. Beady eyes moved between Justin and Vivi. Justin braced himself, and sure enough, the demon spun with surprising speed and rushed at him, fangs bared.

Justin sidestepped the attack easily enough, lashing out to land a blow on the creature's back as it blew by him. It squealed, spinning to glare at him. Rivulets of drool had begun to drip in ropy threads from its mouth.

"Doesn't need to be a vampire to be trouble," Vivi

said. "Lots of these things turn up. And they *never* get the benefit of the doubt."

"Good policy," Justin said as Vivi launched herself at the demon again. In a series of deft moves she'd wounded the creature, which had mostly served to make it angrier. This, Justin knew, was not one of the more intelligent types of *inferi*. This sort was simply bred to cause and thrive on destruction.

A flash of claws, and crimson streaks appeared high up on Vivi's left arm. She didn't make a sound, only bared her teeth as she beckoned the demon with her short, curved blade. The sight of the blood, Vivi's blood, had hunger rushing through him like wildfire. But it was unlike the hunger he'd grown accustomed to grappling with as a vampire. Or at least, there was an element to it that Justin couldn't quite get a handle on.

He didn't have to time to think. All he knew was that he *wanted*. And the demon was in his way.

With a snarl, Justin launched himself at the creature, slashing out with quickly lengthening claws. The *inferi* gave a hideous squeal, then spun, grasping wildly for Justin. A swing of its arm clipped Justin before he got clear, and the jarring blow was a reminder that what these things lacked in brains they made up for in brute strength. He lashed out, drawing blood and a roar. Justin didn't care, growling, waiting as the demon lowered its head and readied itself to charge him. Vivi came out of nowhere, leaping onto the *inferi's* back and plunging her blade through rawhide-tough skin. She struck where the heart would have been, should have been…but she withdrew the length of steel and stabbed through the back of its neck, too, just in case it didn't have one.

Justin stood still, stunned, watching as Vivi completed the kill quickly, efficiently and then leaped to her feet with far more grace than he himself had mustered. Her face and dress were spattered with black ooze, but nothing could mar the brilliant grin she gave him.

"Thanks for the distraction. Might have taken a little longer otherwise," she said.

It took Justin a few seconds to answer. His heart was pounding as it hadn't in ages, shocked out of its normal, sluggish, ancient beat. His breaths came in quick, sharp pants.

He felt incredibly alive. And as he watched Vivi approach him, the keen edge of the strange hunger she inspired in him only sharpened.

"I live to serve," Justin finally said, earning him a soft, musical laugh from Vivi. She came to him across the sand. Her feet were bare, he noticed, her sandals doubtless kicked off on the way to her target.

"You fight like a warrior," Justin murmured, raking over her lithe, taut body with his eyes. "Even in a dress."

"Yeah, well, I try to keep my slaying stylish," Vivi

replied. The glint in her eyes was appreciative when she stopped only a couple feet away to look him over.

"You fight pretty well, too. Not that I'm surprised. You're covered in demon blood, though."

"So are you. And we both stink of sulfur."

Vivi looked down at her ruined dress and sighed. "I don't know why I bother to spend money on nice clothes."

They laughed together, the tension of the fight easing even as Justin felt it replaced by a pull that was even more intense, in its way. She watched him, her laughter fading into a gentle, quizzical smile, as though she were seeing something she was trying to puzzle out. It made him uncomfortable…. But it wasn't entirely unpleasant. He hadn't felt nervous around a woman in centuries. Not in a way that had more to do with sex than violence, at least.

"We're going to need to get cleaned up," Vivi said. Justin felt a sinking feeling in the pit of his stomach. Was his evening with her to be over already? Silently, he cursed the *inferi*. Hell had caused him all sorts of trouble in the past year, between Terra Noctem's new Fallen residents and the fact that his people were now targets for the *inferi* and their masters ever since he'd assisted in preventing the apocalypse.

"Of course," Justin said, unable to come up with a convincing argument to keep her here. Stinking demon blood was hard to get around. Then Vivi quirked a smile at him, stepping closer. She paused, just for a moment, then reached out to take his hand, pulling him forward.

"Well, then what are you standing there for? Come on," she said, and snagged her purse from the ground.

So with the Hunter's warm hand in his, Justin allowed himself to be led. And somehow, for the first time in ages, he didn't care where he was going as long as she was coming, too.

Chapter 8

I've lost my mind. Finally, completely lost my mind.

The voice was a disapproving drumbeat in the back of Vivi's mind, but that didn't stop her from pulling Justin along with her down the beach. She didn't let go of his hand, and he didn't seem interested in breaking the contact. So she smiled and cajoled him and allowed herself the pleasure of feeling his skin, cool as marble, soft as silk, warming against her own.

She knew it was crazy. But so was tag teaming a demon with a vampire king. She doubted anything tonight was going to top the insanity of that.

"Where are we going?" Justin asked. The lines of his face were softer in the darkness. He looked more relaxed than she'd seen him yet, and amused besides. Good. He could use some fun in his life—that was obvious.

"This way," Vivi replied, falling into step beside him. She thought Justin might pull away, but he threaded his fingers through hers instead, cementing the tenuous physical bond between them. Her heart fluttered in her chest, so she continued talking to distract herself.

"I try to stay away from business when I'm here, but sometimes it shows up anyway. Which means I need to know where I can clean up without wandering through Mirage covered in gore and freaking out the general public. Luckily...we're at the beach."

He didn't seem to understand, but she supposed he wouldn't. Not when he'd obviously been *wherever* for so many years.

Vivi led Justin toward a long, darkened set of stairs that descended from the higher land down to the pale sand. On the far side of the steps, at the base, was a wooden platform with a showerhead and a knob attached to the wall in front of it. The beach here was silent, the sounds of humanity distant.

"Ta-da!" Vivi announced, waving a hand at it.

Justin looked at the outdoor shower and gave a nod. "Ah. For washing off the salt from the ocean," he said.

"Or whatever," Vivi agreed, seeing that this was new to Justin. Maybe he just wasn't a beach lover. Or maybe he'd been holed up somewhere weird. Some of the Hunters had some pretty wild theories about hidden cities of vampires, crap like that. The higher-ups didn't take the stories seriously, and neither did Vivi. But it was…odd… that with all the Hunters in the world, Justin had managed to remain just a myth. She wanted to ask how he did it, but knew instinctively he wouldn't tell her. Why would he tell a Hunter a secret like that? She'd only use it against him eventually.

Or maybe not, she thought, pulling away from Justin to rummage in the purse he'd been thoughtful enough to grab for her before giving chase. The thought of using anything he told her against him…or his kind, for that matter…already left a bad taste in her mouth. She was on vacation. He was on vacation. There was no reason they couldn't just enjoy—

"What are you keeping in there?" Justin asked. "You're up to your elbow in that thing already."

Vivi's fingers closed around the travel bottle she always had stuffed in her purse for emergencies. She lifted the small white cylinder out, brandishing it triumphantly.

"We call it Hunter's Helper," she said with a smirk. "Best not to leave home without it." She beckoned as she got up on the platform. "Come on, let's do this."

He followed amiably enough. "If you want to shower with me, I'm not going to argue."

"Ha."

She turned the knob when Justin was beside her under the showerhead, and the two of them were immediately doused with cold water. Not freezing, but it was still a shock after the warm night air. Vivi swallowed most of her yelp, but she still squeaked loudly enough that Justin chuckled.

When she opened her eyes, he was rubbing at the black ooze on his arms with little effect. "Damned stuff," he muttered. "It's like the world's most disgusting glue."

"Here," Vivi said, unscrewing the cap on the small bottle she held. She tipped some of what looked like white shampoo into the palm of her hand, then took Justin's arm and smoothed the substance over it. The demon blood washed right off, along with a lot of the foul smell pouring from Justin. He raised his eyebrows at her.

"You could make a fortune selling this stuff to vampires. Seems like all we do anymore is tangle with *inferi.*"

"That's a thought," she replied, pouring more of the shampoo into her hand and, without really thinking about it, picking up Justin's other arm to smooth the cream over his skin. The familiar scent of the stuff rose around them, herbal and faintly sweet. The sulfur smell vanished without a trace. Vivi's motions slowed as she realized Justin was watching her intently while he allowed her to clean him. She swallowed hard and forced herself to meet his eyes, suddenly very aware that it was just the two of them alone together.

Water dripped from dark, impossibly long lashes, the gaze beneath them inscrutable. Vivi found herself once again very, very aware of the power Justin wore so comfortably. Slowly, he leaned nearer to her, and Vivi held her breath.

"If you would," he said softly, his voice a caress, "I can't see to wash the blood from my face."

"Oh. Sure. Um…sure." Vivi tripped over her words, and just hoped her hands weren't shaking when she lifted them to stroke the shampoo tentatively down Justin's cheeks. The few black flecks that had been there dissolved instantly, but the excuse to continue touching him was irresistible. She ran her fingertips over the ridges of his cheekbones, his strong jaw, over his smooth brow, all while he watched her steadily. The contours of his face beneath her hands were unfamiliar, and yet so compelling. The longer Vivi touched him, the less she wanted to stop. She slid her hands into his hair, working the suds into thick raven locks.

Justin's eyes slipped shut. Vivi couldn't imagine he was comfortable, having to bend down for her like this, but he truly didn't seem to mind. Instead, he looked like there was nowhere on earth he would rather be.

When the water had rinsed his hair clean, Justin opened his eyes again, looked at her pointedly and held out his hand for the bottle. She understood at once: her turn. It was only fair…and it wasn't as though she'd been petting him, exactly…but nerves coiled in the pit of her belly as she handed over the bottle and what remained of the shampoo.

When his hands began to brush lightly over the skin of her arms, Vivi shivered, unable to hold his gaze. For such a tall, powerful man, his touch was incredibly gentle.

"You got the worst of it," he murmured softly.

Her laugh was breathless, nervous. "I usually do."

His only response was a small half smile as he tended to her, working his way up to her shoulders, over her collarbone, all with a touch that was intimate without being invasive. He drew closer when he slid his fingers up into her hair, slicking it back away from her face, massaging the fragrant shampoo into her hair to wash away every trace of *inferi*.

Justin's thumbs brushed her cheekbones. Vivi's eyes closed, her skin nearly vibrating with pleasure. But when Justin's breath feathered her face, she knew he wanted her to look at him…knew he wanted exactly what she wanted.

And no matter how ill-advised it might be, it seemed she wanted it, too.

Vivi caught only a glimpse of Justin's dark, endless eyes, the irises ringed with red, before his mouth claimed hers in a decadent, drowning kiss.

Chapter 9

For a single, drawn-out instant, Justin worried she
would push him away.

Then Vivi's lips parted, and Justin stopped thinking
at all.

She slid into him, as fluid as the water that ran down
her body, turning the thin material of her dress into a
second skin. Justin touched his tongue to hers, a single,
tentative taste before he swept inside. Vivi seemed to
melt against him when his arms went around her, when
he slid his arms up her slender back.

Her arms wound around his neck, her fingers sliding into his hair at the sensitive nape of his neck. Justin
gave a soft groan. Vivi's light touch had his entire body
tingling, hardening. Even knowing how he wanted her,
the intensity of his reaction surprised him. He deep-

ened the kiss, holding her closer, pulling her more tightly against him.

He could feel every soft curve, every taut muscle as Vivi pressed herself to him. She matched every rough stroke of his tongue, slid her nails down to dig into his shoulders while she shifted against the rigid length of his cock pressing against her belly. The kiss turned hotter, more demanding. And deep within Justin's sexual haze, hunger, always waiting, flickered to life.

He tore his mouth away from hers to trail kisses down Vivi's jawline, to nuzzle into the warm silk of her neck. Vivi gasped and writhed against him as he licked and sucked at the tender skin, teasing her—and himself— into brutal arousal. He was enveloped by her scent, sweet and decadent all at once. And beneath it, her lifeblood pulsed, a darker scent, so difficult to resist.

Justin's fangs lengthened even as he struggled with the overwhelming need to be in her, with his teeth, his cock, joined in the most intimate way he knew. He nipped her earlobe, desperate for a taste of her, and suckled at the tiny drops of blood he had drawn.

The taste of her was dark and rich, chocolate and red wine…and more, infinitely more. Justin's head swam. Vivi's essence was unlike any he had known. He teased at her lobe with his tongue, savoring the lingering hints of it, knowing with a sudden, terrible certainty that he needed more. That even the *more* might never be quite enough.

"Vivi," he murmured, every ounce of his longing distilled into that single word.

She surged against him with a soft cry, her entire body tightening in a way that told him he wasn't the only one overwhelmed by this. He let out a shuddering breath and crushed her to him as she rode out her sudden climax, wishing he was inside her to feel her trembling around him.

With a sound that was somewhere between a gasp and a furious cry, Vivi pushed away from him, stumbling backward. She was dripping with water, her eyes wide and haunted. She was shivering violently, and Justin doubted it was from cold. He fumbled the water off, somehow, and took a step toward her. But she was like a spooked animal, tensing immediately for flight.

"We can't do this," she said, her voice uncharacteristically harsh.

"Vivi," Justin said, trying to keep his tone calm despite the storm she'd awakened in him. "Don't go. Please. It's all right."

"It's not all right!" she shot back, lifting one shaking hand to the earlobe he'd nipped. "You...you *bit* me."

"A tiny bite. It won't affect you, Vivi, but I'm sorry if it upset you." His words tumbled out as he realized she was very likely going to run off…. And run away from him, hard and fast.

"Upset me?" She laughed, a humorless, hollow sound that was less angry than simply devastated. "You saw what it did to me. Upset isn't the right word." She wrapped her hands around herself and looked ill. "God. I have to go."

"Vivi, don't. I won't hurt you, I swear. I'm sorry."

She shook her head violently. "It's not you, Justin. You can't help what you are. It just doesn't mix with what I am. I can't…I can't do this with you. It'll ruin everything."

She walked quickly, if a bit unsteadily, to get her purse. Justin didn't move. He was afraid if he did, she really would run. And he would never forgive himself for chasing her off that way.

She looked at him, every bit of her conflict etched onto her lovely face.

"Thanks," she said. "I'll…see you."

"Let me at least walk you back to the hotel," Justin said, but she shook her head, as he'd known she would.

"I need to go cool off," she said, then turned and headed up the stairs to the parking lot above.

He let her go, watching her as he stood there dripping and wondering what the hell had just happened. He'd been completely steamrolled by a nymph with bare feet and a soaking wet dress.

Bare feet. She'd left her shoes out here somewhere.

The realization was the only thing that kept him from running after her, though doing so would probably only have gotten him staked for his trouble. Justin set off back down the beach, easily finding Vivi's discarded sandals a few minutes later.

Just like that, he had an excuse to see her again. He had the rest of the night to figure out how he was going to convince her that a week with him wouldn't make her any less of a Hunter.

And that a vacation with a vampire might be exactly what she needed.

Chapter 10

Vivi sat on her bed, cross-legged, listening to the rhythmic rush of the surf beyond the open doors to her little terrace. Her eyes were closed. She was trying to focus on the sound of the waves, to clear her mind of all the junk she'd been dealing with today.

It wasn't working.

A knock on her door had her stomach in knots even before she opened her eyes. It had to be Justin. Who else would it be? Maybe he had her stupid sandals. They'd been gone by the time she went looking this morning, and it seemed like the kind of thing he might do. Partially because he was a surprisingly thoughtful guy, and partially because she doubted he was just going to let her be after that mind-blowing make-out session last night.

The worst of it was, despite what she'd said to him,

some sleep and some distance hadn't given her any more clarity about whether she wanted more of his attention or not. He was sweet, and funny and a hell of a fighter.... And he'd made her come just by sucking on her *ear*.

He was also about as off-limits for a Hunter as it got.

"Shit," she muttered as the knock came again. She swung her legs over the edge, got to her feet, and padded to the door. She took a deep breath, threw her shoulders back and turned the knob.

"Justin, I—"

She stopped short when she looked into a familiar face that was definitely not Justin's.

"Oops."

Tommy Li, one of her better friends from the Guild, grinned back at her. "Justin, huh? Totally busted on the beach hook up. You work fast, Vivi."

She forced out a laugh and hoped it sounded natural. "I'm trying to *enjoy* my vacation, Tommy. I have to work fast. It's only a week long." It was always good to see Tommy. He traveled a lot, and seemed to have the whole "unfettered" lifestyle down pat, so she was never sure how long they'd go between jobs together. Still, it was hard to be happy to see him when his presence here likely meant her vacation had just gotten a lot more complicated.

"You want to come in?" she asked.

"Nah," he said, leaning against the door frame. "Just

wanted to swing by to give you a heads up. Marina sent a couple of us here to keep an eye on things. She's got some idea that there's a big target in the area."

Vivi pursed her lips. One of her favorite things about vacations was that they tended to be Marina-free. Not this one, so far.

"If anything were going on here, I think I'd know," Vivi said, trying not to say the words through clenched teeth. Tommy picked up on it anyway. His coffee-colored eyes glinted with humor.

"Which is why I didn't argue with her. Parking my ass here for a week is a great opportunity to slack off." He shook his head. "She really has a thing about you."

"No kidding," Vivi replied. "We don't exactly see eye to eye on the differences between the Hunters' mission and all-out vampire extermination. If there's anyone here, Tommy, he or she isn't doing anything."

"As long as it stays that way, I'm happy to lay around and get my beach on," Tommy replied. His smile was easy, and impossible not to return. Tommy was tall, lean, with spiky black hair and cheekbones that could cut glass. Vivi had had a smallish crush on him when she'd first started as a Hunter, but a few years of watching him bounce through one meaningless fling after another had made it a simple thing to look at him platonically. Maybe some woman would take him down someday, but it wouldn't be her. She did, however, hope to be around to watch. With popcorn.

"Who's with you?" Vivi asked.

Tommy wrinkled his nose. "Chase."

"Ugh," Vivi replied, full of sympathy. Chase Ardrey was one of Marina's pets. Naturally. Any mission Marina had a particular bug about always got one of her favorites assigned to it.

"Gonna take him out and get him drunk tonight. Then he'll leave me alone while I hit the beach tomorrow."

Vivi snorted. "Hangover strategy. Well played."

"Want to come with? I know you're not working, but it's not exactly work. Or do you need more special time with—" he fluttered his eyelashes "—Justin?"

"No and none of your business. Smart-ass." Vivi waved him off. "You've got my number. We'll grab food or something. *Tomorrow.*"

It would be best not to ignore Tommy completely while he was here...or Chase, for that matter. She might not be sure what to do about Justin, but she was very sure she didn't want to see him staked for no reason. Protective of a vampire, she thought with a sinking feeling. She'd known this would be a slippery slope. And she was sure as hell sliding down.

"Sounds good. Take it easy," Tommy said, winked at her, and headed back down the hallway. Vivi smiled, waved. Then she shut the door, leaned against it and groaned.

"I am in so much trouble," she announced to the empty room.

It was not a great start to the evening. So it was no surprise when the curtains at the sides of the patio doors fluttered and a dark figure materialized between them silhouetted by the bruised twilight sky.

Vivi sighed.

"Come on in, Count Dracula," she said. "We need to talk."

Chapter 11

The first thing she saw when he stepped into the light was her sandals dangling from one of Justin's hands.

The second thing, which obliterated all prior thought, was the look in his eyes.

Vivi had never seen that kind of longing. It was the sort of need that built up over centuries, far longer than a single mortal lifetime. And it was all directed at her. It took her breath away, even as she wondered how she could possibly merit that kind of emotion. Her mouth went dry, and words refused to form themselves into a string coherent enough to speak them aloud.

"I know what you said last night," Justin began, taking the pressure off of her for the moment. "But I thought you might want these."

"Thanks," Vivi managed to say. Her voice sounded

hoarse and strange. "I...I had another pair, but those are my favorite." She made no move to go get the sandals, though. She was afraid that if she started toward him, she'd just keep going until she wound up plastered against him again.

He wasn't the only one dealing with this hopeless attraction.

Justin tilted his head, ever so slightly, as he looked at her. "What did you want to talk about?"

Vivi blinked, feeling slightly dizzy. "What?"

A ghost of a smile hovered at the corners of Justin's mouth. "You said 'we need to talk.' What about?" He paused. "Did it have something to do with the man you were just talking to?"

"Um. Man. *Oh,*" she said, finally piecing together a few of her scattered thoughts. That was when she realized exactly how grim Justin's expression was. He probably thought... Oh, God, would he really think that?

"That was Tommy. I work with him. *Just work,*" Vivi said, lingering on the last bit to make sure Justin understood. The relief on his face gave her a dark thrill. He still wanted her. He was actually jealous.

Yep. Sooo much trouble.

"Just...come in," Vivi said, waving at the chair tucked in the corner. "Have a seat. What's with the dramatic entrance, anyway? I do have a door."

Justin, who was looking decidedly un-Dracula-like

in a pair of baggy cargo shorts and a navy blue T-shirt, obligingly settled himself in the chair. Vivi finally felt steady enough to walk over and perch at the end of the bed, close to him but not too close.

"I tried walking. Your hallway was occupied."

"Ah."

Vivi fought the urge to fidget under the heat of Justin's gaze. Being anywhere near him was only going to make her think of last night. The way his hands had felt on her. And his mouth…

She cleared her throat. "Tommy is a Hunter, like me."

Justin's eyes darkened. "I see. And why would he be here?"

Vivi sighed. This situation, she thought, was a perfect illustration of the gulf between them.

"Someone tipped off one of my bosses that a 'high-value target' was around here somewhere. Marina doesn't trust me to do what she says, so she sent a couple of on-duty Hunters to stake the place out. On the upside, I don't think her intelligence said there was a vampire in Mirage specifically, but if you're looking for a tucked-away spot where a vamp could go incognito…" She trailed off.

"I am to be killed? I wasn't aware Hunters chased down vampires who were minding their own business," Justin said, his voice cool.

"We don't," Vivi replied quickly. "At least, most of

us don't. There's an element—Marina is part of it—that wants to stake everything with fangs. When I joined, the leadership was really tough on anyone who stepped over the line. We deal with the murderous nut jobs, and that's it. It was like being a paranormal cop, kind of. But it seems like lately... I don't know."

"Things are changing," Justin said. "I see." He was quiet a moment, then said, "I'd heard mutterings of this. The strict code of the Hunters is what has always protected them—you—from my kind, Vivi. If that breaks down, all bets are off."

She scrubbed her face with her hands. "I know. If that happens, then I'm in trouble, too. I won't be a party to the murder of innocents."

Justin looked startled. "I don't think I've ever heard a mortal use that term for a vampire. It's refreshing."

Vivi shifted on the bed, feeling as though she were perilously close to tiptoeing over some invisible line clearly marked *Traitor*. Which, she supposed, said a lot about how things had deteriorated in the past couple of years. Her personal view on vampires was hardly outside the mainstream for Hunters. Or at least, it hadn't been.

"Your average vamp is as average as the average mortal. Most vampires didn't choose to become immortal bloodsuckers. It just *happens*. I'm well aware I'm only dealing with the broken ones in my line of work. Or should be." Vivi looked away for a moment. "I don't want you to die, okay? Tommy thinks this is a joke, but his partner on this job will be taking it more seriously. So I'm warning you. You should probably get out of here."

Justin leaned forward, some intense emotion she was afraid to understand written all over his face.

"Vivi…"

"This doesn't mean I wasn't serious last night, Justin," she said, hating that she was defensive, holding up her hands. "I'm still a Hunter. Last night I could have… I wanted…" She shook her head, wishing the simple motion would clear it. When she felt she could, she looked at him again.

"Look, I like you. Which means any further hanging out by us has impending disaster written all over it."

To her surprise, he chuckled. Vivi frowned.

"What?"

"I'm just wondering what has you more worried: me getting chased by a couple of foolish mortals with stakes, or me kissing you again?"

She opened her mouth to answer, realized she didn't have one, and closed it again with an exasperated little growl.

"Did you hear anything I just said? I've worked with both of these Hunters. They make dangerous adversaries, Justin."

Justin stood, looking unperturbed. "Of course I heard you. I appreciate the warning, Vivi, and the insight into the current Guild leadership. I'll keep it all in mind."

She glowered. "But you're not worried. Obviously."

His lazy half smile was both sexy and infuriating. He had told her he'd been a Roman soldier once, and in that instant she could picture it. There was something about Justin that was very much the warrior, despite the modern clothes. She'd noticed that about the different vamps she'd run into, psycho and not. They might live forever, but they seemed to stay products of the time they'd been born into.

"I've lived a very long time, Vivi. Stronger men than these have tried to kill me. So have demons from the hell pit, creatures that make the one you killed last night look like a fuzzy puppy in comparison. I'll keep it in mind.... But, no, I'm not worried right now. I have better things to worry about."

"Like?"

His expression turned startlingly earnest. "Like how to get you to go out with me again."

"It's a bad idea," Vivi said, knowing the words were true even if she didn't mean them.

"Why? Because you're attracted to me? You might have noticed, the feeling is mutual."

Vivi closed her eyes so she didn't have to look at him,

sitting there, sounding like it was the most reasonable thing on earth for the two of them to have another date.

"You just answered your own question," she said simply.

"That's ridiculous. You had fun. I had fun. We had a drink, killed a demon."

Nearly ripped one another's clothes off on a dark beach, Vivi thought, though there was no way she was bringing up the night's end to Justin. He looked like he was thinking about it anyway.

"Look," he said. "I haven't been on a vacation in years." He paused. "In fact, I'm not sure I've ever been on something that would qualify as a vacation. I thought this week was going to be a bust, honestly. I came here to make my sister happy, because she cares about me, and because she would have kept pushing until she won anyway. She's like that."

Vivi smiled. She liked the sound of his sister.

Justin sighed and shoved a hand through his hair, the first sign of nerves he'd shown. When he looked at her, she could see he really felt he was taking a chance here. It surprised Vivi, to know she already had some small amount of power over him. That she could hurt him. Which made everything even more difficult. Because she could already see that hurting him was not an option she wanted to go anywhere near.

"Last night, I had a really good time with you."

"Well. Yeah. Me, too," she admitted. "Even though it ended sort of abruptly."

"If I'd had my way, it wouldn't have," Justin said. Vivi felt heat creeping up into her cheeks as her mind instantly conjured a vision of Justin stretched above her, gloriously naked, riding her to a mind-bending climax. She cleared her throat and laughed nervously.

"As amazing as it might have been, Justin, after this week, I head back to New York, and you head back to... wherever. You lead vampires. I stake vampires. This week is not real life."

"Exactly," Justin said, coming to sit beside her on the bed. The nearness of him had all of Vivi's senses prickling, every inch of her skin tingling, as though her entire body was wishing for his touch.

"This week is an escape for me," he continued. "A complete break from all the usual rules and problems. That's why I want to spend it with you."

Her heart clenched, just a little, as her eyes roamed over his face. She saw nothing to suggest he was anything less than utterly serious, just as he probably was about everything he did. Justin, she had already discerned, needed more laughter in his life. She could give that to him. She would *enjoy* it, Vivi knew. But it couldn't be for long. When it ended, it would have to be completely. A quick fling wasn't the sort of thing she did with guys, nor deciding to have one a decision she felt she should take lightly.

But…he was beautiful, interesting. And lonely. Just as she was. Maybe they both deserved a week away from the rules. From harsh, cold reality.

"After this week," she began softly.

Though his expression tightened ever so slightly, Justin gave a short nod.

"After this week, we go back to real life. You're not any more suited to my home than I would be to yours. I know that. But I find you…fascinating, Vivi. And for now, for this week, I'd like to enjoy myself." His smile was charmingly self-deprecating. "If I can remember how."

Vivi took a deep breath, sensing her answer would be important to her in ways she couldn't yet fathom. That spending this kind of time with a vampire, considering what she did for a living, would shift things: her preconceived notions, her sense of what it meant to be a vampire…and her heart. Which she would have to protect at all cost if she decided to do this.

Not that she could imagine turning away.

Vivi nodded and slid her hands into Justin's, against skin that was cool and yet pulsed with a vitality that could only be supernatural. She saw surprise flicker in the depths of his eyes at her touch. Maybe, Vivi thought, at her acceptance. Even though she still had no idea how he'd stayed single so long. No woman in her right mind would reject him.

And neither would she.

"Okay," she said. "One week. No rules, just fun. And at the end of it, we walk away, no hard feelings."

"Done," Justin said, his voice husky. He leaned in for a kiss, but Vivi leaped up from the bed, her heart pounding madly. If she let him kiss her, here, now, they wouldn't be leaving this room tonight. And while she wanted that, while she was positive she would end up in bed with him this week, she wasn't quite ready. Not yet.

But soon.

"Come on," she said lightly, pulling him up from the edge of the bed. "The night is young. You want fun, I have ideas."

He complied, but his smile was full of sensual promise.

"So do I."

Chapter 12

Justin had to give Vivi credit.

When she decided to do something, she really threw herself into it. And in this case, "it" was making sure he never forgot this vacation. For a variety of reasons. The most recent of which was Karaoke Night at Dolphin Dave's.

He slouched on his scarred wooden bar stool and took a sip of whatever Vivi had ordered for him. It had a festive pink umbrella stuck in it and tasted like strawberry-flavored lighter fluid. He turned his head to look at her and couldn't suppress the grin, despite the fact that the woman's idea of entertainment was more than a little insane.

"We rule," she said, her face alight. "'Paradise by the Dashboard Light' will never be the same."

"No," Justin replied. "I think it's safe to say we've buried that one for all time. They may outlaw it after that."

Vivi laughed and poked him. "Oh, come on. I never get anyone to duet with me. Everyone clapped for us!"

"Because everyone is drunk," Justin replied. But Vivi's enthusiasm was infectious. It had been worth it to fumble and mutter his way through the Meatloaf half of the song just to watch her belt out her parts with gusto. She was so full of life, he thought. Her blue eyes twinkled at him in the dim light.

They were out beneath the stars tonight, which seemed to be where Vivi preferred it. There was a small stage where a reggae band was now setting up, and a large square of sand in front of it marked off as a dance floor. Beside the stage was the karaoke machine, and the burly, piratical-looking DJ who was operating it. The DJ was watching in obvious horror as the evening's last singer, a bleached blonde with a sunburn and a precariously fastened bikini top, howled her way through a Katy Perry song.

The place seemed crowded for a Tuesday night, with a lot of people just arriving for, Justin guessed, the band. The excellence of the reggae had been Vivi's excuse for bringing him here. The karaoke had been a stealth attack.

And he hadn't felt this good in years.

Vivi leaned over to speak directly in his ear so he could hear her over the din.

"Admit it. This is even better than last night."

"I liked looking at the sand sculptures. They didn't make my ears ring," Justin replied. And he'd gotten to listen to Vivi's chatter, about her family, her life, the other Hunters. She was a sociable creature, and seemed to like talking nearly as much as Dru did. It struck him that she and his sister would get along well.

Immediately after which it struck him that if he wanted to enjoy himself with Vivi, he needed to put any ideas like that right out of his mind. She'd made it clear she wanted to go back to her life after this. And he...ought to want the same thing.

Justin pushed the troubling thoughts from his mind and focused on the night breeze coming in off the Gulf, the way Vivi's halter top showed off her long neck, her fair skin. Keeping the hunger he had for her at bay was no small task. He wanted to lick her, bite her...

A rolling reggae beat floated into the night sky, slow and easy, and a few couples headed quickly into the sand to dance. He saw Vivi's grin and knew exactly what she was thinking.

"Come on," he said. "I ought to redeem myself for the singing."

She laughed and followed him out onto the sand. When he turned, she slid her hands up to his shoulders. Justin settled his hands on Vivi's hips, and she began to sway to the music, her movements sinuous. He'd never been much on dancing—even in his mortal days, he'd preferred to watch beautiful women dance rather than join them—but this was well worth it. She was warm against him, rolling her hips with a soft smile as she let the music take her. All Justin had to do was sort of bob and sway, which he noticed was what most of the other men out here were doing anyway. And that worked just fine. He could focus on watching Vivi.

"You're not too bad at this, you know," she said.

"If you're comparing it to my singing, that's a low bar to clear," Justin said, then smiled when she wriggled her way up against him.

"I bet you dance solo in your creepy vampire palace in your spare time. That's where all this talent is coming from."

Justin lowered his head, speaking so that his breath feathered her ear. The memory of suckling at the lobe, of what it had done to her, immediately made the dancing more uncomfortable.

"You," he said, "have some very strange ideas about me."

There was a hint of reproach in her voice when she replied, "Well, you haven't given me much to go on, so I'm coming up with my own version of your everyday life. Lucky for me, I have a very good imagination."

It was a gentle nudge, he knew, about the fact that while Vivi had taken his "let's break the rules together" offer to heart, talking freely about herself, he'd stayed silent on his own life. But what could he really tell her? Speaking of Terra Noctem to her was forbidden, and he didn't think himself above the laws, king or no. And what else was there for him? The kingdom, the city, *was* his life.

He struggled to find some piece of himself he could give her, something not completely dull.

"I don't dance when I'm alone," he told her, continuing to move with her. "I'm very boring, really. I have a massive study, full of books. Took me centuries to put it together, and I still add to the collection. I love to read."

"Mmm. Cozy," she purred. "I can see that."

"I also like to swordfight."

She laughed. "I can also see *that*. Mr. Serious. Obviously, you needed some karaoke in your life."

What he'd needed was a Vivi, Justin thought with an odd, sinking feeling. He'd been alive for so long he hadn't even noticed the slow, steady way that all the color had leached out of his world. And then all at once, it was back, reappearing in the form of a small, raven-haired hurricane. The scents, the sounds, every sensation had a keen edge that left him hungering for more.

And yet even now, he couldn't enjoy it fully. It was in his nature to worry, and there was already a part of his mind wondering how quickly, once he returned home, the vibrancy of all this would fade back to what it had been.

He thought of his desk, piled high with petitions and requests. He thought of himself behind it, alone.

Justin pulled Vivi a little more tightly against him. "Come back to my room with me," he growled softly into her ear. The need to be as close as he could to her was almost overwhelming.

She shivered a little against him, despite the warm night.

"I—damn it, we need to go. Tommy and Chase are here."

Irritated by the interruption, Justin turned his head to see the man from Vivi's hallway, along with a shorter, stockier companion, moving in their direction.

He turned his head away quickly. Though he passed as mortal most places, a trained Hunter would recognize him for what he was as soon as he or she got close. Vivi's jaw was set, and she tensed in his arms. With a soft hiss of breath, she stepped back.

"I'll have to talk to them. You may want to take a long bathroom break. Like, now."

Justin bristled, both at the order and the intrusion, but he knew she was right. Just as he knew these Hunters were going to be a thorn in his side all week. His instinct was to face them down and tell them in no uncertain terms that they were treading on thin ice with both him and his kind. It was what he would have done in any other circumstance. But these were Vivi's people.

To keep her even this short time, he must do nothing. It was the wrong thing.

It was the only thing.

Justin's hands snapped into fists as he grappled with an ugly burst of fury, along with a hot sense of possession insisting he protect what was his.

She's not mine, he told himself. And, then, almost desperately, *Gods, I need to get out of here before I do something stupid.*

Helpless anger tangled his tongue. All Justin could do was step away, give a small, stiff bow, and walk quickly away from Vivi's apologetic eyes.

He wanted what he couldn't truly have.

And he had no one to blame but himself.

Chapter 13

Vivi watched Justin walk away, feeling a bunch of emotions she would rather not examine tangling into a painful knot deep in her chest. It figured: just when he was starting to open up, her job intruded. She could still feel his hands on her hips, the rush of his breath on her skin as he asked her to go back to his room.

She hadn't even had a chance to say yes.

Vivi watched the top of Justin's head vanish into the building as he circumvented Tommy and Chase. Both gave him curious glances. What if they already knew what Justin was? Her stomach did a slow roll.

She plastered a smile on her face, hoping she didn't look too pained as the Hunters reached her.

"Hey, Vivi," Tommy said easily. "Figured we'd run into you and the mystery guy at some point." He looked at the doors Justin had just disappeared through. "Well, you, anyway. What did we do, scare him off?"

"No," Vivi replied, uneasy at Chase's silence, and the close way he was studying her face. When his eyes dropped to her neck, she knew he suspected the truth. She was quietly thankful that Justin had left no marks on her.

"He got an important phone call he had to take," Vivi lied. "Too loud out here."

"True," Tommy replied. "This is the good kind of loud, though." He looked around, scoping out the place for a fling of his own, she assumed. It didn't stop him from teasing her.

"I took a picture of your PDA moment on my phone. It's going to live in infamy."

She snorted. "You did not."

He looked at her with a wicked grin. "I would have, actually, if your man hadn't taken off so fast. What's his deal, anyway? International superspy? I keep seeing you, but he's hard to catch."

"He's a financial man of mystery. This is a working vacation for him, so I'm not even seeing him much." She smiled. "Keeps it interesting."

Her fabricated story, which she'd spent some time on in case anyone demanded details, worked like a charm. All Tommy did was nod with a knowing look.

"Best-case scenario, then. Just don't get all hung up on him."

She pressed her lips together. "Thanks, Tommy. I already have a big brother. And he's way better at being obnoxious and overprotective than you."

He held up his hands, looking anything but contrite. "Just sayin'."

Chase was looking around, his focus so intense that he didn't even seem to notice Vivi was standing there. Then he startled her by asking her a question.

"Sniffed any vamps out around here, Vivi? You may be on vacation, but the job doesn't stop."

No, it didn't. Something that was really beginning to bother her.

"I ran off a couple my first night here," Vivi said, keeping her tone casual even when her words drew Tommy and Chase's undivided attention. "One older, one younger. Neither was anyone special."

"Nice of you to make that determination for them," Chase said, as his eyebrows knit together in concentration.

She started to bristle. "Better me than you. You only ever make one determination."

"It's the only one that makes any sense," he replied. "This is why you'll never make it as a Hunter, Vivi. You'll save the wrong monster and get gobbled up for your trouble."

Vivi had to struggle not to grind her teeth together. They'd been in the same orientation group, and she'd never liked him. He was a weasel. Unfortunately, he had some of the finest instincts she'd ever seen. She'd gotten in on her innate tracking skills and her nerve, but some Hunters had gifts that were more than a little above and beyond human.

Marina picked her pets well.

"Quit being such an asshole, Chase," Tommy muttered.

"He can't help it," Vivi said sweetly. "It's who he is. He's just pissy because he knows this is a wild-goose chase."

Chase shrugged, an odd glint in his eye. "Maybe."

Tommy shot his partner an irritated glance. "As in, 'completely,' even though Captain Good Times here is trying like hell to find some scrap of something to hand to Marina."

"Speaking of... Is your friend coming back, Vivi?" Chase asked.

Now he was just messing with her. But she knew him, despite not liking him. Chase had figured out something was off, even with just a glimpse of Justin. Tommy hadn't yet. But Tommy trusted her.

Guilt settled like a brick in the pit of her stomach. She was where she ought to be, with her fellow Hunters—but it wasn't where she wanted to be. Suddenly the bar was too loud, too crowded, too *everything.* She wanted her strong, quiet vampire who'd done karaoke with her even though she was pretty sure he would have preferred chewing glass.

Her vampire. For now.

For some odd reason, the thought made her wretchedly sad.

Tommy must have caught the odd look on her face.

"You okay, Vivi?"

"Yeah," Vivi said. "Yes. I'm fine. Just wondering where the superspy went." She forced out a laugh, then frowned a little and stood on her toes to look toward the door, as though she thought Justin might walk out of it at any second. "He looked worried when the call came in. I'm going to go check on him, okay? Only be a minute."

Tommy waved her off. "We'll be here." He was already more interested in a pretty, tan brunette laughing with her friends in the sand than Vivi's mysterious beach fling, and that was a relief. Chase, though, only gave her a small, knowing smirk. She rolled her eyes at him, spun on one heel and flounced into the indoor part of the bar as though she didn't give a damn.

And, unable to shake the feeling that Justin had not only vanished from the club, but from her life altogether, hit the front doors at a dead run.

Chapter 14

Justin stood at his balcony, watching the ocean absently as he listened to his sister's chatter on the other end of the phone. He could picture her, sitting with her feet up on his desk and gloating that he couldn't see her doing it. After two thousand years, he knew her pretty well.

"So do you like it? I was in Mirage once a few years ago to deal with some stupid high-ranking *inferi* who had a foot fetish. The creep loved beaches. Bare feet galore. You remember that? Anyway, it made me think of you."

Justin smirked, leaning against the wall. "The demon with the foot fetish?"

A snort. "You're such a jerk. Do you like the beach or not?"

"I like it," he said decisively. Dru didn't need to know *why* he liked it...but it was true.

He'd gotten back to his room quickly, flustered and angry at no one in particular. It was just that ever-increasing sense of longing for something that wasn't meant to be his. All he could think of was Vivi, warm in his arms, or laughing onstage, or tugging him along the beach as she pointed out every aspect of the sand sculptures that still littered the beach from last week's competition. Her life was full. And yet she'd carved out a little space for him.

His life ought to have felt just as full. But what did he have? His sister, yes, thankfully. And paperwork. Meetings. Throngs of supernatural creatures who all wanted something. A part of him missed his study, the cozy solitude of it. He just wondered how alone he would feel in it when he returned.

"...have you met a bunch of loose women in bikinis yet?" Dru was asking as he focused again on her voice. "I hope you're not just hiding in your hotel room."

"Of course not," Justin said smoothly.

"Oh? And where are you now?" Her voice was smug. She knew exactly where he was. But she didn't know the half of it.

He heard a soft knock at the door to the room, and his breath caught in his chest for an instant. Right away he could smell her, feel her presence just beyond the door. *Vivi.*

"I'll have to call you tomorrow night, Dru," he said. "I have company."

Her next words were keen with interest. "*Company? What kind? Is this like, you have to go have a sad conversation with the room-service guy now, or...other?*"

"Good night, Dru."

He hung up in the middle of a barrage of her questions, feeling a little smug that this place, this week with Vivi, was just his. And he did like Mirage. Even apart from Vivi, it was beautiful: small, tucked away, shot through with both luxury and shabbiness. It was different. It surprised him that he could still appreciate the different after so many years of the same thing over and again.

He strode to the door, unlocked it and opened it to see an ashen Vivi. Instantly, his frustration vanished. "Come in," he said. She seemed to want to say something, but finally just nodded and stepped inside the suite. He shut the door behind her, and locked it.

"Chase knows," she blurted out.

Justin lifted an eyebrow and moved to the small bar at one end of the massive room. He picked up a chilled bottle of white burgundy, poured into two glasses he'd had waiting and then recorked the bottle.

"Chase knows what, exactly?" he asked. He'd caught a glimpse of Chase, caught a hint of the stale, faintly sour scent of him. He was not impressed. Justin carried the glasses to Vivi and offered her one. She took it, took a sip without really looking at (or, Justin imagined, tasting) it.

"Maybe not knows. Maybe that's the wrong word. But he strongly suspects you're Marina's target. I think he sniffed you out."

That image made Justin chuckle. "If he's mortal, he didn't."

She shook her head, and his smile faded. "No, *really*," she said, brushing past him, heading out onto the balcony under the stars. Justin followed her. She stood against the wall, holding her wineglass with both hands.

"I'm telling you this because you need to know," she said without meeting his eyes. "I know you're a king, and I like that you're a confident guy, but this ought to matter to you."

And there, haltingly, she revealed something he had long suspected but hadn't ever had confirmed. The Hunters weren't just skilled. They were, in all likelihood, descended from old werewolf bloodlines, gifted with different aspects of their blood heritage. Some more strongly than others. It explained how much more difficult to thwart they were, Justin thought. Just as it explained an innate interest in killing vampires. After all, the night races had not always gotten along perfectly, despite a now longstanding peace. And like the vampires, there were werewolves who had turned their backs on

Terra Noctem, on any notion of living alongside former adversaries.

They had mated with humans, able to produce children where vampires could not. And the result, generations later, were children still being born with that instinct to fight his kind.

Slowly, deliberately, Justin took a sip of the wine. It was tart on his tongue, with a bite that helped anchor him in the present. He had seen plenty of nightwalkers stalk angrily back into the darkness. Some he had considered friends.

"Chase took one look at you and knew," Vivi was saying, her voice strangely thin. "Of course, me bolting out of there is only going to egg him on. You really ought to go, Justin. This is going to turn into a mess."

She looked vulnerable, and very human in that moment, all her fearlessness vanished. All he wanted to do was gather her into his arms and take her somewhere to erase her worry. Which, of course, she would never allow. So he would do what he could in this place.

"Will you go?" he asked softly, putting his wine on the small table that sat on the patio.

She shook her head. "No. It'll look really odd if I take off. Chase can't prove anything right now. And Tommy thinks you're just a rich guy I'm having a fling with."

The way she said it amused him.

"You'd describe me differently?"

Her smile was small, but a start. "Yes. No. I don't know." She shook her head, her hair gleaming as it swung around her face.

He approached her slowly. Somehow, she looked like she might bolt if he moved too fast. It was a relief, in a way, to see she was just as conflicted about him as he was about her.

Gently, he reached out and tucked a lock of hair behind her ear, letting his knuckles graze her cheek.

"There's no wolf in your blood," he said softly, seeing the surprise light her eyes. He traced her jawline, the lovely, pointed face. Now he understood what some part of him had recognized in her immediately. It was why he'd known, on the very deepest level, that he could trust her.

"How did you know?" she asked.

"You're as lovely as any Fae maiden," Justin said, the pieces all clicking into place. "It all makes sense now. You wanted to be a Hunter for the adventure, not for the death, yes? You're curious and brave, graceful and strong. And just. Humans have their stories about the Fae being flighty, but they actually have a very deep sense of right and wrong. Even if they sometimes choose to ignore it," he added with a smile. "Humans and faeries mating is rare. Your ancestor must have been quite something."

He could believe it, and easily.

Vivi looked back at him, an open book. That was

something very human in her. She lacked the guile of the Fae, and he was glad for it.

"I don't even know who it was," she said. "I don't remember most of my grandparents, and the one who's still alive is definitely *not* the one. I didn't know until I made the initial cut for the Hunters Guild training. They told me. And they almost didn't take me because of it."

"Makes sense," Justin murmured. "You have no innate sense of pack order. You follow your whims and your—" he nearly said heart, then stopped himself. "Your instincts. About others. Me being a case in point."

She laughed softly, though there wasn't much humor in it. "So being some tiny part Fae makes me unreliable. Awesome."

"Vivi, it isn't a tiny part. Fae blood is incredibly strong. And it isn't unreliable. It's just being determinedly individual." He paused, stroking his hand down her cheek again. She turned her head into his touch almost reluctantly, as though she couldn't quite help but respond to his touch. He knew the feeling.

"I fought hard for what I have in the Guild," she said. "I had to prove myself. I have to keep proving myself, all the time. This is what I wanted." Her laugh was bitter. "I'm saving the world from the forces of darkness, you know?"

He smiled gently. "Which ones?"

She closed her eyes and groaned. "I'm working on

that." Then she dropped her head, breathed in deeply and raised her eyes to his.

"I don't even know you." Her voice was soft, almost a plea. "I'm wearing a spring-loaded stake in a garter, and I should probably be stabbing you with it. Tell me again why I'm standing in your ridiculously huge suite telling you Guild secrets instead?"

He loved the way she looked in that moment, backlit by the dim light of the room.

"Same reason I'm standing here not biting you or trying to toss you off the balcony, I expect," Justin replied, bracing one hand on the wall above Vivi's head and leaning down until his mouth was just a breath away from hers.

Her pupils dilated. Her breath turned shallow. "Remind me," she said.

"Freedom from harsh reality. Rule breaking. Vacation," he said. He wasn't at all afraid of this Chase, or Vivi's friend Tommy. He was, however, desperately afraid she would just turn at any moment and walk away.

"Because you care," he added softly. It sounded more like a question than he'd meant it to, and he cursed himself silently for sounding like a fool.

But Vivi nodded slowly, her eyes dropping to his mouth.

"I feel like I'm going to give in to one of those whims

we were talking about," she breathed. "Which makes me unreliable. You're going to want to watch out."

"I'll be careful," Justin assured her, and lowered his head to claim her mouth with his.

Chapter 15

Justin swept his tongue into her mouth for a hot, possessive kiss that left Vivi's knees threatening to buckle. But it was the broken moan that escaped him when she pressed into him, digging her nails into his back that nearly sent her over the edge before they'd really begun.

"Justin," was all she managed to get out, her breath no more than a hiss, before he was doing things to her mouth again, nipping, biting, licking at her as though she was the sweetest thing he had ever, would ever, taste. He kissed her like a man possessed, and Vivi could only hold on, caught up fully in the sexual power that was making her thrum like a live wire.

Justin didn't need to thrall her, Vivi thought. His mouth was the most addictive thing she'd ever tasted.

Her head went back when he rocked his hips into her.

"Vivi," he breathed against her neck, teasing her with his tongue. He whispered her name like a prayer, and all she could think of was how good it would feel to have his teeth in her.

She heard her own words as though spoken by someone else. Distant and fuzzy.

"You can... The ear thing... Please."

His laugh was soft, sensual.

"Soon."

"Then I'll nibble on you."

They stumbled toward the bed, fumbling with one another's clothes. Justin's T-shirt bunched beneath her fingers as she dragged it up, wanting to feel the tight skin beneath, wanting him against her so badly she was dizzy with it. His skin, at first cool, turned hot beneath her fingers as she ran them first up, then down the rippling muscles of his stomach that jumped at her touch. She fumbled with his belt, even as Justin covered her mouth with his own again and filled his hands with her breasts.

She gave a soft cry when he squeezed, when he rubbed thumbs across nipples that were already taut and aching. Vivi wanted her hands on him.... And still the damned belt wouldn't give. At her furious growl, Justin scooped her off the floor completely and headed for the bed tucked behind a screen. Vivi wrapped her legs around his waist and held him tight, giving the hollow at the base of his neck a teasing lick.

"Let's see how you like it," she said hoarsely. She scraped her teeth across the sensitive skin, biting just hard enough to leave a mark. She felt his knees start to buckle.

"Bite me again," he said, his voice ragged, "and I'm not going to make it to the bed. It's going to be the floor."

Vivi laughed and began to suckle his ear, loving the way he tightened his grip on her. "Is this better?"

They landed on the king-size bed together, and Vivi quickly stripped off the rest of her clothes, flinging them wherever. Justin did the same, and she took a moment to admire the perfection of him, as sculpted as a classical statue.

Except a thousand times better.

She held out her arms to him. "Now," she said. A question. A plea.

In an instant, he was over her, on her, skin meeting skin as his hands tangled in her hair. Vivi gave a soft cry as skin met skin. She arched against him.

"Yes." She sighed. It was all she had imagined since the first time she'd laid eyes on him…and more. The thought of fighting this now seemed ludicrous. She'd never had a man fit against her as though he'd been created with her specifically in mind, but Justin molded against every curve, every hollow.

"So beautiful," he murmured. His hands cruised down her body as his motions slowed, as he began to explore her in earnest. Vivi ran her hands over his back, feeling the muscles leap and bunch when she lifted her hips against his, feeling the thick, heavy weight of his cock against her.

His laugh was strained.

"I wanted to take my time."

"We have time," she purred. "And I want you *now*."

He touched his forehead to hers, and though his eyes were those of the vampire, dark, endless, the emotion in them was as tender as she had ever seen.

"You taste like sunlight," he said, a reverent whisper.

Something welled up inside of her, something nameless and beautiful. She lifted up beneath him, aching for something she didn't even have a name for.

Justin drove into her without another word, drawing a gasp from her, then a moan. He rode her beyond thought, beyond reason.

Until they shattered together in the darkness.

Chapter 16

Vivi stood on the balcony, watching the sky fade from bruised to black.

She sensed him before his hands slid around her waist, smelled his wonderful combination of male and spice. When Justin came up behind her, she leaned back into him. He kissed her ear, and she shivered.

"What are you thinking about?" he asked.

"The wonders of rule breaking," she replied. "I think I need more practice."

"That can be arranged," Justin said, nuzzling the top of her hair, breathing in. "My office is conveniently close to here."

Then it was her turn to laugh. "Imagine that." Inside, however, she was still trembling like a leaf. Justin's touch had been more than just hands on skin. He'd touched her as though she were a goddess, almost reverently. Vivi turned in his arms to look at him.

"So is this how you lure in the hot women in your secret vampire headquarters?" she asked. "Pull them in with the sweet act, and then ravish them?"

She was teasing, but his look turned serious instantly.

"I would never do that," he said. He appeared to consider for a moment, then continued. "The city I rule is a fairly…closed…society. I know everyone. And I'm not interested in luring any of the women anywhere."

Intrigued, and relieved despite herself, Vivi asked, "Does this city have a name? Portland? Atlanta?"

"Terra Noctem." He lifted an eyebrow with a faint smile. "I shouldn't even tell you that. But since you've trusted me, I can do the same for you."

Warmth flooded her despite the lovely coolness of his skin. It had been a long time since she'd felt this comfortable with a man. Generally they were either nervous, or felt like they needed to prove something. But Justin simply accepted her. Trusted her, despite the differences between them. He knew the blood that ran in her veins and found it a good thing, not inadequate like Marina and her ilk.

The fragile bond she'd felt with him since he'd saved her on the beach strengthened, changed. Dangerous stuff. But she was too euphoric to fight it. Not tonight, of all nights.

"I won't ask where it is," Vivi said, knowing that even now, there had to be *some* boundaries. And he wouldn't be able to tell her. Some rules really couldn't be broken. "Do you like it there?"

He considered the question, looking out into the night. Finally, he said, "Yes, and, no. I don't think I'll be admitting this to her, but Dru was right. I needed to get out and breathe. I just didn't know it."

Vivi grinned. "Happy to be the breath of fresh air."

"You have no idea."

"So it's true. Most of the vampires really are tucked away on their own." She thought about that, about the stories she'd long dismissed as fairy tales. Funny, coming from a woman who carried Fae blood, she guessed.

"Not exactly on our own. I'm responsible for whomever chooses to live among us. It can get interesting, but you'd be surprised at how well everyone manages. We're not all monsters. Some vampires turn out twisted, and sometimes age and circumstance poisons them, but it's far more likely that they'll stay as they always have been. With some slight modifications."

She sighed, thinking about the psychotic types she made a living staking. They always ran alone. Justin made it sound like there were a lot more, the "normal" vampires, who harmed none. She imagined what Marina, or Chase, might do with the location of a city full of average vampires and shuddered. It would be a blood-bath. She couldn't imagine they would live and let live.

If things went south in the Guild, she would have to find a way out. There was no question of that now. All she could do was hope that the balancing forces stayed in place so it never came to that.

"I'm still surprised you saved me," she said, her mind far off. "Some of the Hunters have to be a thorn in your side."

"On the whole, the Hunters have been a force for good," Justin replied, resting his chin on the top of her head. "You have to understand that I rule a city, not a race. The vampires can't police our own kind to the end of the earth, nor do we want to. I protect my own within boundaries, and when it's requested of me outside of those boundaries. Mortals have a right to protect them-selves from threats, as well. We're stronger than you, and dangerous if we choose to be. But if protection be-gins to become extermination, then things will change."

Of course it would. Vivi only hoped she didn't see that day come.

"That's very pragmatic of you," she said softly.

"I've lived a long time. Being hotheaded never got me much more than black eyes and a bruised ego."

She tried to imagine him fist-fighting in a toga and grinned. "Tell me what it was like. Back when you were mortal."

Justin drew back, a curious, intense expression on his face. "Why?"

She couldn't say the words, couldn't tell him that right now, she wanted to know everything there was to know about him, to drink him in until he was an inextricable part of her. So she could carry a piece of him with her when their week was over.

Vivi gave him the only piece of the truth she dared. "I want to know you better."

"I'm very boring."

She laughed. "I doubt that."

He seemed slightly puzzled, but in a good-natured sort of way. "No one has asked me about any of that in... I can't even remember the last time. But if you like, I'll tell you a story or two while I have a drink. I'm a little thirsty." His eyes darkened, and she could see the red within them, glowing like embers. It was the first time she'd seen a vampire's hunger and felt no urge to fight, or in more dire circumstances, to run. Instead, she thought of his teeth scraping against her skin, and wondered how much more pleasure might await her if she let him sink his fangs in, joining with her in every way....

Vivi blinked and looked away, unnerved by her own thoughts. Justin had a veritable blood bank in the mini-fridge to sustain him. And she knew he wasn't thralling her. He didn't have to. This weird interest in being bitten by him was all her.

"I'd like to hear your stories," she said, forcing her thoughts back to the subject at hand. And back to the unpleasant reality she'd been so wonderfully distracted from for the last little while. Morning would come eventually, and with it, a host of new problems.

"I want to enjoy you while I can. Because...honestly, Justin, I'm not sure how we can salvage the rest of the week together. The Chase situation hasn't changed. Neither has anything else. I don't want to take off. I don't want you to take off. But this still doesn't seem very workable. Chase is just going to see my cutting out earlier as confirmation I'm—" she smirked "—sleeping with the enemy. He'll be on me like white on rice. And I don't want trouble."

I don't want him to hurt you, she thought. Though Chase would have to go through her first.

"I know," Justin said. "Which is why I wondered if you might want to just move up here for the rest of the week."

Vivi looked up at him, and found she wasn't really surprised by the offer. Now that the inevitable had happened and they'd fallen into bed, this was the logical next step. There was no sense pretending they weren't going to be wrapped around one another for a good amount of the time they had left. Why keep up the pretense of separate rooms?

"I could text Tommy, tell him I'm heading home for

the rest of the week," Vivi said, thinking it out as she spoke. "I'll tell him I found out you were married. That it killed the vacation. It would explain my taking off earlier. And he trusts me. I don't think he'll bother to check."

She hoped.

"I like it," Justin said. "Then we sneak around...if we decide to go out." His voice indicated he could think of plenty of excellent things to do right here. Considering earlier, she believed it.

It could work. Vivi imagined four more nights here, in Justin's bed. It gave her a dark thrill. One big, sexy vampire king, all to herself. For *days*.

Common sense, buried beneath a formidable pile of wants and needs, whimpered that she ought to get out while she still could. But all Vivi could think of was the way he'd moved in her, how he'd whispered her name like a prayer.

Then she thought of her sparsely furnished apartment back in New York, the lonely bed. She'd be back in it soon enough.

"A vacation in the Royal Suite," Vivi said. "Excellent idea."

"I'm a king," Justin said. "I have lots of good ideas."

She snorted. "You may be a two-thousand-year-old vampire, but you are still *such* a guy."

Justin laughed softly and pulled her back inside, to the soft bed and warm darkness.

"I am," he said, his tone full of dark promise, and she knew Justin's stories might have to wait awhile.

"I have the advantage of experience, though," he told her with a wicked smile. "Come here and let me show you...."

With a grin, she turned the tables, pushing him up against the wall in a single, fluid movement. He allowed it, looking bemused.

"I'm supposed to be doing the ravishing," he said.

Vivi leaned into him, the only barriers between them the hotel robe she was wearing and the pair of shorts Justin had thrown on. She opened the robe and let it slide off her shoulders with a flick of her wrist, taking care of issue one, and rose up on her toes to speak only a breath away from his mouth.

His eyes were like flames in the dark.

"Sorry. It's my turn," she said, shivering as his cool hands came up to skim lightly down her back, pulling her closer.

But he didn't argue.

Vivi kissed him, finally able to take her time, to taste him thoroughly. Justin obliged her, though she could feel how tightly he was holding himself. So much power, she thought as he thrummed beneath her fingertips. So much discipline.

There was nothing about him that didn't appeal to her.

She trailed soft kisses down his jawline, down what

she'd discovered was a very sensitive neck. She heard his breath catch, and felt the delicious knot of pleasure deep in her belly tighten further.

Emboldened, Vivi slid down his body, flicking her tongue over taut nipples, feeling the hard muscles of his abdomen clench when she pressed her mouth just beneath the shallow cup of his navel and slid his shorts to the floor.

Justin's strangled groan told her that he was reaching his breaking point. His hands slid into her hair.

"Vivi," he hissed.

Then she put her mouth on him, getting a single, decadent taste of him before Vivi was lifted, spun around and pressed against the wall. She wrapped her legs around Justin's waist as he drove into her, filling her completely. She throbbed around him, giving a soft cry as coherent thought fled. All she had was need.

Justin's breath was ragged. His eyes were wild. He braced her back against the wall and thrust into her once, then again, each movement threatening to shatter her into a thousand quivering pieces. And still, despite all his strength, he held her as though she was something precious.

Feeling that, knowing that, filled her with an emotion that was as unexpected as it was bittersweet. Vivi wrapped herself tightly around Justin, trying to tell him everything she couldn't say with a fierce kiss.

"Vivi," he breathed against her lips. "Let me taste you. Please."

This time, there was no hesitation. For what time they had, she would gladly give Justin what she had. Because even now, she sensed that no other man would ever measure up for her. Not even close.

"Yes," she murmured.

With the next kiss, she felt the scrape of his fangs against her bottom lip. Then he drew it into his mouth, suckling it.

The first orgasm slammed into her, and Vivi clenched around Justin, helpless as waves of pleasure crashed over her. Then he began to move in her again, hard thrusts that kept her climbing even higher, pushing her toward another blinding peak.

Justin tore his mouth from hers on a harsh gasp, his head rocking back as his own climax took him. Watching him find his release fueled Vivi's own, and she came again, a sensory implosion that rocked her to her core.

She cried out a single word: his name.

As they clung together, Justin shivering nearly as hard as she was, Vivi felt whatever was left of the barriers she'd tried to keep between them give way.

Whatever else happened, some piece of her would always be his.

There in the dark, still joined with him, Vivi accepted it. A part of her was even glad.

And just for tonight, she let herself wish for impossible things.

Chapter 17

The last night of his vacation was warm and calm, the opposite of how Justin felt as he hung up his phone. Phenex wasn't answering, naturally. It was a bad sign. Of course, that was all you could really expect to get when you put your faith in a heavenly dropout. As long as he showed up and didn't get sidetracked by...whatever it was that sidetracked Phenex. The fallen angel wasn't quite as openly awful as some of his brethren, but they all had their vices. In fact, they were proud of them.

Justin looked at his phone, growled and shoved it in his pocket. This could well be his last night with Vivi. He wanted to make it a good one. And he wanted to offer... or maybe just suggest...

He sighed heavily, tipped his head back to look at the ceiling, and wondered whether he had finally lost it altogether. He wanted to bring the Hunter home with him. Maybe for just a while. No, that was bull. If she came with him, he was never letting her go. He just needed to find the right moment to ask her. The perfect moment.

Constructing that moment was making him slightly crazed. Dru would say he was micromanaging it. And she would be right, but he didn't give a damn.

Justin had shooed Vivi out a half hour ago, promising a surprise. He didn't love the idea of her being out on her own with the Hunters likely still lurking around, but her friendship with Tommy had proven useful in easing his worries. Tommy had bought Vivi's story completely, and was still texting her to check on her. It was how she knew that he and Chase were already sitting at the Wayfarer, bored, drinking and hoping to be sent elsewhere soon.

She was safe, out having the hamburger she'd claimed to be starving for anyway. And he was just about ready for her.

He examined the setup one last time. The French doors to the patio were thrown open, and the gauzy curtains billowed gently in the warm breeze. A round table had been brought up by some of the staff and set with white linens and china. A vase of bloodred roses sat on it beside a bucket of ice, tucked into which was a bottle of expensive champagne. Two champagne flutes gleamed in the light of the candles Justin had scattered around the suite.

Perfect, he decided, the tightness in his chest easing

just a little. All he needed was the music. He looked at
his watch again and cursed. Justin turned away from the
doors to text Vivi, asking her to come back as soon as
she was ready. He got a quick response in the affirma-
tive, and his nerves began to plague him again. Preparing for battle was easy, was *nothing* compared to this.
He knew what a sword would do when used correctly.
He didn't have a clue what he might say that would per-
suade Vivi to leave her mortal life behind. All he knew
was that she was the first ray of sunshine that had fallen
into his life in ages, and he didn't want to let go of it. If
he could just get her to agree to come stay for a while…
If he could buy himself some more time to convince her
that "awhile" ought to be "permanently"…

He barely heard the soft rustle of wings behind him.
"You're late."

A voice so beautiful it was like music itself responded.

"I don't see a woman. So either she dumped you already, or I'm not late. Also, bite me."

Justin turned to look at a tall, preternaturally handsome man with short, flame-colored hair and eyes of
heartbreak blue that glowed faintly in the dark. A pair
of massive ebony wings rose from his back, fanned out
behind his broad shoulders. With another dirty look at
Justin, Phenex folded them together and they vanished
from sight.

In his hand was a twelve-string acoustic guitar. From

the look on Phenex's face, Justin wondered whether he was going to play it or beat him over the head with it.

"Thanks for coming," Justin said, and meant it. Phenex shifted uncomfortably, and Justin thought, as he often did, that this particular fallen angel had more heart than most of them, even though there was no understanding what he'd chosen to do with it. But while any mention of romance would send the rest of them running, Phenex often looked wistful.

It was why Justin had asked the most musical of all the Fallen to play for him and Vivi. And it was, Justin expected, why he'd accepted, despite the grousing.

"Just remember, you're paying me for this," Phenex muttered. He put the strap of the guitar over his shoulder and ran through a few chord progressions.

The doorknob behind him turned. Justin took a deep breath. This was it. He turned.

Vivi walked into the room, her face pale, her eyes wide and pleading.

Behind her, urging Vivi forward with the tip of a dagger, was Chase, along with seven or eight other Hunters, all with weapons drawn.

Justin felt Phenex's strong presence behind him, coming to stand with him. These Hunters would be no match for a vampire warrior and a fallen angel, Justin knew. But he wasn't worried about losing to them.

He was worried about losing Vivi.

"You or your friend make a move, we'll turn your asses into pincushions," Chase said. Tommy looked troubled, but he made no move to set Vivi free.

"And what, exactly, have I done to earn the ire of the Hunters?" Justin asked smoothly. "I've harmed no one. Or am I mistaken about what your group does?"

"You're the vampire king," said a tall brunette, stepping out in front of the group. She was attractive, sharply featured. But her eyes were cold, dead things. This, he assumed, was Vivi's hated superior, Marina.

Justin gave a small, condescending bow. Phenex remained silent. Watching, Justin knew. Waiting for the right moment to strike. It was the way the Fallen operated. But the dark angel was hardly innocuous.

"What is he supposed to be? Another ancient like you?" Marina asked, jerking her chin at Phenex. "I'll take it. Two for the price of one."

Justin barely glanced at her. All of his attention was focused on Vivi, the sorrow so clearly written on her face. He saw her take in the champagne, the candles. Her eyes glittered.

"You haven't answered my question. What have I done?"

"As if that isn't obvious. You've thralled one of my operatives. Stolen God knows how many secrets from her. You did a good job, picking a weak link, but I wouldn't expect any less. I can't let that pass."

Vivi bared her teeth at Marina. "I'm not thralled, you bitch! He's done nothing! And this is *not* what Hunters do!"

"I like her," Phenex murmured behind him. "A little altruistic for my taste, but still. Nice."

Justin shot a fulminating glance at Phenex, who looked utterly unconcerned.

Marina looked between him and Vivi, and Justin could see the blood in her then, the feral gleam in Marina's eyes. Bad bloodlines, Justin thought, disgusted. The wolf packs had purged them, but they continued to destroy pieces of the world.

"What, you expect me to believe that the vampire king has found true love with a Fae-blood Hunter? She isn't that stupid. And neither are you."

Love. True love. Even as he thought the words, Justin knew that's what he felt. The tightness in his chest, the nerves, the anxiety, all eased and vanished at once. He didn't just want Vivi, didn't just need her. He loved her.

He opened his mouth, ready to say the words in front of everyone. But Vivi chose that moment to leap forward, somersaulting away from Chase with a lightness and grace that belied her heritage. In an instant she was standing between him and the Hunters, a dagger in her hand. Chase was blinking at his empty hand with a comically stunned expression on his face.

"This is not what the Hunters stand for," Vivi snapped.

"We only destroy those who *kill* humans. We're protectors, not murderers!"

"Naive little Vivi," Marina growled, and Justin could see that the woman was at least a half-blood werewolf. Her eyes took on a yellowish gleam, her fingers hooking into claws.

"The vampires are a scourge. If we don't destroy them, they'll destroy us. It was always going to be this way."

"She's as mad as the ones she hunts," Justin said, moving to Vivi's side. He looked at her friend Tommy, the only one of this group whom he thought might listen.

"This is what you want to do? Start a war when my kind want none?"

"They're talking monkeys, Justin," Phenex said softly. "What do you expect?"

Tommy looked at the Hunters, looked at Vivi and then cursed as he moved to stand with her. He looked at Marina.

"Desmond's going to hear about this. I'm no fan of vamps, but this isn't right."

Marina looked disgusted. "A disappointment." She looked at her followers and barked the order.

"They're both thralled! Kill all of them!"

Vivi fought like a woman possessed.

She launched herself at Marina, more full of fury than she had ever been. She'd already been grappling with the idea of losing Justin to his city. Now, this bitch wanted to take him away permanently, and for no better reason than an ancient, pointless grudge against his kind. She wouldn't let it happen. And she wouldn't let the Guild that had meant so much to her degenerate into being nothing more than vicious killers.

Vivi slashed out with Chase's dagger, drawing a screech from Marina when she drew blood. The room was a blur. She saw the tall redhead with the incredible face pull a flaming sword out of nowhere and enter the fray with a hard grin. One swipe from that blade and half the Hunters were down.

She and Marina circled one another, while Justin barely bothered to toy with an enraged Chase before snapping his neck.

"Weak blood," Marina growled at her. "You've ruined us if he goes free."

"Can't be any worse than what you've already done," Vivi spat.

Marina slashed out with her claws. Vivi felt a strange warmth across her chest that bloomed as she sidestepped a half second too late. There was a shout, and Vivi felt herself jerked roughly back against a hard chest. She caught only a flash of Marina's triumphant smile.

"I knew you liked vamps," a familiar voice hissed in her ear. Then teeth were in her neck, tearing at her flesh. She didn't even have time to scream.

Adam, she thought. The vampire Justin had run off that first night. Marina's sudden fixation on Mirage finally made sense. He'd tipped off the Hunters out of spite, and now he was finishing what he'd started.

Should have staked him, she thought hazily.

Just before the world went black, she heard screams, saw the flash of a fiery blade and heard Justin's enraged roar. Then she was in his arms, one last time.

"No," she heard him say, his voice sounding distant, broken.

"Love," she tried to say, desperate to get out the words she now knew were true, whether he walked out of her life or not. But only the first "I" came out in a whisper.

Then all went silent and dark.

Chapter 18

Three nights later

Vivi awakened to singing.

She stirred from a deep, warm slumber, drifting on the currents of the most beautiful sound she'd ever heard. It was a voice…but a voice in its purest form, crystalline and pure, an enchanted thing. It enveloped her, wrapping her in its light until she had to open her eyes.

It was night here, wherever here was. Vivi blinked slowly, her eyes adjusting quickly to what appeared to be a hospital room. There was just the bed she was in, a table on wheels parked beside it, a television bolted to the wall. And in one of the horrible plastic chairs these rooms always had sat the redhead with the face of an angel, strumming a guitar and watching her with eyes the color of the sky at dawn.

"You," she said, and her voice sounded awful and rusty. Her throat hurt. Her neck hurt.

Everything hurt.

Vivi's body felt stiff and unfamiliar when she tried to sit up. The redhead rose.

"Careful with that," he said, and his voice was the music she'd been hearing. She watched him in awe.

"What are you?" she asked.

His grin was a flash of lightning across his beautiful, moody face.

"Trouble," he said. "Or so I hear. You remember everything?"

She thought back, and the memories collided into one another one by one, a rush of blood and anger and terror that she would never see Justin again....

"Where is he? Is he okay?" she asked hoarsely.

"Oh, yeah. He's a lot harder to kill than that. It was you he was worried about. Talking monkeys are fragile." He smirked. "Even the ones who are pretty badass. Nice fighting."

"Thanks," she said. "Um, where am I?"

"Later. I have to keep singing the guards their lullaby so they stay asleep."

She frowned. "Guards?"

"Your boss, Desmond, wants you guarded until things get sorted out. He thinks he's protecting you from Marina's buddies in the Guild, and us. He's half right. Not bad for a human."

He gave her a small, courtly bow and exited the room, strumming his guitar. She caught a bare glimpse of a few people sprawled in the hallway, heard the sound of snoring, before the door shut again.

"Vivi."

His voice, at least to her, was even sweeter than the redhead's. Justin walked from the shadows by the window. He looked as handsome as ever, the dark vampire king. But his eyes were cautious. That was, until she spoke.

"You. Get over here now." And she held out her arms.

He was in them in an instant, and just the feel of him against her filled her with the sort of joy she'd always thought was reserved for romance novels and fairy tales. She buried her face in his neck, inhaling the scent of him.

"You saved me," she said.

"Barely," Justin said gruffly, holding her tight. "Even when I let him go that first night on the beach I knew Adam would be trouble again. I just never imagined he'd betray me to the Hunters as payback for getting in his way."

"Well, if it makes you feel any better, I didn't expect it, either. That's low even for the kind of vamps I hunt," Vivi said, the horror of what had happened no match for the comfort of Justin's strong arms around her.

"He nearly ripped your throat out," Justin said, and she heard the anguish in his voice. "I wanted to give you a choice, but you almost didn't get one. I've been watching you like a hawk. Tommy threatened to stake me if I so much as looked at your neck, but—"

"Choice?" Vivi asked, confused for a moment. Then she understood. "You would have saved me by turning me. But you didn't want to."

"That's not exactly true. I just didn't want you to hate me for it." Justin kissed her temple, her cheek and then softly on her mouth.

"I love you. I know you said no strings, but you're really sort of impossible not to love." His eyes darkened, going nearly as black as night. "I want you to stay with me. But I couldn't take the choice from you. So few of us get to choose."

She let the words sink in, thinking that there was nothing she would rather wake up to than this. Every night. Forever.

"Are you proposing an extended vacation?" she asked, smiling softly.

He tucked her hair behind her ear, a gentle stroke. "Very extended, yes."

Her smile faded as she thought of her parents, her brother. She couldn't just vanish from their lives, nor did she want to. The idea of becoming a part of Justin's world fascinated her. She'd been a part of the night for so long now that joining it permanently didn't bother her. In some ways, Vivi suspected she might fit into Terra Noctem as a vampire better than she had ever fit in among the Hunters. But she couldn't simply leave every piece of this life behind. Justin seemed to know before she said anything.

"I want to meet your family," he said. "I don't want to take anything you love away from you, Vivi. You can see them whenever you like. Whatever you want, whatever you need, is yours. I've let duty be the only thing in my life for far too long. We can travel. We can explore the world together. As long as you'll be mine." His heart was in his eyes. "You're everything I've ever wanted. I love you, Vivi. I don't want to deal with the rest of forever without you."

It was exactly what she needed to hear, and any remaining doubts vanished in the face of what she knew they would have together. Vivi thought of how it would be, how she would probably install a karaoke machine in his study and get a big, slobbery dog to keep her company while he was busy and how she would likely never, ever stop trying to drag him into dark corners to get her hands on him. How he would be hers, and she his.

"I love you," Vivi said, and saw his heart in his eyes. "I'm probably going to drive you crazy, but I love you. Enough for a permanent vacation. Enough for forever."

"I can't wait," Justin said softly.

And proved it with a kiss.

* * * * *

ISLAND
VACATION
Lisa Childs

Ever since **Lisa Childs** read her first romance novel (a Mills & Boon of course) at age eleven, all she ever wanted to be was a romance writer. With over thirty novels published with Mills & Boon, Lisa is living her dream. She is an award-winning, bestselling romance author. Lisa loves to hear from readers, who can contact her on Facebook, through her website www.lisachilds.com or snail mail address, PO Box 139, Marne, MI 49435, USA.

Chapter 1

Work sucks. For the past four years, Piper Reynolds had spent ten to twelve hours a day, six—sometimes seven— days a week shut in a small, windowless office with only fluorescent bulbs for light. Whatever tan she'd once possessed had long since faded to a pallor so translucent she probably could have passed for a vampire.

If vampires actually existed outside the pages of young-adult novels...

Not that she'd read those novels or anything else. She never had the time or the energy to read anything but reports, ledgers and bank statements. She spent so much time studying numbers scrolling across a computer screen that she had strained her eyes to the point of needing glasses. While she only needed them for reading, she wore them most of the time—since she was usually working anyway. Not today, though, and not for the next thirteen days.

Piper should have been thrilled that she had won the office lottery for the two-week, all-expenses-paid vacation. But ever since her name—well, the one she'd used for the past four years—had been pulled from the raffle basket, apprehension had tied her stomach muscles into tight knots. Maybe that apprehension was just fear of the unknown since she'd never had a real vacation before and she had been working, at one job or another, since she was fourteen.

Or maybe it had been the fact that her boss had called out Patricia Reynolds before he had even completely unfolded the piece of paper he'd drawn out. Had her name really been the one written down? He had never shown it.

But why would he have wanted her to win?

To get rid of her?

That made no sense given how hard she worked. Had she stumbled across something she wasn't supposed to have seen? But like every other employee, she'd signed a confidentiality agreement. She could reveal nothing of what she knew about E. Graves Financial Planning, which despite all those hours she logged, was really very little. She didn't even know whose accounts she was working on; she didn't know whose millions or billions she was investing and tracking.

Maybe her boss had been the one to stumble across

something: her real identity. Given who she had once been, she could understand that he would want her far away from a company known for discretion. He had certainly sent her far away from the office in Zantrax, Michigan.

Boarding the private plane at the airport had been like stepping into a different time zone—a bygone era of luxury and comfort. The leather seats were so big and the cushions so deep and soft that she should have slept the entire flight. But she couldn't relax enough to sleep.

She wasn't afraid of flying. Even though she hadn't been on a plane the past four years, she had logged many frequent-flyer miles before then. It was that damn sense of apprehension keeping her awake.

She had worked so hard to keep her secrets. What if she'd been discovered? But if her boss had discovered who she was, he would have fired her instead of rewarding her with a vacation.

This damn vacation….

Reluctant to leave the security of her windowless office, she had tried to refuse her win. Hell, she hadn't even remembered entering her name in the drawing in the first place. But her boss had insisted she take the two weeks and the trip.

"Miss," the young stewardess said softly as though not to disturb anyone else. But Piper was the only passenger aboard the private plane.

A plane all to herself? A stewardess for only her? What the hell kind of vacation had she won? She hadn't even been this pampered in her previous career.

"You need to fasten your seat belt," the woman advised. "We'll be preparing to land soon."

"Where are we landing?" Piper asked as she clipped her belt back together. It was no canvas strap like on commercial flights but a thick leather belt with a gold-plated buckle.

The stewardess smiled slightly, as if amused. "You don't know?"

"No."

In addition to being all-expenses paid, the vacation was to an undisclosed location. All she had been told was to pack light and bring her passport. No matter how many times she had asked, her boss had refused to reveal any more clues to her destination.

Of course E. Graves Financial Planning was known for its confidentiality; that was why they had so many affluent clients who valued their privacy as much as their stock portfolios. One of them had been so grateful for the firm's discretion and hard work that he had donated the vacation for the company's annual office lottery. The only thing her boss had told her was that this man was their oldest and most important client and to refuse his gift would have been an unforgiveable insult. Piper had picked up on the implication that if she hadn't accepted the trip, she might have been terminated.

She'd been fortunate that Graves's background check hadn't revealed her real identity, but she couldn't risk that a new employer might. And if the media found out…

She shuddered at the horrific thought.

"Then I wouldn't want to spoil your surprise," the stewardess said, her smile widening slightly but not enough to show her teeth. She was beautiful, the kind of polished beauty that only went skin-deep.

Piper had once been that kind of beautiful…when she'd actually cared about how she looked. But along with her tan, she'd lost the highlights in her hair so that it was more mousy brown than blond. And badly in need of a trim, it hung thick and heavy around her shoulders and in her face.

The plane hit a rough patch, sending it bouncing like a stone across water. Piper clutched her seat belt, tightening it around her waist. She cared less about the plane going down than where it was going, though. She asked, "Can you at least tell me if it'll be a pleasant surprise?"

But the stewardess hurried off toward the cockpit, leaving Piper behind with her question unanswered. For now. The plane had leveled out to a more gradual descent; it would land soon and then she would at least know where she was.

But when would she learn why? Because that tight

knot of apprehension warned her that she hadn't won this vacation out of luck. She worried that it might prove to be the exact opposite of luck that had put her on this plane to nowhere.

Anticipation quickened his pulse, sending his blood pumping hard and fast through his veins. The drone of a plane's engine disrupted the eerie stillness of the night. She was *here*. Finally.

Roarke Monterusso chuckled wryly at his own impatience.

Four years. That amount of time was nothing compared to the centuries he'd lived. So why had it felt so interminably long? Because four *weeks*—hell, four *days*—was too long to wait for justice.

She had eluded justice too long. *She* had eluded him too long.

Roarke didn't need her formally charged or convicted of her crime. He only needed to know that she had been punished, and the only way to make certain of that was to personally dole out that punishment.

Bright lights flashed, guiding the pilot to the airstrip on the other side of the twenty-acre private island. The plane landed smoothly. Moments later another engine fired up, and a car brought her around the winding drive to the house. Headlamps flashed in his face, but he didn't so much as blink. The light just bounced off his eyes like a spotlight reflecting back at her.

She stepped out of the door the chauffeur held open for her and directly into the beam. The light shimmered in the tresses of her deep golden hair.

His sources had sworn that Patricia Reynolds was not the infamous Piper. They had assured him that the women looked nothing alike. They had been dead wrong.

She had changed over the past four years, but the changes were slight and superficial and did nothing to disguise her beauty or her allure. She wore glasses and a baggy beige suit. Her hair was long and thick. As disguises went, it was weak.

How had she fooled so many? The media believed she'd disappeared off the face of the earth. But his sources should have been smarter....

Had they lied to him?

Most people were too afraid of him to lie to him and risk his wrath. But maybe they had been more afraid of what he might do. To *her*.

They were right to be afraid. As she climbed up the porch steps to him, she trembled slightly. If it was with fear, she was right to be afraid, too. She had more to fear than anyone else.

Justice...

Beams of light radiated from his eyes, like flames from a torch, and like fire, his stare scorched her. Heat chased away the chill from the cool night air that had

had her trembling when she'd left the warmth of the limousine.

The driver dropped her small bag onto the step next to her. She had been told not to bring a lot of clothes, so she'd assumed the vacation was someplace sunny and warm. Instead the small, heavily wooded island was dark and cold. The car backed away, taking the light with it. She glanced back at the limousine, regretting that she hadn't thanked the chauffeur for the ride. Then she turned back toward the man standing now in complete darkness on the porch, and she regretted taking that ride at all.

With only dim light spilling through the glass door of the mansion behind him, the man was an imposing shadow—tall and broad and totally silent.

"I'm Patricia Reynolds," she introduced herself with the lie.

Patricia had been her mother's name; that was why she had chosen it as hers when she'd needed a new identity. She had never really known her mother, though. The teenager had given her up for adoption shortly after Piper's birth.

The man offered her nothing, not a greeting or a hand to shake. He just continued to stare down at her, his eyes hot even without the headlights reflecting off them.

Piper trembled again—this time with nerves not cold.

"I won this...vacation...from my employer," she stammered, "E. Graves Financial Planning."

He finally spoke, his voice a deep rumble as he asked, "Vacation?"

Her pulse leaped with fear. Had she wound up in the wrong place? Since she had no idea where she was supposed to be, she had no idea if she'd actually arrived at the correct destination. She never should have agreed to this trip. "Uh—uh, you don't know anything about it?"

He continued to stare at her as if she were a UFO that had dropped from the sky over this private island. Maybe to him, she was....

Had he had any idea that she was coming?

After a few more nervous moments—on her part—he replied, "I know about E. Graves Financial Planning."

"Are you a client?" He was too young to be E. Graves's oldest and most important client, especially since her boss had obviously meant richest when he'd said most important. Maybe this man was a grandson or great-grandson of that client.

Who the hell was he?

Still reticent, he replied, "I believe their clients are guaranteed confidentiality."

She swallowed her nerve-induced excess of saliva and nodded. "Yes, they are. We're so good at protecting our clients' privacy as well as their assets that one of them rewarded the office with this all-expense-paid vacation.

I assumed that client was you...." Since he had been on the porch, awaiting her arrival.

Of course he could be a servant; that would have made sense that, like the stewardess and the pilot, he worked for that oldest and most important client. But his dark suit was tailored and expensive and made of a fabric that lovingly framed his broad shoulders and heavily muscled arms. If not for that suit, she might have figured him for a security guard; he was so tall, probably closer to seven feet than six, and so muscular. But the man's whole, cold-stare-down-his-haughty-nose demeanor was more that of the master than the servant.

"One should never assume anything," he advised her.

He was right. She'd assumed that she could trust her employer, that the trip was legitimate. After the night-mare she had lived through four years ago, she should have known better than to ever trust anyone again.

"You're right," she agreed with a shaky sigh. "I thought my boss..."

"You thought your boss was sending you on vacation," he said. "You were wrong."

Four years of no one recognizing her at the office, of no one harassing her, had lulled her into a false sense of security. She had believed that she was actually safe at E. Graves. But then she wasn't at E. Graves anymore.

"So you don't know anything about me?" she asked. "You didn't know I was coming here at all?"

"You're making assumptions again," he cautioned her. "I was expecting you. But you're not here for a vacation."

Now she got it. She wasn't here to relax; she was here to *work*. A breath of relief slipped out between her lips. She would be more comfortable working than vacationing anyway. "Okay, I understand."

"I don't think you do," he said. "Not only did I know you were coming, but I know everything about you, Piper."

Those four years of false security slipped away, leaving Piper exposed in a way no layers of bulky clothes could cover. Her heart slammed against her ribs as her earlier apprehension surged into panic and horror.

Now she knew exactly where she was.

Hell...

Chapter 2

Panic widened her eyes and she glanced behind herself, as if searching for an escape route.

"It's an island," Roarke reminded her. "You can run all you want, but you won't get very far. You'll only get hurt. There are creatures in the forest that you don't want to meet in the daylight, let alone the dark."

"You—you're mistaken," she said.

"No, I'm quite familiar with this island." Because he hated being forced to hide what he really was when he was around humans, he had rarely left the island until four years ago. Then he'd no choice; he'd had to leave to track down a killer.

A human.

She shuddered. "Not about the creatures. About me. My name is Patricia. Not Piper."

She said it almost as if she believed it, or perhaps it was just that she desperately wanted him to believe it. Had she realized that she was finally about to be brought to justice?

"I—I should leave," she said. "The airstrip wasn't far from here. I can walk...." She grabbed up her bag and stepped down, descending the stairs blindly, backward, as she faced him, as if scared to turn away from him. As if he might attack if she did...

He wouldn't do that. He wanted to see her face when she was finally served the justice she'd eluded for so long.

"You can walk," he agreed. He wouldn't physically stop her. Yet. "But you won't be able to fly." Not like he and the rest of the Secret Vampire Society could fly.

The plane had been only for her benefit, to lure her to him—instead of his grabbing her off the street in Zantrax. Once he'd found her, he had barely been able to restrain himself from doing just that, though. But he couldn't have risked something going wrong and her escaping. Here she had no way to escape. Him. And justice.

A motor roared and lights flashed as the aircraft lifted off into the night sky. She stared up at it, as if her gaze alone could pull the plane back to earth, back to her. As the lights grew fainter and smaller than the stars, her shoulders slumped with defeat. Then she lifted her chin, as if rallying. "You must have some other way of getting off the island, like a boat or a…"

"You're not leaving, Piper."

"I'm not Piper." The wind picked up, swirling her long, thick hair around her face and shoulders. She shivered.

Irritation threatened to snap his patience. But he had waited four years. He could wait a few more minutes, maybe even hours to dole out justice. Maybe it would be even sweeter were he to build up his anticipation to that long-overdue moment.

"Come inside with me," Roarke ordered, reaching behind him to push open the door to the foyer. "You're cold."

"I'm not cold," she snapped back with the reply. "I'm scared."

"You have nothing to fear from me," Roarke said, holding open the door for her, "if you're really not Piper.…"

But because she was, she had everything to fear.…

Her eyes glistened in the dark, tears moistening them. "I don't know where I am." And maybe that was why she climbed back up the porch stairs and met him at the door. She tilted her head and stared up at him as if trying to place his identity. "I don't know who you are. And I don't know what you want with this woman you call Piper. I would be stupid if I wasn't scared. And I'm not stupid."

"No, you're not or you wouldn't have managed to disappear four years ago," he said, "especially given that the paparazzi followed you everywhere."

She laughed, but her lips trembled with nerves, not mirth. "The paparazzi would never waste their time following a woman as boring as I am."

He laughed, too—a sharp chuckle of bitterness. "You tried really hard to reinvent yourself as boring." The baggy suit jacket and pants. The dark-framed glasses. Somehow the disguise made her even sexier—made a man fantasize about what might be beneath those ill-fitting clothes....

Made a man want to peel them off and find out exactly how full her curves were, how soft her skin...

But that man wasn't Roarke Monterusso. He wasn't attracted to her; he couldn't be.

"I am boring," she insisted with another shiver.

"You are cold. Come inside." He put his hand on her, just at the small of her back to guide her across the threshold and into his house. Beneath the baggy jacket, her spine dipped in as her butt curved out. And despite her shivering, warmth permeated her clothes and heated his palm. His skin tingled in reaction and his pulse quickened.

Hell, maybe he was that man.

Piper tensed beneath his touch and resisted the slight force he exerted to guide her inside his house. Or maybe she shouldn't assume that the three-story plantation-style house was his. She had already assumed too much like she could trust the employer, for whom she had worked so hard, to not put her in danger.

"And, as I already told you," she reminded the man, "I am not stupid."

But just like her new identity, that was a lie, too. Because if she were smart, she never would have accepted a trip without knowing where she was going and whom her host would be.

"I'm not going anywhere with you," she told him, "until you tell me who you are."

His mouth curved slightly with amusement. Did he find her fear or her weak show of bravado amusing?

"You are hardly in the position to give out ultimatums, Piper."

"Stop calling me that!" she snapped, anger chasing away her fear. That name, uttered in that deep rumbly voice of his, brought back nightmares it had taken her years to get over. Those had just been dreams though, horrific dreams, not reality. Except that hearing her name on his lips somehow made it all seem so real.

"If you're really not her, stop hiding in the dark," he challenged. "Prove to me that you're not Piper."

How could she prove a lie?

His grin widened at her noticeable hesitation. "You can't." Ignoring her resistance, he increased the pressure on her back until she stumbled into the marble-tiled foyer. He shut the door behind her, and the lock ominously clicked.

"I—I don't know who this woman is, so I—I don't know how much I might look like her," she said with a stammer as she grasped at any halfway plausible explanation.

He laughed at her again—as he already had, with bitterness. "You've overplayed your hand, Piper." And as if bored with her lies, he walked through open French doors into a room off the foyer.

She turned back toward the door, tempted to turn the knob and see if he had really locked her inside with him. But even if she could escape the house, she wouldn't be able to escape the island. She had to convince *him* to let her use a boat or to call back the plane to take her home, so she followed him into the den. The dark paneling, coffered ceiling and shuttered windows reminded her of the office where she'd spent so much of her life the past four years.

"I don't know what you think I'm overplaying," she said. "I must look somewhat like her for you to have mistaken me for her."

He opened the door of a small refrigerator concealed in a wall of bookshelves and pulled out a bottle. Nothing fizzed as he popped the top and downed the liquid concealed by the dark glass of the bottle. Was he drinking alcohol?

Maybe he would drink enough to pass out and then she would be able to... What? She was stranded on a damn island, for crying out loud. A bubble of hysteria threatened to rise to the surface, but she forced it back down. Or she would literally be crying out loud with fear and frustration.

"You overplayed your lie," he explained, "by claiming to not even know who Piper is."

"I don't," she insisted. At least she hadn't really known *who* Piper was until she had stopped being Piper. Until she'd become Patricia, she had been too busy *being* Piper to figure out who she really was, to realize what had made her tick, what had mattered to her and what she really wanted out of life.

Anonymity had topped her list.

His gaze growing dark and hard with irritation and something even more threatening, he said, "*Everyone* knows who you are."

Maybe that had once been true. But not anymore....

She shook her head in denial. "No one knows me. I'm just a certified public accountant and financial planner."

"Now," he agreed, as he lifted a long tube off the mahogany desk in the room. The cardboard tube had been the only thing on top of it. He popped the end off of it and tapped out a rolled-up piece of paper. "But you didn't used to be. You've been a supermodel since you were fourteen years old."

She laughed naturally. There had been nothing *super*

about her modeling. Her adoptive mother had forced her into it—to earn her keep. At five-nine, she hadn't been tall enough or, with her bigger frame, thin enough for runway modeling, but fortunately she had been photogenic. Or only the devil knew what else her *mother* might have forced her to do to *earn her keep.*

As if to prove how photogenic she'd been, the man unrolled a poster of one of her swimsuit covers. Sand and water clung to her darkly tanned skin and sunlight burnished her golden hair to platinum blond.

"You were a veritable pinup," he said—but with disgust instead of awe.

He wasn't the only one disgusted at the thought of her poster hanging on people's walls, of people staring at her. She shuddered. "If that was the kind of life I would have chosen for myself—" which it damn well hadn't been "—why would I have given it up to become a numbers cruncher?"

Because that was the career she had actually wanted, the one she had worked in classes toward her MBA around photo shoots. She had been grateful for that education when the nightmare had begun.

"You went into hiding," he said.

Her heart shifted, kicking against her ribs, as fear coursed through her. How had he known? Did he know why? Did he know about the nightmares?

"But your efforts were futile," he said. "No matter how determined you were to hide, I was even more determined to find you." Triumph flashed through his dark eyes. He was like a hunter who had ruthlessly tracked down his hapless prey.

She fought to control the fear that overwhelmed her, causing her to tremble. She couldn't stop shaking. "You found the wrong woman," she insisted. "I'm not who you're looking for...."

Not anymore. She wasn't the woman who inspired men to obsession and infatuation. *She* had never actually been that woman—just an airbrushed fantasy. Like her nightmare, not real.

Piper pointed to the poster he clenched in his fist, the glossy paper crumpling in his grasp. "That's not me."

The sincerity in her soft voice nearly convinced him that he might have found the wrong woman. She wasn't the first person who had told him she wasn't the infamous Piper. Doubts nagging at him, he turned the poster around and studied the image of the supermodel.

He couldn't deny that the young woman was beautiful. But no amount of beauty and allure was worth a man's life....

He knew that beyond a doubt. But he had other doubts now. He didn't know if this woman—the one who called herself Patricia Reynolds, the woman who had just appeared four years ago when Piper had disappeared—was really Piper.

But it *had* to be her.

He studied the woman on that damn poster. The hair was blonder. The skin tanner. The face thinner. And the eyes…

He glanced up at the woman in his den, but he couldn't see the eyes of Patricia Reynolds, not behind the glasses that reflected the light back at him. Were they that same green that sparkled with…what?

He turned back to the poster. Happiness? He doubted it because Piper's lips only slightly curved, as if forced into the smile.

Amusement? That she had fooled so many people into worshipping an empty vessel? She had no heart or soul. She had proved that.

So it wasn't warmth or goodness sparkling in that deep green. Glee—that she had made so much money with so little effort?

Giving that up to go into hiding must have killed her. But she wouldn't have had to give up anything had she not *killed.*

She had escaped prosecution. She had escaped punishment. But Roarke wouldn't let her escape again. She would pay for what she'd done. She would pay for taking away his cousin's immortality—for ending his eternal life.

For the life she'd taken, she would have to pay—with her life.

Chapter 3

Piper held her breath as the man studied the poster. He didn't stare at it as so many others had—with fascination or lust. Instead he stared at it with hatred, his jaw clenched so tautly with the dark emotion that a muscle twitched in his dimpled cheek.

Even angry he was a gorgeous man. His hair thick and jet-black, his eyes soulfully dark and thickly lashed, his body tall and broad-shouldered, he was every woman's fantasy. Just like she had once been every man's.

But this man's. He wasn't turned on by her picture. He was turned off. And enraged.

If she couldn't convince him that she wasn't Piper, she was in grave danger. She had to do whatever necessary to convince him. Or she had no chance of leaving the island alive…not with the intensity of hatred burning in his gaze as he turned his scrutiny on her.

"Take off your glasses!" he ordered.

Now she wished she'd gone for contacts instead, the colored kind. But her eyes weren't really the intense green that they looked on the poster. They were hazel; the green swirled up with brown and gold so that sometimes it was barely noticeable. She pulled off the glasses that she only really needed for reading, and slipped them into the pocket of her loose suit jacket.

He narrowed his eyes and his brow furrowed, revealing his inner debate. "The color's different but the shape and size…"

"Might be right for the eyes, but not the body," she said. Wanting to sway the outcome of his inner debate to her side, Piper reached for the buttons on her suit jacket. Her fingers trembled, but she managed to slip them through the holes and shrug off the loose jacket. "That's not my body on that poster."

He chuckled with real amusement this time, easing the tension in his jaw. "Your shirt's as loose as your jacket," he said. "I can't tell what's beneath it. And the pants…"

"You want me to take off all my clothes?" she asked. Taking off the jacket had required more courage than she'd thought she'd had. The nightmare had stolen away her bravery, leaving her sleepless and afraid of the dark.

He shook his head in denial. Of course a man like him,

devastatingly handsome and wealthy enough to afford a private island, wouldn't be interested in the woman she had become. "I want you to tell me who you really are."

"P-Patricia." She choked on the name, horrified that she'd nearly told him her right one. "Patricia Reynolds."

His eyes narrowed again. "P-Patricia?"

"I'm scared," she reminded him. "You still haven't told me who you are or what you want with this Piper person and now you want me to take off my clothes!"

His lips curved again—into a full-fledged grin that had those dimples piercing his lean cheeks.

Her breath caught, trapped in her lungs with the sheer awe of his good looks. It was more believable that he had been the model than she.

"I didn't ask you to take off anything," he reminded her.

"I don't care," she said, reaching for the buttons of her blouse this time. Her fingers were steadier as she pulled them free and shrugged off the cotton shirt. "If it'll prove to you that I'm not this woman and convince you to let me go, I'll strip naked." But she only unclasped her pants, not her bra. And when she unzipped her pants, she shimmied off only them—not the panties beneath them.

The first time she'd undressed for a stranger, she had been fourteen and on a go-see. She'd had to strip for the designer for him to decide if her body would complement his clothes. That first time she had been horrified and humiliated but then she'd learned that it wasn't personal. Or intimate. After that she had undressed for countless strangers over the years.

And the full-cupped cotton bra and boy-short-cut panties were much less revealing than the bikini she'd worn on the poster. But more of her body showed because she had more body now. Without her adoptive mother and designers forcing her to starve herself and spend endless hours in the gym, she had lost the taut muscles and sleek curves. Her figure was fuller now, her skin pale and soft. She actually liked this body whereas she had always resented the body on the poster.

The man was not the only one who stared at that picture with hatred, remembering how that life had actually kept her from living one. Not that she was living one now since she spent most of her time holed up in a windowless office. Maybe it was time to conquer her fears and learn to sleep with the lights off again.

Or just to sleep at all...

And laugh. And have fun instead of just work. But she would never get that vacation she'd been promised if she couldn't convince this man to let her go.

"See," she said. "Here's your proof." She lifted her arms from her sides, holding them up. "I am not that woman."

He wasn't staring at the picture now. He was staring at *her* and maybe even more intensely than he had the image of the supermodel. Only now she had no idea what he was thinking or feeling....

Lust. It slammed into him with all the force of a hurricane. In all the centuries he'd lived, he had never felt desire so intense. And he had known many women—women far more beautiful than the one who stood before him now in drab beige underwear. The tan cotton made her skin look paler, like alabaster.

His fingers twitched with the impulse—the *need* —to touch that skin and find out if it was as silky as it appeared. But he kept his arms at his sides, his fists clenched, to resist the temptation. Touching her wouldn't prove that she was Piper. He was beginning to think that nothing would.

But just because her skin was a little paler and her curves a little fuller than the woman on the poster didn't mean she wasn't that woman. That picture had been taken five or six years ago—maybe longer. Unlike immortals, humans aged and changed. It was inevitable.

He shook his head, pitying her mortality and her desperation. "This proves nothing."

Except that he was not as strong as he'd always believed he was. He had always been in control of his emotions and his desires...until now when his passion for justice warred with his passion...for her.

"I look nothing like that woman," she insisted, her

voice rising with desperation. "If that's not enough proof, what do you need? DNA?"

Roarke had nothing to compare it to—the crime scene had been cleaned, nothing left behind of either the killer or her victim. His cousin was gone—his body disposed of as the Secret Vampire Society disposed of their dead.

Ashes to ashes...

But Roarke hadn't needed to see the body to know that his cousin was gone. They had been in constant contact until four years ago; they had been more like brothers than the distantly related cousins they'd actually been. And the society had given Roarke proof of his cousin's murder. They had claimed, though, that they didn't have proof of who'd committed it.

But Roarke knew.

Piper, his cousin's human girlfriend, the bloody obsession on whom he'd spent so much money and time. But was *this woman* that psychotic bitch?

"I will give you whatever you want," she offered, her arms spread wide, "whatever it will take for you to let me go."

His traitorous body hardened at the offer, his erection straining at the fly of his pants. His fangs would have hardened, too, had he not grabbed a drink the minute he'd stepped inside the den. If he hadn't staved off his hunger, he might have already bitten her—might have taken what she'd denied his cousin as she'd strung him along with demands for more and more material possessions.

A woman like Piper had only known how to take; she'd never offered to give anything to anyone. She certainly wouldn't have taken off her clothes without a fee. But then that fee was her freedom...

"So what would you give me," he wondered aloud, "if I let you go?"

She blushed, her face and even her shoulders turning pink with embarrassment. "N-not *that*. I wasn't offering to sleep with you. I'll give you money. Hell, I'll give you blood—"

He groaned at the thought of tasting her, of seeing if she was as sweet as she looked and smelled. He dragged in a breath, inhaling the unique fragrance that was hers alone—both floral and light and dark and mysterious.

"Who are you?" he asked. And this time he was willing to listen to her, willing to consider that she might not be lying to him.

"I told you—Patricia Reynolds," she replied, her voice steady—the stammer gone with the clothes that lay on the floor of his den. "I'm an accountant at E. Graves Financial Planning."

He forced himself to focus on her eyes; gold flecks glittered against a backdrop of brown and green. They distracted him as much as her body, so that he had to remind himself why he had first begun to suspect she was Piper. "What did you do before you started working for Graves?"

"School," she said. "Undergrad and then graduate school."

"What school?"

"Several," she replied. "I took classes when I could pay for them."

She sounded so damn sincere—a damn sight more sincere than the people who had told him that Patricia Reynolds wasn't the former supermodel. They had just pointed out how crazy it was to even consider that the infamous Piper would have chosen to become a hard-working accountant.

But he hadn't listened to them. He had listened to his gut that had insisted it was her—that she had found the perfect place to hide—where no one would look for her.

But him.

He'd seen her before today—getting into her car in the underground parking garage at E. Graves's offices in downtown Zantrax. He had only caught a glimpse of her face when she'd shaken back her hair before sliding behind the steering wheel. And that one gesture had hit him like a punch in the gut with the conviction that she was Piper. So then he had listened to his gut and no one else.

Until now. He was listening to her, and he was beginning to believe her.

How could he have been so wrong? Had he spent

four years searching for Piper just to terrorize the wrong damn woman?

He couldn't be wrong…because that meant he'd failed his cousin again. He hadn't protected Rick from Piper four years ago. And after even four years, he had failed to bring his killer to justice.

How many more years would it take him to find the real Piper and avenge his cousin's murder?

Piper held her breath while the man withstood his internal struggle. The battle waged in his dark eyes and clenched jaw, a muscle twitching in his deeply creased cheek.

A twinge of guilt struck her. She had lied for years—even before she'd gone into hiding. She had lied to her adoptive mother and to designers who'd asked if she'd liked their clothes. She had even lied to herself. But this was the first time she actually felt bad about lying.

Yet, given the way he'd looked at that poster, he was the last man to whom she should finally start telling the truth.

He stepped away from his desk and that damn poster and closed the distance between them. Standing this close to her, he would see that her bone structure hadn't changed—that she was actually the woman he'd sought with such determination.

He leaned over, his face close to her stomach, which

she automatically sucked in. Not that he would be attracted to her, but he was looking...

Would he notice the scar from the belly-button piercing she'd had back when she'd done that swimsuit shoot?

He reached out, but his hands grabbed up her discarded clothes—not her. She felt a flash of disappointment that the attraction wasn't mutual. Hell, it shouldn't even be one-sided. This man obviously hated who she'd been—enough to lure her to a private island. And do what to her?

Kill her?

The nightmare threatened to return, bringing with it a rush of fear and bloody memories. With a grimace, she forced them back.

He uttered a ragged sigh, one word spilling out with his breath. "Sorry..." He held out her suit, the beige flat and drab against the honey tone of his skin.

Ignoring the burning sensation in her lungs, she held her breath yet. Afraid to reach for the clothes dangling from his hand, she could only stand on trembling legs before him as she waited for more. Just what the hell was he apologizing for? For not believing her lie? For not sparing her whatever fate he'd planned for her?

He met her gaze, his dark eyes full of torment and regret. "I'm sorry. I was so certain...."

Now she didn't dare release her breath because the depth of her relief might give away her lie. She could only nod in acceptance of his apology. Then she parted her lips, just a little, to ease the pain in her chest.

He shook his head with disgust, but this time it seemed as though it was with himself. "I can't imagine what you're thinking...."

She damn well hoped he couldn't.

"You came here expecting a vacation...."

And instead she'd stripped for a stranger. Remembering that she wore only her underwear in front of that handsome stranger, she reached for her clothes. Her fingers grasped the material, and she tugged.

But he didn't release them. Instead he pulled her closer, so that her body brushed up against his. The expensive silk of his tailored suit caressed her bare skin.

The knuckles, on his hand clutching her clothes, pressed against her midriff, right below her breasts. Her heart began to race, even faster than it had with fear; it raced now with desire.

She had never really lived before. And thinking, as she had, that she might not have the chance to live had her desperate to experience everything life had to offer. All those experiences she'd either been too busy or too afraid to try.

Like love...

Not the emotion but the action—the *art*—of making love. She was no virgin, but she had never been promiscuous, either. She had no idea how *casual* sex could be.

Could she make love with a man whose name she didn't even know?

She wanted to—wanted a man who hated who she really was. She was losing it now, even more than she had after the nightmare. She tugged harder on her clothes, desperate to pull them on and escape before she did something crazy.

But he still wouldn't release her clothes. Instead he released another shaky sigh and with it, one word: "Stay."

Chapter 4

Roarke didn't want to let her go. Even though she wasn't the woman he had wanted her to be, or maybe because she wasn't, he wanted her—with an intensity that burned white-hot.

"Stay," he said again.

Her eyes widened with fear and that stammer was back when she asked, "W-why?"

"You were promised an inclusive two-week vacation. Stay here and take me up on that offer," he urged her.

She shook her head, and that long thick hair swirled over her shoulders and breasts and tickled his wrist. His skin tingled at the sensation. She wasn't Piper; she was sexier. So much sexier....

Because Patricia Reynolds had a humility and generosity of spirit that the supermodel had never possessed.

He instinctively knew that she would be an amazing lover.

But she had no reason to desire him and every reason to fear him.

She tugged on her bundle of clothes again, trying to wrest the garments from his grasp. "I—I just want to go home," she said, the fear in her voice now.

"Don't let this misunderstanding scare you off," he said. Misunderstanding was a huge understatement but it was better than telling her that he'd mistaken her for a murderess. "I should have known you weren't Piper."

She lifted her bare shoulders in a jerky shrug. "It's okay," she replied, as if to absolve him of his guilt. She was definitely not Piper. "I never wanted this vacation anyway."

"Island vacations not your scene?" he asked.

From the paleness of her skin, she obviously spent very little—if any—time in the sun. Everyone he'd talked to about Patricia Reynolds, especially her boss, had praised how hard she always worked. That was why the man had agreed to call her name no matter whose he had actually drawn from the raffle basket. He thought Patricia would have fun and relaxation. He'd had no idea that Roarke had other plans for her.

"Vacations aren't my scene," she said with a shaky attempt at a smile. "I've never had one."

Guilt gripped him strongly now, clasping his heart in

a tight vice. This poor woman had boarded a plane full of anticipation for two weeks with no work and no stress. And she'd disembarked to threats and danger.

If he hadn't listened to her…

If he hadn't accepted that she wasn't Piper…

He nearly shuddered at the thought of what he might have done to her, of how he might have doled out justice to her.

And then she would have been as much an innocent victim as his cousin had been. Maybe more because Roarke had warned Rick that the supermodel was only using him. Patricia Reynolds had had no warning.

He had taken her by surprise. And he'd taken away the vacation she'd been promised. "You're definitely staying here."

He wasn't certain he could let her go yet; he couldn't even give up her clothes—let alone the woman who had stripped them off because she'd been so desperate to get away from him.

That desperation was still on her face, which was as full and soft and beautiful as her luscious body. "Please," she beseeched him, "just bring the plane back for me."

"I can't," he lied. With his free hand, he gestured toward his nearly empty desk. "There is no phone."

Her eyes, those glittery gold and green and brown eyes, narrowed with suspicion. "You don't even have a cell phone?"

"It would be pointless," Roarke replied. "There are no cell towers on the island." That, at least, was the truth.

She narrowed her eyes more, which furrowed her brow. "Then how do you communicate with the outside world? Computer?"

He pointed to his desk again. His laptop was hidden and locked away in the bottom drawer. "No internet, either."

She wasn't any easier to convince than he had been. Of course he was lying, though.

"How do you summon the plane?" she asked, her full lips pursed with skepticism.

"I arrange with the pilot, ahead of time, when I need the plane." Which was *never.* "It won't be back for two weeks, so you really have no choice, Miss Reynolds." Because he wasn't about to give her one. "You'll have to stay."

Tears, of either frustration or fear, glistened in those pretty eyes of hers. "I—I can't stay here—not with you…."

"I won't hurt you," he promised.

And now that he'd given his word, he couldn't…touch her. He couldn't make love to her and risk losing all control. With as much as he wanted her, he doubted he would be able to stop himself from taking her completely and for eternity.

* * *

Piper needed to get the hell away from this man. Now. Before he figured out that she had lied to him. And before she did something stupid....

Like take off the last of her clothes and press her naked body against his....

Her legs trembled with the intensity of her desire for him. She stood so close to him that his knuckles still pressed against her stomach as the two of them almost absentmindedly wrestled for control of her beige suit.

"How in the world do you think I can stay here?" she asked. "With you?"

She still didn't know his name. But it mattered less who he was than who she was—who she *really* was.

"I told you that I won't hurt you," he reminded her. "You have nothing to fear from me."

Maybe not from him. But she was afraid of this inexplicable yearning she had for him.

"What about that woman?" she asked. "That Piper woman? Does she have a reason to fear you?"

His already deep brown eyes darkened even more, nearly to black. "That doesn't concern you."

It had much more to do with her than she ever wanted him to realize.

"But you would have hurt me," she insisted, "if I hadn't convinced you that I'm not her."

"Like I said, that doesn't concern you. You're not her."

He didn't deny his hatred of Piper. Just thinking about her had his jaw clenching and his stare intensifying.

Why did he hate her so much?

"But why would you hurt her?" she asked. "What did she do to you?"

He shook his head, as if unable to even put it into words, as if he were choking on his hatred. He closed his eyes, but before his thick lashes brushed against his cheeks, she glimpsed the emotion in his eyes.

Sorrow. It gripped him even tighter than the hatred had. He was suffering. Because of her?

No matter how many millions of people she had met over the course of her modeling career, she knew she had never met him. A woman wouldn't ever be able to forget a man like him. Masculinity radiated from him like an electrical field, charging her every nerve ending with awareness. Heat generated from him to her, flushing her skin—making her want what she'd never really wanted before.

But she couldn't make love with a man who hated her—at least not without knowing why. Did he have a reason for his hatred any more than anyone else had had a reason to love her?

Just because of her damn pictures...?

"You can tell me," she urged him.

He opened his eyes again and stared at her, almost as if beseeching her to drop it. "You don't want to know."

Her breath shuddered out. "Maybe not," she admitted. "But I feel like I should know—since you mistook me for her."

"I won't make that mistake again," he assured her. "You're nothing like that woman."

"What am I like?" she asked.

"Beautiful," he said, his voice dropping to that sexy rumble. He stared down at her, and there was nothing of that hatred in his dark gaze. There was just the heat of desire.

For her? For the way she looked now?

With her free hand she gestured toward that crumpled-up poster on his desk. "Most would consider her the beautiful one."

He shook his head, his sexy mouth twisting into a grimace of disgust. "That's because most people don't know what she's really like."

"You don't know me, either," she reminded him. "You don't know what I'm like." Neither her new identity as Patricia nor who she'd been as Piper.

"I don't have to know you to know that you're not a cold-blooded killer." He released the grip he'd kept on her clothes and stepped back as if needing distance from her, as if he still had doubts about her identity.

But a killer?

Instead of putting on the suit, she let the garments

fall back onto the hardwood floor. How could he think she was a killer?

"You—you said she was a model," she reminded him, "not a—a killer...."

"People are often more than they appear to be," he said, as if warning her.

She could have used that warning years ago. "I don't pay attention to fashion." She hadn't even when she'd been in the business. "So I hadn't heard about that model. But I watch the news. If she'd killed someone, I would have heard about that...."

He shook his head. "Not if it was covered up right away...."

A sudden pain pounded at her temples, as if someone had struck her with a hammer. A haze of red blinded her; she closed her eyes to clear her vision. But the red remained—like the vestiges of that nightmare she'd tried so hard to convince herself hadn't really happened. It wasn't real.

It couldn't be real....

She trembled so hard that her weak legs threatened to fold beneath her.

Strong hands gripped her arms, steering her backward. She dropped blindly onto something soft. Supple leather shifted beneath her bare thighs. She really should have put her clothes back on.

"I told you that you didn't want to know," he said, his

voice such a deep rumble that her skin tingled as if he'd touched her...with his voice...like his hands were touching her. His palms cupped her shoulders, his thumbs tracing over her collarbone. "Are you all right? Do you want some water?"

"No." She didn't want water. She wanted him. But how could he think that she—Piper—was a killer?

That red haze didn't clear from her vision; it continued to blind her—to his handsome face and to the memories of that nightmare that had haunted her the past four years.

Could it have been real? Could she really be a killer?

"Whom—whom did she kill?" she asked.

His fingers moved up from her shoulders over her neck to her jaw. He cupped her face in his palms. "Shhh... none of this has anything to do with you."

Tears stung her eyes. She blinked them back and wrinkled her nose against the sting of them. It had everything to do with her. But she couldn't tell him that. If he truly believed she was a killer...

If she truly was...

"I don't want any of this ugliness touching you." He leaned closer, his breath warm against her cheek. "You're too beautiful.... Much too beautiful..."

She wasn't. Not on the outside and maybe not on the inside, either. Not if he was right about her....

He couldn't be right about her.

But the only way she would know for certain was to let herself remember.

The nightmare....

Fear struck her with the force of a blow, knocking the memories from her tormented mind. The pounding increased, in her blood now—pumping it fast and hard through her veins. The red haze cleared from her vision, along with whatever images had been flitting through her mind, and she focused on his face.

His amazingly handsome face.

Giving in to temptation, she reached out and traced one of the deep creases in his cheek. Her face flushed with embarrassment as she realized what she'd done. Before she could snatch back her hand, he caught it. He brought her fingers to his lips and sucked the tips inside his mouth.

His tongue danced across her skin, sending desire racing through her. Her nipples tightened and her thighs tensed. She pressed her legs together and shifted against the leather cushion. But skin rubbed against skin, making her even more hyper-sensitive of her sensuality.

"You taste so sweet," he murmured.

She pulled her hand from his mouth and pressed it and her other hand against his chest. But she didn't push him away—even though she should. Instead she reached for the buttons on his shirt, needing him to be as bare and vulnerable as she was.

And she needed more than the slide of his tongue across her fingertips. She needed his kiss and leaned in, closing the distance between them. She pressed her mouth to his.

His lips were silky-soft while his mouth was hard, his kiss full of passion. He groaned, and she took the kiss deeper, slipping her tongue into his mouth where her fingers had been just moments ago.

Her hands were busy elsewhere now—baring all his muscle and skin to her hungry gaze and touch. After parting his shirt to his impressive chest with its dusting of dark hair, she slid her hand lower, over his taut abs to the clasp of his pants. His erection strained against the fly. He wanted her every bit as much as she wanted him.

His hands moved over her with the same urgency, stroking her skin, pushing down the straps of her bra and unclasping it so that it fell away—leaving her breasts bare for his gaze and his touch. He moved his mouth down her throat, over her collarbone—raining kisses on her flushed skin.

Then he closed his lips over a taut nipple. Tugging it into his mouth, he stroked first the tip of his tongue over the pebbled point and then the sharp tip of a tooth.

Piper moaned over the onslaught of desire coursing through her body. While he teased one breast with his mouth, he teased the other with his thumb, stroking the coarse pad back and forth over the nipple.

Pressure wound tight inside her, and she whimpered and shifted against the couch, arching her hips. He reached for her panties now, pushing them down her hips. Then he parted her legs and stroked his long fingers over the very essence of her desire for him.

He barely touched her and she came. But it wasn't enough to release all the pressure—it was just enough to make her want him more.

His control must have snapped, too, because he stripped off his clothes as she had hers—with more haste than grace. His body naked and gloriously hard, he pressed her back into the soft cushions—his erection pushing against the core of her.

Finally, realizing what she was about to do with a virtual stranger, Piper panicked and screamed.

Chapter 5

"Stop!"

Sweat beaded on his lip and his muscles quivered as Roarke struggled for control. She had yelled stop—more than once. He had to stop. He couldn't take her against her will.

He was a beast but not an animal.

He levered his arms against the couch, pushing weight off her. But she arched against him, wrapping her long legs around his waist.

"Don't…" she murmured, her breath coming in pants between her parted lips. "Don't stop…. Just wait a minute…."

He was big. Many women had needed time to adjust to his size, but she hadn't even let him inside her yet. "What…?"

"What's your name?" she asked. Her face flushed an even darker shade of red than it had been flushed with passion. "I need to know your name...."

"Roarke..." He paused, something holding him back from telling her his last name.

It had less to do with that E. Graves confidentiality agreement than simple self-preservation. Since she didn't know where he lived or his last name, she wouldn't be able to find him again when her vacation was over; then she wouldn't be able to tell anyone else where to find him if she figured out what he really was.

What the hell was he thinking? He hadn't wanted to take such a risk by making love to her. He hadn't trusted his control; he wanted her so much. But he had stopped—mostly—when she'd told him to. Maybe he could maintain control....

"I need to know," she said. "I need to know what name to scream when you make me come...."

He nearly came then—at just her words. His control shredded, and he thrust into her wet heat. She arched and shifted and took him deep, her inner muscles clutching his shaft.

He thrust in and out, and she rose up, meeting him—taking him deeper each time. He buried his face in her neck, as he buried himself inside her. But he pulled his lips taut over the fangs that distended. He wanted to taste her, really taste more than her skin or her flavor.

He wanted to taste and feed on the very essence of her—her blood.

But he didn't do that. He drank the bottles of nourishment. He didn't feast on humans or other members of the society. Until now he'd never understood why other vampires gave in to such primal urges. But until now, until *her,* he had never had that intense hunger.

Her muscles clutched tighter, her nails digging into his back as she came. And just as she'd promised, she screamed his name. "Roarke!"

He thrust deeper and harder until he came, too. "Patricia…"

Her body, so soft and seemingly boneless just moments before, tensed beneath his. With regret? He couldn't blame her for having qualms about what they'd just done—after how harsh and mistrustful he'd been when she had first arrived.

"Stop," he told her.

Roarke moved his mouth from the temptation of her throat to the sweet fullness of her lips. He kissed her—deeply—mouth open, tongues stroking and tangling with each other.

Panting for breath he pulled back and continued, "Stop thinking."

She stared up at him, the bits of gold glittering in her eyes. Then her pupils grew, swallowing the gold and the green and the brown.

"Just feel." Still buried inside her, he hardened and moved. "Just enjoy."

She moaned and shifted beneath him, arching into him. She clutched his back again, pressing him against her.

"This is your vacation," he reminded her, whispering the words into her ear. "We're the only two people on this island."

She shivered. But instead of fear, there was amusement in her voice when she asked, "So what happens here stays here?"

He wanted her to stay, too, and maybe longer than fourteen days. But he couldn't keep her forever. Once her vacation was over, she would get back to her life in Zantrax.

And Roarke would get back to the promise he had posthumously made to his cousin.

To avenge Rick's death—to kill his killer.

If this was what a vacation was like, Piper wished she had taken one years ago. But any time she'd had between modeling assignments, she had used to take classes. And then—after the nightmare began—she hadn't dared. In addition to not wanting anyone to recognize her, she hadn't wanted to have any time to relax and perhaps to remember what she and everyone else agreed was best forgotten.

But this—making love with Roarke—wasn't relaxing. And as he'd said, she couldn't think about anything. She could only feel.

He felt so good. Muscles rippled under supple skin as she ran her hands all over him—down his broad back, over his shoulders—down his chest. Soft hair tickled her palms.

And his tongue tickled her lips, teasing the corners until she opened her mouth. He thrust inside her mouth like he thrust inside her body.

She matched his rhythm, meeting each of his thrusts with an arch of her hips and a stroke of her tongue against his. He was so hard—his body—and his mouth. She was no virgin. Before she'd gone into hiding, she'd had a couple of boyfriends who'd moved in the same social and fashion circles she had.

But those boyfriends had definitely been just boys. Roarke was a man—one who knew how to please a woman.

Piper had never felt like this—had never experienced the intense pleasure that he'd just given her. Or the pain, as that pressure mounted inside her again—building so tight that she thought she might shred in two.

Then he reached between them, rubbing his thumb against where their bodies joined. And his mouth pulled back from hers. First his lips slid down her throat. His tongue flicked across where her pulse leaped against her skin.

Then his mouth slid lower. He arched back and so did she, lifting her breasts. He tasted her nipples—flicking his tongue across the pink points. And he pushed his thumb harder against her.

And she came, her body exploding in fireworks of ecstasy. She clutched at him with her arms and her inner muscles, holding him inside her—pulling him deeper as the pleasure kept shuddering throughout her—curling her toes and blowing her mind.

He came, too. And as he filled her with his pleasure, he uttered the same lie that he had uttered the first time they'd made love. That lie had had her tensing with guilt then and now. It was the lie she'd told him. "Patricia!"

Guilt chased away the afterglow of pleasure he'd given her. Pleasure he wouldn't have given her had he not fallen for her lies. So she'd stolen it from him—along with trust she didn't deserve.

Sure, she had lied to protect herself because she'd suspected she was in danger if she admitted who she really was. But she had never considered that she might have once posed the danger.

But that nightmare rushed back with that red haze. Blood? Whose blood?

His fingers slid across her cheek to her jaw, and he tilted her chin until she met his gaze. His eyes were dark with concern. "Are you all right?" he asked. "I didn't hurt you?"

She shook her head. If she believed what he'd told her, Piper had been the one who had hurt him. And from the sorrow she'd seen on his face, it had been badly.

"It's been a while for me," he admitted. "So I hope I wasn't too rough with you." He traced his fingertips across her skin, as if inspecting her for bruises.

"Who was it?" she asked, desperately needing to know.

His brow furrowed. "Who was it?" He repeated her question. "You and I are the only ones on the island. There's no one else."

Now. Maybe because of her.

"Whom did you lose?"

She needed to know if it had been his wife or a lover. Had there been someone else between them when they'd made love—another woman in his mind?

"Who do you think that Piper woman killed?"

He tensed now and withdrew—physically and emotionally. He pulled away from her and pulled on his pants. Maybe his hands were shaking too badly to clasp them, but he left the waistband open over the jutting bones and muscles of his lean hips.

She wanted him again. Still. She had never been loved that thoroughly. And she had never been hated as venomously as he hated Piper.

That intensity of anger and vengeance and pain was

back on his handsome face, clenching his jaw and darkening his eyes. "I know she killed him."

"Him?"

"My cousin. My best friend…."

Rick Monterusso. The man smiled.

Not Roarke. He wasn't smiling. But the man in her mind was as he introduced himself to her, as if she should have known who he was. *He stared at her as if he'd already loved her. And he'd never met her before. He knew her not at all.*

So how had he gotten into her apartment? Had he broken in?

Her heart rate increased, pounding frantically with fear as the memories flooded back. And they were memories—not just fragments of a nightmare that she had never quite been able to forget no matter how hard she'd tried.

The feelings overwhelmed the images. So she couldn't focus. She couldn't see. That red haze blinded her again. And she started shaking—really shaking—not just trembling. Her body jerked as if she were having a seizure. And maybe she was.

"Patricia!" Roarke shouted that name—her fake name—as if he'd been calling her but she hadn't heard him.

She could barely hear him now. He sounded so far away. Or was she the one far away?

"What can I do?" he asked. "How can I help you?"

She gasped for breath and fought to form words with lips that trembled uncontrollably. "I—I need my bag."

"Bag?" Confusion and frustration made his already deep voice gruffer.

"On the porch," she reminded him, her mind flitting to the image of her small suitcase she'd left on the front steps. "I—I need the prescription inside."

It had been too long since she'd taken her medication. That was why she was so weak, her muscles a quivering mess. If she didn't get her pills soon, she knew what would happen—she *wouldn't* know what had happened. She would black out completely. Usually she awoke hours later, but she had to force herself awake.

The doctor who'd prescribed the pills had threatened that if she kept forgetting to take them, that one day she wouldn't be able to wake up again. She would lose more than time.

She would lose her life.

As consciousness slipped away from her, she had one last thought: Had she waited too long already?

Was it too late?

Roarke grabbed her bag from the porch and ran back inside his house, leaving the door gaping open behind him. The creatures of the night knew not to enter his house. He wasn't afraid of what lurked outside but of what awaited him inside his den.

He had thought her skin pale before, but she had absolutely no color now. Her body was startling white and lifeless against the black leather. He leaned over her, but he could feel no breath escaping her lips, could discern no rise and fall in her chest.

He reached for her throat, sliding his fingertips across her skin. The pulse that had pounded so furiously only moments before was weak and thready.

She was alive. But just barely…

Was this his fault? Had he been too rough with her? But he'd had no idea that she had a medical condition—something for which she had been prescribed medicine.

Careless of the zipper, he ripped apart her bag and spilled the contents across the hardwood floor. A brown bottle rolled away from the mound of swimsuits and light dresses. He grabbed for it. It had one of those damn childproof tops that had to be pushed down to pop open. He ignored the rules and tore it off. The plastic pinged against the floor and bounced across the room. A couple of pills spilled out, too. He caught the dark capsules in his palm.

What the hell were they? Certainly too damn big for her to swallow as she was, nearly unconscious. But what choice did he have?

He pressed a pill to her lips, pushing it between them.

Then he moved his fingers over her throat, tracing the path of the capsule and making certain she swallowed it. And didn't choke...

Was one capsule enough? Given the size, he would think so, but then he had no idea what the hell her condition was. She had just started convulsing, her body violently jerking until she'd passed out.

Was she just unconscious? He felt for her pulse again. It was still barely perceptible. He leaned closer, pressing his cheek to her mouth. He felt no breath against his face.

Did she need more than one pill?

He turned his attention back to the bottle. The directions were vague—take as needed. As needed for what?

He'd lied to her about having no phone. He had a cell locked up with his laptop—and access to a satellite that gave him phone coverage no matter where he was. He would call her damn doctor and find out just what this medication was and why Patricia needed it. After spinning the bottle in his slightly shaking hand, he found the doctor's name but didn't need to look at the number. He knew it by heart—as did every member of the Secret Vampire Society.

Dr. Benjamin Davison had once been a world-renowned cardiologist until he'd gone into private practice—for the Secret Vampire Society. He worked exclusively on vampires and other creatures of the underworld.

So why the hell had he prescribed something for a human? Unless...

Roarke had accepted that Patricia Reynolds wasn't Piper. But maybe she was a hell of a lot more than just an accountant....

Chapter 6

This was a vacation.

Sex that had her body still humming with pleasure, no matter how weak she was.

Warm sand beneath her feet. A soft breeze tousling her hair around her bare shoulders.

Piper dragged in a deep breath of relief. Despite all Dr. Davison's dire warnings, she had awakened. She'd been disoriented, though, and completely unaware of where she was.

In a bed. A wide, soft bed.

His bed.

But Roarke hadn't been sleeping with her. She suspected he was still in the den. The mahogany French doors had been closed when she'd walked through the foyer and out the front door.

As the doctor had warned, she had no idea how long she'd been out or of how much time she'd lost. There was no sun—just an eerie light shining on the water. Either moonlight or the first light of dawn or maybe even the last light of day....

The water, burnished gold in that eerie light, stretched endlessly. No sign of other land in sight. No sign of life but her. Water rose in rippling waves that crested onto the beach and lapped at her bare toes. She curled them into the warm sand.

Or maybe she hadn't awakened. Maybe she had died and gone to heaven. And if she had, then she wasn't the killer Roarke thought she was.

Or she would have gone to hell.

And then she did go there, as her mind finally let the nightmare come back. The water turned to blood. It flowed all over everything. Her feet. Her shoulders. It spurted down her arms.

And then over her hands. Her hands were covered in blood.

His blood.

She dropped to her knees on the sand, and the water swirled around her legs, soaking the skirt of the sundress she'd found on the bed when she'd awakened. But the water couldn't wash away the blood. Or wash his image from her mind. It reflected back at her from the shimmering surface of the sea.

He hadn't looked like Roarke. In fact he'd been pretty much his exact opposite. Blond. Blue-eyed. Shorter, closer to her height than Roarke's, and slighter of build. But freakishly strong...

Pain ached in her limbs as she remembered the fight. He had clasped her wrists in a grasp so tight that her bones had nearly snapped. Had he been attacking her or just fending off her attack?

Because she was alive. And he was not. He stared up at her from the water, his eyes open with shock and pain. Blood poured over his body, pumping out of the open wound in his chest.

And then his heart stopped beating. It just *stopped*. And his eyes grew vacant with death.

She screamed in realization that the nightmare wasn't about what had happened to her but about what she had done. Roarke was right.

Piper was a killer.

Her scream chilled his blood even more so than when he'd discovered his bed empty, her gone. They were on a damn twenty-acre island. Where the hell could she have gone?

He should have stayed beside the bed, should have watched her. But he'd tried calling the surgeon instead. Ben Davison hadn't answered his damn phone. A message said that he was handling an emergency and would return calls when he was free.

Roarke couldn't wait. He had to know why she saw a doctor no other human had seen in years. Since he couldn't talk to Ben, he would talk to her. If he could find her...

If she was able to talk...

Since her scream had drawn him from the house, he hadn't heard another sound—not a bird chirping, not even the breeze rustling the leaves of the trees in the heavily wooded forest. He followed her footprints in the sand. From the spacing of them, it looked as though she'd walked—not run—down the beach. And it appeared that she had been alone, not running from someone.

Not running to escape him. But then her footsteps disappeared, the waves lapping away at the sand—hiding her path from him. Hiding her...

"Patricia!" he called out to her. "Patricia..."

Finally birds moved, rising up from trees in a frenzy over the urgency in his voice. But the woman didn't move. She knelt in the water that swirled around her legs and soaked her dress. Her body was bent forward, as if she was praying.

Or trying to drown herself in the waves.

He ran across the sand toward her. "Patricia!"

Her hair had parted on the back of her neck, hanging over her face and chest and down into the water. He reached for her, to pull her back, and noticed the scar. There was a strangely familiar mark on her nape—the scarred flesh indented in two distinctive spots….

His fingertips just touched her skin when she jerked violently—as if she were convulsing again. But then her body stilled and she turned toward him, her gold-flecked gaze meeting his.

"Are you all right?" he asked.

Her beautiful eyes filled with tears, and when she shook her head, they spilled over, sliding down her smooth cheeks. He dropped onto the sand beside her and cupped her face in his hands.

"What's wrong?" he asked.

Was she dying? Was that why she needed the pills?

Roarke couldn't wait for a return call from Dr. Davison. He needed to go back to Zantrax. It would take him only minutes to fly there, but he couldn't leave her.

She might not be alive when he returned. He needed to talk to Ben—to get him to come to her. "I'll get you help," he promised, and closed his arms around her to lift her from the water.

But she resisted, pushing against his chest and breaking the hold of his arms. He stumbled back onto the beach while she stood yet in the waves that kept crashing ashore. But she didn't lose her balance. She was strong now—stronger than she'd been when they'd made love and certainly stronger than she had been when her body had started seizing. Maybe the pill had helped her.

What the hell was that medication?

"I don't need help," she said, her eyes still bright with the sheen of tears. "I just need..."

"What?"

Whatever it was, he wanted to give it to her. He just wanted her. Even after making love with her twice, the intensity of his desire hadn't eased. If anything, it was even more intense because he knew how perfectly their bodies fit, how much pleasure they could bring each other....

"What do you need?" he asked.

"You."

His breath caught, trapped in his throat.

"I want you," she said, the longing in her voice and eyes.

This connection between them was so strong—unlike anything Roarke had experienced in all the centuries he'd lived. He had prided himself on never falling for anyone—on never being vulnerable to another being.

After his cousin's death, he'd become even more determined to stay detached. Isolated. Here on his private island.

Then he'd brought her here thinking she was a cold-blooded killer. He had been at no risk of falling for such a woman. But he'd been wrong about her. About her identity and her appeal.

"I want you, too," he said, and he reached for her again.

But she stepped back, into deeper water, and shook her head. "No, you don't...."

"I thought I didn't," he admitted. "I thought I wanted justice." But that desire was so much less than his need for her. "Now I just want you...."

"You have me," she assured him. And she closed the distance between them now.

She was cold and wet against him. He had pulled on his shirt, as he had his pants. But he had left it unbuttoned, his chest and stomach bare so nothing separated his skin from hers but her wet dress. And the cold.

She shivered.

Roarke wrapped his arms around her, trying to warm her. Trying to chase away the chill. But it wasn't just hers. An odd sensation raced up and down his spine, an ominous foreboding.

He couldn't forget that prescription, couldn't forget that she wasn't well.

"Don't think," she advised him, as he had her just a few hours ago. She slid her fingertips over his face to his brows. Then she gently closed his eyelids. "Just feel...."

He felt her lips, brushing across his. And then her teeth nipped at his bottom lip, pulling it open for the bold invasion of her tongue. He tightened his arms around her, holding her close as the kiss deepened.

But she broke free again, as easily as she had only moments before. He would have opened his eyes in protest, but her lips were there, kissing his lids. And her hands were everywhere, running over his chest—pushing his shirt from his shoulders.

Then her fingers brushed against his erection. Metal gave a quick whine as she lowered his zipper.

Like her hands, her lips moved all over him. Down his throat, over his chest. Her tongue tasted a nipple, hardened it to a taut point. She nipped at that point, sending a jolt through his body.

When her soft hands closed around his erection, he nearly came. But then her lips were there, kissing the tip of his shaft before pulling him inside her mouth. She had dropped to her knees in front of him. He clutched his hands in her thick hair, trying to pull her away. But she resisted, matching his strength.

How was that possible? But he couldn't think about that. He couldn't think at all as she made love to him with her mouth.

The pleasure was so intense it was almost painful, building a pressure inside him. His every muscle clenched taut with it—his groin heavy with it—begging for release.

She swirled her tongue around him and sucked him deep in her throat.

And he came, shouting her name. "Patricia!"

How had he ever mistaken her for Piper? She was so generous and loving. And he found himself falling....

He dropped to his knees in front of her and wrapped his arms around her bare shoulders. Her skin was still chilled, still wet as the waves, crashing onto the shore behind her, sprayed her.

Her face was wet, too, but the salt water came from her eyes, which overflowed with tears.

His heart clenched in his chest. "Don't cry," he beseeched her. "Please, don't cry...."

Seeing her like this, so sorrowful and scared, affected him almost violently, as if someone had reached inside him and twisted all his organs into knots.

"What's wrong?" he asked, concern nearly filling his throat—making his voice gruff. Whatever the problem was, he would fix it. Whatever she wanted, he would give her.

Even if what she wanted was to leave? The question made him as sick as her tears. It would hurt like hell, maybe even worse than losing his cousin, but he would let her go.

If that was really what she wanted...

She didn't seem to want him anymore. She'd given him pleasure. But instead of letting him make love to her, she pulled back—tearing herself from his arms. She jumped to her feet and ran down the beach—farther from the house. Except that it was an island and if she kept running, she would circle around to where she'd started.

To where they had started—on the steps of the front porch of his home.

He pulled up his pants and zipper and ran after her. Catching her easily, he closed his arms around her. His hands pressed against her stomach, holding her against him. Then he slid his hands up her midriff to cup her breasts. The wet fabric of her dress was transparent against her skin, her nipples taut against the material.

He brushed his thumbs across the points. They peaked even more, and she shuddered against him. "Let me please you," he said, sliding his lips down her neck.

Would it please her if he nipped her...just lightly with his fangs?

But he wouldn't be able to stop with just a nibble. He would want to bite her, to taste her deeply....

He couldn't be that selfish, couldn't take his pleasure at the price of her pain. He moved his hands down her body, to the hem of her dress. He lifted the wet fabric, so that he could touch her as intimately as she'd touched him. He moved his hand over her mound to the tight nub of her arousal.

But she clutched at his wrist and pulled his hand away.

"Let me make love to you, Patricia...."

"Stop," she whispered.

"I want to give you the pleasure you gave me," he said. "I want to make love to you, Patricia." He was afraid that he was already falling for her.

She turned in his arms and pressed her fingers against his lips. "Stop," she said again, her eyes brimming with more tears. Of regret. "Stop calling me Patricia."

That ominous foreboding rushed back over him, chilling his skin and his blood. "Why?"

"Because Patricia really isn't my name," she confessed.

"Who are you?" he asked even though he was afraid he already knew—that he had always known and had lied to himself just like she had lied to him.

"You were right all along," she said, confirming what had quickly become his worst fear.

Even though he knew she was finally telling him the truth, Roarke shook his head in denial. "No...."

"I am Piper." She sucked in an audible breath. "And I am the one who killed your cousin."

Chapter 7

"Aren't you going to kill me?" she asked. Death—that was the reward she'd expected for her confession. Or at least a physical attack.

She would have preferred those to Roarke's actual reaction: silence. He had immediately turned away as if unable to bear the sight of her. He stood at the edge of the beach, water lapping over his bare feet and wicking up his pant legs.

But he was oblivious to the wet and cold while she stood shivering—probably less from the chill on her skin and more in anticipation of the explosion that had to be building inside him. But he seemed as oblivious to her as he was to the elements.

It was as though she had ceased to exist for him. And after the intimacy and power of the lovemaking they'd shared, that hurt her more than he ever could have wounded her physically. Her heart ached as if she were now the one with a gaping hole in her chest.

"Isn't that why you brought me here?" she challenged him, goading him into acknowledging her presence. "For revenge?"

"For justice," he corrected her almost absentmindedly. And his gaze stayed focused on the water, as if the answers he sought would somehow wash ashore with the waves.

Maybe he wasn't the man for whom she'd found herself falling—the caring, loving man who was haunted by sorrow. Maybe he felt only hatred and rage.

No. She didn't believe that—not after how gentle and considerate he'd been with her. And how badly he had felt when she'd convinced him her lie was the truth— that she wasn't the woman he hated.

"So you already tried and convicted me without even bothering to ask me my side of what happened?" she challenged him again. "When we first met, you warned me against making assumptions. But it seems you're the one who's been assuming the most. And the worst. You've already decided my guilt."

"You admitted you killed him," he said, tossing her confession back at her.

"But you don't know why," she said. "You don't know what happened."

He uttered a ragged sigh, a gasp of pain and anger. "No. And now that my cousin is dead, I never will."

"I can tell you…." What she remembered. But it seemed more like a nightmare to her than reality. There were still more questions than answers even in her own mind.

Maybe he was right. Maybe with his cousin gone, neither Roarke nor she would ever know the truth.

"You've been lying to me since you set foot on my island," he accused her—justifiably. Finally he turned toward her, and the hatred was back in his eyes—maybe even more intense than when he had first believed she was Piper because now he had to feel betrayed, too. "Why should I believe anything you tell me?"

She lifted her shoulders in a shrug, unable to argue with him. Unable to assuage his pain and that sense of betrayal. She could have told him that she was falling for him—for his loyalty and his honor—even though that honor included vengeance. But he wouldn't have believed her. He would only suspect that she was trying to trick him.

He pushed a hand through his thick dark hair, shoving it off his brow. "Hell, give it your best shot," he challenged her, "convince me to spare your life."

She shuddered at the threat, grateful now that she hadn't told him what she was feeling for him. It wouldn't matter. Probably nothing would—regardless of what she said. So she just shook her head.

His patience and control snapped, and he reached for her. Clasping her arms, he shook her but only slightly—not enough to hurt but enough to tip her head back to face him. "You wanted to tell me your side...."

"What's the point?" she asked, "when you're not going to believe me anyway?" And after the lie she had told him, she couldn't blame him.

He shook her again, with a little more force and commanded, "Tell me what happened!"

"I can only tell you what I remember," she said. And for so long that had been blessedly little. "I've spent the past four years thinking that it was just a bad dream. I convinced myself that it never really happened, and I pushed it from my mind."

"You murdered my cousin and *forgot* about it?" he asked gruffly, as if choking on his rage. "You went on living your life as if you'd done nothing wrong?"

"I don't think I did," she said, clinging to that belief. "I think I was just defending myself...."

"From the man who loved you?"

She shuddered at the thought of that kind of sick obsession being called love. "From the man who stalked and assaulted me!"

The nightmare came rushing back. The letters and emails. The strange gifts left in hotel rooms and her apartment. Finding her wherever she'd gone—wherever she had tried to hide.

Roarke pushed her back, as if he didn't trust himself to hold on to her any longer and not hurt her. "You're a liar. You are a damn liar. The two of you had a relationship!"

She shook her head. "Until that night... I'd never seen him before."

"You bitch, you used Rick!" he accused her. Another accusation lurked in the depths of his eyes, that she had used him, too. "You asked him for money and presents and gave him nothing in return—no affection. No attention—"

"I didn't ask him for anything!" she shouted, trying to get through to him. "I never saw him—I never talked to him—until that night, until I found him in my apartment!"

The horror of that moment rushed back over her. Her home had always been an oasis, an escape from the media and her mother. She shut off her cell the moment she opened the door and then she shut out the rest of the world. But that night, she hadn't been alone. She'd locked herself inside with a madman.

"It was *his* apartment," Roarke said, as if correcting her.

She stared up at him, the one who was incredulous now. He knew less than she remembered. "You don't even know where it happened."

"He didn't live there, but it was Rick's apartment," he insisted. "He was paying for it."

Frustration gnawing at her, she shook her head. "You don't have any of the facts."

"I don't think you know what the facts are, Piper," he admonished her.

"Were you there?" she asked. "Did you see what happened?" Someone else must have been there...eventually. Someone had found her and gotten her medical attention.

That muscle twitched in his deeply creased cheek, as if he were struggling to control his anger. "If I had been there, my cousin wouldn't be dead."

And she would be.

Hell, she probably still would be dead. Because he wasn't likely to believe the rest of what little she remembered.

"He attacked me," she said, shivering now even though the breeze was warm and had dried her clothes and skin.

Maybe it was the coldness of Roarke's stare that chilled her now.

"He would have killed me," she insisted, "if I hadn't killed him first."

Damn her. He wanted to believe her again. Even knowing that she had done nothing but lie to him, Roarke wanted to believe her.

But he couldn't take her word—not over Rick's

word—the last words his cousin had ever spoken to him. Rick had loved her so much that he'd wanted to give her everything she wanted.

Roarke hadn't understood—until just a few moments ago, when he would have given Patricia anything to make her happy. But she wasn't Patricia—she was Piper.

"My cousin was convinced that the two of you had a relationship."

She shuddered again as if repulsed at the thought. "I told you that I had never seen him before—never talked to him. Whatever relationship he thought we had was only in his mind."

Rick *had* seemed obsessed with the model. He'd collected every photo she'd ever had taken, even candid shots and childhood pictures. Roarke hadn't believed that his cousin had been in love, merely infatuated with beauty and sex appeal. But he'd thought Piper had encouraged that infatuation for her own personal gain. There had been emails and letters between them, but what if she hadn't really sent them…?

No, Rick wouldn't have forged them—not even to prove to his skeptical cousin that the relationship was real. Because Roarke had had his doubts until he'd seen the correspondence…

"He said you'd asked him to move in with you," he remembered. "That you wanted to spend forever with him." She had wanted more from Rick than his money and presents. She'd wanted immortality. She'd known what he was. And humans weren't allowed to learn about the Secret Society and live because their knowledge posed a threat to the vampires.

She had definitely posed a threat to Rick; she had ended his immortality. She'd taken his eternal life.

"Four years ago I was young and had never experienced love," she said. "I didn't want to spend forever with anyone." She glanced up at him with that longing back on her beautiful face. "Then…"

He ignored the implication that she had changed her mind—that he had changed her mind about forever. He wouldn't let her seduce him again. She had already tricked him into betraying his cousin and his own integrity. He wouldn't fall for her. Again.

"How did you kill my cousin?" he asked.

Her lips parted on a gasp, as if tempting him to kiss her. And to deepen that kiss…

But she was a killer. The most dangerous kind because she knew how to kill beings that weren't supposed to die.

"You—you want specifics?" she asked, that stammer back with a rush of fear and nerves.

"I want details—every last gruesome detail."

She began to tremble but not as violently as she had in his den. She didn't appear about to pass out. But she closed her eyes. "Like I said, I don't remember much about that night…." She shuddered. "And what I do remember doesn't seem real…. Doesn't seem possible at all."

She lifted her hand to the back of her neck, to that scar he'd glimpsed when he had found her kneeling in the water. Now he realized she had probably been trying to wash away her guilt.

But her eyes opened and stared up into his, and he glimpsed no guilt lurking among the glitter of gold flecks. Maybe she truly believed she had killed in self-defense.

"I don't blame you for not believing me," she admitted. "I don't know what's real or not. There was blood. So much blood…."

"His." He would have bled profusely around the stake she'd driven into his heart.

"And mine," she said, clutching at her nape as she must have that night. "When he had attacked me, he could have severed an artery. He must have come close to one. I think I lost a lot of blood." Her breath escaped in a ragged gasp. "That's probably why I don't remember much…."

"You passed out?" The scar was real enough and looked as though it could have been from fangs. Rick's? Had his cousin hurt her?

"I don't even know how long I was out," she said. "I woke up in some strange operating room." She shivered again.

Roarke almost shivered, too, sharing the revulsion of the room she'd mentioned. He had only been there once. He'd had to bring Rick after his cousin had gotten into a violent brawl with another society member in the bar that was in front of the underground operating room. "That was when Dr. Davison treated you?"

She narrowed her eyes as she stared up at him. "You know Dr. Davison?"

He nodded. "How do you know him?"

She shrugged. "I don't remember. I don't even know how I got to that room."

Roarke reeled from the possible implications of what she'd just shared with him. "So Dr. Davison treated your wound?"

She pushed her fingers into her hair again and stroked them over that scar. "He told me that this was nothing." Her voice sharpened with anger as she realized that she, too, had been lied to and betrayed. "He convinced me that none of that had really happened. That I'd had an emotional breakdown and that stress had caused some wild hallucinations."

She wasn't the only one whom Dr. Ben Davison had betrayed. He had been one of the first to swear to Roarke that Patricia Reynolds wasn't Piper. Davison's wife and father-in-law, the bartender at that underground night-club, had supported his claim. No wonder Roarke had trusted his own gut over them; they had all been lying to him.

"And he put you on those pills?"

She nodded. "And he told me to put those memories from my mind, that it all must have been just a horrible nightmare."

"He knew what happened?" Roarke asked.

Her eyes narrowed more and she considered a moment before nodding. "He seemed to know even more than I remembered of my *nightmare*."

"So he was there," Roarke said, his anger shifting from her to the man he might have considered a friend had he ever spent more time in Zantrax. It was the one city in the world where there were probably more Secret Society members than humans. But still Roarke preferred his island. "He's aware of what really happened?"

She shrugged. "I don't know. I remember so little myself...."

"I need to talk to the doctor," he said. But he didn't want to leave her alone on the island. He wasn't so certain that she couldn't escape.

"But the plane won't be back for nearly two weeks," she reminded him.

"I don't need the plane to leave the island," he admitted.

She shook her head, as if disgusted. "Seems like I wasn't the only one lying. You do have a boat."

"Not one that could get me to Zantrax from here."

"Then how do you intend to get there?"

Roarke was taking a risk—making one of those assumptions that he had warned her against making. And if he was wrong, it could cost them both their lives.

But he hadn't been wrong about who she was. He probably wasn't wrong about *what* she was, either. So he shared a secret with her, one no one outside the society was supposed to learn and live and one that could cost the society member his eternal life if he revealed the secret to a human. "I can fly."

Her mouth opened again but not even a gasp escaped her lips. She was too shocked. And too scared. She stared at him as if he'd lost his mind.

So he showed her. He caught her in his arms and rose up from the sand. But she struggled against him, and she was strong enough to break his grasp again. It probably wasn't all she was strong enough to do. She dropped to the sand. But she wasn't hurt because she vaulted to her feet and ran.

As if she were able to outrun a man who could fly....

He could have caught her easily, but he didn't chase her. If he forced her to fly with him, he couldn't be certain that she wouldn't struggle free and fall again. And much farther than a few feet to soft sand.

If he were wrong, she would die. For four years that was all he had wanted—her life for his cousin's. But now he wanted more than her life. But first he had to learn the truth no matter how much that might hurt him. He suspected that losing her would hurt him more.

Chapter 8

Her nightmare was real; every bizarre detail of it had happened. Vampires weren't just in pages of young-adult novels. They were as real as her memories of the night she had killed one of them.

They weren't supposed to die.

But of course that was what she'd read in a fiction novel. The truth was so much…more real. She ducked her head, as if Roarke was still flying over her. But only the coffered ceiling of his den was above her now, as she sat at his desk.

She wasn't the only one who'd been lying. She'd found his desk unlocked and a laptop and cell phone inside a drawer.

But that wasn't all she'd found.

That night, the night she had pulled it from Rick Mon-

terusso's pocket and used it on him, she'd thought it was
a dagger. But in the light of the chandelier glittering over-
head, she could see that it was actually a stake. A highly
polished and sharpened piece of wood that was a more
effective and deadly weapon than any knife or even a
gun. She would never know what instinct had guided
her to shove that stake into his heart or even where she'd
found the strength as blood had spurted from the wound
on her neck. But she had killed an immortal creature.

A vampire.

She'd thought then she'd just been protecting herself
from a crazy stalker. But she had found more than the
stake. She had found a thick folder labeled simply: *Piper.*

And inside were the letters and emails. Not just the
ones she had received from the man she had thought
stalking her. But also the ones she'd supposedly sent
him. They weren't exactly love letters, more like a seduction. They flattered and cajoled and beseeched him
for presents and more.

Money. But the checks hadn't been made out to her.
They had gone instead to her business manager. There
was a stack of them, too, adding up to over a million dollars. Made out to and endorsed by her *mother.*

She must have written the emails and letters, too, leading the man to believe that he'd had a relationship with
Piper. He hadn't lied to his cousin. And after Roarke had
seen all this correspondence and had probably found her

fingerprints on the ivory carved handle of the murder weapon, it was no wonder that he had tried and convicted her in his mind. What was a wonder was that he had let her live.

If she'd had the same amount of evidence proving that he had hurt someone she had loved, she might not have done the same. But then she had never really loved anyone.... Until now.

She had fallen for this man. But yet he wasn't a man. Like his cousin, he was a vampire. She read the last email she had supposedly sent Rick. In this one she hadn't asked for money or presents, she had asked for immortality. Her mother had wanted that for her?

But, why?

Then she remembered that she had started getting turned down for modeling assignments. That, four years ago, at twenty-two, Piper had already begun to look too old for some designers to use. So her mother, as resourceful as ever, had found a way that Piper would have never had to retire; she had found her eternal youth.

Immortality.

So when Rick Monterusso had attacked her, he had only been doing what he'd believed she'd wanted. He'd just been trying to turn her into a vampire.

And she had killed him....

Her stomach flipped and churned with the sick realization that she'd killed an innocent man. Even though

Rick Monterusso had been a vampire, he had also been a victim in another of her mother's mercenary schemes.

Four years ago Piper had done what she'd accused Roarke of doing now: she'd executed a man without giving him a chance to explain his actions. Instead of giving him a chance to talk she'd fought him, just as her email had warned him she would. In that last email she had told him to ignore her struggles, that immortality was what she really wanted.

Now all she wanted was the ability to believe again that it had all been a nightmare. That none of it had happened because she didn't know how she was going to handle the reality of having killed an innocent man. The cousin and best friend of the man she'd fallen in love with.

Roarke would never return that love. He would never be able to forgive her. When he returned, he would have his justice.

She dropped the stake back onto the desk. She wouldn't use it to defend herself. She had already hurt Roarke too much. She would never be able to forgive herself.

Usually Roarke wasn't sensitive to the cold. But something about this room, in the basement of an office building in Zantrax, Michigan, chilled him to the bone. Dr.

Davison had saved many lives here, but then there'd been those beyond saving.

Like Rick. He was gone. Nothing Roarke did was going to bring him back—not when the special surgeon to the Secret Vampire Society had failed.

Roarke shivered, glad now that he had done up the buttons on his shirt. He wished he'd grabbed his coat, too.

"Cold?" a deep voice asked.

"This is an operating room," he said, turning toward the doctor who'd entered through another door than the one Roarke had been watching. "Shouldn't it be warmer in here?"

"My patients usually don't care about the temperature," Dr. Davison pointed out.

The doctor's hair was more gray than black. He had already been in his forties when he'd been turned into one of the Secret Vampire Society. Until then he had been the only exception to the rule of no mortal being able to live after learning their secret. That was because they'd so desperately needed his services and that was why a member eventually turned him, so the society wouldn't lose him, and his special talent, to mortality.

The doctor studied Roarke, as if assessing him for injuries, before asking, "Are you hurt? Do you need my medical attention?"

"No."

"Then why are you here?"

The society was small enough to be close-knit. Davison knew who he was and how seldom he left his island.

"I left you a message," Roarke reminded him, "but you didn't call back."

The doctor shrugged. "I've been busy—haven't even listened to all my messages yet."

Roarke didn't have time for any more lies. "I want to talk to you about Patricia Reynolds."

Dr. Davison arched a dark brow and lied again. "I'm not familiar with the name."

"We've talked about her before, but you didn't tell me then that she's a patient of yours."

"If she's a patient, I can't discuss her with you," the special surgeon replied. "Doctor-patient confidentiality, you know."

Roarke snorted derisively at the weak attempt at avoiding his questions. "The Secret Vampire Society isn't held to privacy laws."

"There is no stricter privacy law than ours," Davison reminded him.

Had Roarke violated that law when he'd flown in front of Piper? He suspected not, but he needed confirmation. He needed to get the doctor talking, privacy be damned.

"Then just listen," Roarke suggested. "If Patricia Reynolds is a patient of yours, you're about to lose her."

"Is she hurt?" Ben asked, all concerned physician now.

"Not yet," Roarke said, "but she will be soon. I'm going to kill her."

"Damn it, Monterusso," Ben cursed him. "I told you she's not Piper."

"She said the same."

"So listen," the doctor urged him.

"Then she admitted that she really is Piper and that she killed my cousin."

Ben's breath, along with a pithy curse, hissed out between his clenched teeth. "You're lying."

Roarke shook his head. "I'm actually the only one who hasn't been lying."

Ben paced the small room, as if trying to escape the web of deceit he'd helped spin. "She wouldn't admit anything to you."

"She wouldn't tell the truth?"

The surgeon cursed again and then replied, "She doesn't know what the truth is. She doesn't even know what happened."

"It was just a nightmare," Roarke said. "You really convinced her of that."

"It was easier and safer for her to believe than the truth." He arched that damn brow again. "Easier and safer for you to believe it's all a nightmare, too."

Roarke slammed his fist onto the metal gurney between him and the doctor. "I want the truth. After four damn years of not knowing exactly what happened, I need to hear it all!"

"You're right. You should know." Ben settled onto the edge of the gurney, as if he needed to sit down just to tell it.

Fearing what he was about to learn, Roarke thought he might need to sit, too, but he just leaned back against the brick wall behind him. "Did my cousin attack her?"

Ben nodded. "He nearly killed her. She'd lost so much blood. She was out for weeks. I didn't think she'd come back."

His stomach pitched at the horrible thought of a dead Piper. And just a few short days ago, he'd wanted to be the one to kill her. "So she told me the truth about that."

Ben sighed. "I'm surprised she remembers any of that night."

"She's forgotten more than that night," Roarke shared. "She forgot that she had a relationship with my cousin."

"She didn't."

Roarke fisted his hand again but he didn't swing at the doctor or the gurney. "I saw the emails and letters between them."

"Check the email address again. It wasn't her. It was her mom—*adoptive* mom. She was using both Piper and your cousin," Ben explained. "She set the whole thing in motion."

"Why?"

Ben shrugged. "Greed. Desperation. Pure evil."

Roarke shuddered as anger surged through him. And finally he could direct that anger at the right person. This was the woman he needed to kill for what she'd done to Rick and for what she'd done to Piper. She'd promised to love and protect Piper, and had instead put her in grave danger for her own personal gain.

"She's gone," Ben said, as if he'd read Roarke's mind. "When she found them...like that...in Piper's apartment, she found my number on Rick's phone and called me. It was already too late for him, Roarke. I'm sorry...."

The surgeon had already told him that—four years ago. He'd just kept the rest from him to—rightfully—protect Piper. He was the first person who ever had. Roarke nodded in acceptance of the apology.

"I'm sorry," the doctor repeated. "But you know it was only a matter of time. Your cousin was reckless and impulsive. He never thought things through. Carrying that stake on him was the reason he died. If he hadn't had it on him..."

And now the guilt was all Roarke's. "What about the mom?" he asked, needing to know if the woman was really gone or if the surgeon was trying to protect her, too. "What happened to her?"

"Someone from the society learned what she'd done, what she knew..." Ben shrugged again, not overly concerned about the woman's death. "You know the rule."

And if anyone had posed a threat to the society, it had been that woman. He believed she was really gone.

"What about Piper?" he asked.

"She recovered."

He shook his head. "Then why did you prescribe her the pills? What are they?"

"You know about the pills?"

"I had to give her one," he said. "She passed out. I thought she was dead."

Ben sighed in resignation, as if giving up on the whole privacy thing. "I'm only telling you this because I don't think you really want to destroy her anymore. But there is only one way that you'll be able to kill Piper."

As he'd suspected, Roarke hadn't broken the Secret Society rule when he'd flown in front of her. She wasn't human. "She's a vampire?"

"Yes." The surgeon straightened his shoulders, as if he'd just shrugged off a heavy burden. "But she doesn't know it."

And telling her had just become Roarke's burden. "Why did you keep that from her?"

"I didn't think she could handle knowing it was all real, knowing that she'd killed a man."

"She's stronger than you think she is," Roarke said with pride and hope. He didn't really know her. Maybe she wouldn't be strong enough to accept the truth of what had happened and what she was.

Moments after saying goodbye to the surgeon, Roarke walked into his house. He found her in the den, toying with the sharp point of the hand-carved and finely honed stake.

Because Rick had always been getting into fights, Roarke had given that stake to Rick.

For protection. It was the worst kind of irony that it was how he'd actually died.

How could Roarke blame her when he was equally, if not more, to blame for what had happened to his cousin?

"Piper."

She tensed and clenched her fingers around the ivory handle of the stake. Was she going to use it as she had before—to protect herself? Would she use it to kill him?

That would be the ultimate irony for Roarke. But maybe it had served the purpose he'd intended it for; it had been used for protection and would be again. Her protection.

And that was most important to him now—now that he could accept what his feelings for her were. Love. But no warmth flooded him at the thought. Instead his blood chilled as a horrific thought occurred to him.

What if he told her what she was and she used that stake on herself?

Chapter 9

"I'm sorry," she said, her heart clenched with guilt. And love. A love that Roarke would never be able to return. He hated her. And with good reason. "I'm so sorry."

"You were only defending yourself," he said. He crossed the room and held his hand, palm open, over the desk.

He wanted the stake. But Piper couldn't release the handle. Instead she stared down at the sharpened stake with morbid curiosity.

"He wasn't trying to kill me," she said, tapping the tip of the stake on the thick folder. It sliced easily through the sheaf of papers. "He thought it was what I wanted."

"He was wrong."

"He was used, just like you thought," she said. "You were right about him."

"But I was wrong about you," he said. "None of this was *your* fault."

Somehow he'd learned what Piper fervently wished she had known four years ago. His cousin would be alive if she'd realized just how devious her mother could be. "Did you find her?"

"She's already gone."

On some level Piper had known that. Since the day she'd adopted her, that woman had never left her alone. Until that day Piper had awakened in that strange room.

"Is she why you went into hiding?"

"Partially," Piper admitted. But if the woman had been alive, she would have found her—just as Roarke had— no matter how well she'd hidden. "And then there was the nightmare that I couldn't forget…. Finding that man in my apartment…"

Now she knew that he'd had his own key. Hell, the lease had been in his name—not hers like she'd believed. She had been living an even bigger lie than she'd realized.

"You were hiding from potential stalkers, too," Roarke guessed, his deep voice so very gruff that he cleared it after speaking. It probably choked him up thinking about his cousin being mistaken for a deranged stalker.

She nipped at her lip. "I had them before. People who became obsessed with an image, with an air-brushed fantasy."

He leaned across the desk, his face close to hers. "It doesn't sound like you enjoyed modeling."

"I hated it," she confirmed. "The only thing I hated more was my mother."

"Then why didn't you get away from her?"

She dropped her gaze from his. A man like Roarke wouldn't understand her cowardice and helplessness. She stared down at the stake. It might have taken that to escape the woman. She hadn't been a vampire but she'd certainly been a bloodsucker. "I was afraid of her."

"You had every reason to fear her," he pointed out. "She was evil."

"After what happened," Piper shared, "I was afraid of everything. The dark. The light. My own shadow...."

"I'm sorry."

She flinched at his pity but then marveled at how he could feel it—how he could feel *anything* at all for her. "You're the only one who doesn't have any reason to be sorry," she said. "You've done nothing wrong."

He chuckled but with bitterness and no humor. "I have the most reason to be sorry."

Because he had believed her lie? Because he'd made love with her?

He gestured toward the weapon in her hand, and his fingers had a slight tremor to them. "I gave him that stake."

"Why?"

"For protection," he explained. "Rick was impulsive and hotheaded. He was always getting into fights." He reached out and closed his hand over hers. "He would have never lived forever—not the way he lived. If not you, someone else would have taken his immortality."

After everything he had lost, he was trying to make her feel better? She had already suspected that she'd fallen for him. Now she had no doubt that she was helplessly, hopelessly in love with Roarke Monterusso.

His face, all those handsome angles and hollows, was so close to hers. He stared at her as intensely as he had before, but she couldn't see any hatred in the rich brown depths of his soulful eyes.

"Why are you being so nice to me?" she asked.

If it was a trick, a way of bestowing justice for his cousin's death, it was far crueler than simply killing her. Because it gave her hope that he might be able to forgive her, and she knew that wasn't possible—not after everything she had done: the murder, the lies, the betrayal...

"You have every reason to hate me."

Like her fingers around the stake, his heart clenched at the pain and sorrow on her beautiful face. She was so racked with misery. "I don't hate you," he assured her. "I could never hate you."

"That's because you're such a good man."

He laughed at the compliment. "Oh, sweetheart, I am anything but a good man."

She glanced from the stake to his chest. "You're a vampire."

He was worried about his heart but not because he thought she might plunge that stake into it. But because he was afraid she might not return his feelings…because of what he was.

She didn't know that she was the same. And he didn't know how to tell her, not while she held the stake.

"Yes, I am a vampire."

She smiled wistfully. "You're going to live forever."

"Maybe," he agreed.

She dropped the stake, as if worried that he might consider that a threat to his immortality. She was only a threat to his happiness.

"I—I'm not supposed to know about you, am I?" she asked, the stammer back. "That's why Dr. Davison wanted me to forget about…everything."

"He was worried about you," he admitted, "worried that you might not be able to handle those memories." Could she handle knowing everything?

"I hate that I took a life," she said. "And you should hate me for taking that life."

"I could never hate you," he repeated and then he drew in a deep breath and told her why. "Because I love you."

Tears flooded her eyes; a couple brimmed over to cling to her long, golden lashes. "Don't…"

"Don't what?" he asked, his heart thudding heavy and hard with dread. He'd known that she might not want the love of an eternal creature.

"Don't lie to me," she murmured, her voice breaking with fear. "Don't lie about loving me."

Along with the file and the stake, the laptop and cell phone lay on his desk. So he couldn't say that he'd never lied to her. But he had never lied about his feelings.

Maybe he needed more than words to convince her of his love, though. Maybe he needed action….

He grabbed her hands and tugged her up from the chair. Then he led her around the desk. But he wasn't about to make love to her on the leather couch again. He lifted her in his arms and carried her up the stairs to his room. If she noticed that his feet didn't touch the treads, she made no comment.

Piper said nothing as she stood before him, at the foot of his bed. Her eyes were wide, and she swayed on her feet, trembling almost as uncontrollably as she had that first night they had made love. He picked her off her feet again and settled her onto the mattress.

"I'm not lying," he assured her as he followed down onto the bed. "I love you…."

She moved her head back and forth against his pillow, tangling her hair around her shoulders. "You can't."

"Why can't I love you?" he asked. "Because you're so beautiful." He kissed her lips, intending just to brush his mouth across hers. But passion ignited, and he deepened the kiss, sliding his tongue through her lips. He fought for control and pulled back. "You're so sweet. So generous. So loving. Why can't I love you?"

"Because of what I did," she said, "because of what I took from you. How would you ever be able to forgive me, let alone love me?"

"You defended yourself," he reminded her. "You were attacked—that's all you knew. You had to protect yourself. That warrants pride—not forgiveness."

Tears welled in her eyes again—of hopefulness now. "You do understand...."

He nodded, and the tightness eased slightly in his chest. "And I really do love you."

"Roarke..." Her voice cracked with emotion.

He levered himself up and tore off his shirt. Then he ripped open the zipper and his fly and kicked off his pants. His erection jutted toward her.

"I know you want me," she said. "But can you really love me?"

"I told you that it doesn't matter what happened in the past." He reached for her dress, tugging it up and over her head. She wore no bra beneath it and only thin cotton panties. "What matters is the future...."

He kissed her again. Deeply as he caressed her skin.

First he stroked his fingers just along the edge of her jaw and then down her throat to where her pulse pounded madly.

Was she scared of him? Or turned on?

He lowered his hands to her breasts, pressing his thumbs against her nipples. They pebbled, and she arched, pushing her breasts into his hands. And she moaned, parting her lips. She sucked his tongue deep into her mouth.

She wanted him. Even knowing what he was, she still wanted him.

More of that tightness in his chest eased as hope joined the love he felt for her. He pulled back from her kiss. "I love you...."

Heat flickered in her eyes, igniting those gold flecks so they glittered like sparks from a fire. "Roarke..."

He moved down her body, kissing her throat and then her breasts. After laving her peaked nipples with his tongue, he moved lower yet. He ripped off the panties and loved her with his mouth. He slipped his tongue inside her, and she clutched at his shoulders, rising off the bed.

"Roarke!" She sank her nails into his skin as she dragged him back up. Then she reached between them. Closing her hand around his erection, she guided him inside her.

He tensed, resisting the urge to thrust. "Don't rush this," he said. "Take your time...."

But she didn't listen. Instead she gripped his butt and pressed him against her. He slid deep inside her. She was wet and ready for him. If she could want him so much, maybe she could love him, too.

She arched and lifted her legs, wrapping them tight around his waist. And she met his every thrust, her muscles clutching at him, pulling him even deeper inside her. So deep that he didn't even know where she ended and he began; he had never been so close to anyone before. And he wondered why he had always been such a loner—when it was so much better to be a couple.

Ignoring the heaviness in his groin that begged for release, he stilled. And he waited until she opened her eyes and met his gaze, then he beseeched her, "Marry me."

Her breath audibly caught, and she tensed in his arms. "I'll only marry you if you can promise me forever."

"Of course—"

"Not human forever," she interrupted him. "Your forever. I want to spend eternity with you."

"You love me?"

Her lips curved into a slight smile. "From nearly the first moment I saw you." Her smile widened. "Even when I thought you were going to kill me...."

"I wouldn't have been able to do it," he assured her.

"Even when you hated me?"

"Even then. I've never hurt anyone," he said. "I usually keep to myself."

That smile kept curving her lips higher, making her eyes glitter even brighter. "Here on your private island."

He nodded. "It's easier than keeping secrets, than being with humans."

She tensed, as if insulted. She had no idea yet what she was. "You have to turn me."

"Are you sure you want this life?" he asked. "This isolation? And its limitations?" He needed to know if she could handle it...before he told her everything.

"I've been isolated and alone," she said.

"The past four years."

"Even before that, even when everyone knew who I was and watched my every move, I was alone. Maybe even more so than when I was in hiding," she said. "I don't want to be alone ever again. I want to be with you. Forever."

"Then bite me." It was an offer that, in all the centuries he'd lived, he had never made to another. No one had ever tasted his blood before.

Holding her against him, he rolled onto his back, so that she was on top, straddling him. Her skin paled, and she began to tremble. She pressed her palms to his chest, holding herself up. "I—I didn't hear you right. What did you say?"

"Bite me." At the thought of her fangs sinking into his flesh, he grew even harder and longer inside her.

Her eyes widened in shock. And fear...

Did she understand what he was telling her? Did she realize what she was?

She couldn't have heard him right. He couldn't mean...

Her trembling turned to shaking. It was happening.... Not only had she forgotten her pills, but she didn't even know where the hell they were. Not now. She couldn't pass out now. "I—I need that prescription...."

She glimpsed the bottle on the nightstand and leaned across Roarke's muscular chest, reaching for it. But he caught her wrist, holding her back. She was too weak to fight him now.

Was that what he'd waited for? Her weakest moment to take his vengeance. He hadn't really forgiven her. He didn't really love her. The thought hurt as badly as that stake through the heart must have hurt his cousin—because she felt torn apart.

"You don't need the pills," he said. "You need to bite me."

"I—I don't know what you mean...."

He tunneled his free hand into her hair and pressed her face into his neck. His fingers traced over that scar on her nape. Was it one scar or two? Whenever she touched it, she noted two separate points.

Two points?

She'd never been able to figure out what she'd been attacked with, what had caused her blood to spurt as it had. Fangs?

"I want you to bite me," he said, as if that explained anything at all.

She shuddered at the thought of doing to him what had been done to her. "No. I don't want to hurt you."

"You can't," he assured her. "Only a stake through my heart can really hurt me."

"B-but I can't...."

"You have to," he said.

Her trembling increased, her body beginning to jerk more violently.

"Now," he urged her, pressing her face tighter against his throat.

Her tongue flicked out, and she tasted the salty sweetness of his skin. And as she did, something happened. Her body stirred where they were joined, her muscles clenching him inside her.

But something happened in her mouth, too. Teeth grew—just two—into sharp points, digging into her lips. She pulled them back, opening her mouth wide.

"Bite me!" he yelled. And instead of fear, his voice was gruff with excitement.

He wanted this. And she wanted to please him. So she sank her fangs into his throat. Blood spurted over her tongue. She moved to pull back, scared that she had actually hurt him.

He groaned, but it wasn't a groan of pain but ecstasy. He clasped her to him and ordered, "Drink."

She wouldn't have thought she could…. She considered it disgusting. But it wasn't. It was rich and sweet and more intimate even than their making love.

Because now his blood flowed through her, pumping through her heart now as it had pumped through his. They were connected more intimately than humans could ever connect.

She wasn't human. Must not have been for the past four years…

She couldn't think about that now, though. She could do nothing but feel.

As she drank, he began to thrust inside her. His control snapped, his pace frenzied. He groaned and writhed beneath her. His hands clutched her hips, grinding into her, as he came.

And he screamed her name. Her real name. "Piper!"

She pulled back and licked her lips. "Bite me," she invited him.

He grinned. But he accepted her offer. As his fangs sank into her neck, his body hardened inside her again. She rocked her hips against him, riding him as the pressure wound tight within her. He sucked at her, and she came, that sensation releasing the pressure inside her.

The orgasm was intense, shuddering through her so passionately that it caused her to nearly convulse.

He pulled his fangs from her and clutched her close. "Are you all right?"

Her heart beat the same rhythm as his, with the same blood. She settled against his chest with a soft sigh. "I love you."

"Will you love me forever?" he asked.

"Forever and always."

"You understand, then?" he prodded her.

Her lips curved into a smile. "I was turned...four years ago."

He nodded, his chin bumping gently against her head. "And no one told me?"

"Dr. Davison didn't know if you could handle the truth."

"I'm stronger than he thought."

"That's what I told him," he said. "You're stronger than even you realized."

Superhumanly strong. Everything made so much sense to her now. Felt so right. "This has been one hell of a vacation," she said. "I'm only a few days in and I've already gotten engaged."

"We'll get married before your vacation is over," he said. "I can't wait."

"We have forever," she reminded him. "I'm not going back to work for E. Graves. I'm sick of the long hours.

Of the hypervigilant confidentiality and secrecy. I never even found out what the *E* stood for."

His sexy mouth curved into a grin. "Empty."

"Empty Graves?"

"Their clients are all members of the Secret Vampire Society," he explained.

She giggled. "You really are their oldest and richest client. But don't worry, I'm not marrying you for your money."

"My body?" he asked, growing hard inside her yet again. He was insatiable—nearly as insatiable as she was.

"I'm marrying you for your love," she said. "Nobody has ever loved *me* before."

"I'll love you forever and always," he promised her.

Tears stung her eyes. She blinked them back, too happy to cry. So she laughed instead. "And maybe I'm marrying you a little bit for your island."

"Really?" He grinned.

"Yes, living here will be like taking a permanent vacation." This life seemed like a fantasy compared to the life she had been living.

"Sounds like you're really enjoying this vacation," he teased.

"Definitely," she agreed. She was happier than she ever could have imagined she could be. *"Work sucks."*

* * * * *

HONOUR CALLS

Caridad Piñeiro

Chapter 1

Michaela had been tracking the vampire since she'd sensed the elder during her scouting mission in Central Park.

He wasn't the one she sought, but the heightened thrum of his power told her he had just killed. Reason enough to pursue him until she could find the right vampire and dispatch him.

Then and only then could she leave New York City for a kinder, gentler place.

She discovered the elder vamp's victim just beyond one of the jogging paths. The kill was fresh, the scent of the elder strong on the female runner who had been tossed into the underbrush like garbage. As Michaela bent to examine the jogger's body in its shredded clothes, she realized the vampire had not just been content to drain the woman of blood. The victim had been sexually assaulted as well and in the most brutal of ways—ripped apart by the vampire sating his lust.

Michaela opened her senses to pick up every last scintilla of the elder's trail, from the metallic taste of the victim's blood on his breath to the unique wake of energy the immortal left behind.

She reached the southern end of the park and something ahead of her spooked one of the horses attached to a hansom cab waiting along Central Park South. The animal reared up, hooves flailing.

She darted behind the cab and caught a glimpse of a blurry figure speeding through Grand Army Plaza. As she raced to the fountain in the center of the square, the pulse of undead power beat at her more strongly, signaling that she was getting closer to the ancient vampire.

Another indistinct flash weaving through the pedestrians on Fifth Avenue confirmed the immortal was within her reach.

She focused on that vague shape, keeping a watchful eye and a respectful distance as she chased after him. She could not engage the vampire elder out in the open where either humans or other vampires might see what was happening. To do so might expose her presence in the city and possibly bring down the wrath of the vampire council.

Despite her caution, the elder must have sensed that he was being followed.

He increased his speed, weaving in and out of the humans on the sidewalks, climbing to the rooftop of a building in lower Midtown Manhattan and leaping from one structure to the next before dropping to the ground. The vampire moved at an almost frantic pace, as if he knew the nature of her mission.

Michaela kept up her determined pursuit, patiently waiting for the moment when the time would be right. She dodged pedestrians and vehicles as the vampire attempted to elude her, well aware that she had to act before the immortal reached the safe haven of the Blood Bank.

If he made it there, she would have to pull back and wait for another night. There were too many undead in that place to risk a confrontation within its doors.

Too many, and she was just one against them.

She drove back the crush of loneliness that nearly choked her, reminding herself that there was no other way. Her life held too much death and destruction; it hindered any kind of personal commitments.

The few people she had allowed to get close had run away when they discovered the truth about her existence.

The truth about her.

Or they'd ended up dead.

In Union Square, the vampire geared down to human

speed, using that pace to lose himself amongst the many mortals still present in the park. The beat of the humans' life forces and their scents served to disguise his presence.

Michaela paused at the far edge of the square, examining the walkways, attempting to separate the humans from her undead prey, but she was unable to pin down the immortal. She waited, hopeful that once the elder moved beyond the boundaries of the crowded area, she would be able to pick up his presence once again.

Her wait was futile.

Long minutes passed with no activity that she could discern.

She finally acknowledged that she had been bested by his subterfuge, but that didn't mean the chase was over.

She knew just where the vampire was likely to go.

If she could beat him there, she still might be able to take him out before he reached the safety of the nightclub.

Hustling at breakneck speed, she arrived at the mouth of the small cobblestoned street that led to the Blood Bank. At the club's door was the ever-present vampire bouncer and crowd of humans waiting to mingle with both wannabe and real vampires. Not to mention the occasional shape-shifter brave enough to cross into bloodsucker territory.

Michaela had never understood the human fascination with the undead, the near veneration for the amoral creatures who had taken so much from her and others.

Vampires weren't meant to be idolized, she thought.

They were meant to be exterminated.

As she felt the presence at her back, she realized she had guessed right about the vampire elder.

She had barely half turned to face him when he lashed out at her, nails as sharp as eagle's talons raking across her jacket. The leather did its job, keeping his nails from tearing into her flesh.

Bending backward, she avoided the deeper thrust of another vicious swipe toward her midsection and then dropped down to sweep the vampire's feet out from under him.

He landed with a thick thud, while she was immediately back on her feet after a quick jerk and launch of her body, a nice sharp wooden stake in her hand.

"Not what you thought, fang boy?" she taunted as she stood, arms akimbo, above the prone body of the stunned elder.

With a swift move of his own, the vampire surged to his feet, fully transformed. His eyes glowed with a piercing teal-blue light. Long deadly fangs erupted from his mouth and ended at a point below his chin. Such a prodigious length of tooth testified to his longevity. The strength of his elder power jabbed at her senses, threatening just by its very existence.

This vamp would not go quickly, she thought as the elder issued a warning growl and lunged at her again, beginning a dance that could end in only one way...

With one of them dead.

Frustration clawed at his gut as he stared at the picture of the latest victim found torn apart in a downtown alley. As he flipped through the status report on the investigation, a familiar name appeared in the FBI case report.

The Blood Bank.

FBI Assistant Director in Charge Jesus Hernandez expected a fair share of crime in a city like New York, but judging from how often the edgy Goth bar appeared in the reports provided to him, the Blood Bank appeared to be crime central.

He supposed the easy way to find out more about the club would be to ask any of the agents in his bureau what to make of the place. But he hadn't gotten to be one of the top agents in the New York City Bureau by taking the easy way. On the contrary. He believed in personally getting involved when it was necessary.

As he picked up the file again and examined the photo of the body parts found a couple of blocks from the bar, he raked his hand through his short-cropped hair and blew out a disgusted breath.

He'd read the witness statements. Tales of creepy happenings and Goth clubgoers who might be a little more than they seemed.

Even his top agent—Diana Reyes—seemed to believe in the possibility of an underworld that was less than human.

It was definitely time for a visit to the Blood Bank to get his own impression.

Memorizing the address, he rose from his desk and slipped on his suit jacket. For a moment he considered going by his apartment to change, certain he would look out of place in his expensive suit.

But his apartment would be seriously empty. His last lover had moved out nearly a year earlier, complaining about the time he devoted to his job. Considering that the living room still boasted only the recliner and the plasma television he'd bought after she'd left, she had probably been right.

Plus, as he mentally reviewed the contents of his closet, he knew he had nothing suitable to wear to a Goth bar anyway.

Best just to drive by the place, scope it out and decide what to do next, he told himself. For good measure, he checked to make sure his gun was loaded and tucked snugly into the holster at his side.

The one thing he knew about the Blood Bank: it wasn't the kind of place you went without protection.

Chapter 2

Shit. The small street on which the Blood Bank was located was not wide enough for the passage of a car. His intent to just drive by wouldn't be possible.

As Jesus rounded the block for the third time, he scoped out a free parking spot a short distance away and then headed on foot toward the club.

He hadn't gone more than a few feet before the heat and humidity of the August Manhattan night had him sweating beneath the weight of his suit jacket. Since he was armed, removing the jacket wasn't possible. He was starting to regret that he hadn't gone by his apartment to at least change into a T-shirt and jeans.

Swiping at a line of perspiration along his brow, he paused at the mouth of one of the older streets in the city.

It looked more like an alley, which seemed appropriate for the place he was about to visit.

Ahead of him and about four small blocks down was a line of people at a nondescript building—the Blood Bank, he assumed. The line was relatively long, considering the hour, and it was filled with a decidedly rough-looking crowd clad in black leather and metal. That at least was not very different from what he had expected.

As he proceeded along the cobblestones, bright with the light from a full moon and uneven beneath his shoes, he kept a wary eye on the smaller, narrower side streets and tight gaps between the buildings. It was at the mouth of one of those alleys that the last body had been found.

Or at least, parts of the body.

A grunt, loud and painful sounding, snared his attention. Two turn-of-the-century brick buildings, built so closely together that the moonlight did little to illuminate the area between them, did a good job of hiding whatever activity was going on in the gap.

Another grunt was followed by the din of metal trash cans crashing together.

Definitely a fight and, judging from the sounds of it, someone was getting their ass kicked.

Jesus pulled out his Sig and advanced to the opening of the alley. He took a step within and let his eyes adjust to the lack of light, revealing the two people locked together in combat. One was tall and much bigger than the other, and as they grappled together, the light from a side-door lamp illuminated their features.

The smaller one was a woman, while the other...

Eerily bright blazing eyes shot a glance his way while long white fangs gleamed under the artificial light of the lamp. The creature growled at him, the sound like the rumble of a mountain lion, but then turned back toward the woman.

Jesus blinked, unable to believe what he was seeing, but another glimpse of the creature's face confirmed what he was—a vampire. Or at least, someone posing as one.

The much smaller woman had her arms braced against the creature's jacket, trying to keep those wickedly long fangs away from her face, but with the vampire's greater height and bulk, Jesus feared she might be fighting a losing battle.

No, he cursed as she continued with the fight, totally ignoring his presence.

The creature spun the woman around and as the light swept over her face, he could tell she was young. Mid-twenties, he guessed before she whirled out of sight again, struggling to break away from the demon's grasp.

With a quick upward jab of her arm, the woman snapped the creature's head back. It emitted a louder growl, but the woman's blow did little to slow the demon. It reached behind to grab the woman by the scruff of her neck and whip her against a brick wall. She hit with a thick thud and fell to the ground dazed, prompting Jesus to action.

"FBI. Stop or I'll shoot," he called out, training his gun on the demon as it took a step toward her.

The thing actually halted and looked at him. What he guessed passed for a smile erupted on its face, but then a second later the demon reeled back, grabbing at its chest with long taloned fingers.

The woman had buried a wooden stake deep into its chest.

Shock filled the creature's face, mirroring Jesus's own surprise as he realized she had just killed someone...

No, make that some*thing*, before his eyes.

Blood leaked from around the edges of the stake, staining the off-white shirt the man-beast wore. It stood, hands flailing, long nails clacking against the stake, disbelief on its face before the look became blank and the creature dropped to the ground.

"One down, too many more to go," the woman said, her voice deeper than what he would have expected from someone so petite. She nudged the creature's body with the toe of her black boot and then bent to examine it, as if to make sure she had finished the job.

One down, huh? He turned his gun on her and warned, "FBI. Put your hands up."

She faced him and just for a moment he thought he

saw a hint of fang at her mouth and a glow in her gaze, but then she stepped into the puny shaft of light from the side lamp on the building.

Her face was anything but demonlike.

She stood before him, her hands outstretched at her sides, her totally human face serene and beautiful, reminding him of the pictures of the saints his mother used to have on the wall of their fifth-floor walk-up apartment. Of course, the black leather encasing her slim body was anything but saintlike.

Too beautiful and too young, it occurred to him as she took a step toward him.

"FBI. Stop or I'll shoot." He held his gun steady and aimed straight at her head.

A wistful smile played across her face as she stepped toward him tentatively. "This is none of your business. The FBI has no power here."

"Here? This is New York City, lady, and in case you didn't notice, I've got the gun and the badge." For good measure, he drew aside the edge of his jacket to reveal the silver-and-gold badge clipped to his belt.

She surprised him by laughing, a sexy husky sound that pulled at his gut, confusing him. His confusion only increased with her next words.

"This may be New York, but that gun and badge won't help you against vampires. Especially ones like him."

She motioned to the body on the ground. "Or the ones up the block in the Blood Bank."

Certifiable, he thought, because now that he had time to think, he knew the demon on the ground had to be a man in costume. Vampires were not real and a stake to the chest would kill most anybody. But then the body on the ground did a funny little twitch and began to shrivel up before his eyes.

Following his gaze, she peered over her shoulder. With a shrug she said, "The older they are the faster they dry up. Harder to kill, though. Age makes them stronger."

He shook his head and, for the barest of seconds, closed his eyes to refocus, blaming what he had seen on the lack of light. But when he returned his gaze to the body, it was still slowly disappearing, sublimating like dry ice, and the stake remained buried deep in the middle of its chest.

When he looked back at the woman, he realized she had walked right up to him. The barrel of his gun was barely an inch from her face. Her very young and attractive face.

After she finished perusing him, she wrinkled her nose and said, "You don't strike me as the type to believe in anything that doesn't go by the book."

She was right, which frustrated him; despite his better judgment, her power and self-assurance called to him.

As their gazes met, he detected loneliness in her.

The same emotion that lived in him, thanks to the demands of his job.

Fascinated, he said, "So make me believe."

She smiled and motioned to the entrance of the alley behind him.

"Follow me."

Chapter 3

Michaela watched the bewilderment on his face fade and be replaced by something…

Dangerous, she thought, sensing his attraction to her, sensing the want in him that could make him risky. Somehow that wasn't enough to deter her from fulfilling his challenge. She would make him believe.

When he holstered his weapon, she brushed past him, trying to ignore her response. She wasn't usually the suit-and-tie type, not to mention that he was older than the other men who'd been in her life.

Of course, that was because dead or gone was her typical type. Not old. Especially since old was something she would never become.

Ignoring her contradictory emotions, she put a sexy roll in her walk as she moved toward the Blood Bank.

A quick glance over her shoulder told her that he was totally buying in to her challenge. A thrill of anticipation shot through her.

She smiled, pleased that he seemed intrigued, and headed straight to the bouncer. The big man glared at her until she allowed a hint of her gleaming gaze to emerge. He hesitated, maybe sensing the difference in her power, but then she repeated the action and added a bit of fang.

The bouncer relented and, with a broad sweep of his arm, lifted the red velvet rope for her and the FBI agent. As they slipped beneath the boundary, the bouncer emitted a low growl, as if to warn her that the two of them were not fully welcome.

She ignored him and plowed forward, the FBI agent close to her back. After they entered and moved out of hearing of the bouncer, he leaned forward and asked, "Bouncer is a vampire?"

His tone was laced with disbelief, but she nodded as she navigated through the crowd with him nearly plastered to her back. The bar was full tonight, packed with dozens of human Goth and wannabe vampire types, as well as the real deal. Colored spotlights skittered unevenly over the crowd. On the small stage at the far end of the club, glaring light illuminated a band playing loudly and aggressively, half singing half screaming indeterminate lyrics. The strong thumping bass and heavy drumbeats pulsed across the club and incited those on the dance floor to thrash and jump in rhythm.

The lights and noise bothered her senses. She hurried to the back of the club where it was quieter and dimmer, creating a feeling of false intimacy. The area was crowded, but in the farthest corner was an empty table for two.

She sat down with her back to the wall, not wanting any surprises. Unexpectedly, he plopped down right beside her rather than across from her.

When she arched a brow in question, he shrugged and said, "Don't want to have to watch my back, either."

Understandable and yet provoking.

His physical presence was difficult to ignore, and his dark brown eyes seemed fathomless in the dim light.

She hoped he would not prove as fascinating as he appeared.

"So you expect me to believe the bouncer was a vampire and that there are other ones here, as well?" he said, examining the interior of the club.

There were definitely vampires present. She sensed the push of their undead force, but before she got into proving it, she wanted him to buy her a drink. She was low on cash and most men disappeared once they discovered the truth around them.

The truth about her.

Raising her hand, she signaled a waitress.

When the young woman arrived, Michaela said, "Cuervo shooter."

Slipping a glance at her companion, she realized he was checking out the waitress, in a vamp way, not that she expected him to pick up on the signs so quickly. She shook her head.

He understood and ordered a shooter, as well.

The waitress hesitated and Michaela explained, "You're new. You've got to pay up front."

He snorted in disgust, but quickly dug into his pocket, peeled off a twenty from a moderate wad of cash and tossed the bill on the scarred black Formica table. The waitress immediately scooped up the money and walked away to place their orders.

"Must get nice clientele in here," he said as he tucked his money into his pocket. The motion pulled his suit jacket back, exposing the butt of his gun. At an adjacent table, one of the patrons noticed the weapon and quickly scurried away.

Jesus wondered why the man felt compelled to run. In his line of business, it was an obvious sign of guilt, but in here…

For all the patrons' Goth rebelliousness, they were quite uniform in their manner of dress; lots of black, from the leather and jeans to their hair.

"You said you'd make me truly believe," he reminded

his companion just as the waitress came to the table with their drinks.

The waitress placed the lime, saltshaker and shots of Cuervo on the table. His companion bit into the lime, skipped the salt and then downed the tequila in one gulp before ordering another.

"Thirsty?" he asked as he paid in advance once again.

"Once guys see how things are, most of my dates don't last beyond the first drink." She fidgeted with the empty shot glass.

"Didn't realize that buying you a drink made this a date," he said, perplexed by her, by the self-assurance on the surface that seemed to hide a well of vulnerability.

"Not your usual type, I suspect," she said and fully faced him.

Not his type?

He wondered about that as he sipped his shot of tequila and studied her. Her dark, nearly black hair fell in choppy layers against her roundish face. Cerulean-blue eyes bore an exotic slant and hinted at extreme intelligence, while pale, creamy skin appeared to be as soft as satin sheets.

The black leather jacket she wore fit tight against her body, accentuating both her slimness and slightness of stature, but the tank top beneath the jacket exposed the lushness of her curves.

He imagined exploring those curves. Raising that lean, strong body against his and slipping within.

His type, he thought, fighting back his body's response. Now that they were up close, he guessed her to be at least a decade younger than his thirty-eight years.

"Don't have a type and I'm not the kind to drink and run," he said, taking another sip of the Cuervo to quell the desire awakening within him.

She laughed, the tone of her merriment rich and uninhibited. It had been a long time since he had allowed himself that kind of freedom, but she clearly was not one to hold back.

That only intrigued him more, especially when she challenged him with, "You may be the kind to run after you see what goes on in here."

Elegantly raising her hand, she gestured to the far corners of the club, close to where they sat. He could barely make out the shadows of people engaged in various activities.

Leaning close to him, she said in a hushed tone, "Look carefully if you dare."

Her warm breath against the base of his neck was sweet. He imagined the kiss of that breath elsewhere and decided it warranted the risk.

"I dare."

Chapter 4

He followed the surprisingly long line of her index finger, which pointed to a doorway guarded by a muscular bouncer. He was another very pale man who exuded a power that Jesus could feel even across the distance separating them.

Yet one more vampire? he wondered before turning his attention to the door.

In the distant corners, so dark they were almost devoid of light, he finally recognized the activity going on.

Sexual, he thought as he watched one woman writhing against someone, her legs wrapped around a waist. Heat raced through him as he imagined his companion riding him like that, but he quickly tamped down the thought.

Beside that couple was another in an intimate embrace. The woman straddled a man's thigh, grinding against it, clearly seeking satisfaction. Her companion had one hand tangled in her long blond tresses. Before Jesus's eyes the man pulled the woman's head back, exposing the long line of her neck. There was a familiar weirdly bright blue-green gleam in the man's gaze and a flash of white fang before the man buried his face against the woman's throat.

Jesus imagined he could hear her sharp gasp of surprise. He saw the jerk of her body, confirming that he wasn't imagining the attack. When the man shifted his head for the barest of seconds, a dark line of blood became visible against the woman's skin.

Instinctively Jesus began to rise, determined to interrupt the assault, but his companion laid a hand on his arm.

"Don't get involved. She came here for that and the vampire knows the rules."

Vampires did not exist and what he had seen so far that night could be explained by...

He didn't know what would explain it, but surely there was a rational reason somewhere.

"The rules?" he asked, sitting back down and picking up his shot glass. He hoped her answer would provide a more plausible explanation for what he had just seen.

"No siring the humans in public. I'm even surprised he put the bite on her like that. Foley—"

"Foley?" He finally downed his shot, wincing as the heat burned down his throat.

"Foley's the owner of this place. He usually has a 'no public biting' policy," she replied easily, but a furrow of worry was etched in the middle of her forehead.

"Not good that they're getting so bold," she added.

The waitress came over at that moment with their next round of drinks and he placed another order.

"Not running?" she asked as she picked up the wedge of lime.

"Not sure. But before I make up my mind…who are you?" He dragged the shot glass close and slowly shifted it between his hands.

She wiped the lime juice from her hands against her jeans and then introduced herself. "Michaela Ramirez."

He eyeballed her hand, then shifted his gaze back to her face as he took her hand in his much larger one. "Jesus Hernandez."

Raking her gaze over his attire, she said, "Special Agent Hernandez?"

"Assistant Director in Charge," he corrected.

"The boss man."

It explained the air of power about him and confirmed what Michaela had already suspected—he was the kind of man who knew how to take care of himself. But it also meant he was the kind of man who would not understand the mission to which she had dedicated her life, and her eventual death.

He played by the rules. Her existence defied such constraints.

Arching a brow upward, he asked, "And what is it that you do? You know, your job when you're not busy staking the undead."

She didn't have an answer she thought he would accept, so she took her time, perusing him once again.

His suit was expensive and well tailored to his big, muscular body. Despite his age, thick dark brown hair showed not one hint of gray. The few wrinkles on his face were the smile lines at the edges of his very sensual mouth and dark brown eyes.

Eyes that twinkled with amusement at her inspection, at her stalling tactic.

Surprising.

"What's a guy like you doing in a place like this?" she asked, wanting to shift the focus back to him.

"Maybe starting to believe."

He downed his shot of tequila just as the waitress brought the third round.

When she reached for the lime and shot glass, he covered her hand with his deliciously warm one. His palm was rough against the back of her hand. She imagined that roughness rubbing other parts of her body and a

hot flush erupted within her, dampening the spot between her legs.

"Sure you can handle another? You're kind of…small,"
he said, dragging his gaze over her figure.

His look lingered at her breasts, yanking a more obvious response from her. Her nipples beaded into tight
points, which only convinced her that it had been way
too long since she had last satisfied herself.

Way too long, she thought as she turned her hand and
grasped his, running her fingers along the fine hairs on
the back of his wrist. She stroked his bare skin, edging
beneath the cuff of his shirt.

"You'd be surprised at how much I can handle." She
grinned when she felt the tremor beneath her fingers.

Jesus held his breath as her simple touch jerked his
body to life. It had been so long since he had done this
little dance with a woman. He wanted to confirm that
he wasn't misreading the signals.

"Just need to make sure you know what *you're* doing
in a place like this," he said and half turned in his chair
to be certain that he didn't miss a millisecond of her reaction.

"What I'm doing?" She looked down to where her
hand still stroked the sensitive skin at his wrist.

He took her question as an invitation and grasped her
hand in his. He noticed the slight chill of her skin and

wondered at the reason for it, but he thrust aside the niggle of concern.

"Nervous?" he asked, narrowing his eyes to read her reaction. If anything, she'd been assured, strong and complex so far. He was anticipating experiencing more of the same from her.

"Just...cold," she answered and twined her fingers with his. "As for where this is going... Are *you* sure you're ready to handle all of this and more?"

Jesus shot a look around the club and then back at her. She seemed so much a part of this place and yet removed from it. That might explain the hint of loneliness he had sensed in her.

"If the 'and more' involves the two of us alone together somewhere, I'm ready."

Shaking her head, she smiled, but there was no mistaking the sadness in her voice as she said, "You may be sorry you said that."

He cupped her face with his free hand and explored the soft skin of her cheek. He shifted his thumb downward over her full lips. Her warm, sweet breath exploded against his finger, as if she was shocked by the intimacy of his touch.

"If I promise not to be sorry, can you do the same?"

She sucked in a shaky breath and he saw how her pupils widened with desire. Against the pad of his thumb, her lips quivered before she worried her bottom lip with her perfectly white teeth.

Perfectly white *fangless* teeth. The thought brought some relief that he wasn't about to engage one of the supposed undead in what he hoped to be some very satisfying sex.

"Well?" he prompted, her delay both worrisome and frustrating.

She released her bottom lip and finally said, "I won't be sorry."

Chapter 5

"Good." He rose and stood by the table, obviously waiting for Michaela to choose where they would go for their tryst.

"Where" definitely not being the flophouse where she was staying while she completed her mission. She suspected that Jesus, too, would not volunteer where he lived for their encounter.

Which left only one immediate choice—one of the back rooms at the Blood Bank.

She stood and inclined her head toward the rear of the club. "We can pay for a private room in the back."

Jesus narrowed his eyes, seemingly doubtful, but he didn't hesitate to follow her as she led him to the bouncer by the door. He stood with tattooed and muscular arms across a broad chest barely covered by the metal-studded leather vest he wore. He kept an unwelcoming glare on his face until Jesus reached into his pocket and extracted some cash.

"What will it be for the best room you have?" Jesus asked.

The bouncer looked at her and replied with a snicker, "I guess such a fine *lady* only deserves the best. A hundred dollars until dawn."

"Dawn?" he asked, even as he peeled off the bills and handed them to the man.

"A virgin, are you?" the bouncer said with a sneer, but Michaela shot her hand up to silence him.

"The key is all we need from you."

When he held out the large brass key, she snagged it from his grasp and rushed into the hallway containing the private rooms.

The hall was narrow and relatively short. The walls were painted black and seemed to devour the light from the dated wall sconces located near each door. The floor beneath their feet was carpeted with a thick shag rug in deep crimson. It was matted down in the center, testifying to the traffic that passed this way.

Jesus followed Michaela as she checked the number on the key against the ones on the wooden doors of the rooms. Finally, at the door farthest away from the club and all its noise, a brass number eight marked the room as theirs.

"What did he mean that we had the room until dawn?" Jesus asked, towering over her. His physical presence rattled her calm, causing her to falter while she tried to unlock the door. He immediately covered her hands with his and helped steady her as she turned the key and opened the door.

She had heard about the Blood Bank's private rooms, but she had never been in one. The room was surprisingly more than what she had expected.

A queen-size four-poster bed took up one side of the space, the bed's surface lushly appointed with a satin comforter, an assortment of pillows and remarkably clean sheets.

But it was the accessories on the opposite side of the room that subsequently snared and held both her attention and Jesus's.

He walked to the wall where an assortment of whips, chains, cuffs, knives and other toys were conveniently displayed. Running his index finger along a pair of fur-lined wrist cuffs, he shot her a half-lidded glance as he once again asked, "Why dawn?"

"Why do you think?" She removed the wrist cuffs from the wall and examined them more carefully, even going so far as to undo the strap on one of them.

"It's when the vamps go home after a night of play," he said.

A rough edge tinged his voice. Was it from fear or

from imagining their own night of play, fur-lined wrist cuffs included?

"It takes a lot of trust, don't you think?" she asked, slipping on one cuff and holding out her arm the way one might do when examining a bracelet.

It would take a lot of trust, Jesus thought. More trust than existed in their newborn relationship. He reached out and slipped off the cuff, tossed it aside, encircled her fine-boned wrist with his hand and urged her close.

"Tell me what you want, Michaela." He enjoyed the contradictions she presented, but he needed something concrete on which to begin this night, on which to— perhaps—build something more. Because he suspected that with a woman as complex as Michaela, one night just wouldn't do it.

She laid a hand on his chest and stepped so close she had to tip her head back to peer up at his greater height. Softly she rubbed her hand against the fabric of his shirt and said, "I want normal."

The longing in her voice was unmistakable. His own yearning responded in sympathy.

It had been way too long since he had done normal.

Gingerly, aware that she was a little skittish and might bolt, he eased his arm around her waist. Slowly he urged her to move that last little bit, until her body brushed his. But he moved her no farther, not wanting to intimidate or overpower. Somehow, he understood that Michaela needed equal footing.

She needed a partner, he thought as he bent from his greater height to put his face level with hers.

"I think I can do normal," he teased, a playful grin on his face as he sought to begin her night of respite.

Their evening of pleasure.

A smile crept to one corner of her mouth. She cradled his cheek and traced the lines of his mouth with her thumb, shifted it to the dimple beside his lips.

"You have a nice smile. You've done it often during your life," Michaela said. At his puzzled look, she slipped the pad of her index finger across the faint lines on his face.

His grin turned wickedly sexy. "There's something to be said for maturity in a man."

Dipping one hand while bringing the other upward, she placed both on the cotton of his shirt, exploring the gloriously sculpted muscle beneath. As she closed the final distance between their bodies, the hard jut of his impressive erection pushed against the flatness of her belly.

She pressed against him, shifting her hips back and forth. "Maturity doesn't seem to have affected your 'something,' because it's definitely saying—"

"I want you, Michaela. You're...unique." He buried

his hand in her shoulder-length hair and cupped the back of her head.

Unique?

He couldn't even begin to guess just how different she was, but she had asked for normal tonight. Any explanations could wait until she'd experienced the wonder that he had promised.

"You sweet talker. I bet you charm all the women with lines like that."

The playfulness faded from his face, replaced by an intensity that nearly stole her breath. "Not much for talk, Michaela. I'm an action kind of guy."

At the back of her head came the gentle pressure of his hand, urging her to her tiptoes until his lips were a breath away from hers.

"Are you an action kind of woman?" he asked and his tequila-spiced breath spilled against her lips, creating an intense pull of need within her.

"Yes," she replied.

Chapter 6

A shudder ripped through his body at her answer. He knew then that no matter how much she wanted a normal night, there was one thing he couldn't do...

"I'm not sure I can go slow," he said.

She chuckled and tipped her head upward once again to lock on his gaze.

"That's okay. You can go slow later."

Later, he thought, and groaned as he imagined taking her again and again until the dawn came and maybe even beyond that. But for now...

He slipped his arm beneath her buttocks and raised her until they were face-to-face.

"I think later sounds great." He smiled, which prompted her broad, unrestrained grin. A smile so real and inviting that he had to feel it against his lips. He traced the edges of her welcoming smile with a series of impatient little kisses until the contact wasn't enough for him.

Or for her.

She bracketed his head with her hands, kept him close, as she tasted him and then slipped her tongue into his mouth. Raised her legs and wrapped them around his waist, welcoming him elsewhere.

Jesus kept on kissing her even as he walked with her toward the bed on the other side of the room. When he bumped the mattress with his legs, he dipped down to let her sit on its edge. Michaela grabbed his lapels, the fabric expensive beneath her hands, although she itched to have the more luxurious texture of his skin against her palms.

She urged the jacket from his shoulders, exposing the well-worn and cared-for leather of his holster, the menacingly black grip of his gun and the slick cotton of his shirt. Grasping the fabric, she jerked, sending buttons flying but accomplishing just what she wanted.

As the shirt hung open, she laid her hands on his skin. Hot like a winter fire. Surprisingly smooth since he had little chest hair. The rich caramel color of his skin matched the warm brown of his eyes, which were glittering brightly as he glanced down at her, a deliciously receptive grin on his face.

"I guess I'm not the only one who can't go slow."

"Guess not," she said, wrapping her thighs around his legs once again, imprisoning him tightly. Leaning back against the soft surface of the bed. Challenging him to action.

He didn't disappoint.

He teasingly brushed his hands across her breasts before helping her ease the leather jacket from her body. As the jacket came off, he tossed it to the side, seemingly ignoring the unexpected weight and metallic thud that hinted at some kind of weaponry in the garment. Instead, he immediately grabbed the edge of the black tank top she wore, pulled it up and over her head and exposed her upper body to his gaze.

Between her legs came the jump of his erection. He emitted a low rumbling moan a moment before he put his fingers at the front clasp of her black bra. The slight tremor of his fingers confused her.

"Jesus?" she asked and laid her hands over his.

His name on her lips nearly undid him; it had been so long since a woman had said it with such a mix of need and doubt.

He wanted all doubt gone.

Needed all doubt gone.

"Be sure, Michaela."

She slipped her fingers beneath his hands at the clasp of her bra and parted the fabric to reveal herself to him.

"I'm sure, Jesus. Incredibly sure."

He dragged his hands away from her breasts, to her shoulders, where he ran his thumbs across the fragile lines of her collarbone before inching down the straps of her bra and removing it. Then he slowly passed the pads of his fingers down the softness of her skin until he cupped her breasts. He ran his thumbs across the hard peaks of her nipples, intent on savoring all the differences between them: the paleness of her skin against the darker tones of his; the size of him, immense against her slight frame, reminding him of her physical fragility. But as she encircled his wrists with her hands and urged him onward, her actions spoke instead of the strength of her spirit.

He circled the hard tips of her nipples with his thumbs then pulled on them, dragging a response from her as she raised her hips and ground herself against him.

Bending, he replaced his fingers with his lips, sucking and teething. He thrust his hips against her center, building her need. Enticed by the soft gasp of pleasure and the shiver of desire that came beneath his lips, that slipped from her skin to his as his body brushed against hers.

Michaela grabbed hold of his shoulders as he loved her breasts. She rocked his body against the center of her, creating a deep sensual clenching that wanted more.

While he tongued and sucked on her nipples, bringing her to the edge, she reached down and undid her black jeans. Parted the fabric there.

He sensed her motions and responded, lowering one hand down her body until it rested on the gap of skin exposed along her belly. His thumb circled the indent of her navel, while the tips of his fingers brushed the hair between her legs.

She shifted her hips and he raised his head from her breasts, locked his gaze on hers and dropped his hand down the last few inches.

His eyes were dark with emotion when he parted her with his fingers, seeking the center of her. Intense as he slowly circled the nub between her legs, building her pleasure. Warmth and damp erupted between her legs at his caress and she once again urged her hips upward.

Again he didn't disappoint.

He eased first one finger and then a second within her and brought his thumb to her clitoris, the pressure and thrust of his movements sure. Demanding.

She grabbed hold of his shoulders. Powerful. Stable. A solid place where she found purchase as she moved her hips, seeking her pleasure and release.

Jesus loved the look on her face, in her eyes. Part wonder. Part desire.

All woman.

Strong, certain female.

He had warned her that he couldn't go slowly and her actions only made it even more impossible to hold back.

As much as he regretted leaving her, he ripped his

hands from her body and made short work of stripping off her boots, socks and jeans, revealing impossibly long legs and the nest of curls at the juncture of her lush thighs.

He stared down at her, appreciating the beauty she offered.

Fierce femininity, he realized. Sexy strength wrapped around an intensely private and vulnerable soul.

A soul that needed this night's satisfaction and respite.

He intended to give her the evening she desired.

Quickly he undid his belt and pants. He dropped them, but didn't bother to remove them.

He secured her hips in his hands and poised his erection at her entrance. The ripple of her desire beneath his fingers and at the tip of his penis urged him on.

Michaela gasped as he penetrated her in one sure thrust and then waited for her to accommodate the size of him.

So large.

Scalding heat within her, igniting her ardor.

She held her breath, overwhelmed by the sensation of him. Overwhelmed by his barely controlled passion.

Then he destroyed her.

He tenderly brushed his thumb across her cheek as he whispered against her lips, "Let go, Michaela. I'll be here to catch you."

Chapter 7

Let go.

It had been so long since she had allowed herself such freedom. Since she had been able to trust anyone enough to permit herself such liberties.

Now, here he was. Promising so much. Unaware of the impossibilities of his promise.

But for this one night, she intended to believe as he did.

With a subtle roll of her hips, she accepted what he offered and took him deeper within.

He dropped his head to kiss her, his mouth open on hers, tasting her. Sucking in her breath while he drove into her, his movements steady and sure.

She cupped the back of his head and played her tongue against his, mimicking the movements of their bodies, but then he shifted away to lick and bite her nipples.

She held him near as her body answered the call of his, rising ever higher. Need tightened into a knot deep within that had her rocking her hips in rhythm to his thrusts and arching her back so that he might more easily savor her breasts.

Then suddenly it came, wrapping around the center of her and stealing her breath. Forcing her ever higher against him as the sharp explosion of passion burst throughout her body. Dragging a strangled scream from her as she dug her nails into his shoulders.

He stilled his thrusts, kissed her lips and whispered, "Let go, Michaela."

She did.

A second later the full force of her climax washed over her, so intense that her body shook from the power of it. Around his erection, her muscles tightened, as if afraid he would leave, but then he slowly pulled out and the slick friction of his withdrawal yanked a protest from her.

Jesus answered that protest, driving in again and again, his forehead leaning on hers. His mouth swallowed her gasps and sighs of pleasure as he drew out her release until unbearable pressure built inside him.

She must have sensed it since she reached down and cupped him, caressing him and dragging a finger along the sensitive gap right behind his scrotum.

Her touch undid him.

With a sharp, swift inhalation, he buried himself so

deeply it almost seemed he might split her in half. He spilled his seed in her womb, his body taut. His back arched as he closed his eyes and experienced every nuance of her body, became intoxicated by the smell of her, now marked by his sweat and release.

Michaela watched him as her own climax ebbed around him, the last fluttering motions rippling across his erection as it nestled within her. Milking the seeds of life that could never find fertile soil within her.

His arms were braced at her sides until she laid her hands on his forearms and ran them up to his shoulders. With a gentling touch, she said his name and urged him down onto her. He came willingly, laying his head beside hers, his larger body nearly engulfing her as she lay pressed beneath him.

"Am I too heavy?" he asked and she shook her head.

"No," she replied, welcoming the protective weight of him. She continued her caresses, wanting this tenderness after the intense way they had taken one another.

He brought one hand to grasp her waist, slowly running it up and down her side in a soothing motion. He waited until the tremors had left both their bodies and their breathing had slowed to a regular tempo. Only then did he pull away from her to remove the rest of his clothes. Almost before she could notice his absence, he was back by her side.

He urged her upward on the bed until they were once

again lying beside one another. Her head was pillowed on his shoulder; her one thigh tucked between his legs while his arms held her close.

She had wanted physical satisfaction and gotten it.

She hadn't counted on this.

The loving caress of his hand along her back.

The way she was surrounded by him, and not just physically.

There was unexpected security in his embrace. A surprising sense of dependability.

Not that it would last.

Jesus sensed her pulling away from him even though she had barely shifted physically. It was more in the way a slight tension had crept into her body. When she looked up at him, that furrow of worry was back between her finely shaped brows.

"Running already?" he asked softly, but he didn't stop the gentle glide of his hand along her back.

"Is that what you think I do? Hit and run?"

She moved away from him then and he immediately felt the absence as the night chill replaced her warmth.

"Am I wrong?" He spread his hands across her back to keep her from escaping.

She shook her head and looked away, but much as he was determined not to let her leave, he would not abide her hiding her emotions from him.

He cupped the side of her face and tenderly urged

it upward. That was when he noted that her eyes were bleeding out to the weird blue-green gleam he had seen earlier that night.

Fighting back the fear he suspected she wanted to see, he injected calm into his voice. "Who are you, Michaela?"

"You mean *what,* don't you?" she asked, a low inhuman rumble in her tone. A slight bit of fang nipped just below the edge of her full upper lip.

He could take a guess at the what, although he was still finding it difficult to believe, even with the proof staring him in the face. He mustered control over his gut reaction to the unexpected, then realized he was neither fearful nor repulsed.

She'd made him feel more than he had ever felt before. Because of that, he was willing to suspend his usually strict approach to learn more about her.

"No, not what, Michaela. Who? Who are you and why are you doing this?"

Christ, she thought, completely at a loss on how to deal with him.

With her vampire powers engaged, there was no missing the slightly hurried beat of his heart and the chill and tension that had crept into his body. Sure signs of fear, not that he was revealing it.

Or giving in to it, she thought, totally puzzled and unbalanced by his reaction.

By him.

"You're afraid of me, but you're not fleeing?"

He laughed harshly. "I didn't get to be an ADIC by shitting my pants and running at the first sign of trouble. So you can cut out the whole creature-of-the-night routine—if that's what it is—cuz I'm not going anywhere."

She morphed back to her human state and realized his response proved what she had initially thought about him—he was a man used to dealing with danger.

A man who might be prepared to deal with her.

So she gave him his answer, praying that once she did, things would return to the way they should be so that she could figure out what to do about him.

"I'm a dhampir."

Chapter 8

He shot her a perplexed look and raised one full dark brow. "A dhampir? Care to explain?"

"Half vamp, half human. Stronger than a human, but weaker than a vampire."

With his thumb, he traced the lines of her mouth, parted her lips to reveal the now perfectly straight edges of her teeth.

"Do you bite? Humans, that is?" he asked.

She bit down on his thumb with her teeth, making his erection jump against her belly.

"Guess a little fang in a girl doesn't bother you?"

He shrugged, clearly guarding his reaction. "Depends on the girl. Depends on why she's busy staking vampires in my city."

"*Your* city?" As if to prove just how little was truly his, she reached between them and stroked him, fully rousing his erection to life, loving the jerky jump of his body that prompted a sympathetic twitch between her legs.

Jesus knew he'd be hard-pressed to deny he still wanted her despite the discovery of what she might be. She held the proof of his desire in her very capable hands. But he suspected he wasn't the only one who couldn't resist.

Cradling her breast in his hand, he idly rubbed his thumb across the hard tip of her nipple.

"*My* city. My rules," he stressed.

She chuckled and increased the pressure of her hand. She inched upward on the bed until her lips were against his and the spill of her breath flavored his every inhale.

"I warned you before. Your FBI rules have no place in my world and the vampires have no place in yours."

He kissed the edges of her lips. Tasted the sweet straight lines of her teeth with his tongue before he said, "Wrong, *querida*. I came to this place because its violence has already touched my world and I need to stop it."

"Like you may one day have to stop me?"

"Yes. I will stop you if I need to."

Her body went rigid. She ceased her caresses and moved away from him both physically and spiritually. As he met her gaze, the gleam of unshed tears shimmered in her eyes, but she held them back as she said, "I won't let you prevent me from what I have to do. Honor demands that I finish what I've started."

"What have you started? Why did you stake that vamp?"

She shook her head and bit her bottom lip before she finally faced him. "They raped my mother. That's how I came to be born. She managed to escape them, but they came after us."

Jesus grabbed hold of her fisted hands. "They wanted you dead?"

She nodded and a lone tear escaped, tracking down her face.

"They wanted my mother dead. They got their wish," she said, and told him her story.

New Jersey Shore
Twenty Years Earlier

Her mother was bleeding.

Michaela could feel the warmth and wet of it drip down onto her as her mother held her hand and dragged her through the tall marsh grasses along the edges of the dunes. The stalks, dry from a lack of summer rain, crackled, the noise overly loud in the silence of the night.

Too loud, Michaela thought, recalling the creature that had attacked them. The creature who would surely hear them pounding and crashing through the grasses as they tried to escape.

Suddenly her mother stopped short and shoved Michaela away toward a larger patch of foliage.

She fell to the ground, the sharp edges of the grasses biting into her palms as the tall stalks swallowed her up. The saw edges of the plants cut her hands and arms, but she bit down on her lower lip to stifle her cry of pain, aware the sound would reveal where she was.

Aware that her mother was ready to sacrifice her life to hide her daughter.

Holding her breath, Michaela tried not to move as she peered through the ever-shifting mass of dune grass.

Her mother stood, her chin at a defiant tilt. Blood dripped down the side of her face from a large gash above her brow. The blood looked black thanks to the palette of the night. Her face was washed to a pale green hue by the light of the full moon.

"You didn't think you could run from me again, did you?"

The tone of the creature's voice was low, almost soothing, with an odd rolling sound beneath, like the purr of a cat.

Her mother said nothing for a moment, then picked up her chin another rebellious inch. "You will not take me again. I will not allow it."

The odd rumble in the creature's voice intensified as he laughed and said incredulously, "You will not allow it?"

Something flashed before her mother. A bright white blur so close to her...

A gush of dark liquid erupted from her mother's throat and spilled down the front of her bright yellow sundress.

Her mother brought her hand to her throat, but the creature yanked it away, laughing cruelly. "I will have you now, as you die. I will have you after, as your body cools. But first..."

The creature wrapped an arm around her mother's waist, holding her up as her knees buckled, burying his head against her ravaged throat.

The horrible sounds of his sucking and her mother's moaning carried across the still night.

Michaela covered her ears, but it was too late to avoid hearing him say, "But first I will have your blood."

Curling into a tight ball, Michaela tucked her head against her knees, brought her arms over her head and closed her eyes. She tried to escape from what was going on just a few feet before her. She imagined other places and times. Prayed for her mother to be safe. Thought about the yellow sundress her mother wore and how they had bought it at the thrift store just earlier that week.

The rough shake of the ground beneath her body pulled her back from where she had gone.

Only then did she realize the night was now almost quiet. The only sounds were those of the stalks as the wind moved them and the faraway susurrus of the waves washing against the shore.

She was alone. Or at least she thought she was.

Peering through the brittle green stalks, she saw what had made the resounding thud that had snared her attention.

Her mother's body lay less than an arm's length away, staring sightlessly at the moonlit sky. Her dress was torn, exposing her breasts and the bite marks on them. The cheery yellow was bloodied from the hideous hole where her throat had once been.

Michaela wanted to keen and cry, run to her mother, but instead she grabbed hold of her knees and forced herself to remain still, fearing that the creature lingered nearby. Knowing that her mother had given her life to save her. She could not dishonor that sacrifice with her fear.

A second later the ground shook again and suddenly there were shafts of light piercing the night, moving back and forth across the dark sky. Other tremors came beneath her and she realized they were footfalls. Coming closer and faster as the intensity of the lights increased. Suddenly there were blue pants legs standing before her hiding place.

"Shit. Holy shit," the man said and passed his flashlight over her mother, across her still-beautiful face and sightless eyes.

Michaela cried then, a puny wheezing sound, but it was enough to snare the man's attention.

He parted the grasses before her and the silver-and-gold badge on his chest gleamed brightly against the royal blue of his uniform.

"Jesus, Mary and Joseph," he said as he reached for her.

Chapter 9

"The officer who found us—Joe Santos—had been sweet on my mom." Michaela dragged in a long tortured breath as emotion choked her.

"He didn't turn you in to the authorities, did he?" Jesus asked and swiped away another silent tear from her face, his gaze fixed on her.

She nodded. "He gave me a home and kept me safe. Taught me how to protect myself and use a gun."

"He knew about the vampire?"

Her fists were clenched so tightly they had begun to hurt. She relaxed her hands and he took advantage by twining his fingers with hers as he asked, "Did he know about you?"

She tried to pull away from him, wary of what he made her feel. Of the emotions he had forced her to relive. But he increased the force of his grip. He couldn't have held her if she wanted to escape him.

But she *didn't* want to escape.

There was something safe and secure about his presence. Something that reminded her of the policeman who had adopted her.

"When I hit puberty, things changed. I got stronger. Started needing less sleep. Craved—"

"Blood?" He jumped in.

Regretfully she nodded. "Joe never adopted me, but he was a father to me. He realized something was going on and finally gave me a letter my *mami* had written that he had found and read years earlier. He had put it in a box of things he collected to give me when the time was right. The letter explained about the vampire who had raped her—the one who came back to kill her."

"The vampire didn't know about you?" Jesus asked, caught up in the story she was telling him. Concern for the child who had suffered tangled with his fascination for the woman she had become. As she had promised earlier that night, he was coming to truly believe that vampires were all too real. But even if they were, in his heart he knew Michaela was different.

"If the vampire had known, he would have killed me. Full vamps don't care for half-human abominations like dhampirs."

"And you have no love for them either, only—"

"You can't stop me from honoring my mother by killing the creature who murdered her. By exterminating others like him who care nothing for human life," she urged, pleading her case.

"Honor calls to you, but it does to me, as well. I can't let your violence create havoc with the laws I'm supposed to enforce."

"I don't hurt humans, Jesus. And I promise you that I won't let the demands of my honor spill over into your world." She laid her hand on the side of his face, stroking the rasp of his evening beard. "But if somehow it did, I understand that this thing between us—"

"Won't protect you from what I'd have to do," he finished, regret already wrenching his gut at the thought of having to choose between her and the laws he had sworn to uphold.

A sad smile crept onto her face, but she inched closer until her lips brushed his. "Then we have a truce?"

A truce, he thought. He confirmed it by bringing his lips to hers, his kiss tentative, tender.

There was none of the urgency of their earlier coupling as he explored the contours of her mouth. Treasured her breasts with his hands. Eased his fingers down to the center of her. Explored the slickness of her lips and the wetness of her vagina.

Her soft, soughing breaths drove him on as did the strong strokes of her hand along his erection.

When he entered her again, he waited, wanting to prolong the union for as long as he could. He needed to experience all the nuances of her as they continued to kiss and caress. This time, their passion grew slowly until they were both shaking.

Rolling onto his back, he urged her to straddle him, letting her set the pace of their loving as he worshipped her breasts. He urged her on with the slow upward lift of his hips, deepening his penetration.

Michaela moaned at the sensations he created as he buried himself deep into her center. Biting her lower lip to control the urge to scream, she rocked her hips, riding him. She sucked in a strangled breath as the climax rose within her and the motions of her hips became more forceful as she sought her release.

He placed one hand at her waist, guiding her as he rose up and licked the tip of her breast. Teething the tip of it gently, the sharp moment of pleasure/pain released not only her climax, but the demon she thought she had tamed.

Jesus sensed the surge of her release as it washed over her, followed by a strange inhuman push of power.

As he met her gaze, the bright blue-green glowed powerfully and a small hint of fang extended beneath her full lower lip.

"You want to bite me?" he asked even as he braced

one arm against the surface of the bed and rose up so he could be face-to-face with her.

"I do." The animal purr tinged the tone of her voice and her gaze dropped briefly to his neck before locking back on his eyes.

"What if I bite first?" he asked, but didn't wait for her answer.

He surged forward and laid his mouth on the spot where her shoulder met her neck. He licked up and down before playfully taking a bite that he then soothed with a whispered kiss.

She shuddered against him, bringing one hand up to the middle of his back and the other to cup his head, urging him on.

"More, *por favor,*" she pleaded and rolled her hips, enticing him to finish. To allow his own release to erupt.

He bit down gently and then sucked on the spot once more as he surged upward with his hips.

Against his throat came her rough cry followed by the sharpness of her fangs as they skittered along his skin. He stilled for a moment, awaiting the piercing pain, but the warm wet of her tongue arrived instead, licking upward until she brushed the shell of his ear with the sharp points of her fangs.

"More." The rumble of her voice vibrated against him.

He kissed her throat and drove his hips upward. He gave her another love bite and caressed her breast with his free hand, answering her soft moans of pleasure with tenderness until he was barely able to hold back his own climax.

She lowered her head again and whispered, "Let go, Jesus. I'm here to catch you when you fall."

He groaned and closed his eyes as her strong arms came around him, supporting him. Her hands pressed against his back while her hips pumped up and down, helping him along to his release.

But he had to see her face as he came.

He met her gaze.

Her human gaze, the demon apparently under control, only...

She lowered her head to his throat and gently nipped it with her teeth.

Human teeth.

She sucked on the spot to soothe it, and the tender pull of her mouth sent him over the edge.

A mangled groan escaped him as he drove upward one last time and spilled himself into her. Felt the wash of his climax ripple from deep within and surge through his body.

She wrapped her legs around his waist and her arms around his shoulders, uniting them at every possible spot—hips against hips, her midsection and breasts tucked tight to his. Her heart beat quickly against the wall of his chest as her breath washed over his cheek. Her mouth took his, her kiss tender and calming, restoring something within him that had been empty for too long.

He returned the kiss, burying his hand in her hair to keep her close. His mouth opened on hers, accepting the enticing bite at one corner that prompted his smile. A smile that dragged a playful chuckle from her.

As he looked up at her, her eyes glittered with satisfaction and relief. Somehow he knew his reflected the same.

"Life sometimes brings you unexpected pleasures," he said.

"Nothing says it only has to be tonight," she replied and brushed another kiss across his lips.

He was surrounded by her in every possible way and yet didn't feel trapped. She was a dhampir, inhuman, and yet he didn't feel threatened.

Or fearful.

For the first time in a long time he didn't feel alone.

"I assume you have somewhere to stay while you're in town?"

Shock froze her in place as she considered his question.

A place to stay?

She thought of the run-down hotel whose halls smelled of stale urine. Of the indiscriminate stains on the mattress and mustiness of the room that was barely bigger than a closet.

Then she thought of a different place.

A place where someone might be waiting for her at night. Waiting to hold her. Waiting to make love with her. Waiting to share both triumph and disappointment.

But not just anyone, she thought, gazing down at Jesus's handsome face.

She would be coming home to *him*.

Slipping into bed beside *him*. Having *his* arms hold her and keep the monsters at bay.

Those monsters had destroyed her life, but they had also brought her to this place.

Brought her to him.

"Not really, but…are *you* sure you're ready to handle all of this and more?" she asked.

He surprised her by chuckling and shaking his head. "I'm sure of only one thing. I want to explore whatever this thing is between us. Can you accept that?"

Amazingly, she could.

She could accept that uncertain promise because up until now, her life had been empty of any promises except one…

The promise of death.

His vow, unsure as it was, promised life. Possibly love.

Bringing her lips close to his, she said, "I can accept that."

"You won't be sorry," he vowed as he met her lips with his.

Michaela knew she wouldn't be.

Honor had called for her to go on this journey, one that had been filled with pain and loss. But the journey had now given her this night and this man.

A man with his own sense of honor.

As he began to make love to her once again, she realized her journey had offered her another path.

She would no longer walk the lonely road alone.

She had him and the promise of love to keep her company.

She smiled and gave herself over to honoring that promise.

* * * * *

IN THE SERVICE
OF THE KING
Laura Kaye

New York Times and *USA TODAY* bestseller **Laura Kaye** is the author of nearly a dozen books in contemporary and paranormal romance. Laura grew up amidst family lore involving angels, ghosts, and evil-eye curses, cementing her lifelong fascination with storytelling and the supernatural. Laura lives in Maryland with her husband, two daughters and cute-but-bad dog, and appreciates her view of the Chesapeake Bay every day.

Chapter 1

Kael paced the length of his private sleeping chamber, avoiding the plush emerald carpet and keeping to the uncovered stone floor at the edge of the room. After an hour of ceaseless movement, the cold of the large polished slabs bit into the flesh of his bare feet and gave him something to focus on besides the Proffering, which he loathed but required. Three months had passed since his last feeding, and the Warrior King needed the blood of either his mate or a human virgin to maintain his immortality and the strength of his humanity. He had no mate, and no intention of acquiring one. But Kael the Fair never felt less like his name than when he stepped into his feeding chamber and found the Proffered waiting within.

"My lord? It is time." Liam's deep voice sounded through the door.

Kael halted before the wide carved mahogany door, his layered dark green and navy tartan robes settling around him. He rolled his shoulders, tilted his head to the side to stretch his neck. The familiar weight of the intricate jeweled braid on the left side of his head moved as he tried to release the tension seizing his muscles. The jewels were the most obvious of the physical marks of his royal rank; the rest were written into his skin. Tonight, of all nights, he felt the burden of the duty and obligation they represented.

"My lord?" Liam pushed the door open and stepped back.

Kael sliced his fangs into his tongue to keep from snapping at the man who had stood at his side for the past seven hundred years. Equally ancient and nearly physically matched, Liam was the brother Kael never had and knew the king as well as any living being could. On many occasions they had stood together against their enemy, the Soul Eaters, so named not just for draining the blood of their human victims, but for consuming their souls as well by drinking through the last stutter of their hearts. Then removing and eating it. All vampires required human blood, but only the Soul Eaters gave in to the lure of exsanguination, became addicted to the kill, and murdered their human prey. And their selfish and increasingly brazen actions were making it harder to hide their collective existence from the mass of humanity.

Kael and Liam didn't speak as they navigated the worn stone corridors of the king's ancestral estate. The underground compound was located far beneath the ancient walls of Castle Dunluce, within the craggy cliffs on the coast of County Antrim in Northern Ireland. Kael's clan, the MacQuillans, had inhabited the land since the late sixteenth century and transformed a small existing tower house into a sprawling, indomitable fortification meant to provide Kael and his vampire brethren the privacy and security they required. In modern times, Kael chose to dispel unauthorized prying of the aboveground ruins by turning over their management to Northern Ireland as a state historic site. The arrangement provided maintenance to the castle remains and landscape during the problematic daylight hours, dedicated security, and humans loyal to the MacQuillan "descendants" who visited the site occasionally and supported its preservation with large, regular bequests. It was rather like hiding in plain sight.

The normally busy halls of the castle's central manor house were empty, as Kael preferred on the Night of the Proffering, and only dimly lit by occasional wooden torches. The compound possessed every modern convenience and security mechanism, but firelight comforted the Warrior King, and put him in mind of times of old, before the conflict with the Soul Eaters had become so constant and tiresome.

On the castle's walls, medieval tapestries hung next to Renaissance portraiture and modern art, but Kael gave his priceless collections little regard. He wanted the strength that feeding provided, but hated the means by which it was obtained. To be sure, the Proffering sustained him. He required it. But it also reminded him of all he'd lost, and what he'd never have again.

Finally and too quickly, they arrived at the antechamber to the set of apartments used by the Proffered when on the grounds. Liam opened the door and stood back, bowing his head of shoulder-length brown hair—braided at the left in the way of the warrior, and allowed the king to enter ahead of him. "After you, my lord."

Kael stepped into the oval room and huffed. "Would you cut the 'my lord' crap already?" He rolled his neck again. As a room, it wasn't particularly remarkable—it was bare except for a small altar at one end and hooks for his robes and a few ceremonial implements at the other. But it was so loaded with everyone's expectations that the air felt thick as he drew it down his throat.

Liam grinned before schooling his expression. "As you wish, my lord."

Kael growled and rolled his eyes, knowing even as he'd uttered the words Liam wouldn't heed them. Fat lot of good being king was sometimes. But Liam was too steeped in the traditions of their people. He often treated Kael just as one of the warriors—which only a handful of the warriors were comfortable doing—but not on the Night of the Proffering. Tonight, to Liam, he was Kael the Fair, Warrior King of the Vampires, Chieftain of Clan MacQuillan. Like it or not, he had a role to play for his people, obligations to his men, and needs that required fulfillment. Out of tradition and deference, once the Night of the Proffering was scheduled, the rest of the clan warriors would not feed until their king had his sustenance, so despite Kael's desire to put this night off—and his ability to go punishing stretches without feeding—he was acutely aware that denying himself meant denying his men. And the war with the Soul Eaters required well-blooded warriors. So Kael fed even when he might have gone without, and Liam's adherence to the traditions helped him remember the significance of the night. It was bigger than his needs, his desires, his fears.

A familiar clattering sound drew Kael from his thoughts. He turned to find Liam on his knees, carefully covering the jade dais with hundreds of small, faceted emeralds. The stones looked nearly black in the low light of the single torch, but Kael could see their exact vivid shade of green in his mind's eye. The emerald was the sacred stone of his people, representing life and renewal. Liam recited an old Celtic prayer to the spirits of the Chieftains as he worked, then he swiftly backed away and cleared the altar for the king's sacrifice.

With purpose, Kael stepped up to the dais, opened his robes, and knelt onto the jewel-encrusted alter. The traditional pose required his knees, shins and feet be flush against the surface, and that he sit back but not relax his bottom against his heels. He had to hold the position for ninety-three minutes—one minute for each day since his last feeding—but his massive thighs never quivered for an instant, never once belied the strain his muscles endured as they settled his six-and-a-half-foot frame in a semiseated position.

Crimson and emerald mixed together on the platform almost immediately as the king's blood dripped out of the dozens of cuts and punctures the jewels inflicted as a sacrifice on his lower legs. Liam stepped up behind him and removed the robes. Kael centered his mind and concentrated, easily tuning out the quiet sounds Liam made as he crossed the room to hang the garments. Later, after the Warrior King entered the feeding chamber, Liam would collect the bloodied stones into an ancient glass urn for display in the Hall of the Chieftains—the ceremonial center of the compound. The urn's contents reaffirmed the ancient belief, "life gives blood gives life," and its appearance in the hall signaled the warriors they could feed.

Kael chanted these ancient words in his head, words of life, bonds, sacrifice, honor. His focus was absolute— neither pain nor apprehension nor Liam's efficient movements around the room distracted him from the precision of his position and prayer.

Instinctively, he knew when he'd served his sacrifice. He blinked open his eyes, which strained a little against the flickering yellow light. Liam was long gone, but he'd readied everything Kael needed, as he always did. Carefully, the king rose to his feet, stepped off the jeweled dais and gently removed the stones that were embedded in his flesh then returned them to rest with the others. He retrieved the cloth laid out on the edge of the altar and wiped the blood from his wounds. He healed quickly and cared little about the injuries, but there was no sense scaring the Proffered with unnecessary gore. She was probably already nervous enough.

His skin cleaned, Kael picked up the leather knife holster and strapped it to his thigh. The dagger it held was lean and vicious, but used correctly offered a quick and nearly painless cut that saved the Proffered from the piercing of his fangs into her soft flesh. Or, perhaps more accurately, the knife saved him from learning whether the woman could be his mate. Only by fully joining his body with the Proffered—by feeding directly from her veins as his cock took her virginity, could he determine

if she had the potential to walk beside him as his partner in leadership, life and love.

But Kael didn't want to know. Kael didn't want a mate.

He'd had one. Meara and their newling son had died
in childbirth following the stress of an attack by the Soul
Eaters on Dunluce, the very attack that brought ruin to
the castle and drove them to expand the existing underground apartments into a full-out compound. While
Kael and his men had eradicated that fiercest and most
troublemaking band of Soul Eaters of the eighteenth century, his clan's losses had been great. Ever since, Kael
had vowed never to chance again the lives of those he
loved. Given the dire state of the war in recent years,
that meant never chancing love again.

Yet, Kael's very biology yearned to seek out the mate
connection so strongly it was nearly painful—his fangs
throbbed in search of the satisfying pressure of teeth
slicing mated flesh, his balls clenched for the release of
his unrealized progeny, his chest tightened against the
centuries-old loneliness.

Still, he held fast, wanting to protect himself and the
Proffered and her family. He would take only what he
had to from her, and no more. He wouldn't take her affection. He wouldn't take her humanity. He wouldn't risk
her life. No matter how much she or his people might
want—no matter how much, in those dark, nearly for-

gotten corners of his mind, *he* might want—he wouldn't fall in love.

So the dagger was necessary. He'd soothe the Proffered using his hypnotic words and eyes, then bleed her into a goblet before sealing her wound with a quick swipe of his tongue—the closest he allowed himself to drinking from her, and then, only out of necessity. As the virgin blood from the goblet infused his system, his ancient chemistry would allow him to do no other than slake his body's primal thirst for carnal connection with the woman in front of him. But there would be no biting, no feeding directly from her vein and, therefore, no chancing the mate connection.

The Proffered were specially groomed for this role by human families around the world in alliance with the vampires. The seven surviving vampire kings, related by ancient kinship ties or blood rites, each ruled over a region of the world. Together, they coordinated their offensive campaigns against the Soul Eaters. Over the years, one strategy they'd developed was the careful cultivation of influential human allies, known collectively as the Electorate. In exchange for the Electorate's silence on the vampires' existence, their assistance where necessary in diverting human attention from the war, and their providing of the Proffered—required because a vampire could only be born and not made, and all vampires newlings were male, the vampire kings repaid them with their protection and their blood, which cured disease and slowed the aging process significantly. The Electorate understood that mating their human daughters with the kings and their warriors would enshrine the Vampire-Electorate Alliance for all time, cementing a partnership through familial relations that otherwise existed through diplomacy alone.

But, as with Kael, the war had left many of his vampire brethren hesitant to develop emotional ties that could be used against them. Without mates, fewer newlings were born every year.

Knife holster in place, Kael walked to the hooks at the rear of the room and retrieved the innermost robe—a dark green silk that skimmed over his weary body and billowed behind him as he walked. He tied the belt around his waist in a careless knot and approached the feeding chamber.

Taking a deep, centering breath, the king eased the heavy wooden door open and stepped inside.

Kael pierced his tongue with his fangs to keep from making an utterance he had no business making. But for the love of all that was holy, the creature before him was magnificent.

Perfectly posed despite the thundering sprint of her heart, her long black-brown hair was braided and intertwined in the traditional way, ribbons and flowers threaded throughout. The sheerest of white silk robes did little to hide from his vision the sexy muscularity of her body. She was not thin, which pleased him. He had once turned away a Proffered for being too thin—he was 250 pounds and nearly feral once blooded, and he'd feared crushing her. Instead, this woman appeared strong, athletic. She was young, to be sure, but also womanly, with curves where women should have curves, with rounded flesh that would fill his exploring hands and strong grip.

He stepped before her kneeling, submissive form and swallowed the blood his fangs had drawn into his mouth. "Tell me, young one, what is your name?"

Chapter 2

After years of imagining this very moment, he was speaking to her. And, oh, God, what a voice. Deep, resonating and slightly accented, it dragged over her like a caress.

Oh, he asked me something...what did he ask? Her brain engaged again and her lips fell open. "Shayla, Your Highness, Shayla McKinnon."

"It is a pleasure to meet you, Shayla. I am Kael, Son of Iain, Warrior King of the Vampires, Chieftain of Clan MacQuillan."

His introduction set her insides to trembling. Vampire. At one time, the concept had been impossible to conceive. But she'd been forced to confront the reality of their existence one cold winter night when men in uniforms and dark suits had arrived at her family's home and delivered the news her older sister had been murdered. At fourteen, Shayla had been completely devastated. Though she realized her father's position as editor in chief of a major Irish newspaper made him a prominent figure in their community, she'd known nothing of her parents' high-level role in the Electorate Council. Hadn't known it existed at all.

But once she found out, knowledge was power, and the only thing that provided any solace to her grief was learning there were other vampires, good vampires, who fought the vile creatures who had harmed Dana.

From that moment on, purpose and a sense of mission filled Shayla's life. She vowed to find a way to join that fight, a role she could fill in advance of inheriting her parents' positions on the Electorate Council upon their deaths. So, when the offer to become one of the Proffered arrived, she jumped at the chance. If she could do nothing else, sustaining the warriors battling evil would make a contribution, if small. But she wanted to do more. A restlessness to help fueled her, driving her to overload classes and take summer school such that she graduated high school before her sixteenth birthday. She began university and the Proffered training in tandem, completing the latter at nineteen, readying her to perform her duties for one of the vampires some time during her twentieth year. College graduation occurred soon after. Toward what end she did all this, she didn't quite know, but it felt right. And the fire in her gut demanded action, cried for vengeance.

The king padded across the mostly bare floor, circled her. The weight of his observation settled over her. She girded her muscles to brace against the tremors she almost couldn't help. "Do you know why you are here?" he asked as he stopped before her once more.

Shayla inhaled to speak, but froze. *You're going to have to try harder than that.* She mentally high-fived herself for not making such an elementary slip. He hadn't specifically told her to respond, now, had he?

Excitement and adrenaline made her stomach flip-flop. How Shayla had hoped this man, this vampire king, would live up to her years of fantasizing. Once she'd learned, during her Proffered training, of his incredible exploits against the Soul Eaters—and his losses— the idea of meeting him, *serving* him, had quieted her restlessness like nothing before. She'd busted her butt working to the top of the class of Proffereds, earning the notice and mentorship of the most experienced and connected trainer. Her interest in this Warrior King ignited an academic curiosity about Celtic history and culture, and she'd built on her training by pursuing those studies at the graduate level. All for the chance of serving Kael the Fair, a chance she was so very thrilled to have this night.

Just being in his presence was a dream come true, and

she determined to face her duty with strength and courage no matter what else happened. Though, the thought he would need her, might find her attractive, desirable even, was such an incredible turn-on she'd had no problem protecting her virtue from her few suitors over the years. Imagining what he'd seen in his long lifetime and what she could learn from him inspired her interest in the medieval history of the British Isles, now so central to the intellectual identity she'd developed for herself. So, her innocence was his to take, if he would have it. She felt no shame in that.

She only wished he would want her time and time again, but knew that wasn't his practice.

Shayla frowned and internally chided herself for letting her thoughts run away with her. If she wasn't careful, she would make a mistake. She inhaled a deep, cleansing breath and cleared her mind, assessed her position. She held the pose just as she'd been taught: knees on the floor and spread, bottom resting on her heels, back and shoulders erect, hands resting on her thighs palms up, head down, eyes diverted. Her submission was part of her offering; it communicated the voluntary nature of her presence before the Warrior King. As she knelt there, the thin white silk robe the only barrier between his blazing eyes and her flesh, she'd never felt more brave, more in control of herself...more alive.

She drew strength from those feelings and awaited the king's command.

Kael smiled down at the top of her head, and felt a little like testing her. He didn't practice domination with all of his sexual partners, though the challenges inherent in it thrilled his intellect and his libido. But, given how tightly he had to control himself in order to restrain his natural instincts when in the presence of the Proffered, he'd long ago realized restricting their behavior, words and actions would enable his own control.

"You may answer my question, Shayla. Do you know why you are here?"

A light pink bloomed on her pale cheeks. "I am here to offer myself in whatever capacity might please you, Sire."

The king tilted his head as his gaze raked over her, absorbing every detail of her appearance, observing every quiet shift in her downcast expression. "Indeed," Kael murmured. He reached down and grasped a long braid, stroked his thumb over the length of it. Her hair was silky and fine even through the weaving. He tightened his fist around it to break his urge to plunge his hand into the beautiful mass of hair.

Finally, he dropped the fine strands of dark chocolate and came round to stand in front of her. "Look at me."

She responded immediately to the direct command, tilting her head back but keeping her expression passive.

That didn't stop him from noticing the dilation of her eyes as they settled on him.

He sucked in a breath. He would've been impressed with her responsiveness if he hadn't been so completely enthralled by those eyes. Her left iris was a brilliant emerald, nearly rivaling his own in the intensity and clarity of green. Her right, however, was a bright turquoise, touched by green to be sure, but without question a deep, dazzling blue. The effect of her mismatched gaze, paired as it was with her fair, creamy skin and dark tresses, was arresting. His mouth gaped in rapture of her beauty.

Powerless to resist, he leaned down and cupped her left cheek in his hand. He stroked his thumb across her cheekbone, his finger playing with the ends of her eyelashes. "You have been touched by magic."

Her breathing stuttered and her eyes grew glassy. She blinked the threatening tears away. "Thank you, Your Majesty," she whispered. She pressed her face into his hand, just the tiniest bit.

That one small movement seemed weighted with emotion and affection, drawing Kael into personal conversation he rarely offered the Proffered. "Am I to understand that tonight actually marks your birthday?"

Shayla bit her lip and nodded.

The image of her teeth buried in plump flesh made his body tighten. Her birthday, how wonderfully unusual. It happened, of course, though the Proffered's blood was most potent any time during her twentieth year. "Well, Shayla McKinnon, I will try to make it a good one for you, yes?"

Her smile was warm, glorious. "Thank you, Sire."

The way she looked at him sent ripples of electricity through his blood. His fangs elongated. Kael pressed his lips together and dropped his hand, backed away.

Something like confusion shadowed her face before she straightened her expression and lowered her gaze once more.

Those eyes are going to be a problem. He was drawn to them, to her. He wanted to pull her up from the floor and onto the bed, and lay her out on her side as he rested facing her. He wanted to learn about her as he stared into those magical eyes. And he *never* wanted to learn about any of the Proffered. He never allowed himself to imagine them as companions. He was on dangerous ground.

But her face was like a mask of his people's mythology. One eye offered the green of their sacred stone, and the other the hue they cherished for its representation of fidelity, loyalty. Her porcelain skin reflected the purity of intent the diamond in his hair stood for, and her dark red lips were the color of life-giving blood. Her face was a mirror of the sacred stones—emerald, sapphire, diamond, ruby—hanging in his hair.

It had to…mean something. Didn't it?

No!

He hadn't realized he'd growled in response to his thoughts until Shayla jumped. Kael resumed his earlier pacing, growing more frustrated at himself and the situation as he thought about the dangerous impossibility of his emerging desires for her. He was half tempted to send her away, but he couldn't bring himself to do it. And that turned his frustration into anger.

He marched to the large cabinet in the corner and wrenched open the doors. The left one banged against the wall and ricocheted back at him. He yanked out a drawer and drew a heavy black eye mask from among the items displayed within. He had to hide those eyes.

He stalked across the room and stopped just behind Shayla's now-trembling form. Remarkably, he noted in passing admiration, it was the first fear she'd demonstrated since he'd walked into the room....

He shook his head. "Rise, Proffered."

Shayla complied immediately, but was as confused by his suddenly harsh tone as by him calling her by her title rather than her name. She'd been warned he might do so, but he'd been using her name so freely just moments before. Not only that, but his declaration—*you have been touched by magic*—had been so affectionate and earnest it filled her heart with the acceptance and appreciation of her appearance she hadn't always found growing up. Kids had teased her about her "mutant eyes," and it wasn't until adulthood that she'd come to prize their uniqueness and ignore the mean comments and staring gazes. The admiring tone in his words had fueled the secret hope she harbored that tonight would lead to something more, something meaningful.

Blackness cut off her thoughts. Cool fabric covered her eyes and she swayed at the unexpected loss of her vision. His large hands on her shoulders steadied and inflamed her, and she immediately regretted the loss of their heat when he drew them away.

"Hold out your left arm." His voice held none of the warmth of before, none of the soothing welcoming tone that had calmed and reassured her earlier. She followed the command, reining in her rising disappointment as she did so. How stupid of her to read anything into his kindness. She'd been warned what would occur this night—and what wouldn't. And yet, she'd allowed her imagination to run away with her, and she'd formed impossible expectations.

"Come." Kael supported her arm and led her across the room. She resisted gripping onto his wrist, despite the instincts that implored her otherwise, and soon she was following his command to sit.

The chair was hard and forced her into the straightest posture. Kael arranged her arm on the wide downward-slanting surface of the armrest. Her wrist and hand hung off the end. Knowing what was coming, Shayla's heart rate spiked and her breathing became shallow.

Something threaded between her arm and side, and warmth grazed her left breast. She barely restrained a gasp. A stretchy band bit into her bicep over the silk of her robe. None of this was unexpected, though she had thought she would have the use of her eyes to watch him work. She took a deep breath and forced her shoulders to relax.

Focusing on her memory of his appearance helped. God, she'd barely been able to breathe when she'd first laid eyes on him. He was...the most fascinating man she had ever seen. The vibrant deep green of his eyes was surreal. Dim lighting seemed to reflect out of them and, like an animal's eyes, they glowed and flashed. His amazing mane of bronze hair hung down over his shoulders, and a braid with green, red, blue and clear stones tied back the hair on one side of his head, revealing the incredible angularity of his masculine face. His brow was strong, pronounced, and his cheekbones were high and sharp. His square jaw framed a mouth so full and expressive her own mouth filled with saliva at the thought of getting to taste him. Lust and desire had barreled through her veins, making his mood change all the more disorienting.

No matter. What *she* wanted wasn't their purpose. A cold wetness washed over her wrist before being wiped away. What mattered most was what *he* needed—to

maintain his strength in the war against the Soul Eaters.
And she was willing to give. It was why she was here.

Kael needed to get this over with. Shayla's—no, the
Proffered's—presence seemed to be sucking the very
air out of the room and, with it, his control. There was
just something about her. He needed this to be over and
for her to be gone.

That would fix everything.

He rushed through his preparations, not taking the
usual time to reassure the Proffered, to ease her fear. He
appreciated the sacrifices they made for his well-being,
and so his normal practice was to take every precaution
to limit their fear, reduce their pain. Now, he did the
minimum, drawing solace from her poise and calmness.
She didn't seem to need the same bolstering as some of
the other Proffereds. He admired her for that, which was
the problem in a nutshell.

Kael pulled the wooden stand holding the ceremonial
goblet in front of the corner of the Proffered's chair and
positioned it to catch the blood that would flow from
her wrist.

"Listen to my voice," he began. Normally, he would've
used his eyes too, the combination of voice and eyes
being the most effective at completing the hypnotism,
but he just...couldn't. "I wish to have your blood. You
will not feel pain, and I will make it so you bear no last-
ing injury. Do not be frightened. I wish you only to feel

pleasure in giving me this most sacred of gifts and to know how much I appreciate your offering." Kael rushed through the words and felt a little odd he couldn't see his assurances reflected back in her expression.

He removed the blade from its holster.

"Do you give your blood freely, Proffered?" The knife hovered over her wrist.

She didn't answer, and he glanced from her wrist to her face.

He hadn't given her permission to answer. Such discipline, despite the stressed scent of her adrenaline in the air. Just who was testing whom here? "Answer me."

"Yes, Your Highness, I give you my blood freely. It is yours." Her voice was clear, firm.

He had no idea what possessed her to add on that final declaration, but he had no business liking the sentiment as much as he did. An odd tingling skittered over his right hand and his cock stirred under his robe. He shook off the rising fog of arousal. He had to do this. Now. Kael drew the dagger across the soft unblemished skin of her wrist. A red ribbon bloomed immediately, along with the rich, spicy aroma of her lifeblood, and Kael placed the knife on the edge of the stand next to the golden goblet.

"Beautiful," he whispered. He glanced at her face. Her cheeks had paled, but otherwise she was silent, still. Her heart sounded out the same staccato beat as before. "You are doing so well, Proffered. Be at ease."

As crimson droplets pooled in the deep cup, Kael reached up and released the tourniquet, increasing the fragrant flow. He swallowed thickly, his body anticipating, responding. Desire set his muscles on edge.

The cup filled steadily, perfectly. Kael inhaled and the heady scent of her offering collided with every nerve in his body. He gasped and his mouth dropped open. Though he wouldn't need them, his fangs elongated further and demanded he taste the thick warm liquid, quench his endless thirst. Ancient instincts whispered dark promises in his ear and urged him to claim her, skin to skin, mouth to throat. His erection roared to life at his imaginings and pushed easily against the thin silk of his robe. Nearly panting, he licked his bottom lip repeatedly. Had he ever felt such hunger?

When he glanced up at Shay...er, the Proffered's face, her bottom lip was quivering.

Kael frowned as his mind raced and unease settled like a rock in his gut.

Though the cup was not quite filled, he bent immediately and licked his healing saliva across her wound. The exquisite flavor of her lifeblood exploded inside his mouth and his cock twitched and wept.

A single tear rolled out from under the right side of her eye mask.

Kael's loins deflated as he sucked in a breath. Dread slid like ice down his spine. He reached out and eased the mask up and off her eyes. The strap on one side tangled in a braid and pulled it loose. A white flower fluttered down into her lap.

Her eyes, so beautiful, so expressive, told him how badly he'd messed up.

What have I done?

Chapter 3

Shayla couldn't meet his eyes. If she did, she knew the tear she'd been unable to restrain would turn into the first of many. The relief of his tongue's caress had just been so beautifully complete, easing her after the slicing cut of the blade had ignited a conflagration up her whole arm. She hadn't really believed the bloodletting would be fully painless—how could someone make a knife wound painless, after all? But she also hadn't expected it to hurt quite so bad. She'd been worried she wouldn't be able to hold out against the stinging pain, that her weakness would disappoint him. When it was finally over, she'd lost control, just for a moment. She was so pissed at herself for crying in front of the king.

"You must tell me—" the king's voice was tense, words clipped "—did you feel the blade?" Dark energy rolled off him like a storm. The hair on her arms and neck raised, prickled.

Not meeting his gaze, she nodded once.

"Say it."

Shayla inhaled a deep breath. "Yes, Your Highness, I felt the blade."

He shot to his feet and held his hands out from his body, imploringly. "And you did not think to say so? You must have known from your training that wasn't…right."

She shook her head and shrugged her shoulders. His disappointment in her was like a punch to the gut.

"Answer me!" His voice reverberated around the stone room.

Her gaze turned to his. It was the first time she'd violated her submissive role, meeting his eyes without permission, but his anger stirred up hers. "I endured it for you. I did not wish to displease you, but it appears I have done so anyway. So, I'm sorry I have not lived up to your expectations, but I didn't know what else to do." She held his gaze, annoyed that she found him so damn sexy even though she was angry. None of this was her fault. Was it? No.

Preternatural light reflected out from behind the emerald of his eyes. She could only describe his expression as bewildered, and his loss of control, even if only in hiding his reaction, softened her anger. Finally, when she could take his intense observation no longer, she dropped her gaze back into her lap.

Could this night go any worse? She thought about what remained to happen between them and sagged against the unyielding wood of her seat. *Oh, God. Yes, there was every chance this night could get worse. Please, God and any other deity listening, don't let me disappoint the ancient sex god vampire warrior king in bed.*

Kael threw his hands in the air and growled. The sound startled Shayla but it also stirred a tingling sensation low in her belly. In another situation, his feral outburst, so full of power and otherworldliness, would have been entirely arousing. He paced again, and though she knew by his clenched jaw and fists he was angry, she was almost amused at what she assumed was a nervous habit. Head still down, she watched him from beneath her eyelashes. The movement of his lithe body mesmerized her.

Kael's chest clenched and his stomach soured with his guilt over harming her. His weakness had driven him to cover her eyes, led him to rush through his normal preparations, kept him from assuring the needs of the Proferred—caused him to hurt her. His voice should've been enough, had been enough with others, but somehow he wasn't surprised to find something else distinctive about this woman. About Shayla.

Not in three hundred years had he failed someone

this egregiously. The comparison to Meara was so unexpected, he faltered in his step. Not since her had a Proffered twisted him up inside so badly. What was going on with him tonight?

He chanced a sideways glance at the beautiful source of his turmoil.

Over his seven centuries of life, many blades had pierced his skin. He knew the awful burn of sharp metal against unprotected flesh. Yet, she'd sat there so silent, so stoic. *To have done that...God, her strength.*

Not to mention the way she'd defended herself. When was the last time someone had addressed him so forthrightly, had dared to express anger at him? Well, Liam did occasionally, but few others. Her actions put her in rather elite company.

And she was right. None of this was her fault. It was his, all his. He should send her away, now, before he made things worse.

He stopped pacing and faced her. The chair forced her into an erect posture, causing her breasts to thrust forward against the robe. Her dark nipples visibly pressed into the thin fabric. Kael's fangs ached to bite into the mounded flesh of her ample breasts. He saw himself in his mind's eye: striding across the room, falling to his knees between her parted thighs, pulling the gauzy material apart and devouring her slowly but surely....

The exact opposite of what his own best judgment told him to do.

As his eyes raked over this imagined scene, they fell on the goblet still perched under her hanging left wrist. The smell of precious lifeblood hung thick in the air. He salivated. Primal need demanded he have it, *now*. The urge was almost magnetic, cosmic.

But the way it had been obtained…

As he debated, Shayla drew her shoulders back, exaggerating her posture, as if she was girding herself for something. Her fingers fluttered for a moment before gripping the arms of the chair. She shook her head. Finally, she drew a breath. "May I speak, Your Highness?"

The steadiness of Shayla's voice intrigued him. Once again, she surprised him, and yet her approach in initiating a conversation fell entirely within her role. Strong, disciplined, magical, sensual, beautiful…her appealing attributes multiplied with each passing minute. Wary, Kael nodded. "Speak freely."

Her body eased forward on the wooden seat, setting off alarm bells in Kael's head. Almost in slow motion, Shayla sank to her knees in front of the chair and assumed the waiting position in every manner except one: rather than rest her hands palm up on her thighs, she reached with her left hand and grasped the goblet, then cupped it in between both hands and held it above her head, up to him. "If it pleases you, Your Highness."

Kael's heartbeat stuttered, then took off at a sprint. Her initiative was daring and so damn sexy his groin tightened in anticipation. He unthinkingly added courageousness to her growing résumé. And fuck if the dramatic gaping of her robe wasn't the most decadent thing he'd ever seen. The top of the silk opened in a plunging V that revealed the rounded, heaving flesh of her breasts. But it was the bottom of the robe that exposed previously hidden territory. As she'd slid to the ground, her knees had pulled the hem back, and her open-kneed pose gave him a direct view of the dark triangle of hair between her strong, shapely thighs.

The spiciness of her body's natural lubricant combined with the rich, thirst-quenching promise of her dark offering proved an overwhelming aphrodisiac, spoke to parts of his soul he thought long dormant. Blood pounded through his head. His fangs throbbed. His cock jerked.

"Aw, hell," he muttered as his instincts took over and cast his thinking consciousness into a dark corner. He stalked up to her and pulled the goblet from her hand, then placed it back on the stand. His hands threaded under her arms and, with little effort, pulled her to her feet.

Holding her lovely face, he pressed his mouth to hers.

Shayla's mind erupted into a cacophony of joyous confusion. She'd been specifically told there would be no kissing. The king did not kiss. But, *holy hell!* Did the king ever kiss.

His large frame bent down over her, surrounding her in his heat. His full lips sucked and pulled at hers and his tongue demanded entrance and exploration, which she freely granted. His hard muscles bunched and thrummed around her, setting her body on fire everywhere they touched. The scent of powerful masculinity filled her nose, and the exquisite flavor of his tongue in her mouth intoxicated her. And, oh God, every time she felt the passing hardness of his fangs as they kissed made her whimper and moan. Her body readied itself immediately for his, moistening, opening.

Having shielded herself from physical relationships, she was astounded to learn her body had the ability to produce this crazy, urgent euphoria. Her brain scrambled to process each new, maddening sensation. In that moment, she would've done anything to maintain the feeling. Was it always like this?

Kael growled low in his chest as his mouth came at her again and again, and Shayla felt the vibration of the feral sound against her breasts. She squeezed her thighs together, seeking friction to satisfy even a little of her now uncontrollable lust. Her mouth was so filled with his probing tongue it was difficult to get enough oxygen, but his kisses convinced her she could live without it as long as he continued to devour her so intensely.

Never had she imagined the expression of physical love could make her feel so wanted, so needed.

His obvious pleasure throbbed against her stomach and flooded her with unbelievable feelings of power, and just a little fear. Because they were off the grid now, outside the bounds of the rules and expectations she'd been taught during her training. And she was thrilled it might mean he was as affected by her as she was by him. Wherever the king was leading them, she was only too happy to follow. In truth, she felt powerless to do otherwise.

A sharp, piercing sensation nicked the edge of her tongue. She gasped into his mouth. He bit her! They said he wouldn't—

All thinking abruptly halted as he sucked on her tongue and fed. The intense suction made her knees go weak and her cunt clench. She sagged against his chest and threw her arms under his and up around his broad back so she could grasp onto his shoulders for leverage. The suction pulled through her tongue again and again, lighting up her entire nervous system and promising to make her come if it continued. She dug her nails into his bunching muscles as he rocked his thick cock against her belly. She pushed up onto tiptoe to bring her aching, dripping center closer to where she knew instinctively they both needed it. He gripped her tighter as he bent his knees and rolled his hips against her lower pelvis, teasing her by inching ever so much nearer her quivering clit. She could hardly tolerate the pressure building inside her. He sucked and sucked at her until the overwhelming pleasure of it all sent her into a dizzying and explosive orgasm unlike any she had ever had by herself.

A long, high-pitched moan ripped up her throat. Her legs lost all feeling and she fell against him entirely as all the muscles in the center of her body pulsed and clenched. His hands flew down to catch her weight and he pulled back from the kiss for the first time in what seemed like hours, glorious, ecstatic hours.

Trembling shudders rippled through her body over and over. The waves of sensation trapped her, lifted her up and spun her around. Finally, her muscles quieted. Sheer amazement and a deep, warm satiation flooded through her blood. Struggling to focus, she smiled up at the king.

Kael's expression visibly chilled in the moments after she met his gaze. He shook her lightly and pushed her away from his body. "Stand."

Shayla stumbled one step then caught herself, but her mind was still flying just enough she couldn't fully make sense of his actions. "Sire?"

"No." He shook his head and wiped at his mouth. His fists clenched.

Shayla's stomach plummeted into her pelvis. Her equilibrium faltered and she stumbled another step as the room seemed to bend and twist.

The king stalked to the door in the back corner through

which she had entered and hammered two swift blows with his fist against the wooden surface. "Retrieve the Proffered."

"What? No!" Shayla didn't know whether to be pissed at the king's mixed signals or mortified at his apparent displeasure in kissing her, in bringing her to orgasm. But what she didn't want to know was his rejection. Not when he was her best hope for quenching the vengeful fire burning in her gut. But, more than that, the girlish dream that she could find a connection with someone as magnificent and mysterious and powerful as Kael the Fair didn't seem so childish anymore. Not after what she'd experienced tonight. She might be inexperienced, but she knew what she felt, and she hadn't imagined it. Some sort of primal, magnetic pull existed between them. She felt it in her bones, in her blood. Her heart squeezed and thrummed in recognition of the odd, compelling sensation.

She had to make him believe in it, too. She resumed her submissive standing pose and lowered her head. "I will do better, Your Highness, please."

"Leave." He paced from the back door toward the ornate one through which he had entered.

Her whole body trembled at the impossible direction of their conversation. "No. Please. We can still—"

"Go. Now!" His words roared and echoed through the stone chamber.

Shayla jumped. Her tears flowed unbidden and she turned to retreat. Her first shaky step knocked her into the stand on which the goblet of her own blood still sat. The cup bobbled threateningly, a splash of crimson spilling out and staining a line of dark red against the bright white of her robe, before she caught and righted it. The sight of the crimson stain brought a whimper from her tightening throat and set her into a flat out run to the door.

She hadn't seen it open, but her trainer stood there, face etched with disappointment and confusion, waiting to escort her away from the chamber, away from the Warrior King of the Vampires.

Chapter 4

"Damnaigh sé go léir don diabhal!" Kael's damning curse roared through the empty chamber.

Fucking hell, he'd lost his goddamned mind. Lost all control. Fed from her.

The knick of his fang against her sweet tongue hadn't been intentional, at least he didn't think so, but once he'd tasted her luscious blood, there was no going back. Each pull had warmed his chest, flooded him with power, and reverberated directly to his cock, driving him to get in her. He'd imagined the tight velvet clenching of her pussy around every inch of his length, unleashing the urge to thrust against her, seek out her wet entrance. Her allure was like a siren spinning dark promises in the night. Promises of paradise in the slick heat of her woman-hood. Promises that, just maybe, forever existed in the cradle of her thighs.

And then she had come. If he'd thought her beautiful before, it was nothing compared to her magnificence at the peak of ecstasy.

But as he watched her ride out her high, his mind came back to him in starts and stops. He'd kissed her. She'd embraced him. He'd *drunk* from her. And he'd been about to fuck her standing right there in the center of the room as he devoured her lifeblood down his throat.

Kael paced and tugged at his hair, spitting out a stream of expletives and plaintive pleas for guidance and assistance in his native tongue. "Cén bhrí atá ann? Cad é cuspóir an Céilí Dia ann?" If only the gods would answer him and explain his purpose—and why he felt so lonely fulfilling it.

Ancient grief joined the raging river flowing through him and filled him with the need to destroy. He glared at the offending goblet of Shayla's blood, but couldn't bring himself to waste something so precious. Kael whirled, nearly upsetting a long mahogany console table, and unthinkingly cleared it in one violent swipe of his arms. Candlesticks and a vase of flowers clanged and crashed against the floor.

The ornate door exploded open and a trio of massive bodies filled the entryway, guns and blades drawn.

"My lord?" Liam rasped, his eyes wild as he surveyed the room. Braeden and Daire followed suit, braced for a fight.

Kael shared a blood connection with the highest-ranking warriors that gave them the ability to sense his emotions, so he wasn't particularly surprised by their appearance, though the last thing he wanted was an audience for his stupidity.

He glared at the bewildered men. The scene was almost comical. Liam, still in his full regalia associated with the feeding ritual, Braeden and Daire dressed only in boxing shorts, their taped fists revealing they'd come directly from a sparring match in the compound's massive training facility.

"Jesus, smell that," Daire whispered to Braeden as he lowered his weapon.

Kael leveled his narrowed gaze at the young warrior. Braeden placed a warning hand on his mouthy brethren's chest.

Liam watched the exchange and turned to his men. "All is well. Leave us."

Braeden bowed his head and stepped back through the door first. "Come on, Daire," he bit out.

Daire inhaled deeply, taking the myriad scents still so thick and fragrant in the room into himself. Finally realizing everyone was waiting for him, he shook his head, bowed it and retreated.

Liam secured the door before nailing Kael with a questioning stare.

The king turned away and resumed pacing and ranting under his breath.

"My lord, how may I be of service?" came Liam's voice after a while.

"You can leave."

"I cannot."

Kael flashed in front of him. "You can very well fucking leave." His fangs elongated as he lashed out.

"I will not!" Liam stepped forward, apparently refusing to be cowed. "You really want to do this?"

They hadn't come to blows in ages, but it had happened before. The king bored his gaze into Liam's, but finally stepped back.

Liam eased his stance. "Where is she?"

"Gone," Kael said as he looked down at the ground. His shoulders sagged as some of the fight went out of him. Everything just felt so...wrong.

"Did you—?"

Kael rolled his eyes at Liam. There was no way he didn't smell that goblet of blood. "What do you think?"

"And, why—?"

"Christ, what are you? The Inquisition?" He drilled his angry stare into his brother in arms. Guilt flooded him. Minutes passed. "I hurt her."

Liam frowned. "What happened, Kael?"

The thought of recounting all the ways in which he'd failed her exhausted him. "It doesn't matter."

"That's bullshit and you know it." Liam sheathed the silver dagger and holstered his weapon. "I've known you my whole life. You would never hurt a female. Not intentionally."

"What do you want from me, Liam?"

"I want to know why you sent her away. Why her life-blood sits there wasting. Why you are more distressed than I can remember seeing you in aeons." He held out his arms.

"Oh, for the love… Fine. Her eyes were mismatched… one green, one blue. I covered them, because they were too damned fascinating. And then the hypnotism didn't work. And she felt the cut of my blade, endured it without complaint. And I…I didn't even fucking notice her pain. Then, as if she hadn't proven herself worthy, she implored me to partake of her blood anyway, despite the way I'd failed her. I kissed her, Liam. And I drank from her. And then…"

It had felt so damn right.

But now she was gone. Her absence weighed on his shoulders, depressing him, squeezing his chest. Oh, the way he'd dismissed her… He groaned and scrubbed at his face with rough palms.

Liam gaped at Kael's rush of words. "You drank from her?"

"Did I not just say that?"

"Kael, did you claim her? Is she—?"

His heart clenched. "Of course I didn't. I cannot." He met Liam's questioning gaze. A dark realization rose up from his psyche, demanded to be voiced. "Liam," he finally whispered, "I did not have to claim her. Somehow, I could tell..." He shook his head.

Liam sucked in a breath and his eyes went wide.

Though the righteousness of the admission nearly drove him to his knees, Kael resisted the truth of it. He sighed, a sound full of defeat and resignation. "Like I said, it does not matter. She's gone. And it is better for her that she is."

"Do not be a fool, brother."

"Watch your tongue, Liam."

The warrior ran his hand through his brown hair, then grasped Kael's shoulder. "Don't assume you know what's best for her. Bring her back. Let her choose." Kael shook his head and dropped his gaze. "You must, Kael, you cannot continue this way."

Kael shoved the hand away and stepped back. "I do not see you seeking out a mate. Or most of the others."

Liam scoffed. "I have not found her. But I *look*. As for the others, *you* are their role model. They follow your lead."

Kael's gaze cut to Liam's. "What?"

Liam heaved a breath. "It is time. Meara has been gone for three hundred years." Outrage erupted in Kael's gut, but Liam pushed on. "She would want you to be happy. She would want you to have comfort. You know damn right well she would kick your ass if she knew how you denied yourself."

Kael braced his hands on his hips and hung his head. Well, that was true. Meara had been a fierce woman, full of life and laughter and aggressively loyal. And she'd believed in love. Kael would go as far as to say she'd taught him what love meant, why it should be valued.

"Jesus, Kael, if you've possibly found your mate, how can you even think of letting her go?"

Kael inhaled a shuddering breath and rubbed his lips with his hand. *Fuck. I let her go. No. I sent her* away.

And now she was out there, somewhere. Unprotected. Vulnerable. The Soul Eaters had found his clan's stronghold once. Though that particular band of evil had been eradicated, nothing said it couldn't happen again. Meara hadn't been his fault, he knew that in his heart of hearts. But if trouble befell Shayla after he'd thrown her out, that would lie at his feet. And it would crush him.

Icy cold panic sloshed in his gut, seized his spine. "Shit, Liam. I was horrible to her."

Liam stabbed him in the chest with his pointer finger. "Then make it right."

Kael nodded, massaged his forehead. Wanting her wasn't the question. Impossibly, he did, in every way and soul deep. But could he allow himself to be so vulnerable again? His heart panged and his hand dropped to his chest, applied counterpressure to ease the awful tightness there. Who was he kidding? Her loss already pained him. Resolve filled his gut and straightened his spine. "Get her," he whispered, his tone urgent and strained.

A smile full of boyish mischief and fraternal affection transformed Liam's face. "Right away, my lord, right away."

Kael glared and Liam straightened his face as he sprinted from the room, but he moved with so much enthusiasm Kael couldn't resist the buoyancy of good humor that inflated his chest.

It constricted just as quickly. He needed to know she was safe. He needed to look into that mystical gaze. Anxiety tossed his stomach as he anticipated seeing her again. He couldn't imagine what she must think of him, how she must be feeling. Christ, she wasn't even down from the high of her orgasm when he threw her out.

Kael braced himself. Every likelihood existed she wouldn't want to return. And though that decision would level him, he wouldn't blame her one bit.

If Shayla never saw a blindfold again, it would be too soon.

With her eyes covered to keep secret the rural location of the vampires' compound, she reclined against the leather of the luxury sedan's backseat. Having asked her trainer for some space, she rode alone. It was the middle of the night, just hours into the twentieth anniversary of her birth.

Happy freaking birthday to me.

She shifted and pulled her legs up under her on the seat. Unthinkingly, she rubbed her left hand, massaged her palm. At some point it had started aching, but she couldn't remember hurting herself. The gentle hum of road noise was soothing, at least. Anything to distract her from her thoughts.

The previous evening, the trip from Belfast had taken a little over an hour, so she knew it wouldn't be long until she was back at her hotel near the airport. She'd be returning to London tomorrow, and she could definitely get into the idea of losing an afternoon browsing the shelves of the Waterstone's at Piccadilly Circus. Anything normal would be nice right about now.

The car slowed and veered to the left, and gravel crunched beneath the tires. Then they were still, only the soft purr of the idling engine filling her ears. The driver was separated from her by a privacy screen.

Shayla threw her hands out to brace herself as the car eased into what had to be a U-turn.

"Um, hello?" She reached forward until her hands found the facing seat and then shifted her body to reach the dividing window. She knocked. Nothing. "Oh, come on. Hello?" she called louder. She flopped back against the seat.

What is going on? Maybe her trainer, a man she called Master Simon, needed to ride back with her after all. That must be it.

In the quiet lull of the resumed ride, all she could think about was how different the night had gone from what she'd expected. Yesterday, she'd been so excited, nearly giddy, as she imagined what the evening might hold for her. How meeting the king could very well be the answer to a variety of prayers. Now, she was just depressed… and, frankly, a little annoyed. Kael might be gorgeous and fascinating and sexy, able to make her come by kissing her alone, but he was just a *guy. For God's sake.*

Oh, who am I kidding?

Kael was everything she'd ever fantasized, and so much more. Powerful and magnificent in his otherworldliness. Gentle and kind, at least when he wanted to be. So damn hot her novice body and mind could barely process it. Her best shot at getting justice for Dana, vengeance against the Soul Eaters.

Shayla hugged herself and laid her head back against the seat. She'd find another way. Somehow. As for Kael, well, the Proffered never had more than a few hours with him, did they? Her rational mind knew that, expected it. Any hopes she held out otherwise were just the last hangings-on of teenage fantasies. Now she could put her daydreaming aside and focus on a realistic path to fighting the evil in her world. If nothing else, there was her future role on the Electorate Council. Surely there were also other contributions she could make she didn't yet know enough to conceive. That thought eased the tension from her neck and shoulders.

The car stopped again, drawing her attention. She'd been so distracted she couldn't tell how much time had passed. Her door clicked open. From somewhere outside, voices bit back and forth at one another. She slid her blindfold off and set it on the seat beside her.

Shayla's eyes blinked and watered as they adjusted to the fluorescent lights of the cavernous garage—she'd guessed right, then, they'd returned. Through a squint, she was finally able to make out the shape of her trainer, a tall, thin man in his mid-forties, and—she was certain from his size and long braid—a vampire warrior. Chills raised the hair on her arms as she stepped out of the car. Why was the warrior here if the point of her return was to collect Master Simon?

The men's conversation halted, and both turned to look at her. Their expressions were studies in opposites. Master Simon's entire face was frowning—it was his "concerned" expression, rather than his "angry" one, and she was a little relieved at that.

The big warrior, on the other hand, wore the most welcoming smile. He nodded once. "Hello."

His manner was open, friendly. It put her at ease.

"Hey." She glanced at Master Simon, who was watching them, wary.

The vampire stepped forward and offered his hand. "I am Liam."

She looked at him for a minute, then placed her hand in his engulfing grip. "I'm Shayla."

He grinned as he shook her hand. "It's very nice to meet you, Shayla."

Shayla returned his smile, then bit her bottom lip. She had no idea what was going on and therefore what protocol was appropriate. She had a million questions, but no idea if she was free to voice them. A long moment passed with no one saying anything, unleashing a nervous energy inside her she could barely restrain. Finally, she couldn't keep herself from breaking the silence. "Uh, so..."

"Come, Shayla. Let's talk." Her trainer held out his hand in invitation and directed her back the way they'd come just an hour before.

She glanced between them for a minute and smiled wryly as Liam nodded encouragingly. "Yeah. Okay."

The three of them entered the reception area, passed through security, and threaded their way through several corporate-looking hallways until they returned to the posh apartment where she'd readied herself earlier. Simon offered her a seat in the living area and she settled into an armchair and crossed her jeans-clad legs. A glass of orange juice and two of her favorite kind of chocolate-chip cookies sat on the side table. She smiled at Master Simon and took a long sip of the cool sweetness.

The men chose seats around her. Master Simon and Liam traded looks, then Simon said, "The king would like to see you again."

The words were so far outside her expectations she merely blinked at them. Hope flared in her gut, but she tamped it down. Hard. No one saw him a second time. She tucked her long loose hair behind her ears. Finally, she managed, "Why?"

Liam smiled and sat forward, but clamped his mouth shut when Simon glared at him. Her trainer's protective-ness warmed her heart. She'd always liked him, even when he was a pain in the ass. But he'd given her every confidence she'd be able to handle this night. She trusted him.

"He regrets what happened and would like to see you again," Simon replied.

Shayla pulled her eyes from Master Simon's guarded expression to Liam's eager face. The weight of what wasn't being said hung in the air between them. The question was: did the why matter? If she put her hurt at Kael's earlier rejection aside, the answer should be no. Nothing had really changed. She'd committed to doing this, wanted to, even, and now she had the opportunity again.

This would truly be her last chance...for so many things.

"I see," she said as her brain analyzed what was really going on. She nibbled the edge of a cookie.

Liam's smile flagged a little as he watched her. His mood shift puzzled her. He seemed so invested in her decision.

She narrowed her gaze at him. "May I make a request? Uh, two, actually?"

"You may make them," Master Simon replied, "but I cannot guarantee to honor them."

Shayla had expected his response, but from the vampire's demeanor, she guessed she had a bit of negotiating power. And she planned to use it. "May I have an hour to prepare? I could use some time to...get my head screwed on straight again."

"That's an excellent idea, Shayla. Of course. And your second request?"

There was no way Simon was going to say yes to this one, but asking it couldn't hurt. "Well, um, may I have permission to, uh...ask the king a few questions?"

"No, Shayla—"

"Yes, definitely," Liam interrupted. He winked at her.

Master Simon gaped at Liam's outburst and Shayla pressed her lips into a line to keep from laughing. She liked Liam, liked the feeling he was somehow her ally in...whatever this was.

Simon shook his head. "Yes, then, apparently. Does that mean you are willing?"

"Yes, Master Simon." Anticipation shot down her spine. She couldn't believe this was happening. Maybe she still had a shot, after all.

"Then, take your hour and be prepared for me at—" he looked down at his watch "—three-thirty? We will treat everything from then exactly the same."

Chapter 5

Kael stood on the hidden balcony carved into the basalt cliff face and soaked in the view of the crashing waves along the Antrim Coast. In the far distance, the volcanic formation known as the Giant's Causeway was just visible under the moonlight.

How many centuries had he admired the beauty of this harsh, unforgiving seascape? How many nights had he come here hoping the rhythmic motion of the sea would imbue him with the peace and tranquility that war and loss had leached from him so many lifetimes ago?

Footsteps approached from the stone corridor behind him. Kael braced against the thick ledge, expecting the worst. Deserving it.

"My lord?"

Tension drained from Kael's shoulders. Liam's voice

told him the news was good. He breathed in the cleansing sea air and turned to his brother. "Thank you, old friend. She is well?"

Liam grinned. "She's great."

Kael's gaze cut to Liam's. "You spoke with her?" Liam nodded. "And what did you speak of?"

"Just introductions, really. Oh, and she wants to be able to ask you some questions."

Kael hitched an eyebrow. "Does she now? About what, exactly?"

The warrior scratched his chin. "Didn't say."

"And you didn't think to ask?" Kael's layered robes caught the wind and danced around his legs.

He shook his head and shrugged. "Figured it didn't really matter."

Kael nodded and ran a hand through the unbraided side of his hair. "Fair point." He stepped toward the entryway and Liam moved to the side, allowing the king first passage. Liam secured the stone-faced door, constructed in such a way it was indistinguishable from the rest of the rock wall on the outside. "So, did she, uh, say anything about me, or, uh…" Kael pinched the bridge of his nose.

"Did she say anything about you?" He chuckled. "No, but I could pass her a note in study hall if you like."

Kael's fist connected with Liam's bicep before he'd really thought to do it. Damn, that little release of tension felt good.

Liam grabbed his arm and spit out an old Gaelic curse. His glare was indulgent, bordering on a smug smile. "Feel better, my lord?"

Kael clapped him on the back. "Much. Let's return to the chamber, shall we?"

Liam smirked. "She'll be up in about an hour."

Kael halted. "An hour?"

"She asked for some time."

Kael ignored the humor coloring his old friend's expression. "I guess I can't blame her." They resumed walking down the twisting passageway single file until it intersected with a main corridor. Liam secured a second door—this one modern, reinforced steel, before they continued on.

What the hell was he going to do with himself for another hour? As it was, he could barely restrain himself from showing up at the door to her apartment and begging her forgiveness. He shook his head at himself as they returned to the ceremonial anteroom to the feeding chamber.

"I don't suppose we need to replicate the cleansing ritual, do we?"

"I shouldn't think so." Kael braced his hands on his hips. "Then again, this is a bit irregular."

"Yes." Fraternal affection shone from Liam's eyes.

Kael turned away. Hope was the most dangerous of all the emotions. He would let Liam harbor enough of it for both of them, at least for now. Kael was trying hard to manage his expectations. Exactly how this would all work out remained to be seen. And maybe it wouldn't work out at all.

Sighing, he walked to the feeding chamber door and opened it. He knew something he could do to pass the time. But when he looked to the floor by the far wall, the mess he had created was gone. The tabletop stood empty, and the shattered glass, broken candlesticks and crushed flower stems had been removed. Kael turned to Liam, knowing without question he'd taken care of it. "Thank you, and sorry."

Liam waved him off.

A new idea flashed into mind, and it was brilliant. "Ah, I'll be back."

"My lord?"

"Ten minutes."

"My lord, this is highly unusual."

Kael's smile hurt his cheeks. "Yes, it certainly is."

"What if she returns before you do?"

Kael halted in the doorway to the antechamber. "Ah. Fair point. You wait here and tell her I'm sorry to keep her waiting but will only be a moment."

"What?"

"Thanks, Liam," Kael said, the rightness of his actions driving him away from the room. He marched through the empty halls to the small industrial kitchen. Although vampires could only consume the flesh of animals or liquids, particularly spirits, they kept other foodstuffs around for the few mated females, who retained most of their human physiology and still required regular nutrition, as well as for their human employees and the occasional human guest. Whistling, Kael pulled open the refrigerator door, unsure what he might find. He didn't spend much time in this room.

But he was determined to lay out an offering for her— one his own hands prepared.

A hearty sausage frittata sat on the center shelf. Perfect. He pulled it out and placed two thick slices on a plate. A container of paper-thin prosciutto caught his eye. He retrieved it and some cut-up melon, and wrapped the ham around the juicy, orange chunks. His chef swore by the combination of the sweetness and saltiness, even if Kael couldn't enjoy the fruit. Next, he ladled marinated olives, artichoke hearts and red peppers from a covered dish into a bowl. It was likely he'd just raided the human staff's breakfast, but suspected he could find a way to make it up to them.

Kael cleaned up his mess and turned to the pantry. He added apples, oranges and mixed nuts to the tray. The meal was turning into quite a feast, igniting a satisfied warmth in his gut. He yearned to see her nourished at his hand. He added a chilled bottle of water and a crystal goblet to the tray. He debated wine, but wanted them both clearheaded for the conversation he hoped they'd have.

As he wandered back through the halls, he whistled again as he juggled his load. Liam sprung from an armchair in the corner of the feeding room when Kael breezed in. The warrior's eyes went wide as he surveyed the contents of the weighted-down tray.

Kael settled the meal on the round table next to the bed, then poured the water into the glass. Satisfied, he turned and surveyed the room. The goblet of Shayla's blood and his dagger still sat on the stand across the room, and the blindfold and a single white flower lay on the floor.

They needed a clean slate. Those things had to go. He glanced at Liam. "I've got it from here."

Liam nodded. "As you wish, my lord." He didn't even try to hide his smile as he left the room. The ornate door clicked behind him.

Kael busied himself picking up and putting away the blindfold, cleaning and sheathing his dagger, and placing the small white flower on the edge of the plate of food. All of this allowed him to avoid deciding what to do with her blood. He hated to waste something so precious—precious not just because it was a virgin's blood, but because it was *her* blood. But if she rejected him, he wouldn't deserve it. And if she didn't, well...hopefully he'd never have to feed from a cup again.

He stared at the goblet a moment longer, then finally placed it on a shelf inside the large cabinet. His fangs stretched out in his mouth as the scent of it infused his consciousness. His throat burned and constricted as he secured the doors. Hunger clenched in his gut. Hunger for blood, for companionship. For love.

Before long, footsteps echoed in the exterior corridor and a knock sounded at the back door.

Kael swallowed hard and strode to the center of the room. "Come."

Simon Freneau pushed through the door and stopped on the threshold, bowing his head. "Good evening, Your Highness."

Kael stepped forward and offered his hand. "Simon. Good to see you again." He nodded and shook Kael's hand, but his furrowed brow didn't speak of pleasure. Kael knew how protective the trainers were of the Proffered. He clearly had some amends to make. Kael's mistake, the failed hypnotism in particular, had made Simon look bad too. The women were told the pain of the whole experience was minimal to none, and that was true. Usually. "It won't happen again."

Not the least because he hoped to never again require the services of the Proffered. But that was up to Shayla— and the mating bond, though Kael swore the mystical connection of a blood match had been weaving its tendrils around him all night, drawing him to her. Body, mind and soul.

Simon nodded again and the muscles in his face relaxed, though he still didn't smile. "May I present to you the Proffered?"

"Please." Kael swallowed. He could smell Shayla, hear her small movements in the hallway. She appeared in the doorway, a vision in a fresh white silk robe and styled mahogany hair. She stepped in and cleared the door, then took her standing position with her hands behind her back and her head bowed.

Simon looked between them once, leveled a pointed stare at Kael, and stepped backward through the door.

Shayla was counting her breaths again, trying to rein in her emotions, but his very presence was nearly undoing the past hour of relaxation she'd attempted. She'd started out with a quick yoga routine, stretching and working her muscles, then soaked in the tub. The concentration the braiding took also provided a great distraction, but it still seemed time had sped up when Master Simon knocked on her door. Now that she was before Kael again, her neck and shoulders tightened as her apprehension increased.

"Shayla, look at me."

As much as she'd been waiting for his voice, it still startled her. His use of her name. His tender, regretful tone.

She knew she must obey, but was afraid if she did, she'd lose control of her emotions—and she wasn't sure whether hurt or anger would win out. Neither was appropriate to show, and both were likely to result in tears.

The king stepped toward her until he was easily within arm's reach. "Young Shayla," he whispered, coaxing her. A long moment passed. And then he fell to his knees before her, his face tilted upward so their eyes could finally meet.

She gasped and her mouth dropped open. He was more fascinating, more gorgeous, than she had even fully recalled. Fire danced behind his eyes, and flashes of gold shined out through the emerald. He was smiling, and it highlighted the strong masculine angles of his jaw and cheeks so vividly it stole her breath. A reaction amplified by the appearance of the sharp tips of his fangs. Shayla licked her lips.

Despite being on his knees, he radiated such palpable power she could feel it jangling in the air between them. *Oh, God. He's on his knees.* A throaty sigh escaped her as she dropped to her own. She was always to be below him.

"Now I can't see you again." The warm, amused tone was back. "Please look at me."

Taking a deep breath, Shayla finally obeyed. Her gaze raked over his intricate tartan robes before finally settling on his handsome face. When their eyes met, the smile he let loose dazzled her, and she smiled back. His playfulness, the incredible sense of ease now possessing him, made it harder to hold on to her anger.

"Thank you," he said. She nodded. "I have some things I'd like to say to you. Are you willing to hear them?"

"Of course, Your Highness."

Kael frowned for a moment, and Shayla didn't have time to figure out why before he spoke again. "I hurt you, and I owe you an apology."

She inhaled to speak, but he cocked his eyebrow and she fell silent. She nodded again instead.

"I don't just mean for hurting you with the knife, although I am...beyond sorry you had to endure that." He grasped one of her hands in both of his and her lips fell open. His touch was so warm, so encompassing. "I lost control and it compromised your safety, your well-being, and that is my first responsibility to the Proffered."

Shayla's shoulders and gaze dropped as he referred to her title again. She internally reprimanded herself for expecting anything else.

The fingers on his free hand nudged her chin up and beckoned her to look at him. "Shayla, I lost control because I...I felt something, with you. Something I don't feel...ever. I..."

She should've been focusing, listening, but... *Did he just say he felt something for me? With me? Lost control because he felt something...as in, he has feelings? For me?*

He chuckled. "Where did you go, young one?"

Shayla shook her head. "I'm sorry, Your Highness."

He squeezed her hand and dipped his head to look up into her once again diverted gaze. "Shayla, could you please call me Kael?"

Her eyes flew to his and she gaped. "Yes?"

His grin brightened his whole face. "Was that a question?"

"No, Sir—er, Kael." A blush bloomed hot on her face.

"Mmm, that is lovely. And so fragrant." He fingered her cheek. "I would like to taste you, Shayla."

She gulped and shuddered as her heart took off at a mad gallop. "O-okay."

"Okay," he whispered as he leaned in.

This wasn't the wild kiss he'd claimed her with earlier. His lips found hers gently, reverently, as if he was savoring small tastes of a rare gourmet meal. One large hand grasped her shoulder and the other cupped her cheek—both brought her closer to him. He pulled and sucked at her lips, his hair falling around their faces as he rose up over her. She opened herself before he even demanded it of her—her body remembered his exquisite taste and begged for its return. Their tongues stroked and explored, but she needed more. She pushed forward just enough to suck his whole tongue deep into her mouth.

Sweet fulfillment exploded against her taste buds, dragging whimpers and moans from her. He groaned and her hands flew to his hair. Her left hand found masses of thick silky bronze she gripped and tugged as she held him to her, but her right hand fell on his jeweled braid. Knowing the significance of it, she yanked her hand back, afraid she'd offended him.

But then his big hand grasped hers where it rested against his chest and pulled it back up to his head. "Hold me," he whispered against her lips. "Touch me."

Shayla moaned her assent as her fingers wrapped around the braid and the jewels bit lightly into her skin.

Kael wanted to go slow. He wanted to seduce her— not just her body, but her heart, her mind. But his body was nearly vibrating with the difficulty of restraining himself. Her lust and adrenaline were heady scents in the air, but nothing compared to the tantalizing aroma of the sweet cream of her arousal. Except maybe the deep sense of psychic calm that had invaded him since she'd returned.

His cock came to life, his fangs stretched out and rubbed dangerously against her tongue and lips. He pulled back. When he bit her this time, he didn't want it to be an accident.

"Can you forgive me, Shayla?" He searched her blue-green gaze. His life seemed to hang in the anticipation of her words.

She was breathing heavily and trembling. Her gaze was just as searching. "You hurt me."

Her words crushed him with guilt and enlivened him

with pride in her for standing up for herself. The multiple sides of her personality fascinated him. She could be both submissive and fierce, obedient and challenging. And he adored that about her. "Yes."

"Don't do it again." The cocked brow above her blue eye enchanted him.

This wasn't a woman he could push around. This was a woman who would push back. He was thrilled. He bowed his head. "You have my word." She studied him, then nodded. He smiled. "Yes?"

"Yes," she whispered.

He grasped her cheeks and pressed his lips to hers. "Thank you." He tilted his head and kissed her right eye. "Thank you." Then her left. "Thank you."

She giggled as she fisted her hands in the thick folds of his robes. The delighted sound made his chest expand.

"My Shayla." *Ask her. Tell her*. Kael pulled back and licked his lips.

"What is it?" She reached a tentative hand up, her eyes asking permission. He nodded and her small, warm palm cupped his cheekbone, stroked his brow, tucked a thick strand of hair back off his face. Each gesture left him with the overwhelming feeling of being cared for.

It has been so long....

"I need you to understand me." He grasped her hand and kissed over her life and love lines. She tilted her head. "I want you."

"Good." She smiled. "You have me."

Chapter 6

Shayla meant it. She'd fantasized about this man for years now. She'd had her first orgasms at the mere idea of him. Later orgasms had involved the only image she'd ever seen of him—a portrait in which the artist had well captured his powerful otherworldliness that attracted her so. Not all her fantasies involving him had been sexual, either. She'd dreamed of fighting by his side, gutting a Soul Eater from navel to sternum and watching the life bleed out of his eyes. She knew that wasn't likely, of course. Though she was trained in martial arts—as were all the Proffered, she knew enough to know she didn't have the expertise to be anything but liability in a real fight. But that didn't keep the violent images out of her secret imaginings.

Now that she'd met him, though, felt the unbelievably

intense pull to him, she knew her attraction was to more than just the idea of him, the fantasy of him. It was to Kael, the man.

And he wanted her, too.

"You have me," she repeated. "Have me."

Kael's mouth dropped open and Shayla gasped as she caught the white flash of a sharp tooth again. She was darkly fascinated by this side of him and shivered at the thought that the man before her was not just a man, but a *vampire*. Wanting him to know she was serious, she extended her wrist to him.

In one swift motion, he grasped it and pulled both of them to their feet. She gasped and fell into him. "Not this time. Come. Please."

She frowned but followed him to the massive iron bed. She watched, fascinated, as he unclasped his magnificent tartan robes. He still wore the thin green silk robe from before underneath, but she was distracted from thinking about that when he turned toward the bed and, in a graceful flick of his wrists, unfurled the layered tartans out over the bedding in a soft, gentle pillowing of fabric.

Shayla was glad he turned back to her so quickly. She wanted what was about to happen and her body ached for things she didn't even have the words to name, but if he gave her the chance to get nervous, to overthink it, she might.

He didn't give her the time.

He grasped her shoulders and pulled her against him, his mouth finding hers as if they'd never left off earlier. As her lips and tongue responded, he wrapped his arms around her. One large hand cradled her head while the other smoothed down over her back and settled just above her rear. The strength of his embrace pressed their bodies together. He was hard and thick and long between them. She writhed and pushed against him.

They kissed and explored each other until Kael was all that existed. His heat surrounded her. His male spice filled her nose and excited her palate. His touch, tender and possessive at the same time, set every nerve ending on fire.

He pulled away from her mouth and she gasped for breath, then moaned as he trailed openmouthed kisses and licks and long teasing drags of what had to be his fangs along her jaw and down her neck. He sucked on the pulse point below her ear. "I will take care of you, Shayla," he whispered. She shivered and tilted her neck for his exploration.

She cupped the back of his head as he leaned down to explore her body. The cool silk of her robe slid off her shoulders under the direction of his hands, then settled around her biceps like a shawl. He fumbled at her waist and the belt dropped, freeing the robe to swing open. He raked his gaze from her face to her legs. His observation set off an electric current down her center. His lips glistened as he licked them.

When he met her eyes again, his were blazing. The brilliant green hue wavered and intensified. He yanked the tie to his own robe free and the fabric fell open, revealing a swath of muscular and marked male flesh from throat to groin. An intricate black design pulled her attention from his face to the light golden skin of his chest. Mostly visible between the hanging green silk was a large round tattoo of a series of interlocking Celtic knots surrounding a regal Pict horse. The Celts' knot work represented the complexity of life, and the more overlapping the lines, the greater the protection against evil was supposed to be. If the symbolism was true, Kael should've been well served by this beautiful mark.

Every inch of his body was lean golden muscle, much of it decorated by beautiful Celtic artwork. Every rippling of his shoulders and clenching of his defined abdomen radiated leashed power. Her eyes bulged and she whimpered when she took in the thick, long shaft protruding from the bronze curls covering his groin. She might have been a little scared if her pussy hadn't tingled in need and anticipation.

For long moments, she drank him in. When she noticed the faster rise and fall of his chest, she finally looked back to his face.

He was watching her observe him—his mouth hung

open and his Adam's apple bobbed in a rough swallow. The lengths of his fangs were completely visible to her for the first time.

Her eyes widened and dilated. She shifted her stance, adjusting to the moisture between her legs. She couldn't stand the distance between them and closed it with a sure step. With one hand against the horse on his bare chest, she reached up with the other and cupped the back of his head and pulled him down to her. She was stunned to feel a rhythmic beat under her hand and realized how much about him she wanted, *needed,* to know. Later…

This time it was her mouth that claimed his. His fang pinched her lip and she moaned. Then she wrapped her tongue around the other fang and flicked it repeatedly. His mouth tasted like danger and ecstasy. Embracing his nonhuman side so wantonly felt decadent, but also like the most natural thing she'd ever done.

Kael fisted his hands in her hair but couldn't decide whether to pull her away or hold her there forever. Definitely forever. Now that he'd accepted the magic weaving around them, he felt it down deep. Being with Shayla this way was as right as breathing, as drinking blood. Her tongue curled around his right canine and he sucked in a breath and growled. His fangs were so fucking sensitive and her tongue was relentless. Pre-cum slicked the skin of her stomach where he thrust against her. She lifted a leg and wrapped it around his thigh. The spicy-sweet scent of her arousal exploded into his senses, called him home.

He groaned, then grabbed her shoulders and forced her backward until her body met the tall column of the iron poster on the bed. It took a little effort and even more resolve to release her from the kiss, to give up her stroking of his fangs. But his patience had just run into the negative.

Shayla gasped as her back bumped into the cold metal, which he imagined got colder as he pushed the robe the rest of the way off her arms.

"Arms up and grasp onto the post."

Breathing harder, she responded immediately and the pose perfected her posture and lifted her breasts.

"Yes. Yes, Shayla. Beautiful." He hummed in appreciation and pulled the belt off his robe, then shrugged out of it altogether.

Desire and need drew a low growl from his chest as he reached up with the silk tie. Seconds later her hands were secured to the bedpost above her head. Kael ran his nose up her cheek to her ear and inhaled deeply. "I don't want to drink from you just yet—" he licked the shell of her ear "—so we're going to keep your hands up there where they won't be able to urge me to do something I'm not ready to do." He nipped her earlobe and she rubbed her cheek against his smooth jaw. He leaned back to find her gaze intense and aroused. Her teeth sank into her bottom lip. He narrowed his eyes at the sight. "And, so long as I can't bite you, no biting yourself." His thumb pulled the plump skin free of her teeth then rubbed across it. He couldn't begin to allow himself to imagine *her* doing the biting. "Fuck."

Now that she was so exposed to him, he took full advantage. He started on the breasts he'd been admiring so greedily all night. They filled his hands with warm weight and he licked and kissed and suckled her pebbled nipples deep into his mouth. He worked back and forth between them, his fingers massaging and tugging the mound his lips weren't worshipping. She moaned and pushed herself further into his mouth and squeezed her thighs together.

Kael smiled at her squirming and dropped to his knees. Giving no warning, he pulled Shayla's legs out from under her and lifted them over his shoulders until her thighs rested on them. Her gasp of surprise morphed into a guttural cry when he anchored his mouth against her swollen, wet lips. He sucked and licked and penetrated her with his tongue. Her juices flooded his senses and coated his throat, taking the worst of the edge off his demanding thirst, but it wasn't enough. It would never be enough, with her.

Shayla whimpered and pleaded between cries and moans. "Kael," she rasped, igniting a wave of his own pleasure at her free use of his name. "Ka—" His name trailed off into a throaty scream as her orgasm exploded around his mouth and radiated through the rest of her body in a series of muscle spasms. Her euphoria was magnificent.

"More, Shayla. Again." Making sure her sensitive flesh was well coated with his soothing saliva, he nicked her swollen lip with his fang. She screamed and bucked when he surrounded the cut and her clit with his lips and sucked her flesh and blood over and over again.

Kael's body was in heaven and hell. His cock swelled and leaked against his thighs. His sac, high and tight, ached for release. But her taste was so fucking rich and luscious—and, *Christ Almighty*, her blood was thick and warm and totally life-giving—he couldn't give any of it up without at least one more fast flow of her cream down his throat. And he wanted her delirious and bone-less with pleasure.

Her keening and clenching muscles told him when she was on the verge. "No, no. I...I can't. No more. Mmm, Kael...oh, God, don't stop—"

Her babbling cut off abruptly as her orgasm stole her breath. Her thighs squeezed his face and her whole body thrashed. Kael supported her entire weight to insure the restraints didn't harm her wrists or shoulders. But her ecstasy was glorious and unleashed a raw feeling of mas-culine pride in his chest. He devoured every bit of her release, relished her sweet taste, her complete submission to his will. And what he willed was her pleasure. Tonight. Forever.

When Shayla's muscles quieted, her whole body sagged. Kael eased out from under her, rose and, with a quick flick of his wrist, removed the bonds. She collapsed against him, her movements so fluid someone seeing her might've thought her drunk.

"Shh, dear heart. I have you."

She nuzzled her face into the crook of his neck. Competing reactions erupted. The gesture was sweet and comforting, and tugged at his heart. But the proximity of her mouth to his throat also spiked his arousal as it conjured imaginings of her opening her mouth, drinking.

Sucking in a breath that failed to calm, Kael lifted Shayla into his arms and gently laid her atop his tartan robes on the bed.

Shayla blinked her eyes open and found herself sprawled out on the bed. Her arm brushed something soft and comfortable, and she recalled Kael spreading out his robes. She stretched and fought the urge to curl up and snuggle into them. His scent lingered all around her. *Kael.*

She turned her head and found him. His hard body pressed against the length of her side. A light sheen of sweat covered his brow and his lips glistened with her juices and his saliva. A passing thought urged embarrassment, but she was too blissed-out to feel anything but gratitude and contentment, especially when he looked at her with such hunger.

Teasing, dragging fingers caressed her from throat to pubis. His voice was raspy. "Are you ready for more, Shayla? I don't mean to rush you, but I—"

She reached out and pressed three fingers against his full lips. "Don't even think of apologizing for needing me."

He hitched an eyebrow and kissed her fingers, then pulled them away. "Was that a command, milady?"

She blushed. "Take it how you will." She bit her bottom lip to restrain the smile threatening to erupt.

He growled. "What did I tell you about biting yourself?"

The tension in his voice and flashing gold behind his dilated eyes thrilled her and reawakened her body. "Well, someone ought to," she whispered.

His mouth dropped open and she watched in awe as his fangs elongated. She squeaked as he easily pushed her further up on the bed and crawled between her thighs.

"Just someone, Shayla? Anyone?" He braced himself with one arm while his other hand rubbed the head of his cock through her slick folds.

"You," she breathed.

"Say it again," he growled. His muscles trembled and his eyes nearly glowed.

Her heart thundered against her breastbone, deep need making her crave his body in hers. She almost couldn't hold herself still the urge was so intense. "You. I'm yours."

"Your body?" He pushed the thick head of his cock into her wet pussy and stilled.

She groaned and looked down between them. The erotic vision of his dick entering her body made her cunt clench. He bit out a curse in what sounded like ancient Gaelic. Her gaze flew to his. "My body is yours."

"Yes." He pushed in further and Shayla gasped at the incredible stretching and filling. "Your blood? Who can claim your blood?"

Shayla found it difficult to speak through her panting. "Only...you."

His weight fell upon her and he braced himself on his elbows near her shoulders. One of his hands tangled in her braids and lifted her head up for a searing kiss. Finally he pulled away and trailed kisses to her ear. Under her hands, his taut muscles radiated leashed power. "Your virginity, Shayla, your womanhood," he rasped.

"Yours," she pleaded.

His body exploded in movement. He thrust his hips until he was fully seated within her. He threw his head back and roared in a sound that could only be described as ecstatic triumph, then as quickly dropped his face to her throat and buried his fangs deep within the yielding flesh of her neck.

Shayla was overwhelmed, awash in competing sensations. The speed of Kael's actions surprised her and his pleasured shout drowned out her gasped whimper. She'd cried out as her body adjusted to his full presence, and then his bite seared her neck. But all of that seemed as if in a different lifetime, because the very first sucking pull of his mouth against her throat removed every bit of pain from her body.

His movements possessed her, claimed her. He wrapped his body over hers as he hunched and thrust between her thighs. His hands cradled and held her as he moaned and sucked at her throat. Her body had broken out in a sheen of sweat and she was slick everywhere, easing his way as he slid his massive taut frame above hers. She wrapped her arms around him and dug her fingers into his shoulder blades, his lats, his ass, as she tried to anchor herself to reality.

The suction at her throat pulled through her whole being until her toes curled against his calves. Her legs fell open and she ground her center against his hammering thrusts. Each suck of his mouth throbbed in her pussy until she was mad with need.

Shayla whined and pleaded and nuzzled his hair and writhed against him. Kael growled as he fed and the sound vibrated through her chest. Impossibly, her body detonated again. She arched back against his robes while her muscles clenched and pulsed around his. For a split second, she went insane with the pleasure. Her mind couldn't handle it. The world disappeared in a floating blissful haze as she shuddered and moaned and gasped for oxygen. It was glorious. And totally overwhelming.

Kael licked the wounds closed on her neck and looked down at her. "That's right, Shayla. So good, you are so fucking good."

Her heart swelled at his praise. She had nothing to compare him to, of course, but he was proving himself an amazing lover—passionate, attentive, and impossibly sexy. She couldn't imagine needing—or wanting—anything more than him, than what he was giving her. The fear of losing him at the end of the night burst into her brain and stole her breath for just a moment. It was true. It could happen. So she shoved the useless emotion away and focused on the incredible man atop her. She wouldn't waste a moment worrying. She would burn every touch, every sensation into her memory. In case that's all she had come morning.

Satiation surged through Kael's system. Her powerful blood fed his muscles and reinforced his humanity. Shayla was magnificent beyond his hopes and expectations. Her body was decadence personified. Her eyes blazed with life and acceptance. Her hands held and touched him and made him *feel.* And her words, the longing and...*familiarity* with which she called out his name. It was their first time together, but it felt as natural as if they had always been.

Her orgasm played out, Kael withdrew from her and sat back on his haunches. He pulled her into a sitting position and kissed her, long, languid twists of lips and tongues that spoke of much, much more than lust. "Turn around," he whispered against her lips. "I want to watch you as I claim you."

Trembling and nearly limp, Shayla moved until her back was to him. He pressed a large hand against her spine and she fell forward onto her hands and knees.

"It's so much deeper this way. And I want every inch of you." He pushed home and they both groaned. He went slow, tormenting them both with his restraint. When he'd first entered her, Kael the Fair had disappeared in favor of a nearly feral vampire who craved blood and carnal pleasure in equal amounts. That raw male remained in him, just under the surface. But Kael wanted to draw this out, wanted to revel in every sweet sensation. It had been so long since sex had been about more than just slaking a physical thirst.

Wrapping his arms around her abdomen, Kael pulled Shayla into a kneeling position over his lap. Every bit of his skin screamed for contact with hers, and this way he could hold her as he took her.

And there was another benefit as well. He cupped her chin and guided her eyes across the room to where their movements were reflected in a huge gilded mirror hanging on the wall. "Watch," he commanded.

With one hand, Kael fondled and teased Shayla's full breasts. Using his other hand and his massive thighs, he set a hot, satisfying pace gliding in and out of her velvety heat and chasing what he knew was going to be massive orgasm, one that hopefully delivered a revelation that would change the rest of his life. Shayla urged him on with her searching hands, first gripping his hips, then reaching back over her shoulders and tangling in his hair. She murmured a string of whispered encouragements full of belonging.

The energy in Kael's body congregated in his groin, tightening his muscles and stealing his breath. "Shayla," he panted as he thrust and observed the beauty of their joint movements, "I want you. I want you."

"Yes." Her hand fisted in his hair and she reclined her head and kissed his cheek. "I...want you...too."

"Please," he cried, begging her, imploring the ancient blood magic that joined mates together. Unable to wait a moment longer, he sank his aching fangs into the yielding flesh of her throat.

His body was wound so tight from the intensity of

the whole night with her, this time the first hot pull of her life-giving fluids unleashed his orgasm. He clamped down tighter—his mouth on her neck and his arms around her body—as he bucked against her. His cock pulsed again and again, releasing his seed deep within her. He devoured her blood, unable to stop sucking but knowing he needed to. She would already be drained from her earlier blood loss and the sheer vigor of their lovemaking.

Finally, he eased his fangs from her neck and licked her wound, his body still shuddering Around him, the room seemed to spin. He anchored himself to Shayla, held her close and prayed.

As the last streams of his cum filled her, Kael felt it: a sharp tingling radiating out of their still-connected loins, up his chest, and down his arm to his right hand. He gritted his teeth against the biting burn and squeezed Shayla in reassurance when she cried out at the sensation.

Her head went slack against his shoulder and she unleashed a deep, sleepy sigh. He tilted his gaze to the ceiling and whispered strained, fervent words of gratitude in the ancient language.

He laid her down on the bed and stretched out alongside her. She immediately turned her body toward his. Their gazes met for a brief moment. The corner of her lip raised in a half smile. And then she fell asleep.

Lifting his hand, Kael admired the intricate mating

mark, a series of symbolic knots that wrapped around the front and back of his hand. He was amazed by it, in awe. His heart ached with fullness and hope. Long-lost joy flooded his mind, enlivened his soul. Joy not just for the chance at a mate again, but because it was her. Shayla. Her beauty and grace and strength had already breached his heart.

He fingered the unique pattern, different from the one he'd shared with Meara. Its disappearance from his skin upon her death had been salt in the devastating wound of her loss. Never again. His life would be first and foremost about protecting Shayla's. Assuming…

He shook his head and focused on the decadent sight of her luscious curves, curled up against him, so trusting and vulnerable in her repose. He wished she would awaken so they could join hands and see the way the marks flowed from his right to her left in a continuous, conjoining pattern. But as her heart settled into a normal pace again, he resolved to let her rest and recuperate.

Hopefully, there was no rush. They would have all the time in the world.

As long as she wanted him the way he wanted her. Completely. Totally. Forever.

Chapter 7

Shayla was deliciously dazed, sated like she could never need anything again in her whole life. She stretched against the soft covers and her muscles ached in a way that reminded her how she and Kael had used one another so thoroughly. She rubbed her eyes, trying to remove the grogginess from her head. Unexpected color caught her attention and she stilled.

Beautiful, thin black knots covered her left hand.

She gasped and bolted upright.

Kael appeared out of nowhere, wearing the emerald silk robe again, and settled on the bed beside her. He placed a tray near her knees and held out a glass of water which she gladly accepted, nearly draining the entire thing as if she'd been lost in the desert. She lowered the glass against her leg and raised her hand, then looked at Kael.

He grasped her left hand with his right and kissed it. Her eyes drifted to his mirror markings and she gaped. The hair rose on her arms and neck. "What...?"

Kael shifted onto his knees on the bed. "Shayla McKinnon, this mark proves what I already suspected. You are my mate. You are destined to walk beside me, rule with me, share my blood and, through that, my immortality."

"Mate?" Shayla's mind raced as she traced the incredible marking with her fingers, then followed her tracings onto his hand. "What...I mean, I don't..."

"I know, dear heart." He kissed her forehead and sighed. "Just relax for a moment. We have time to talk." He folded a length of tartan over her legs and waist and scooted the tray and then closer to her. "You must be hungry, yes? I brought you some food. I know it's not much, but..." He shrugged.

She tugged the robe up to cover her breasts and glanced at his face, found him a little shy for the first time. "I'm starving, actually, and this looks and smells delicious." She picked up some cashews and popped them in her mouth, all of a sudden ravenous for the feast before her. "Thank you."

His smile was dazzling, proud, and grew as she polished off her piece of the savory frittata and, at his insistence, half of his, the spicy olives and artichokes, most of the nuts, and an orange.

With a satisfied groan, she pushed the tray away. Kael's eyes flared at the sound, which unleashed a new hunger low in her belly.

He inhaled deeply and chuckled, ran his hand through his hair. "I like the way you think, Shayla, but perhaps we should talk first?"

For a split second, his words confounded her, but then he took another slow, deep breath in through his nose and licked his lips. Could he...? Oh, jeez. He could! He could smell her. She crossed her legs where they were extended in front of her.

Kael frowned and gently encouraged her ankles to part. "Never apologize for needing me," he said, echoing her earlier words in a low, serious voice that amped up her desire further.

Shayla shook her head, blushing and smiling at the expression she swore could only be described as adoring. She drew her legs up to her chest and embraced them, rested her head on her knees so she could see him.

"Okay, well, about this mating..." She admired the design on her hand. Realized the ache she'd earlier felt was gone. Interesting.

"Yes. It pleases me. Greatly. I want you to know that. I hope it pleases you, too." He tucked his right hand into her grip, once again joining their marked hands.

She thought of all she'd hoped for from this night. "It does, Kael, more than you know." She squeezed his hand. "But what does it mean? How does it work?"

He tilted his head. "More than I know? Tell me what it is I don't know, then. Please?"

She nodded. "I will. I promise. But please explain all this first. I need to understand."

He stretched forward and kissed her cheek. "Of course. In my world, Shayla, blood is magical, powerful, the source of all life. Some blood, when joined together, is especially strong, especially right. For a vampire, that rightness can manifest in a bond that identifies mates who would be a good match, who would bear strong offspring. And it is a rare, special thing."

Shayla studied her hand, his words opening up new worlds in front of her, worlds she'd only dreamed of and never once thought would truly exist for her. "So, we're mated now?" A cacophony of reactions flooded her mind.

Kael's eyes flared. "No. Not yet. The mating mark lasts for three days. If the mating ritual isn't completed within that time, the mark will disappear along with the chance to ever be together. If you agree, on the other hand, there will be a ritual ceremony to affirm the bonding and celebrate the start of our life together, with you as my queen, sharing my world, my blood, my immortality."

She frowned and struggled to make sense of her

thoughts. *Queen? Immortal?* So, getting what she'd always wanted came along with some things she hadn't imagined. Did that really matter? "I see," she said as her mind worked, compiling pro and con and to-do lists, weighing options, and imagining alternate paths. She knew she couldn't accept the mating without some sacrifice on her part. She was twenty years old with a world of opportunity and possibility in front of her.

But then she looked at Kael and realized that everything that had ever motivated and interested her, everything she'd ever imagined would make life worth living, was sitting right next to her on the bed.

She could have eternity to ask him her questions about his life and times.

She could have justice for Dana. Vengeance against the Soul Eaters.

She had to tell him. "Before, when I said there were things you didn't know?" He nodded. "When I was fourteen, my older sister was murdered by vampires."

Kael gasped and moved closer, one arm threading around her shoulders. That preternatural light flared in his eyes, but it was darker somehow, more menacing. "Soul Eaters," he growled.

"Yes. Before they drained every drop of blood from her body, they raped her. Then, when she was dead, they slit her open and ripped out her heart. That was how she was found. Those are the images my parents have to carry around in their heads." Shayla held her breath and refused to surrender to tears and grief.

"Were you close with her?"

She smiled and released her breath. "Yeah. I mean, you know, we drove each other crazy like siblings do. But she was my hero. She'd just graduated high school…" She shrugged. "What happened to her, well, I have to play a role in bringing justice to the animals that did that. I've never known what that role would be, exactly, just that I *had* to do something. What do you think of that?"

He studied her for a long moment, then leaned forward and dragged his nose along the skin of her arm. Pressed a kiss there. "Many years ago, I was mated, and she conceived a child."

"Yes," Shayla whispered, reaching out and trailing her fingers through his hair. She'd learned Kael's history, of course, it was part of why she imagined he might understand what drove her, but hearing it from the man himself was something else all together.

"When Meara was in her sixth month, the Soul Eaters attacked Dunluce. We'd been betrayed by one of our own whose treachery went as far as allowing them entry to the castle, and we were caught completely off guard. The assault began at four in the morning when they used our own cannon against us to destroy the walls, insuring there would be no protection from the sun when it rose. Meara shepherded the women and children to the relative safety of the dungeons. There is no telling how many lives she saved. But she went into labor. It was too early and she was bleeding. I was above, engaged in the fight, pinned down and outnumbered when my blood felt her alarm. By the time I could get to her, it was too late. The newling was gone and she'd hemorrhaged so badly feeding her could not save her."

"I'm so sorry," Shayla said. Could she ever replace such a woman?

He turned his face and kissed her hand, still stroking him. "Thank you, but that is not why I told you about her. You asked what I thought of your need to act on behalf of your sister. I understand it, completely."

His words stole the breath from Shayla's throat and wrapped themselves around an old, damaged part of her soul. He wasn't only her dream. He was her dream come true. She threw off the covering of his robe, embraced his big shoulders and climbed into his lap, straddling him. She swallowed his groan as her center ground against his cock, already waking under her. The kiss was intense and sensual, full of compassion and shared grief and understanding.

Kael pulled back and rested his forehead against the bridge of her nose. Then he met her gaze again. "*You* must understand, though, my dearest heart," he began in a strained voice. "I could never expose you to the kind of danger that took Meara from me. My intention would never be to stifle your dreams or impose my will as if…"

She lifted an eyebrow. "As if you were my king?"

One side of his full lips quirked up. "Is it wrong that I like the sound of that?"

The heat of a blush warmed Shayla's cheeks. Truth be told, she did, too. "No, as long as you don't think it's going to get you your way in everything."

"Sometimes, though?" His fingers made slow, teasing drags up and down her spine, igniting delicious shivers and chills.

She grinned. "Maybe."

"Maybe." He threw his head back and laughed. His expression grew serious again. "I only mean to say, I understand your need, Shayla, but I could never toler-ate you out there…exposed…fighting." He grimaced at the words. "My warriors are many, strong, well-trained. They will fight for you. As will I."

His words were a promise, fierce and true and utterly male. She knew he was right about the fighting, but her heart ached at the idea there wasn't *something* she could do. "I know, but, isn't there anything, anything at all—"

"Of course there is." He crushed a lingering kiss against her mouth. "You can stand by me, and give me the strength to face the fight. You can advise me—I'll never hide from you the difficulties we face. You can fa-cilitate our relationship with the Electorate Council, and secure the alliance between vampires and humans. You can feed me, and make me strong. You can feed me, so, in turn, my warriors will feed more frequently, as they must, as they should've been doing all along. You can bear our children, and bring new warriors into the fight."

So much passion imbued his words they brought tears to Shayla's eyes. He made her believe she really could make a difference. For Dana. For herself. For him. "Oh, Kael."

"And, another thing, I spoke with Simon while you were asleep. I wanted to assure him of your well-being, well, after earlier." The lightest of blushes colored his cheeks. He shook his head. "I have learned you are quite a scholar, Shayla, of the history, culture, and languages of the British Isles, of the Celtic people in particular."

She was almost embarrassed at the pride filling his voice. She hugged herself and nodded. "Yes. Though, how would mating impact my ability to finish my degree? Would I have to give it up?" The thought made her stomach flip-flop. On the one hand, he personally embodied the very history and culture that had fascinated her all these years. On the other, her twenty-first-century mindset balked at giving up her education and career to marry and have babies. Not that she didn't want those things, for she truly did. And Kael's words only bolstered that desire.

"Simon suggested the reminder of your studies might

be doable through telecourses. We have archival collections and rare books here you could use for your research. Maybe you could even impose some order on our library, insure the records of my people are known among us and well preserved. And—" he twisted his lips and looked down "—we could send security along with you on any trips you might *have* to make to complete your degree."

She wouldn't have to give it up? Would long-distance course work even be possible? Would her program allow it? And, what might be in his records, documents surely no one had ever studied before? Questions fired through her brain and energized her with the idea there might be a way to have both, do both. "Kael. Thank you. Even if that can't work out, just the fact you inquired about it, entertained the possibility." She grasped the skin over her heart. "It means so much."

"I'm pleased you are happy." He tucked a thick strand of hair behind her ear, the gesture so full of caring. "So, does this mean…"

Only one other concern held her back from an enthusiastic acceptance. He said the mating bond pleased him, but would it ever be more than that? Would he ever love her? Could she ever replace the love he must've felt for Meara? A warm fullness in her chest told her she was falling for him, maybe had fallen for him already—after all, she'd had years of imagining them together. Having met him, she now knew that his beauty, his gentleness, his fierceness, his playfulness, his power—they comprised the real man, not just fantasy. But she wanted him to want her for her, to *ask* her to be his. She rubbed her hands together and studied the stunning, intricate markings. She wanted it to be more than just some...mystical...biology that drew them together.

Kael let out a deep sigh and gently moved her off his lap. He rose and cleared the tray from the bed. Then he turned to her. "This is a lot to take in. And I'm sure the pressure of the deadline is difficult. I will prepare an apartment for you. Anything you need will be provided—"

"Wait. What? Why?" She scooted herself until she was sitting on the edge. Though she was entirely comfortable being nude in front of him, the air was chilly against her tired body. She pulled the robes up over her lap again and tucked them under her arms to cover her chest.

"I need you to be close until you've made your decision. I cannot send the woman who may be my mate out into the world unprotected. But I don't wish to pressure you any more than necessary, so I will give you your own—"

"I can't be with you?" Shayla didn't know the protocol. No part of her training had covered *this* amazing possibility. But didn't the mark mean they were to be together?

Kael's mouth dropped open and his eyes flared. His

cock stirred the silk of his robe "What are you asking, Shayla?"

She shook her head and pushed off the bed, then situated the robes around her shoulders. Kael hummed at the sight and the sound connected with every nerve in her body. "I guess—" she inhaled a bolstering breath "—well, I'm...not asking anything."

"I do not understand." He cupped her face in his hands. "Please, dear heart, do not torment me."

Shayla smiled and held up her hand. "Is this just... chemistry? Biology?"

Kael frowned down at the pattern on his palm, then looked back to her eyes. He studied her for a long moment, then sank down to one knee and grasped her marked hand in his.

"Our mating is chemistry and biology. My body, my blood, needs you on a fundamental level. *You.* Your body brings me peace, comfort. Your blood restores my immortality and humanity. But I wanted you before this, Shayla. I brought you back because I knew, even then." He held their joined hands to his heart. "You are more beautiful than my eyes can take in. Your eyes enchant me and hold me to you. You are brave and fierce and strong and bright and these are just the things I've learned in the few hours we've been able to share. I want to know more."

Shayla bit down on her lip, trying to restrain the tears

and joyous sob that threatened. Kael reached up and pulled her lip from her teeth with his thumb. He arched an eyebrow and she couldn't hold in the laugh-cry that escaped.

"Be mine, love. Please."

Love. Her heart exploded in her chest. "Yours? Forever?"

His smile was beatific. "If we're lucky."

She closed her eyes against his magnificent image and breathed deeply. Life flowed through her, and she knew at once it had led her to this moment, this man, this love. "Yes, Kael. My answer is yes."

Chapter 8

Kael paced his sleeping chamber, his bare feet sinking into the plush emerald carpet. He smiled. That was where the differences with the previous night ended. He could hardly believe only twenty-four hours had passed since he'd walked the length of this room cursing the Night of the Proffering.

Tonight, it was nerves that had him wearing a path into the thick pile. He and Shayla would be mated this night, in a little less than an hour. Anticipation threatened to explode him apart.

"Just an observation, my lord, but you have a big night ahead of you. Keep pacing like that and you're likely to wear yourself out."

Kael halted and whirled on Liam, arms crossed and leaning against the wall by the door. The warrior's smirk was good-natured, and Kael chuckled and shook his head. He'd nearly forgotten Liam's presence in wondering what Shayla would look like. But as his second in command, he'd helped the king ready his clothing and adorn his body for the ritual. His garments all shared the deep crimson and gold of his clan crest, though the red was more significant for its reference to the blood that would bind him and Shayla together. The leather hugged his thighs, tormenting his already sensitive body. He couldn't don the cloak, though, until the blood marking his skin fully dried.

In front of a mirror, Kael carefully fingered the red smears coloring the knot over his heart. He twisted his torso to see the marks on his arm and back, too.

Liam appeared in the mirror behind him. "Dry?"

Kael nodded, simply mesmerized by a sight he thought he'd never see again—the ancient symbols for fidelity, fertility, protection and eternity painted over his skin in his own royal blood.

They would serve as Shayla's first tastes of him and fuel the blood hunger her mating mark would already have unleashed within her. A growl rumbled low in his chest at the thought.

Liam laid a hand on his shoulder, careful to avoid any of the marks, and squeezed. "I believe it is time, my brother. You don't want to be late to your own mating."

Kael nodded, emotion tightening his throat. He turned

and faced Liam, whose eyes were alive with happiness and pride. "Thank you, old friend."

"You deserve this, Kael. It has been far too long since I've last felt joy flowing through your blood. I am honored to stand up for you this night."

Unable to respond, Kael clasped his grip around Liam's forearm, who returned the ancient warrior handshake. "You are a good man, Liam."

"Come. Let me help you with the cloak." He released Kael's arm and gestured to the bed.

Kael turned away and awaited the heavy fabric to fall upon his shoulders. Warmth surrounded him. He slipped his arms into the long, loose sleeves. The fine velvet was soft and thick, of the same deep crimson as his pants. Using the mirror again, Kael fastened the three ornate gold clips that held the cloak together over his chest.

Liam crossed the room to Kael's dressing table, and eased open the lid on an antique carved wooden box sitting there. Liam lifted the crown, encrusted with the same jewels Kael wore in his hair, and returned to stand before him.

"Your crown, Your Highness." Liam bowed his head and held the golden circle up in both hands.

Like the blood adorning his body, Kael had not expected to wear one of these again. As the sovereign, he had several crowns for different occasions. This mating crown had been made new, completed just a few hours before by the Warrior Ronan, who was also a skilled goldsmith. Kael settled the metal atop his head and adjusted it. "The hood, please," Kael managed in a raspy voice.

"Yes." Liam lifted the wide hood over Kael's head, careful not to snag the pointed ornaments on his headdress or the jewels in his braid.

Now he was ready.

Together, the men made their way through the manor house to an older part of the underground compound. Once again, the halls were empty and candlelit. It seemed to take forever to arrive at their destination, but finally Liam was opening the arched doors to the Hall of the Chieftains, where the mating ritual took place for all who lived herein.

All eyes turned to Kael as he entered the room. Six clan warriors formed a circle around the center of the room, each standing at a marked symbol tiled into the floor—symbols that represented elements of the heraldic badge of Clan MacQuillan. The vampires present were his senior clan warriors, his oldest compatriots, the closest thing he had to a blood family. Indeed, he was tied to each of them by a blood connection.

Kael watched as Liam crossed to the far side of the room and disappeared through a similarly arched door.

Then Kael took his place at the center of the circle, dropped to one knee, and waited.

* * *

"I do believe it is time for you to be mated," Ciara announced.

Shayla nodded and accepted the woman's hand. With assistance, she rose from the seat in front of the ornate vanity where she had been readied for the ceremony. Nervous energy gripped her, but so too did something else. An urge she'd never before felt, and somehow knew would only be eased by Kael's presence, flowed through her, held her muscles taut, resonated in an empty ache in her gut. She clenched and released her left hand.

"Thank you," she said, smiling at Ciara and Maeve. The women had spent the day with her while the men assisted Kael, or at least that's what she'd been told. Ciara and Maeve were warriors' mates and great sources of information and reassurance for Shayla. Ciara was the mate of a warrior named Marcas, and though she appeared Shayla's age, she'd been born in 1922. Even more stunning was Maeve, who was mated to Ronan and had been alive for three hundred years.

Shayla had taken an immediate liking to both of them. They'd helped prepare her for the mating ritual and surrounded her with friendship and sisterhood, easing the pang in her heart that no one from her family could share in the ceremony. Kael had explained the previous night that they would be notified and invited for a special wedding dinner soon.

She was the only human who could attend the mating ritual.

Ciara helped her put on the velvet cloak over the rich silk gown she wore. With its plunging V neck and thin lace straps, it was more lingerie than gown, but it was gorgeous, bejeweled with glittering beads along the neckline, empire waist and bottom hem.

"Lower your head," Maeve said. Shayla stooped down and bowed her head. Maeve and Ciara lifted the cloak's hood over the bridal circlet, careful not to muss the intricate braiding and bejeweling of her hair.

"Now, remember," Ciara said with warm smile, "that should be the last time you bow your head to anyone, save your king. In an hour's time, you will be queen."

The very idea made Shayla's head spin. Flustered, she tried to speak but no words came out. She didn't know what to say. All three women fell together, laughing.

Finally, she calmed herself. "Well, my new friends, my future husband does not strike me as the most patient man. So, should we go?"

Ciara and Maeve led her through stone hallways where priceless art decorated the walls and sat atop pedestals. But Shayla's need to see Kael was intense and she could not pay the pieces the attention they deserved. Forever seemed to pass in the time it took to arrive at the arched wooden door of the room they'd shown her earlier in the day. The Hall of the Chieftains.

Liam waited next to the door and offered her a warm smile when their eyes met.

"Liam will take you from here," Ciara said, her expression affectionate.

Shayla nodded at her new friend and exchanged hugs with both women before they departed.

Liam turned to her and held out his left arm. "It would be my honor to escort you to your mate."

Trembling, not out of fear but out of an urgency she could not fully explain, Shayla grasped Liam's forearm with her unmarked hand. He opened the door and guided her forward.

Shayla's gaze fell on Kael's kneeling form and he was all she could see. The desire to run to him made it feel as if her insides were vibrating. She licked her lips and released a shaky breath. Her left hand tingled and she fisted against the maddening, arousing sensation.

Kael's eyes glowed the brightest she'd ever seen. He was magnificent, regal, and more beautiful than she'd remembered after just a day's painful separation. A fierce masculinity rolled off him and curled around her until she swore she could smell him, taste him, feel his touch on her skin.

Liam paused at the outside of the circle and dropped his arm.

And then Shayla stood before the man, the vampire, she knew without question owned her, heart and body.

They joined marked hands and she barely resisted crying out. She sucked in a sharp breath as the most wondrous current of belonging shot through her—she simply didn't know how else to describe it. By the trembling of his hand in hers, she knew Kael felt it, too.

She sank to her knees. They were so close her chest nearly touched his. Only their clasped hands separated them.

Then Kael began to speak. She didn't know the ancient language, but she understood perfectly well the emotion behind the words. Her heart swelled at the passion with which he spoke. Tears bloomed in her eyes at the glassiness she saw in his. Their hands clutched tighter and the feeling was simply, fundamentally right.

She was so focused on Kael she didn't even react when he paused and the warriors chanted in a fierce yell and fell to one knee around them.

After a moment, Kael's deep, fervent voice continued. "I am on my knees before you because we will always be equals, partners in all things. I hold your hand in mine, because we will always be together. I look into your eyes to see into the real you, and let you see into the real me. I pledge to take care of you, protect you, and cherish you for all time." Shayla's heart thundered in her chest. A single tear quietly rolled down her cheek. He raised their hands to his mouth and kissed her fingers.

Her lips dropped open and her mouth salivated at the

picture of his mouth tasting her. That foreign urge flared within her.

"The ancient blood magic has deemed us a good match. I agree with all my heart. Shayla McKinnon, will you be my mate?"

She swallowed hard and smiled. "Kael the Fair, Son of Iain, Warrior King of the Vampires and Chieftain of Clan MacQuillan, I will be your mate. I, in turn, pledge to take care of you, protect you, and cherish you for all time."

Intense heat flared between their palms, stung and burned, and then the pain disappeared completely. Kael flipped their hands over and pulled his wrist back enough to reveal new identical knot-shaped marks covering their palms. Unlike the rest of the mating mark, the knot was colored in greens and reds and blues. It was stunning.

Another roaring cheer rose up around them. The warriors bowed their heads.

Shayla was dying to kiss him. It was almost painful to keep her mouth away. She bit down on her lip, hard, and chewed. With her eyes, she pleaded with him.

His gaze narrowed. "I understand, dear heart. Soon."

She undid the fastenings on her robe as he undid his. She exaggerated the lift of her hood, not wanting to catch the jewels in the circlet of her hair. Kael did the same, revealing a magnificent crown that made her hands itch with a need to bury themselves in his glorious hair. They both dropped their cloaks behind them.

Then Shayla gasped. Her gaze trailed down to the golden skin of his chest, painted with red markings. She breathed deeply and exhaled a needy moan she couldn't restrain. "My lord?" she whimpered, completely over-whelmed by his scent. It was him, only magnified by a million, and it drove her crazy. She shook and panted, was on the verge of begging for...she didn't know.

"What do you want to do, Shayla? What urge are you fighting? Give in to it."

Her gaze cut from the red to his flaring eyes.

"Give in. Do it. Now."

Chapter 9

Shayla licked her lips as she gazed at the red-painted knot over Kael's heart. She wanted to…to…

She sprang at him and opened her mouth over the red. The moment her tongue touched his skin, she groaned, a nearly strangled sound from deep in her throat. This was the urge she'd been feeling all day. She licked and sucked at the spot over his heart until only his clean tattoo remained. She drew back, whimpering. Not enough. It wasn't enough.

"Here," he rasped. He pointed to another symbol painted on the bulge of his bicep.

Needy sounds spilled from her as she pulled his arm to her mouth. She feasted on the mark, but it, too, was gone too soon.

He held his hair away from the left side of his throat. "Again."

She moaned and climbed up him. His other arm strapped her against him, held her in place while she sucked and licked the red away. Kael grunted and shook under her frenzied attention and it drove her on.

It was blood. His blood. It sang to her, beckoned her. She needed more. So much more.

Kael couldn't decide which ached worse, his throbbing fangs, elongated in preparation for the blood exchange, or his cock, which had hardened when Shayla walked into the room and approximated something like steel the moment her eyes discovered his blood. But she was so magnificent in her bloodlust that he reveled in every wanton lick and rough suck of her mouth on his skin. Her need and enthusiasm was more than he had hoped, and so sexy he feared he wouldn't be able to restrain himself from burying his shaft in the wet heat he could already smell right here in the Great Hall.

There were too many eyes here for that, though. The witnesses were there to affirm the worthiness of the chosen, testify to the strength of the blood match and communicate to the human mate her acceptance into their community. In his case, the warriors' presence also assured the acceptance of whatever newling heirs he and Shayla might have—having witnessed the match, his brethren would be able to defend the child's birthright if ever challenged. Beyond what was required for the ceremony, though, Kael would never share her naked body with another male, not even just to watch. The very thought made him prone to violence.

Shayla whimpered and panted against Kael's left ear. "More? Please?"

"My back," he said, his voice a raw scrape.

She spun around him and pressed up tight against him as she feasted on the large mark that spanned his shoulder blades. Her arms wrapped around him and her fingernails dug into his chest muscles.

Nearly three hundred years had passed since a female had fed from his veins, since he'd had the deep satisfaction of nourishing a woman from the fruit of his body. His soul nearly sang for the return of such raw, primal pleasure.

Shayla's arms circled his throat. "Oh, my God, Kael, what's happening to me? I...I..."

"One more, Shayla. You're doing so well." He hauled her body around his and laid her head in his lap. He took a deep breath that failed to calm, then stuck his thumb under the buttons of his leathers and pulled down, opening his fly on one side to expose the flat expanse of his lower abdominals.

Fingernails dug into his clothed ass as her mouth latched onto the fertility symbol. She sucked so hard he was sure she would leave a bruise, and he relished the idea of her marking his body, claiming him in every and any physical way.

She whined, and he knew the blood was gone. Triumph surged through him.

Nearly frantic to have her, he threaded his hands under her arms and drew them both into a standing position. She swayed at the sudden movement, but he easily steadied her. For the first time, he had a full view of the incredible silk gown that skimmed over her luscious feminine curves. Her eyes refocused and raked his flesh, and he felt it as an almost physical caress.

It was time. He was so hungry for companionship. For love. He had no doubts now, none at all, about what he felt for the woman before him.

Kale reached up to his crown and grasped the central ornamental spike. Pushing a concealed release on the back, it clicked free and became the handle to a small hidden dagger. Shayla gasped when she saw it, then her face went pale when he placed the glinting blade to the taut base of his neck and sliced into his carotid artery.

Blood flowed freely in a dark, pulsing stream over his collarbone to his sternum.

Shayla's thoughts had completely devolved to animalistic urges and she reveled in it. The heady spice of his blood—its taste and scent—unleashed an erotic euphoria within her that she didn't think she would ever be able to give up or live without.

So as the thick red spilled down his chest, Shayla's whole body ached to have it.

She hesitated only a second before gripping the corded muscles of his lats and curling her tongue around the heavy bead of blood running downward. The life-giving nectar exploded in her mouth, tasted about a thousand times more powerful directly from the source.

The source.

Her gaze fixed on the wound. Licking fast and greedily up his chest, Shayla arrived at his collarbone, swallowed the savory fluid coating her mouth, and latched her lips and teeth around the cut.

Shayla was utterly unprepared for the ecstasy of drinking directly from him. On the first full pull of his blood, she came so hard she went blind for the full duration of her orgasm. Brilliant light filled her entire visual field as every nerve and muscle in her body seized and jerked. Her juices trickled from her and slicked up her thighs.

Kael's tight embrace supported her and he cried out a victorious roar that echoed through the hall.

Her entire physiology seemed to explode and remake itself as his blood completed the alterations she now knew the mating mark had begun. Almost instantly, she felt lighter, healthier, stronger, invincible.

And then his fangs punctured the tender spot at the

base of her throat, and Kael began to feed from her as she fed from him.

An approving shout rose up from the surrounding men at his actions.

Her embrace with Kael was every bit as intimate as having sex. Maybe more. Because blood was central to sustaining his life and, now, hers too.

She drank and drank until she felt glutinous, but could not pull herself away. He devoured her in the same uncontrolled, needful way, setting off a deep satisfaction within her chest, between her legs. The longer it went on, the more attuned to the blood's movement she became, and she realized they were literally exchanging blood. She flowed into him. He flowed into her.

Her heart felt as if it might rupture. Surely, such a small organ could not contain emotions this intense.

I love him. Oh, God, I truly love him. Kael. My Kael.

As I love you, my dearest heart.

His voice in her head startled her so much she nearly released her suction from his neck. His hand tangled in her hair and held her down, petted her, encouraged her to take all she wanted.

Do not fear, Shayla. We are a part of one another now, inside each other. Our blood connection creates a telepathy that is strongest when we feed and make love.

Shayla was in awe of the rightness of his voice in her mind, like he had always been there, providing solace, comfort, companionship. But, just in that moment, there was something else she desperately needed.

I need all of you in me, Kael. Please. I'll go crazy if I can't have you.

A possessive growl rumbled against her breasts. *We are fully mated, love. I wait only for you to be sated before taking you back to our chamber and making love to you until the sun rises. Over and over again. Until neither of us can move a muscle.*

She moaned against his neck. *Just a little bit more. I just...* She rushed and gulped at the life-giving sustenance.

We have all the time in the world. Slow down. Take your time, dear heart. Savor. Remember? Never apologize for needing me.

After a few more minutes passed, Shayla's thirst was finally quenched. Slowly, she released her mouth from his neck, shocked to see the deep impressions of her teeth marks in an angry circle.

She gasped. *Oh God, I'm sorry.*

For what? For being enthusiastic? For being a little rough? My fangs are still buried an inch into your flesh, yes? Teeth marks come with the territory. A warm chuckle accompanied the thoughts. *I know what I said, Shayla, but I need just a bit more of you. You taste so good, I don't want to stop.*

Whatever you want, whatever you need, it's yours,

Kael. She stroked his hair and held him, adoring that he needed her as much as she did him. Her earlier urgency subsided, though it didn't disappear altogether. Deep down, under her skin, a low-level need remained, maybe would always remain. She hoped so. She never wanted to lose this feeling.

Free from her earlier bloodlust, Shayla became aware again of the men surrounding them, heads bowed and eyes averted, but still witnessing their union. The embarrassment or self-consciousness she might've expected never came. Her conviction in the rightness of all she had shared with Kael made it impossible to feel anything but confidence and pride and love.

Kael released her flesh and licked the wound closed. Because of his body's natural healing powers, his cut had already knitted together.

He threaded his fingers into her hair and ran maddening openmouthed kisses from her chest, up her throat and over her chin. Finally, he claimed her mouth, tenderly, reverently. Minutes passed, or hours, she couldn't really tell, before he broke off the kiss. Their marked hands joined, Kael pulled Shayla to his side. The warriors formed a line before them with Liam at its center. The fierce masculine approval they each wore made her feel she was one of them.

"My brethren, I present to you my mate, our queen,

Her Majesty Shayla MacQuillan," Kael said in a strained, proud voice.

All seven lowered to one knee in a coordinated movement, bowed their heads and declared in one voice, "Your Majesty, we are at your service, now and forever."

Tears pricked Shayla's eyes and words spilled from her lips before she'd thought what to say. "As I am at yours, and our king's."

Approving murmurs and nods moved through the men.

"Rise now, brothers, and be merry."

The group surrounded them, clasped arms with Kael and offered him their wishes. To her, they bowed and complimented the match. A deep sense of family and community embraced Shayla, and she knew this was where she belonged.

But, just then, her interest didn't lie in bonding with the warriors assembled around them, great as they seemed to be.

She wanted Kael.

The floor dropped away from her feet as he swept her into his arms. He winked and pressed a kiss to her forehead.

The men laughed and applauded.

"Well, my friends, if you'll excuse me. I would like to have my mate to myself for a while." A crooked grin brightened his face. "A long while." He backed toward the door, still carrying her. "You see, I, too, plan to be in the service of the queen."

Shayla gasped at his brazenness but couldn't help her laughter, especially once the warriors started throwing catcalls at their retreating forms.

Good humor radiated from her lover, and his pleasure lit up her insides in return.

Kael paused outside a room she'd never entered. "Our private apartment," he explained as he carried her over the threshold. He kicked the door closed behind them.

She could live on the adoration she saw in his eyes. *"Mo chuisle mo chroí,"* he murmured. *You are the pulse of my heart,* she heard in her mind.

"I love you, Kael." She pressed a lingering kiss to his full lips.

"I love you, too," he murmured around the edge of the kiss. "So much."

She pulled away and rested her forehead on his, looked deep into his eyes. "I meant what I said in there, my love. I will always be in your service."

"We are partners, now, Shayla. Equals. We will be in one another's service, in all things."

"I love the sound of that."

"Mmm, so do I." He turned on his heel and crossed the large living room. "And I suggest we begin right now."

Shayla laughed as he picked up speed and pushed through a door into a large bedroom. In the center of the space sat a king-size poster bed with layers of gauzy, sheer panels hanging down from the four corners. That was all she had time to notice before Kael threw her onto the bed and sprawled on top of her.

His kisses started soft, but quickly became demanding, needy. She felt his urgency and returned it. They kissed and shared whispered declarations of love and removed each other's clothing until nothing in the world stood between them.

Everything she'd ever wanted she held within her arms and the cradle of her thighs. Her Vampire Warrior King. Her Kael.

Then he was in her once more.

And they well served each other all that night. With love and passion. Over and over again.

* * * * *

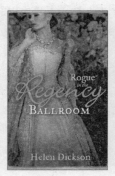

The World of Mills & Boon®

There's a Mills & Boon® series that's perfect for you. We publish ten series and, with new titles every month, you never have to wait long for your favourite to come along.

Blaze®

Scorching hot, sexy reads
4 new stories every month

By Request

Relive the romance with the best of the best
9 new stories every month

Cherish™

Romance to melt the heart every time
12 new stories every month

Desire™

Passionate and dramatic love stories
8 new stories every month